The WINEMAKERS

Have I already read this book? Write your initials here.	

ALSO BY JAN MORAN

Scent of Triumph

The
WINEMAKERS

Jan Moran

ST. MARTIN'S GRIFFIN

NEW YORK

To all who love wine and words

THE WINEMAKERS. Copyright © 2016 by Jan Moran. All rights reserved. Printed in the United States of America. For information, address St. Martin's Press, 175 Fifth Avenue, New York, N.Y. 10010.

www.stmartins.com

Library of Congress Cataloging-in-Publication Data is available upon request.

ISBN 978-1-250-04891-2 (trade paperback)
ISBN 978-1-250-09118-5 (hardcover)
ISBN 978-1-4668-5003-3 (e-book)

Our books may be purchased in bulk for promotional, educational, or business use. Please contact your local bookseller or the Macmillan Corporate and Premium Sales Department at 1-800-221-7945, extension 5442, or by e-mail at MacmillanSpecialMarkets@macmillan.com.

First Edition: April 2016

10 9 8 7 6 5 4 3 2 1

Acknowledgments

While researching and writing this book, I had the pleasure of traveling to Napa Valley and visiting with a former classmate from Harvard Business School, MaryAnn Tsai, and her husband, Larry Tsai, who are founding partners of Moone-Tsai Wines. As past president of Luna Vineyards, MaryAnn shared a wealth of knowledge from her tenure there, as well as from when she was with Beringer Wine Estates. MaryAnn and Larry also poured their exclusive Moone-Tsai wines, which set the bar for excellence high, and have graced the tables of heads of state by request. Thank you for the extensive tour of the Caldwell cave (which inspired the cave in this book), and for sharing your expertise, as well as a plethora of stories—past and present—about the California wine industry.

Very special appreciation to winemaker Miljenko "Mike" Grgich, co-founder of Grgich Hills, with whom I was honored to celebrate his ninetieth birthday at a marvelous vintner's dinner at the Meritage Resort and Spa. Thank you, Mike, for conveying your amazing, trailblazing accomplishments in the wine business. His 1973 Chardonnay, created for Chateau Montelena, garnered top accolades for white wine at the Paris Judgment of 1976, a wine competition in France that inspired the contest in this saga. Much gratitude to his daughter, Violet Grgich, and the gracious Maria Luisa Moreno.

Thanks to those who were so generous with their time, knowledge of winemaking, and memories of Napa: Mike Moone, partner in Moone-Tsai Wines; Elizabeth Vianna, winemaker and general manager of Chimney Rock Winery; John Caldwell of Caldwell Vineyard; Jim Morris of the Hess Collection; Ken Morris and Maryanne Wedner of Grgich Hills; and Tom Fuller of Fuller & Associates Public Relations. My gratitude to the Culinary Institute of America in St. Helena for sharing history of early winemaking, and to the Westin St. Francis in San Francisco for supplying period details.

On a quick side note, Brother Timothy was indeed a real person; he was a wine chemist at the Christian Brothers winery. Furthermore, the actual date of the earthquake in this story is fictional, but as anyone who lives in California knows, the occurrence of such tremors is quite real.

Sincere appreciation to my publishing and editorial team, which is headed by the extraordinary Jennifer Weis at St. Martin's Press, and my amazing agent, Jenny Bent, founder of The Bent Agency. Heaps of gratitude to Sylvan Creekmore, Mollie Traver, Victoria Lowes, and Charlee Hoffman. A toast to my marketing and publicity teams, including Lisa Senz, Staci Burt, Jessica Preeg, and so many others.

To my dear friends Vana Margolese and Wayne Hunkins, who've meant so much to me—how can I ever thank you enough? To friends Josette Banzet and Tommy Roe, Francesca Daniels, and Aly Spencer, and to the writers with whom I am honored to share this privileged journey of storytelling: Rebecca Forster, Anita Hughes, Jane Porter, Belinda Jones, Juliette Sobanet, Melissa Foster, Rachelle Ayala, Allegra Jordan, Allison Pataki, Bennett Zimmerman, Michelle Gable, Jennifer Coburn, Tina Sloan, Samantha Vérant, Gill Paul, Liz Trenow, Hannah Fielding, and so many, many others.

My deepest heartfelt love to my family: Jeanne Hollenbeck, Eric and Ginna Moran, and their newest addition, little Zoë. And to Steven, for chauffeuring me around California and preparing gourmet meals while I wrote.

To read more about my wine travels, visit my blog at www .janmoran.com.

Cheers and *cin cin* to everyone!

The WINEMAKERS

"Sign here, Miss Rosetta." The attorney slid several typewritten documents across his immense oak desk. In his gnarled outstretched hand speckled with brown age spots was a pointed mother-of-pearl fountain pen.

Seated across the desk, Caterina pressed her fingers against her damp collarbone. *How can I do this?* The writing instrument might as well have been a dagger for her heart.

Caterina fanned her face with a cherry blossom paper fan she'd bought in Chinatown. *Where is the breeze off the San Francisco Bay?* It was an unseasonably humid day in the city, a day so scorching it rendered her mind sluggish. Or was that only an excuse for evading the decision she could not bring herself to make?

Fumbling in her purse, she drew out a wrinkled monogrammed handkerchief embroidered by her own hand. The linen held the milky, sweet scent of her little girl, now a year old. *Marisa.* She dabbed her neckline and face, stalling the inevitable. She placed the handkerchief and fan in the lap of her light wool skirt and struggled to compose herself.

In the outer office, a typewriter's staccato rhythm jangled her nerves, each strike an assault on her sanity.

"Miss Rosetta, we've been through this before. My clients are growing impatient." Harold Exeter straightened his crooked frame and stood behind her. "I must have your signature today."

Today.

This was her last day with her daughter. Tomorrow morning, Caterina would hug Marisa and kiss her good-bye forever. Her throat closed and her breath became shallow.

She swallowed the lump in her throat and fought to lift her leaden wrist, but she could not. To her horror, the lawyer clenched her hand, wrapped her trembling fingers around the pen, and positioned it over the contract. He clamped her shoulder with his other hand. All at once, the air in the office grew thick. She gasped for breath.

His bony grip on her hand tightened. "You have already agreed to their offer."

Indeed she had. Nevertheless, she instinctively flung her hand from his grip, dropped the pen, and pushed the documents away as if they were contaminated. Dark ink splattered like wine across neat pages that threatened to extinguish the only pure joy she had in her life.

"Is it more money you want?" Mr. Exeter's voice had an edge she hadn't heard before.

Caterina snatched her purse, dug out the lawyer's crumpled check, and flung it onto the desk. "I don't even want the money you gave me," she snapped. Distraught, she sank her face into her hands, her breath coming in short rasps.

"That was for your medical bills and rent." The attorney shifted on his feet and waited for her to regain control. Once she did, he eased himself into a chair next to her. His demeanor softened. "Miss Rosetta, I'm a father and a grandfather. I know how difficult this is for you. But adoption is the best alternative. If you love your child, how can you subject her to a life of shame?"

Caterina's eyes glistened, and a moan escaped her lips. There was nothing she wouldn't do for Marisa. Yet the motherly instincts of her heart and the rational judgment of her head warred within her.

"Do you want her to suffer the brand of illegitimacy for life?" His voice dropped a notch. "Don't make your child pay for your mistake. She needs a family."

She agreed. And she'd tried to do just that, though she had failed. Faith, the kind woman who ran the small maternity home where she'd been living, had warned her. The longer she waited to give up her baby, the more gut-wrenching it would be.

But Caterina *had* to know, beyond any doubt, that this was the best decision for Marisa. She could bear nothing less. Clutching her handkerchief, she intercepted the tears that spilled from her lids. "I must meet them."

"I beg your pardon?"

"The new . . . couple," she managed to say, instead of parents. Caterina's skin crawled with unease.

"I'm afraid that's impossible."

Caterina shoved the fan and handkerchief into her purse and sprang from the chair.

Immediately, Mr. Exeter placed a firm hand on her arm. "That is, it's highly irregular." He shook his graying head as if it were the worst imaginable deed. "But I can inquire." He glanced at his wristwatch. "We hadn't much time left. Will you sign the documents today?"

Caterina bit her lip. "If I like them."

"My dear, they are the finest people. Your question should be, will they love and care for your daughter? I assure you, they will. However, I shall try to contact them with this unusual request. Nevertheless, in good faith, your signature will be required first." He scooped up the documents. "If you'll wait in the reception area, I'll have this first page retyped."

Caterina felt as if she were suffocating. "I need air. I'll wait outside."

Once she was outside, her step faltered, and she leaned against the brick building, gulping air thickened with humidity. She watched steam waffle from the pavement in waves. This cloying summer heat was nearby Napa Valley weather—good for ripening grapes— but it was a temperature seldom seen in San Francisco.

Although she had a decent job in the city, she ached for the panoramic views from her mother's high-perched vineyard, the scent of soil rich enough to yield the finest wine, and the sound of birdsong on breeze-cooled evenings. She had grown up at the vineyard; it was an idyllic setting for a child.

And yet she could not return with Marisa. *Illegitimate.* Why did society pin labels of hatred on innocent children? Why were families robbed of their precious children, all in the name of propriety?

Marisa. All at once, Caterina sensed an inexplicable draw toward her little girl. She brushed salty tears from her cheeks.

Her skin crawled with a sudden urgency. *Marisa needs me.* As if in a trance, she turned and began walking in the direction of her car.

In the logical recesses of her mind, she knew she should stay and sign the final adoption papers. "It's the loving thing to do," Faith had told her this morning before she'd left the house. Caterina had agreed. She was not a young woman prone to dereliction of her duties.

She had seen other women at the maternity home give up their babies, some mere hours after giving birth. A few girls were heartbroken over lost lovers, while others bravely maintained they were glad to be rid of the product of rape or incest. Yet she had witnessed the tears and agony etched on each face after they'd handed their tiny offspring to a nurse, never to see their child again. Never to feel a heartbeat flutter against their chests in the small hours of the night. Never to see the first loving smile of recognition or hear the first cry of "Mama."

Their inconsolable sobs still rang in her ears.

Something is dreadfully wrong. Her heart palpitating, Caterina quickened her step, brushing past people on the crowded sidewalk.

At first, she'd refused to give up Marisa, hoping to hear from her child's father, the man she loved. *Praying for a miracle.* "You've waited too long," Faith had told her months later. "You must make a decision for the good of the child."

Caterina sniffed the air, detecting a trace scent of thundershowers. Clouds shadowed the sun.

"Excuse me." Caterina pushed past a group of meandering students. She stepped off the curb and dodged a taxi pulling to the corner. Her chest tightened. Her car was parked in the next block down the hill. She shed her jacket and broke into a trot.

Breathing heavily, she increased her pace. She *had* to reach Marisa. Was it a mother's instinct? Frantic now, Caterina ran down the hilly street, her purse knocking against her side, her high heels clattering on the sidewalk.

She reached her car and flung open the door of her turquoise Chevrolet Bel Air with pointed rear fender fins. Her mother had given her the car when she'd moved to San Francisco for college. She turned the key in the ignition and pumped the gas pedal. She *had* to reach Marisa as soon as possible. She didn't know why, but she knew it was dire.

A fat raindrop splattered her windshield, and then another, and another. She flicked on her wipers and pushed the large sedan as fast as she dared on city streets. By the time she arrived at the maternity home, sheets of rain were battering her car.

She parked down the street and then raced through the downpour past old Victorian homes, which lined the way like pastel macarons. Turning in, she hurried up the steps and passed under a canopy of ornate fretwork freshly painted in lemon yellow, mint green, and cornflower blue. Panic rose in her throat. She pushed open the door and pounded up the stairs, leaving a trail of water in her path.

Caterina gripped the doorjamb of the children's nursery in the old home overlooking the bay. Half a dozen playpens with babies lined the perimeter. Paintings of giraffes, monkeys, and elephants adorned the walls, mocking her with their cheerful countenances.

Marisa was pulling up on her railing, teetering on strong, developing legs. A well-dressed, middle-aged couple stood next to Marisa's playpen, exclaiming over her.

"What are you doing?" Caterina demanded, brushing damp hair from her forehead. *They've come too soon.* Terror seized her. She wasn't ready.

Faith O'Connell hurried to her side, embarrassment stamped on her reddened face. "This is Mr. and Mrs. Anderson. They wanted to visit today while you were out. You're back early," she added in an apologetic tone, fumbling with the top button on her green-checked housedress.

A woman with perfectly coiffed blond hair jerked her head around and glared at Faith. "You said she wouldn't be here." She turned a withering gaze on Caterina.

Mrs. Anderson's lips twitched with disdain as she took in Caterina's rain-stained shoes and wet hair.

Caterina flicked away errant strands plastered to her flushed cheeks. She shrugged free of Faith, but before she could reach Marisa, Mrs. Anderson picked up her baby. Caterina's heart thudded.

"How are you, darling?" the woman cooed, kissing Marisa's cheek. "Would you like to come home with us?"

Marisa's lower lip began to tremble, and her eyes sought out Caterina.

"Get away from her. I'm her mother." Fuming, Caterina crossed the room in long strides, intent on rescuing her beautiful dark-haired girl from the woman's pale arms.

Mr. Anderson wore a charcoal suit and a grim expression. "We came here to adopt this little girl. We can give her a good home. Don't you want to do what's best for her?"

Caterina yanked her daughter from his wife and pressed Marisa's trembling little body to her chest. She turned her back to the couple, shielding Marisa from their prying eyes. She *couldn't* let her go. "I *am* doing what's best for her."

Her russet curls quivering with distress, Faith hurried to Caterina's side. "A child needs a mother *and* a father, dear."

"We wanted a little blond-haired girl, but we'll take her," Mrs. Anderson said. "She has such a pretty smile and the brightest blue eyes we've ever seen."

"And a sweet nature," her husband added. "We adopted a boy last year, and this girl is for my wife. It's her birthday today."

Caterina was livid. "You *can't* pick out a baby like a birthday gift. And certainly not *my* child."

"Mr. Exeter assured us we had an agreement." Mr. Anderson jabbed a finger in the air. "You must be reasonable. How will you care for her?" He looked at her with contempt.

"I have a college education and a good job," Caterina said with pride. "I'm a sommelier at the St. Francis Hotel."

"Isn't that like a bartender?" Mrs. Anderson narrowed her eyes and shrank back with disgust.

"Surely you're exaggerating." Her husband snorted. "No place would hire a woman as a sommelier."

Caterina ignored his jibe. "I'm not giving her up, and that's final." Marisa began crying at her mother's distress, and Caterina patted her back. "It's okay, sweetheart. Mommy's here."

"Oh dear," Faith said, wringing her hands. "You must understand that Miss Rosetta is distraught."

"Rosetta? Well, she's a hotheaded Italian. That explains everything." The woman peered down her nose at Caterina. "Come,

Fred, I don't think we want *this* one after all. She'd probably grow up to be just as willful as her mother."

"Get out," Caterina said through clenched teeth.

The woman shifted her large leather purse on her arm and wedged past Caterina, her sharp heels clicking on the wooden floor, punctuating Marisa's wails.

Her husband trailed behind her, glaring at Caterina. "You've spoiled her birthday, you know. And you'll regret this decision."

After the Andersons stormed out, tears welled in Caterina's eyes. She rocked Marisa in her arms, soothing her.

Faith clucked her tongue. "My dear, you must think of Marisa's welfare. It's been a year now. If you wait any longer, it's going to be very difficult for her to adjust to a new family. The Andersons were good people. They would have grown to love her."

"But I love her. I'm enough for her."

"You must face facts. Why, a lovely girl like you can start over and marry a nice boy. No man wants another man's child." Faith paused. "You never heard from the father?"

The father. Caterina shook her head, feeling as if her heart had surely sustained injury. For years they'd been the closest of childhood friends, delighted in each other, read each other's mind, and only recently, as adults, had succumbed to a newfound passion. But now, Marisa was all that remained of their expression of desire. "My mother was widowed, and she raised me alone. I can do this."

"There's a vast difference in our society between a widow and a single woman with an illegitimate child. Think of the stigma she will suffer. Is that what you want for your child?"

Caterina looked at her little girl. Marisa's tears had dried, and a smile crept onto her face. Caterina's heart melted like sweet honey. Her little girl's vivid blue eyes were round and innocent and perfect replicas of her father's eyes. Caterina couldn't let her go. Marisa was all she had of the man she would love forever. "She stays with me."

"We only want what's best for you." Faith heaved a great sigh.

Caterina peppered Marisa with kisses, relieved that she'd gotten there in time. Faith and Patrick O'Connell were fair with the unwed mothers who came to them, and Caterina knew they wouldn't have allowed the Andersons to take Marisa without her permission—unlike some of the other oppressive maternity homes she'd visited—but the mere thought of strangers fawning over Marisa curdled her stomach.

Caterina vowed never to let anyone try to take Marisa from her again. She would do whatever it took to keep her child, and as far as she was concerned, society and its snotty judgments could go straight to hell.

"It's not that we don't love you and Marisa." Faith's expression was earnest. "But you must know you're running out of options, dear."

Caterina squeezed her eyes against Faith's stinging words. Faith had once been a nun, and her mission in life was to be of service to others. But Caterina found it difficult to face her dilemma.

Instead, she closed her eyes and savored the warmth and pressure of Marisa's body against her own. Her sweet, powdery scent always brought a rush of joy to Caterina, but today her emotions were in tatters. A swath of wavy dark hair soft as duckling's down lay against Marisa's smooth, olive-toned cheek. Caterina stroked her baby's skin in a feathery caress. "My precious girl," she murmured. Marisa closed her eyes, snuggling against her bosom. Caterina stroked her hair, stifling a cry. *How could I have thought to let her go?*

Faith put a hand on Caterina's shoulder. "If you won't consider adoption, can you go home to the vineyard in Napa? Perhaps your mother will relent if she meets Marisa."

Caterina shook her head vehemently. "Going home to Mille Étoiles would be disastrous. My mother will never forgive me." Years ago, when Caterina had crossed the threshold into womanhood, her mother had warned her against the mistakes a girl might make. Sex before marriage, pregnancy, illegitimate children. *Utterly unforgivable.*

Her mother's words rang in her ears. She'd heard her reproaches a thousand times. "I'd disown you if you ever made such a mistake. Only common trash behaves that way. Those girls should give their babies up for adoption; it's the only decent thing to do. There's nothing worse than being forced into marriage."

Faith ran her hand over Marisa's hair and kissed her forehead. "If only your mother could see these happy eyes gazing up at her. I think she'd love her immediately, don't you?"

"You can't imagine the wrath of Ava Rosetta." Caterina frowned. Faith seemed to be driving at something, but before Caterina could ask, Marisa turned her eyes up to her, and her heart lurched. Once Caterina had seen her baby's bright blue eyes—*his eyes*—blinking back at her, trusting her, needing her, she couldn't bear to part with her. When she'd finally agreed to "do the sensible thing," as Faith had implored, it had felt as if she were halving her very soul.

Adopting their babies out might have been the right decision for some girls who selflessly gave their children to those who could provide for them, but it was not for her. Maybe those girls were stronger than she was, or maybe they were in more desperate situations. Caterina would sooner take a knife and carve out her own heart—that's what it had felt like when she'd been asked to sign the adoption papers.

Faith rested a hand on her arm. "Aren't you going to Napa this weekend?"

Caterina nodded. Her mother had asked her to help choose wines for a wine-tasting competition. Ava Rosetta was a respected winemaker who had standards so lofty that Caterina had often wondered if she could ever match her mother's stature in the industry—or in life.

"Why don't you take Marisa with you? It is your home."

Why not, indeed? Guilt prickled her neck. Each day that Caterina concealed the truth of her mistake, her lies by necessity grew larger and more complex. She squirreled away cash and constructed elaborate excuses for her whereabouts. She couldn't continue her charade much longer. Her stories had swirled into a vortex of lies that was sucking her spirit from her.

More than that, she wasn't being fair to Marisa. There had been no doubt in her mind that the day would come when she would have to choose between the love of her mother and the love for her child. The bleak thought tore at Caterina's soul.

Faith's reddish curls framed a freckled face drawn with concern. "I must tell you that we have a new girl coming in two weeks. We're going to need your room."

Caterina blinked back hot tears. "I'll tell her this weekend." She'd been in denial; now it was time to accept the consequences of her actions. She'd have to ask her mother if she could live at home with Marisa, at least until her sublet apartment was available again. She clutched Marisa in her arms.

Whatever her mother had to share with her this weekend surely paled in comparison to the truth Caterina planned to reveal.

2

Ava swung open the arched wooden door and stepped outside the main entry of the château just as a shiny red-and-white Corvette convertible peeled past toward the property exit, which was flanked with rows of towering Italian cypress. She stiffened, her defenses on high alert. Santo must have been visiting his older cousin Raphael, who was like a father to him, at his cottage. *He has every right to be here,* she reminded herself, but his presence made her nervous. *At least Caterina isn't here.*

Watching him, Ava slid her hands into the pockets of her slim cotton slacks in an effort to appear nonchalant. She recalled the private conversation they'd had nearly two years ago. Though Santo might think her obdurate and unyielding, he didn't know the real reason behind her decision. And she had no intention of reopening wounds of the past to tell him. Santo rarely came to Mille Étoiles, but when he did, they kept their distance from each other.

Gravel crunched behind her, and she turned.

"So what do you think about that fancy new car?"

Raphael walked toward her, his thumbs hooked in the belt loops of his dungarees, his bronzed face in stark contrast with his white shirt. He had strong cheekbones, a well-defined jaw, broad shoulders, and a muscular, athletic build.

Ava tented her hand against the sun. As he came closer, she said, "Nice sports car. Santo must be doing well."

"He is." Raphael stopped beside her and lifted a strand of hair that had tangled in her discreet diamond stud earring. "I'm awfully proud of him."

The citrus scent of Italian bergamot surrounded him like an aura. Ava appreciated how it melded with the enticing aroma of his sun-warmed skin.

"He has several well-paying clients, and he's been lecturing on viticulture at the university. Told me he's been saving money for the future, but he received a windfall and decided to splurge on the car." Raphael spoke with an Italian accent, his baritone voice reverberating in his broad chest.

"He's a smart young man. Just like you." Ava smiled up at Raphael. What would she do without him? A seasoned foreman, a *vigneron* from Montalcino, Raphael was an expert in viticulture and managed the vineyard workers. Years ago he had brought young Santo to Mille Étoiles to live. Because of her husband's actions, she'd always felt guilty about the poor orphan.

"What's on your agenda today, Ava?"

"Overseeing preparations for the party this weekend." She nodded toward the grand stone château behind her. Mille Étoiles was designed after her family home in Bordeaux, France. "I fear the ivy will take over if it's not trimmed soon. Do you have workers who can tame this wild mess?" Creeping strands of ivy stretched toward twin turrets and crept along tall arched windows crowned with wedged keystones. She had important guests this weekend. Everything must be pristine. Mille Étoiles had a stellar reputation that she worked hard to maintain.

"We'll see to it," Raphael said. "Do you have time to look at the new equipment?"

"Of course." On Raphael's recommendation, Ava had purchased new grape de-stemmers and crushers for the upcoming harvest. "We sure paid enough for it. Is it gold plated?"

"It's a good investment, Ava."

"I know it is." She'd borrowed heavily for the new equipment. "A couple of good seasons will pay for it. But if the weather turns foul, Mille Étoiles will be financially strained." Too much sun, rain, or ice could ruin a crop or compromise the quality of wine. So far, weather conditions had been nearly perfect this season, but all that could change in an instant. Every year brought a new set of challenges.

"Making wine requires a gambler's steely nerves. But you've bet well so far."

"I always worry, Raphael." Ava gazed out from their vantage point. A foggy morning marine layer drifted beneath their mountainous perch, partially obscuring the patchwork agricultural valley below. They walked across the property, kicking up dirt with their boots and stopping to inspect pristine grape clusters—or berries—as they went. The vineyard's lacy vines were groomed to perfection.

At this altitude, where the rigors of nature heaped stress upon the grapes, the cabernet sauvignon berries were compact, their juice intense, and their tannin levels enviably high.

Ava and Raphael were guardedly pleased. The more environmental stress, the better the potential for a fine red wine, due to the higher ratio of skin to interior fruit.

They inspected the equipment and spoke to a few workers, satisfied they were as prepared as they could be for harvest. Ava left Raphael in the vineyard and returned to the house.

In the kitchen, shiny copper pots and dried herbs hung from wooden rafters, and hand-painted tiles brightened stone walls. Even on the hottest days, the thick walls kept the interior temperature cool.

The housekeeper, a plump Mexican woman with black and gray hair wound into a thick bun at the nape of her neck, stood at the counter paring potatoes. She glanced up and flashed a smile. "You just missed that nice young man from New York again."

"I have the papers he left." Frowning, Ava poured cool water from a pitcher on the table. Nina had been working at Mille Étoiles since Caterina was a baby. Nina's daughter, Juliana, had grown up with Caterina; they were as close as sisters. Ava and Nina had also grown to rely on each other over the years, especially during the lean years of the Depression.

"Do you know he said he'd never tasted guacamole? But he sure liked mine." Nina's face lit with pride.

"Did he say what he wanted?" Not that she wanted to talk to that investigator. After his first visit, Ava had been ignoring his calls. She lifted the water glass to her lips. *Caterina must not learn of this.*

"He said he didn't need to talk to you again." Nina inclined her head toward a business card on the counter. "He left his card for Caterina. He said something about an inheritance from her father's family. Wouldn't that be nice?"

Ava shrugged, feigning disinterest. "I don't think there's much to it. But I'll tell her tomorrow when she arrives." She slipped the card into her pocket and changed the subject. "How are the party preparations coming along?"

"Don't worry, everything will be done," Nina replied with a smile. "It'll be good to see Caterina. We don't see much of her anymore."

Ava sipped her water. She wished Caterina would return home to live. She hoped someday Caterina and her husband would run Mille Étoiles.

"Ted and his parents are coming," Ava said. Ted and Caterina had been going steady throughout college. Everyone thought their marriage was a fait accompli, but Caterina had called off their relationship. Afterward, she'd been vague about her reason. Ava still wondered why Caterina hadn't confided in her.

Nina looked up with surprise. "Does Caterina know Ted is coming?"

"Not yet. But Ted is still crazy about her. I think she was skittish about marriage. Now that she's been working, maybe she's had time to reconsider." When Ted's mother had told her that Ted had stopped seeing his girlfriend and still talked about Caterina, Ava started planning to reunite them.

She hoped Caterina and Ted would take up where they had left off. It needn't be a long engagement. Ava smiled to herself. If Caterina became pregnant soon, she'd welcome a grandchild. A whole houseful of grandchildren someday, that's what she prayed for. Then, her job would be complete.

In the meantime, she had to nip this investigator's actions. There was nothing that Caterina needed from Italy.

After dinner, Ava retired to her bedroom. She was worried the New York investigator might not give up. All day she'd thought about what to do.

Ava sat at her antique French writing desk. She slid open a drawer and removed a thick sheet of creamy writing paper embossed with the star-studded grapevine imprint of Mille Étoiles. *I'll write to the probate attorney,* she thought, pursing her lips. *I'll insist that Caterina's inheritance be rescinded.*

Outside her bedroom window, a full moon ignited the heavens with silvery light that spilled onto her desk. Ava sighed. Caterina would have every right to be upset. Yet if she didn't know the truth, it couldn't hurt her.

As it hurt me.

Ava had shielded Caterina from pain and heartache since the day she was born. Why should Caterina—a beautiful, modern young girl with her life ahead of her—care about something that had happened so long ago? In America, one could revise one's life, far from the eyes of ancestors.

And their transgressions.

Her enameled fountain pen hovered over the paper. Caterina had come into the world with curiosity blazing in her luminous, gold-flecked green eyes. After *Mama* and *Papa,* her next words had been questions. *Why? Where? How?*

As a mother, it was Ava's duty to look out for Caterina, to help her get started in life. She passed a hand over her face. Being a single parent was challenging.

Ava peered outside and saw Vino, one of Santo's white Italian Maremma sheepdogs, running in circles and acting strangely. He was probably on the scent of a rodent scampering through the property.

With a heavy heart, Ava realized it was too late to cancel the inheritance. She put down the pen and massaged the sore joints in her hands. Work at the vineyard was physically demanding. Caterina had worked beside her until she'd left to attend the university in San Francisco. She missed her daughter, but more than that, she feared once Caterina discovered the truth, she'd never speak to her again.

The truth. Ava had been telling her edited version for more than twenty years. If Caterina uncovered her secrets, it could have dangerous, devastating consequences. She flexed her fingers and noticed her hands were shaking.

Ava sank her face into her hands. *Why can't people leave well enough alone?*

3

After winding her way up Howell Mountain, Caterina turned into the gravel drive that curved to the magnificent stone château on the property. As she drove, she saw silvery shadows dancing in the breezes that flowed through meticulous rows of wizened vines. Caterina had always thought they looked like little gnomes in the moonlight.

After greeting Caterina, Ava led her to the wine cellar for a tasting before dinner. Caterina decided this was the best place to tell her mother about Marisa; there, no one would hear the inevitable argument.

"Which wines will we taste tonight?" Caterina perched on a hand-carved stool and waited for Ava to pour the wine.

"Why don't you tell me what they are?" Ava arched a finely drawn brow as she took in the outfit Caterina had changed into after her drive from San Francisco.

Caterina sat up straighter. Already she felt scrutinized. She wore a full-skirted, white cotton piqué dress with a short matching jacket. As she fiddled with the pearls around her neck, she realized she'd chosen quite the virginal outfit for her confession. Would it make any difference? In contrast, her mother looked elegant in a slim, wide-necked burgundy silk dress.

The cellar had been constructed in the old European fashion, using stones from their property to build the underground room where racks of wines were stored to age. Though the air in the cellar beneath their castle-like home was cooler than the sun-drenched fields on their Napa Valley property above, Caterina felt perspiration gather around her torso.

She shifted as she watched her mother open a bottle of wine, her familiar movements etched in Caterina's mind. Ava kept the label turned away from Caterina.

Everything Ava did was precise. The flick of her wrist, the set of her jaw, the tilt of her chin. A steady draw on the cork, taking care not to damage it. Next, the inspection, her dark eyes trained to quickly capture the slightest imperfection. The sniff of the cork, followed by an almost imperceptible nod of approval as she eased the wine from its dark womb, its color that of the garnets glittering on her earlobes. A swirl to aerate the oxygen-starved elixir, a glance at the streaks left on the crystal balloon, and a steady inhalation. Her eyes were half-closed in concentration, evaluating the wine.

Ava's superior standards had lifted Mille Étoiles's wine to the upper echelons of the industry. Under Ava's constant evaluative eye, Caterina had been taught perfection. Now, watching her mother was like gazing into a mirror.

Caterina chewed her lip in thought. Not only had she violated her mother's principle of perfection—and those of her religion—but she'd also violated her own standards. She was her mother's daughter.

Caterina moistened her lips to speak, but the words lodged in her throat. *What shall I say?*

Her mother offered her a wineglass. "Tell me what you think, *ma chérie*," Ava said, her French-accented voice reverberating in the cellar.

Caterina met her mother's gaze. Ava was testing her, challenging her. Had her mother ever made a mistake? She always displayed confidence. That was one of her secrets.

Rage was another—and perhaps the only point where her mother fell short of the mark on perfection. When crossed, Ava would unleash a furious tirade, her face contorting like some demon-possessed goddess. Ava was a beautiful woman—slim, elegant, and well mannered. No one—outside of the vineyard, that is—would imagine her potential for wrathful anger. And only Raphael could calm her.

Caterina had often puzzled over the source of her mother's anger and strictness. Ava had everything—Mille Étoiles, a fairly obedient daughter who loved her, and the admiration of all who knew her. And yet, Ava Rosetta remained a woman of contradictions—she had a soft heart, but a stern spine. Was she angry over her husband's early demise? Did she feel cheated out of a larger family?

Whatever the reason for Ava's interminable anger, Caterina needed all the courage she could muster this weekend.

Caterina swirled the wine and then sniffed it. She held the wine to the light, inspecting its opacity. Next, she tasted, holding the liquid in her mouth, dissecting nuances. She shifted the wine farther back on her tongue, detecting different impressions, observing the evolution. Plum, apricot, oak . . . and a sharp burnt flavor.

Caterina spat the wine into another glass. She felt the weight of her mother's inquisitive stare noting every slight movement on her daughter's face. The lift of a brow, the tug of a lip, the twitch of a nostril. These had meaning to Ava. Caterina kept her expression stoic.

"Well?"

"It's rot, and you know it. That's not our wine."

A shadow of a smile crossed Ava's face. "Popular rot, nevertheless." She reached for the open carafe and poured a glass. "Well done. Your reward, *ma chérie*."

"Why would you do that to me?" Caterina drank from a glass of water, swishing cool well water in her mouth to cleanse her palate. "I'm a trained sommelier."

"You have to know the popular competition, as well as our fine competitors," Ava said. "There's always something to be learned."

That much was true, Caterina acknowledged. The future of their vineyard and wine label depended on Ava's—and soon, Caterina's, too—ability to recognize, create, and promote excellence. She brought the glass to her nose, inhaling the familiar bouquet, and then repeated the tasting process. This time she allowed the wine to linger on her tongue, savoring its complexities before swallowing.

Caterina and Ava exchanged nods of approval.

"This is the one we should enter into the competition," Ava announced.

"I thought you asked me here for my opinion," Caterina said. "I'd like to try others before we decide. What about the '52 Howell Mountain cabernet?"

Ava held her glass in midair. "We'll have that tomorrow."

Caterina cleared her throat to speak. *Now is the time to tell her.* But before she could part with her secret, her pulse quickened, beads of sweat formed on her upper lip, and her jaw seemed to freeze in place.

"Maman—"

Ava paused. "Yes, what is it?"

Caterina stared at her. The words she longed to say were thick on her tongue. *I want you to meet someone . . . her name is Marisa, she's your granddaughter, and she's beautiful.*

Her mother smiled. *This could be the last moment she'd ever see her mother smile.*

"Nothing." Caterina shrugged.

Ava started up the stone steps, and Caterina followed her, carrying the wine. She had missed her opportunity. A sour mixture of relief and regret coursed through her.

Caterina wound through the high-ceilinged living room. Its

French-paned doors stood open to the balmy evening breeze, which carried the scent of summer basil from Nina's herb garden.

Nina was already preparing dinner. The middle-aged woman wore a vivid yellow cotton dress festooned with colorful embroidered flowers in the Mexican tradition. She turned when she heard Caterina come in.

"Welcome home." Nina smiled and folded Caterina to her ample breast. "You look tired, *pobrecita*. And you've lost weight."

"That's good." Ava glanced at Caterina with a critical eye.

"My last year at school was stressful," Caterina replied in defense. *In more ways than you can imagine.* "What's for supper, Nina?" Caterina hugged their housekeeper again, inhaling the familiar scent of garlic and cilantro that seemed part of her cherry-brown skin.

"Coq au vin. It's your mother's old recipe with my wild mushrooms and onions, a crumble of bacon, our pinot noir, and a little cognac. And flan for dessert." She winked. "If your mother approves."

"She can have whatever she wants," Ava said with a wave of her hand. "She's a grown woman. Why, at her age—"

Caterina rolled her eyes. "I know, you and Papa had already immigrated, planted the new vineyard sections, and bottled the old vine wine."

"*And* I was a mother." Ava paused. "Ted Thornwald has been asking about you again."

Caterina sat at the kitchen table and shot a look at Nina, who was arranging food on plates.

Ava filled their wineglasses. "I was thinking of having a little party tomorrow night."

Caterina recognized the studied lightness in her mother's voice. "It's all planned, isn't it?" Calmly, she sliced into the tender, fragrant chicken Nina had served.

"*Sí, señorita,*" Nina said with a quick smile. She slid a tray of sliced cheese onto the table. Ava began to nibble on a slice of brie with apple.

Her mother shrugged and went on, "Ted and his family are coming tomorrow. I don't know what happened between the two of you that made you want to go to Los Angeles for a semester—which delayed your graduation—but he's willing to overlook it all. I told them you got cold feet."

"I don't need your help finding a husband."

"Well, apparently, you do. Plenty of girls would like his attention, but I think he's been waiting for you."

"I doubt it. I sure haven't been waiting for him." Caterina thought of the last time she'd seen Ted. He'd asked her out to celebrate New Year's Eve at the St. Francis, and she'd stood him up.

They had dated during her sophomore and junior years—before that unforgettable encounter with Marisa's father in the summer before her senior year. She was fond of Ted, but she'd never been in love with him. Yet, her coolness hadn't dissuaded his ardor. Nina's daughter, Juliana, Caterina's closest friend since childhood, had told her Ted had asked for her opinion on a wedding ring. He'd planned to propose on New Year's Eve.

But Caterina had already started thickening around the middle and had missed her monthly cycles. She told everyone she was taking a semester of art illustration for marketing classes in Los Angeles to learn how to design wine labels and advertising campaigns. And it was just far enough away that Ava, with her night blindness, wouldn't drive to visit her.

"You could do worse than Ted, you know," Ava said with a haughty sniff. "You're twenty-five. The city is full of magic for you now, but I won't live forever. I'd like to see you married and settled before you take over the vineyard. Everyone thought you and Ted would marry."

Caterina glanced at Nina, silently pleading for help.

Nina shoved a pan into a cupboard. "How about that nice young man from New York?"

Caterina swung back to her mother. "Who's that?"

Ava dismissed the question with a wave of her hand. "Just a man who dropped by the vineyard. Some salesman." Ava touched her wineglass to Caterina's, the rounded tone ringing like a bell marking the moment. "At least talk to Ted, and give him a chance."

Nina wagged her head and turned back to her work.

Caterina kissed her mother on the cheek. "I'll speak to him," she said in an effort to appease her. Ava smiled, and Caterina was glad she was in a good mood. Though the opportunity to speak to her in private about Marisa had passed.

Ava retired to her bedroom, relieved that Caterina had at least listened to her this evening. The only thing that could derail her plans was the news of Caterina's inheritance she'd received, although she certainly hadn't shared that with Caterina. *A house in Montalcino.* She wondered if it were the same cottage where the course of their lives had been changed.

That house must be sold. Caterina mustn't return to Italy, not now, not ever. Ava tried to dismiss the growing sense of dread that gathered heavily in her chest.

A soft tap sounded on her bedroom door, and she rose to open it.

Raphael's broad shoulders filled the doorway. "How's Caterina? I was worried about you this evening." His eyes were clouded with concern.

Ava relaxed her brow. She could smell the ripe sweetness of sun-baked grapes on Raphael. He was more than the vineyard foreman; he had become a trusted advisor and a close friend, even closer now that Caterina was no longer living at Mille Étoiles. He was responsible for the grape production. Without his expertise, as a winemaker she would have no fine palette with which to paint.

"Caterina seems well, and I'm glad you came." She rested her hand on his muscular forearm. A fresh sprinkle of gray hair glinted at his temples against his wavy black hair, giving him an air of authority.

Raphael had the toned, muscular physique of a man who used his body every day. Though he was nearing fifty, he showed no signs of slowing down, and men half his age couldn't keep up with him. Only the silver threads of hair and laugh lines around his eyes betrayed his age.

Ava gazed into his warm brown eyes. "Ted and his family are coming tomorrow."

Raphael stroked his stubbled chin. "How does Caterina feel about him?"

"They had a little rough patch. It happens. But they're meant for each other."

"Caterina has her own mind, Ava. She's not a little girl anymore."

"There's no one else in her life. It's time she made a decision." She didn't want Caterina to go through the difficulties she'd had.

Frowning, Raphael shook his head. "Give her some time to follow her heart."

"She's had enough time," she snapped. "She could have met someone at the university." *Men don't understand.* She stopped herself; she didn't want to argue with him. And she didn't want to tell him about the news she'd received from the investigator. Raphael would only say he'd warned her. "I'm tired, Raphael. Tomorrow is a busy day. Good night."

Ava pressed her lips against his cheek and firmly shut the door. *Dear Raphael.* What a good man he was. Even if he didn't understand the ways of the world.

4

It was a sunny Saturday morning, and Caterina had dressed in dungarees to inspect the vineyard before the party tonight. Holding a cup of coffee, she peered from the kitchen window. She couldn't wait to see how the grapes were ripening.

She'd resolved to speak to her mother about Marisa this weekend. She'd missed her opportunity last night, and her mother had already planned the party for this evening. Tomorrow would be the dreaded day. Her coffee cup shimmied in her hand as she thought about it.

Through the window, a flash of chrome caught her eye. A blue car was weaving its way through the cypress-lined drive. Curious, she drained the last swallow from her cup and then made her way through the living room.

A knock sounded on the front door just as she reached it. With Nina in the garden and her mother in the vineyard with Raphael, there was no one else around except for Vino, who stood guard nearby.

She opened the door. "May I help you?"

A tall, lanky man stood on the front steps in shiny oxfords, a fat briefcase by his side. "My name is Anthony Martoni, and I'm an investigator working on an estate case. A law firm in New York, Paxton & Brueger, hired me to locate Caterina Rosetta regarding an inheritance." He spoke with a clipped New York accent.

"I'm Caterina Rosetta." Her curiosity was aroused. *An inheritance from whom?*

"Then I have some important papers for your review. It's good news, I suspect," he added quickly.

"Please come in." She swung open the arched wooden door for him. Vino trotted in after him. "Would you care for coffee?"

He stepped inside, his eyes taking in the soaring grandeur of the home. "Yes, that's very kind of you, thank you."

Caterina showed him to the expansive table in the formal dining room where Ava often conducted private wine tastings. A pair of antique French marquetry and marble-topped cabinets flanked the room, and multicolored bouquets of roses from their cutting garden burst from crystal vases. A Persian carpet muffled their footfalls. Though the home was stately in proportion, it was still gracious and inviting.

When Nina appeared at the doorway, Caterina signaled for her to bring coffee for them, and she sat down. Vino plopped by her feet.

She thought of finding her mother, but Ava could be anywhere on the property. She decided to hear him out first.

The investigator sat down and carefully placed his briefcase on the polished table. Nina bustled in to pour two cups of coffee.

"Thank you, Nina." Anthony smiled and lifted the cup to his lips.

"You know Nina?" Nonplussed, Caterina looked from one to the other.

He cleared his throat. "I've been here before, looking for you. Your mother told me you weren't available."

Nina quickly disappeared into the kitchen.

"Then go on," Caterina said, rubbing Vino's neck. Why hadn't her mother mentioned this?

Anthony took a sip and began. "You've been named in your

grandmother's will. Specifically, you've inherited a house from Violetta Romagnoli Rosetta of Montalcino, Italy."

Caterina looked at him in bewilderment. "That's impossible. My grandmother died before I was born."

"There's no mistake." Anthony opened his briefcase and withdrew several documents,

"A house in Montalcino?" she repeated in disbelief. "What kind of house?"

"A cottage. I understand it needs some work." He gave her a letter and some documents from an attorney in Italy, and as she read, he swung around, peering at wine bottles displayed in an ornately sculpted iron wine enclosure. "May I look at your wines?"

"Of course. We collect other wines, too." She sipped her coffee as she flipped through the pages.

He rested a hand on the ironwork and peered inside. "A Brunello di Montalcino. That's one of my favorites," he added with relish, touching the bottles with reverence.

"You certainly know your wines." Though he was clearly mistaken about her grandmother. "My father was born in Italy. He died when I was a baby, and, as I understand, his family was gone long before that."

"And who told you that?"

"My mother, of course." Questions began to swirl in her mind. Surely her mother had told her the truth. Ava Rosetta didn't keep secrets. *Unlike her daughter.* She pressed her temple to alleviate a throbbing vein.

Caterina rose from her chair. "I appreciate your visit, and I wish I could help you, but I'm probably not the right woman."

"Oh, but you are." He colored slightly. "When I spoke to your mother, she didn't think you'd be interested, but I have a duty to uphold. Today I thought I'd try one more time to deliver your documents before I had to return."

She narrowed her eyes in thought. None of this was making sense.

Anthony consulted his notes. "And we have orders to arrange your passage to Italy on Pan American Airways."

"Orders?" Caterina laughed and drew herself up. Even with her low boot heels, she stood at eye level with him. "No one orders me to do anything." *Except my mother.* Though his offer was ridiculous, she found the prospect of flying across the ocean in an airplane intriguing, and she'd always wondered about her father and his heritage.

"I meant that we have authorization to pay all expenses." The investigator shuffled through his briefcase and withdrew a thick sheaf of papers with an old photograph clipped to the top. He handed the packet to her. "Review the documents, Miss Rosetta, or have an attorney look at them, but there is no mistake. You have inherited a house in Montalcino from your grandmother."

As he finished speaking, the wine bottles began to rattle in their racks. Instinctively, Caterina shoved him away from the tall racks and into a doorway between the living room and dining room. Timbers creaked and groaned around them. The wine racks were secured against earthquakes, but as a native Californian, Caterina had an ingrained habit to seek shelter. Anthony's briefcase clattered to the floor.

With her arms outstretched, Caterina pressed her palms against the doorjamb. Anthony scrambled to mimic her actions and flushed at finding himself cheek to cheek with her as they braced against the vibration. After a few seconds, the bottles grew still.

"Is that it?" Unnerved by the tremor, Anthony looked around with wide eyes.

"Probably. Now you can say you've been in a real California earthquake. But that was just a little shake, nothing to worry about." Taking it in stride, she stepped away. She had far larger problems to think about this weekend. Especially tomorrow.

"Will there be another one?" His face was bright pink and beaded with perspiration. He pulled out a white linen handkerchief from his suit jacket and mopped his forehead.

"You never know. That might have been a precursor to the next big one."

"Glad I'm leaving." He grabbed his briefcase and snapped it shut. "I'll call you next week to make further arrangements." He stumbled out in haste.

Before she secured the latch on the wine rack, Caterina checked the dusty Brunello di Montalcino bottles, mulling over the possibility she'd had a grandmother she hadn't known.

As a girl, she'd often wished for a kindly grandmother. It would have been a lonely childhood, if not for Nina and Juliana. Her mother had never allowed her to mix with the farmworkers, except for Raphael, who ran the vineyard and let her play among the vines. He'd also taught her how to care for their precious grapes, for their entire existence depended on the vines.

Caterina removed a bottle that had moisture around the cork. Her thoughts reeled back to the investigator. Why would her mother have masked the truth about her grandmother, her father's mother? She'd never known her to lie about anything.

There must be another explanation. Ava Rosetta was a woman beyond reproach. Everyone in the valley knew that.

Caterina thumbed through the documents the investigator had left. They were in Italian, which she could read fairly well, though her French was much better. Her father had been brought up in Montalcino, but she'd learned Italian from Raphael.

Ava was a superb vintner, or winemaker, born to the craft in Bordeaux, where she'd been brought up on her family's vineyard. She and Raphael had elevated the wine label of Mille Étoiles to nothing short of magnificent. Some wine merchants who visited the vineyard even thought they were married, the way they finished each other's sentences. But Ava hadn't even dated since her husband's untimely death.

Caterina peered at the tattered black-and-white photograph. The stone cottage was perched on a hill, and she could see vines on the sloped hillside that fell away to one side. Her heart quickened. *Did the land go with the house?* She traced the shadowy structure. *A home in Montalcino. Italy.* Her home now, if these documents were true.

Or were they? Perhaps there was another woman with her name, or maybe the will was an old one. Who knew what went on in Italy, a country so far, far away?

She'd always dreamed of having a family and her own vineyard where she could practice her art. There weren't many women vintners in the world of wine, but she knew her business. She rubbed her furrowed brow, contemplating the photo. What secrets did those walls conceal?

She'd complicated her life, possibly beyond repair. She touched the house in the image again. Maybe she *should* go to Montalcino.

She squinted at the old photo. What did her mother know about this? She would ask her tomorrow, after the party tonight. And she'd tell her about Marisa, too. *Seems we both have secrets to share.*

The fine hair on her neck bristled. Even now, she sensed there was more to the story than her mother would be willing to share. Why would Ava have kept a grandmother from her all her life?

Vino brushed against her legs, whining. She patted her thigh. "Come on, Vino. Let's go talk to Nina before we head to the vineyard." She had a great deal to do before the party; she had to prepare herself for Ted and his parents and come to grips with the thought of reuniting with him. If she did as her mother suggested, it would only be for Marisa, for a chance at a better life for her daughter.

Could she really do it?

5

Juliana let out a low whistle. "Look how chic you've become since moving to the big city." She pushed herself from a chair in the corner of Caterina's bedroom at Mille Étoiles. "You look just like Audrey Hepburn in *Sabrina*."

"Do you really think so? I loved her in that film." Caterina checked herself in the full-length mirror. She'd decided on a slim-fitting black cocktail dress that she hadn't worn since before Marisa was born. A pearl choker and earrings accented the wide neckline and her upswept hairstyle.

"We should go see her new film, *War and Peace*."

Caterina met Juliana's almond-shaped eyes in the mirror. They were large and expressive, just like Nina's. "I'd like to, but I've been spending every moment I can with Marisa." She flicked a new black Helena Rubinstein Mascara Matic on her lashes. The cosmetics magnate often sent Ava gifts of test products before launch for her refined opinion, just as Ava offered Helena the first choice of prized vintages for her wine collection.

"Is this too much for you, Cat? I mean, I understand; I wish I'd had a baby with Al, but most single girls—"

"No," Caterina cut in. "I can do this. I'm her mother." She sat on a tufted rose-colored window seat to adjust the tiny buckled straps on her ebony high heels. "And I have to tell my mother about her this weekend."

Juliana grimaced and sat next to her. "Want me to be there with you? She'll blow up like Mount Vesuvius."

"Thanks, but I need to do this alone." Caterina gazed from the window across the darkened vineyards. "What happened to the lives we once imagined we'd have?"

"I guess we grew up." Juliana smoothed her lipstick-red dress, which had a full flounced skirt nipped into a tiny waist, a copy of the Christian Dior style the fashion editors had dubbed "The New Look" after the Second World War.

Caterina watched her friend, proud of what she was accomplishing in her life. Juliana had been a baby when her father had deserted her mother and returned to Mexico. Shortly afterward, Ava had hired Nina at Mille Étoiles.

After her fiancé died, Juliana had tried to find work at a vineyard, but because she was a woman, few were willing to hire her. Through Caterina, Juliana made friends with wealthy women at the St. Francis and was helping several of them create wine cellars for their husbands and their business associates. She was also arranging advertising for one winery and helping another with special events. Slowly she was building a reputation as a wine publicist, her dream job.

Juliana had overcome a tragedy; surely Caterina could overcome the challenges in her own life. She rested her chin in her hand, her elbow on the windowsill. "Remember when we used to climb to the top of Howell Mountain and share our secrets? If the moon was full, like it is tonight, we imagined our wishes would come true."

The mountaintop spot was where they'd confided their deepest secrets to each other over the years, where Caterina had told Juliana she was pregnant, and where Juliana had cried in her arms over her fiancé's death.

Caterina chuckled softly. "Good thing most of our wishes didn't come true. Remember Jeremy?" She winked at her dearest friend.

Juliana dissolved into gales of laughter. "Oh, Jeremy, my first crush. I haven't thought of him in years." She dabbed her eyes and smiled. "I've sure missed you, Cat. And how is Marisa?"

"She's adorable, and she's getting so big." Caterina blinked hard, thankful she hadn't adopted her out.

A shadow crossed Juliana's face. "Have you tried calling her father again?"

"He doesn't want to hear from me," she said, perhaps a little too sharply. She wished Juliana wouldn't talk about him.

"I see him sometimes in Napa. He's working a lot."

"Jules, what do you want me to say? I've tried." She had once spent long hours with him, testing and refining wine in the cool, stone-lined cave at Mille Étoiles, which was burrowed into the side of Howell Mountain. She pushed the memory from her mind.

"Have you ever met his fiancée?" Juliana widened her dark eyes. She'd wound her straight black hair into a chignon, which made her deep brown eyes loom even larger in her pretty, well-defined face.

"No."

"You have to tell him about Marisa."

"Why? So he can reject her, too?" Caterina huffed as she stood to check the seams in the back of her stockings in the mirror.

"He's a good guy, Cat. I've always thought he'd do the right thing if he knew."

Caterina glanced over her shoulder. "Oh, come on, Jules. He dodged my calls for months. Even sent my letters back unopened, marked 'return to sender.'"

"He has a right to know, don't you think?"

"He had his chance." Caterina raised her eyebrows. "You haven't told him, have you?"

"No." Juliana's eyes darted away, and she picked at a thread on her dress.

"Jules, you promised you wouldn't say anything."

"And I won't. But now that Marisa's older, maybe *you* should. He's her father."

"I've got a lot on my mind right now. Faith needs our room." She tugged on her hose with vengeance to straighten a rear seam.

"Careful. You'll tear your hose," Juliana said. "What about the apartment you sublet?"

"I can't return with Marisa. I just found out the landlord won't let single mothers live there. Evidently there's a morals clause in the lease." Landlords could be choosy. There were so many people who'd left the armed services after the war and started families that apartments often had waiting lists.

"What a jerk. Well, you can stay with me for as long as you like." Juliana had rented a room in a boardinghouse in the village of Napa, much to her mother's consternation. Nina insisted unmarried women should live with parents until they were married. Juliana argued that she'd already been engaged, so she was practically a widow.

"Thanks, Jules, but I'm sure your landlord would have something to say about three people living in your room. No, I'll have to find an apartment as soon as I return." She blew out a breath. "Being a mom is so difficult at times. I think some women, like Faith, must have a natural gene for it." She leaned toward the mirror, picked up a tiny brush, and swept on red lipstick.

"You're a good mother to Marisa, and you love her. So what if Faith is better with a diaper? It's not like Marisa will be in one forever."

Caterina pressed her lips together and smiled at that thought. Juliana was right. She sat next to her and bumped her shoulder.

"Look, I can't imagine what you're going through," Juliana said. "But I know you; you'll make the right decision. You're the best person I know."

"If that were true, I wouldn't be in this mess."

"It took two, didn't it?" Juliana squeezed Caterina's hand.

"Look!" Caterina cried out, motioning toward the sky. A star shot silently through the Milky Way. "You can make a wish now."

Juliana turned toward her with a pointed look. "I already have."

Caterina shook her head. "I'm not telling him."

"Someday you will."

An Elvis Presley song came on the radio, and Juliana jumped off the window seat to turn up the volume. "Oh, I *love* this song. Come on, Cat, let's put our troubles aside and have a good time tonight. We both need it." She swirled around in her red satin dress, snapping her fingers to the music. "Heartbreak hotel," she sang.

"So who are you planning on dancing with tonight, Jules?" Caterina watched Juliana sway to the music. Her gaiety was like a shower of sparklers in the night, even if sadness lurked beneath her sheen. At least Juliana was trying. How long had it been since she'd felt free enough to enjoy herself?

Juliana whirled around. "You know I'm not looking for anyone."

"You don't have to. All the guys are looking at you. Maybe you should give one of them a chance." Juliana had dated Alfonso Villarreal throughout school. He'd worked in army intelligence and had been sent to South Korea. A week before he was scheduled to return, he'd been killed in an ambush. Heartbroken, Juliana hadn't dated since. Caterina removed a stopper from a perfume bottle and dabbed it against her neck and wrists.

A shadow crossed Juliana's face. "I'm not ready yet, but that doesn't mean I can't dance." She sniffed the air. "Smells pretty. Chanel No. 5?"

"Ted's favorite."

"Hmm. Chic. But I thought you had another favorite." Juliana twirled around, humming. "Something richer, sexier."

She did. Shalimar—an exotic, sultry floral blend enriched with vanilla. She'd never worn it again after the night Marisa was conceived. The perfume bottle was stuffed in a box in the back of her closet, along with other photographs and mementos.

Caterina had been up half the night thinking about what to do with her life. She'd dated Ted for a long time in college. She had fond feelings for him, but it wasn't the passion she'd experienced that one, fateful night. Had that been love or merely lust? If she'd never discovered the depths of her passion, maybe she'd be satisfied with Ted now.

And would Ted even accept Marisa?

Juliana waved to her. "Hey, where'd you go? You look like you're a hundred miles away."

"Thinking about tonight."

"Come on, dance with me," Juliana said, twirling around. "Put a smile on that gorgeous face, Kitty Cat. You look like you have the weight of the world on your shoulders." Juliana put her arm around Caterina. "Chin up, tonight everything is copasetic." She winked conspiratorially.

Caterina hugged Juliana, smiling at her use of the old nickname she hadn't heard in years. Juliana was irrepressible; that's what she'd always loved about her. "Come on, let's go, Jules. The party has already started."

The two friends glided down the stairs and opened the French doors to the patio, which was lit with colorful Japanese lanterns. The night air was balmy, and a thousand stars twinkled overhead. A band played in one corner, where a Pat Boone look-alike crooned out the latest love songs—her mother's concession to the young people there.

Juliana tugged her arm and nodded to the crowd that had already gathered. The editor of *Wine Appreciation* magazine was there. To his left was a wine broker who sold to the important restaurants and hotels on the West Coast.

Two other winemakers stood nearby; Caterina could hear them

discussing the pending harvest. Everyone was hoping the favorable weather would hold out.

Last year, some vineyards had lost their entire crop when the grapes were slow to ripen. They'd removed leaves to let in more sun, and then the temperature had soared, scorching the exposed grapes. The weather was the winemaker's fickle partner.

"Look, there's Ted and his parents," Juliana said. The Thornwald family was speaking to Ava. "Shall we?"

"Give me a moment." Caterina accepted a petite vegetable terrine from a silver plate of hors d'oeuvres a server offered to her, along with an aperitif—a tradition to which her French-born mother strictly adhered. Tonight it was a raspberry-flavored cocktail blended of sparkling white wine and cassis.

Caterina smothered a laugh as she watched a woman pick at the terrine in puzzlement. While the rest of America was eating meatloaf and deviled ham, French fare still reigned at Mille Étoiles. Ava would have none of the American hot dogs or commercially canned vegetables. The only alternatives were Nina's fresh Mexican seafood and tortillas and Raphael's pasta.

"*Vive l'apéro,*" Caterina said to Juliana as they toasted.

"Caterina, how nice to see you."

Caterina turned around. It was the editor, Gilbert Waters, and his wife, Bessie, a woman of her mother's generation who had gone to school in France. They exchanged kisses on the cheeks in the customary manner, and Juliana followed suit. "How have you been?"

"Busy, busy," Gilbert said. "We've been traveling so much."

Bessie glanced around and spoke sotto voce. "Have you heard about the new international wine competition in Paris?"

Caterina perked up, although she tried not to appear too interested. "No, I don't believe I have."

Bessie's eyes lit. "It's a blind competition pitting international wines against one another."

At that, Caterina shook her head. "The French will never allow that. Other wines compared against theirs, on their soil? Never."

Gil cast a sly look at her. "Won't that be interesting? It's being hosted by a wine broker. Mille Étoiles should be there."

Caterina raised an eyebrow. "Do you really think a newcomer could enter?"

Juliana shrugged. "Why not ask? Gilbert, do you know how to find out more about entering?"

"I think I can get details and a contact for you," Gilbert said.

Juliana darted a look at Caterina before answering with nonchalance. "Maybe I'll call you later, Gilbert."

Mr. and Mrs. Waters excused themselves to speak to other guests.

Caterina grew quiet, thinking about their amazing Howell Mountain cabernet. If it had aged as well as she thought, it might be a contender. It was a phenomenal wine, a true wine of the terroir, with a distinct sense of place that reflected the soil, climate, and altitude. She recalled the nuances it held, hints of toasted oak, chocolate, spice, blackberry, minerals, and even volcanic matter. But was it good enough to compete on the world stage?

The traditional French style of winemaking held that terroir, or where grapes were grown, was of prime importance. American-style winemaking emphasized the type of grape, so wine in America was sold by the name of the grape, such as pinot noir, rather than the terroir, or place, such as Saint-Émilion, or Médoc, in France.

"A competition could backfire on us," Caterina said. "But see if you can get more details."

"I sure will." Juliana's eyes lit with excitement. "Think of the publicity you could get if you won."

The competition intrigued Caterina, and she longed to showcase California wines. Six decades before, John Patchett had planted his first vines in Napa and hired Charles Krug as his winemaker. The Korbel brothers were producing sparkling wine. Gundlach

Bundschu, Beringer, Inglenook, and Buena Vista had also staked their claims and were producing both reds and whites.

The old vines on Mille Étoiles had once produced a wine that had won a medal at the grand Paris Exposition in the latter part of the last century. However, when her parents acquired the land in 1929, the vines were dormant, casualties of Prohibition.

Looking in her mother's direction, Caterina saw Ava nod at her. "I've been summoned, Juliana."

"Shall I go with you?" Juliana squeezed her arm.

"No, I'll face this on my own, thanks. Go mingle—it's good for business."

Caterina wove through the guests, acknowledging one here and another there with a few gracious words and a smile. Napa Valley was such a small intertwined area, where somehow everyone knew everything about their far-flung neighbors. Caterina swallowed against the anxiety welling up within her. *Or so they thought.*

"Hello, Ted, Mr. and Mrs. Thornwald." Caterina met her mother's eyes. Ava was beaming.

Ted swung around. "Hello, Caterina. You're looking quite nice tonight." Ted was cordial, but Caterina could sense hurt under his polite veneer. Perhaps her mother had been wrong about him.

"Indeed, I must say, you look quite worldly now," Mrs. Thornwald said, peering down her nose at Caterina. Ted's mother was a woman who took pleasure in the finer things in life. Impressive jewelry, an impeccable coiffure, the perfect family. She'd traced her lineage to San Francisco's founding fathers and made sure everyone knew it.

Here it comes. Caterina arranged a pleasant expression on her face. "Just a little older, ma'am."

"And still not married?" Mrs. Thornwald sniffed haughtily. "You young girls simply don't have time for what's really important in life, do you?"

Caterina shot a look at her mother, whose smile was frozen on her face.

"Now, Hilda," Ted's father cut in. "This young generation does things differently from the way we did before the war. Caterina, Ava tells us you're doing a fine job at the St. Francis as sommelier. We should dine there soon. Ted, you've always liked the St. Francis, haven't you?"

"Thank you, sir. That would be delightful." Caterina slid her gaze back to Ted. He'd gained some weight, but he was still slender, tall, and blond, with the sort of icy eyes that always seemed to be holding something back.

"May I freshen your drink?" he asked, his pale blue eyes resting coolly on her.

"Caterina, show him where to go, please," Ava said, taking charge of the situation. "Go with him."

Her mother was determined to put them together again. Ted offered her his arm—as courteous as always—and she rested her fingertips lightly in the crook of his arm. They made their way across the patio.

"It's been a long time, Caterina. How've you been?"

"Terribly busy," she said with a wave of her hand.

"Seeing anyone?"

"I haven't dated anyone since you, Ted." That much was true.

A smile spread across his face. "Look at you. You're a beautiful girl, and you're not dating?" He steered her off to the side patio where they could be alone and then turned to face her. A lantern above them cast an eerie red glow on his face. "Cate, I think I understand why you bolted like that on New Year's Eve."

"It's still Caterina." She'd never liked the nickname he used for her. An old memory surged through her mind. Ted had once told her that her name was too ethnic. *Cate,* he had said, *is much more sophisticated. Cate Thornwald, now doesn't that sound better than Caterina Rosetta?*

She stared at him. She liked her first name. Everyone pronounced it in their own way—her mother softened the *r* with her French accent, and Juliana and Nina rolled the *r* with their Spanish pronunciation. And then there was Marisa's father, with his throaty baritone and mesmerizing accent that elevated her name to poetry. And sometimes, to him, she had been simply *cara*. She lowered her lids to mask the pain in her eyes.

Ted smoothed his hair. "Okay. Caterina it is."

She was curious. "So why do you think I left?"

"My father told me nice girls are sometimes scared of intimacy. I want you to know that I respect you."

Caterina held his gaze. "I *was* scared, Ted." That much was true. Only not about what he thought. She forced herself to think about Marisa and what was best for her.

He ran his knuckles along her jawline. "I'd like to start over with you. We can build a life together. And I still love you."

There it was. The validation of his intent. Though his touch didn't thrill her as another man's had, she softened her eyes and allowed a smile to creep onto her face. "It might be complicated."

"I'm sure there's nothing we can't work out. I can run the vineyard for you and your mother." He put an arm around her and drew her to him. "It's so good to see you again," he said. "Hmm, you're still wearing the perfume I gave you."

She put an arm on his shoulder to balance herself. It would be so easy to begin dating him again, become engaged and married. Let Ted run her life. She thought of her friends Donna and Beth and the marriages they'd settled for. They'd married because they had no other options. But she had a profession, and supposedly, a house in Italy. She had options. Yet she was also a mother, and her little girl needed a family. Her *own* family. Would Ted agree to adopt Marisa? "Ted, we really need to talk."

"I can't imagine what you might say to change my mind this time." Ted placed a finger on her lips. "Maybe you needed time then, but I know we are meant to be now." His lips curved into a smile. "And I can't tell you how much it means to me that you've remained pure for me."

Had she heard him correctly? She inclined her head. "Would that have been a problem?"

"You are, so it doesn't matter, does it, Cate?"

Again with the *Cate*. She lowered her eyes. "No, it doesn't matter, Ted."

He nuzzled her neck around her collarbone, which was exposed in the wide neckline she wore, and planted a soft kiss on her lips. When she pulled away, she caught a glimpse of someone at the edge of the party. She let out a small gasp.

She recognized him at once. The broad span of his shoulders, his long legs, his thick hair. His confident stance, hands on his narrow hips. A shiver coursed along her neck. He looked like a Roman god. She *couldn't* face him. Not here, not at a party.

The thought of him—and what love *really* felt like—yanked her back to reality. She took a step back from Ted.

"What's wrong?" Ted grabbed her hand.

Her head was spinning with conflicting emotions. "For a moment, I thought I saw a ghost."

He chuckled. "There's nothing to be frightened about. I'm here for you now."

She glanced over Ted's shoulder, feeling the captivating draw of another man's charismatic presence. Her breath constricted in her throat, and heat gathered in her torso. The memory of his touch flamed within her.

She dragged her gaze back to Ted. She would never feel the love for him that she felt for Marisa's father. That wouldn't be fair to either of them. *Or to Marisa.* Yet she yearned for the feel of another man's arms around her.

How could she possibly pretend with Ted? She squeezed her eyes shut for a moment, knowing that she was dashing Marisa's chance for a father, her mother's hopes for a union, and Ted's abiding love for her against the haunting memory of one unforgettable night. But she had to. She couldn't live with herself any other way.

And in her heart, she knew he would never fully accept Marisa. "Ted, I'm sorry, but on second thought, I don't think we're meant for each other, after all."

Ted's mouth opened in astonishment. "Cate, what's the matter with you? Have you lost your mind again?"

"No, in fact, I think I just came to my senses." She and her daughter could be happy by themselves. Or as well as they could be.

She stared past him, her heart pounding, but now she saw nothing. *Where did he go?* Had he seen her yet? *I have to get out of here.* She turned and hurried toward the house, skirting the patio lights and ducking into the shadows as she went.

As she reached for the brass doorknob that led to the kitchen, a man's hand covered hers, scorching her with its energy.

"Caterina." His deep voice reverberated in his chest.

She whirled around. Beneath a slash of dark eyebrows, a duplicate of Marisa's blue eyes blazed into hers. The natural lure of his magnetism heightened her senses, and her pulse picked up. The air between them seemed charged with electricity.

Santo Casini was still dangerously attractive.

6

"What are you doing here?" Caterina cried. Of all times for Santo to reappear in her life, why tonight? She leaned against the rear door of her house to support herself. His mere presence had unhinged her; his attraction was instantly as powerful as it had ever been.

His sun-bronzed hand on hers rooted her to the spot, and a current crackled between them. "I have to talk to you."

"I . . . I can't." She tore her gaze from the depths of his azure eyes. She saw her mother charging across the crowded patio toward them, slicing through the festive partygoers with hardly a glance around her.

Though Caterina loved her daughter more than life itself, she'd already made one drastic, irrevocable mistake with this man. However, despite her resolve, if Santo beckoned again, she would fall. Already her limbs tingled as if her will were seeping from her body.

"Caterina, I must speak to you." Santo's words were urgent. His musky masculine scent drew her in with every breath she took.

Caterina clung to the sanity of her pragmatic mind. He had avoided her many times before. What could be so pressing now? A thought sprang into her consciousness, and she tamped down panic. *Does he want to tell me he's getting married?* She couldn't bear to hear those words from his lips. "Please leave me alone." Caterina spun away from him and flung open the door.

Santo called after her, but she couldn't stop.

Once inside, she fled across the tile floor and sought sanctuary in the bathroom. Locking the door behind her, Caterina splashed water on her face, not caring whether her mascara and eyeliner trickled down her cheeks or not. She had run away from Santo, terrified by his presence. And before she'd raced into the house, she'd seen the anger etched on her mother's face.

Soon there would be hell to pay.

She unbuckled the straps on her high heels and stepped out of them, wriggling her toes on the cool tiles, stalling for time. Wrapping her arms around her torso, she swayed to the muted music playing outside, her heart shattering as she remembered the last time she'd danced with Santo. If she hid in the house the rest of the evening, Juliana or her mother were bound to come looking for her. She couldn't hide forever. She dabbed her eyes, trying to repair what was left of her makeup.

A hard rap sounded at the door, and she leaped back, stumbling over the mauve velvet fainting couch her mother had positioned just so in the large guest bathroom. *Is that Santo?* A basket of rose petal potpourri tumbled to the tile, releasing its scent as she hyperventilated.

"Caterina, are you all right?" Ava's voice pierced the thick oak door.

"I'm fine. I was just a little warm." Struggling to breathe, she knelt and scraped up shriveled rose petals and dried orange rinds.

"I'd like to talk to you, *s'il te plaît.*"

Caterina replaced the basket and stood on shaky legs. She leaned into the gold-framed mirror to inspect herself before facing her mother. She smoothed her cheek rouge and drew a ruby nail under her matching lower lip, wiping the slight smudge Ted had left when he'd kissed her. She fastened her shoes and then opened the door.

Her mother was a vision in a Jacques Fath white satin cocktail dress. Beyond her, outside the French-paned doors, the party continued. *Where is Santo?* She could see the Thornwalds sweeping away, with Ted lagging behind his parents, his hands thrust into his pockets. But Santo was nowhere to be seen.

Her mother's eyes flashed with anger. "What did you say to Ted?"

"Can't this wait until morning?"

"You must go back to him."

"I will not. Besides, they're leaving, Maman." Caterina nodded toward the door.

"You've driven them away." Ava clasped a hand over her mouth. "How could you behave like that?"

"Like what?" She folded her arms and cocked her head. "I will not marry a man I don't love."

Ava pressed her temples. "Can't you see that I'm trying to help you, Caterina?"

"What about what I want in life?" Caterina stared at her. *And where is Santo?*

"Don't be so quick to decide I'm wrong." Ava blew a puff between her perfectly red lips. "We're women; we don't always get exactly what we want in life."

How well I know that. Yet she shot back at her mother. "You had your family and a business, Maman. Why can't I?"

"I made the best of the hand I was dealt, from your father, to Prohibition, to the Depression when we nearly lost it all, to the war—"

"Oh, don't be so *tragique,* Maman."

"How dare you be so impertinent? We lost young men across the valley—Juliana's Alfonso and boys younger than you. We all mourned them." Ava's voice sounded strained. "What do you know of hardship? Why, in Italy—"

Ava stopped, but Caterina latched on to her words. "What about Italy? You never speak of your life there."

Ava's eyes were like hard, glittering stones. "What does it matter? Leave it alone."

"You've had your struggles, and I've had mine." Caterina swallowed her fear. "I want to do the right thing now." Whether it included Santo or not.

"You always do exactly as you please," Ava hissed, turning around. "You always have, you willful child." She wagged a finger in Caterina's face. "You should marry Ted while you have the opportunity. You're getting older, and you have no prospects for marriage. When do you plan to have children?"

Caterina hesitated for half a beat. "I *have* a child." There, she'd said it. Her entire world slipped on its axis.

Ava inclined her head. "What?"

Her words burst out like a coiled spring. "I have a little girl, she's a year old, and her name is Marisa." Caterina watched as her mother's lips parted in astonishment. Guilt surged through her. She should have confided in her mother long ago.

"No, no, no." Red splotches dappled Ava's chest, and she pressed a hand to her throat.

"It's the truth." She looked past her mother, but Santo was gone. *Just like before.*

Ava swiftly regained her composure and smirked in disbelief. "Oh really? And just when did this occur?"

This was the bitter anger Caterina had sought to avoid. She closed her eyes, struggling against a torrent of conflicting emotions. When she opened her eyes, she spoke in a flat voice. "I had her at the end of the spring semester. I told you I was taking an art course in Los Angeles. That's why I graduated late."

As realization settled heavily on Ava's shoulders, she touched the wall for support. "You gave birth in Los Angeles?"

"No, in San Francisco, at a private maternity home."

A pained expression crossed Ava's face. "You were afraid to tell me. This is horrible."

"She's a beautiful baby. I'll bring her here, Maman."

"Who forced himself on you? Tell me," Ava demanded, rage rising in her voice.

"No one forced me. It was . . . mutual. It was love." Caterina glanced through the doors, but there was still no sign of Santo.

"Love? What do *you* know of love?" Ava's trembling lips were rimmed with white fury. "Why, you reckless, wanton child. How dare you! You are ruined with Ted and any other respectable man."

Caterina turned back to Ava and folded her arms. "I don't care if I ever get married. I have my little girl, and I'm not going to hide her from you anymore." She paused, summoning strength. "I need help, Maman."

"You have shamed yourself, you have shamed me, and you have shamed Mille Étoiles." Ava's voice cracked. "How could you?" She huffed with derision. "You're a stupid girl. I can't even look at you."

Though Caterina had known her mother would reject her for this—Ava had always warned her, hadn't she?—her words still hurt, slicing through her heart like a scythe.

"You must adopt her out. You cannot keep an illegitimate child."

"Of course I can." Caterina straightened her spine, drawing herself up over her mother. "And I'd like to bring her here."

"Here? *Non!* Don't be ridiculous. You must get rid of her, give her to a family who can care for her. You cannot do this alone."

"You did." Caterina saw Nina behind them, closing the doors to the patio, where guests were turning curious faces their way as their voices rose above the music. "She's my daughter, and I've been caring for her just fine—*without* your help." She paused, still yearning for a word of comfort, a touch—anything from her mother. But Ava stood resolute. "Not that you're offering to help, obviously."

"No, indeed. You must go to confession at once." Color drained from her face, and her eyes widened. "Is she Ted's child?"

Caterina glared at her mother. "No."

"Then who *is* the father?"

49

"It doesn't matter." She didn't matter to Santo, so why mention him? Then Raphael would be involved . . . it was far too much to imagine. They were too incestuous here on the vineyard, removed from the village of Napa and the city of San Francisco, cloistered above the fog line.

Ava clutched her arm. "You *must* tell me." Then her voice dropped to a strangled, feather-thin whisper that Caterina had never heard before. "It's not Santo, is it?"

"And what if it were?" Caterina couldn't look away; Ava's face was stilled in the most tortured expression she'd ever seen.

"You'd be horribly . . . *ruined*. Anyone . . . but him."

Why? Something in Ava's voice signaled a dire warning. *Why such a dramatic response? Why does she so loathe Santo?* Caterina swung her head slowly to one side in disbelief and then came back to center. As she did, Ava dissolved with relief, clearly assuming that she meant *no*.

"Thank God. Who, then?" Ava demanded. "A boy at school?"

Caterina shrugged. Not exactly lying, not exactly telling the truth. She'd learned that from observing her mother.

"And he left you. Does he even know?"

"No." That was the truth.

"Then do the right thing—get rid of that baby."

Caterina watched her mother's emotions churn through her. "No. 'That baby,' as you call her, is *my daughter*. I'd sooner cut off my arm. Surely you can understand that." Caterina's worst fear was unfolding before her.

"Insolent child." Ava raised her hand to Caterina's face, but caught herself. Her voice cracked. "She will wreck your life. Do not bring that baby here. I have no desire to see her."

"That's fine, because I will *not* subject her to your abuse." Caterina bit back the hurt that enveloped her. She jerked away from Ava's grasp and started across the room.

"Don't come back until you've gotten rid of her."

Caterina stopped and whirled around. "I'll leave in the morning." She clenched her teeth and strode from the living room, clattering up the stairs two at a time as tears burned in her eyes. Her heart seemed to splinter, just as she'd known it would, torn between Marisa and her mother. *And where did Santo go?*

When Caterina reached her room, she sank to her feet and collapsed against the wall in the dark, her chest heaving with sobs that racked her body. She had clung to a tiny hope, small as a grape seed, that her mother would yield, fold her into her arms, and forgive her. Isn't that what their religion taught?

Caterina sat in the blackened room for what seemed an eternity. As the burnt-orange moon climbed high in the night sky, Caterina vowed that she and Marisa would survive. *Without Ava. Without Santo.*

Ava sat alone in her room. The party was over, and the guests were gone. Raphael and Nina had gone to bed. And Caterina might never speak to her again.

She turned over the dilemma in her mind. She could hardly remember a time when she hadn't had to conceal the truth. As a teenager, she had nearly destroyed her life, and she'd rather die than let Caterina make the mistakes she had.

Ava knew her angry outbursts weren't productive, but she couldn't help herself. She was a passionate woman, and it took every bit of strength she had to control her emotions and keep their lives and business on track. She was often tired and short fused; unfortunately, she directed her frustration toward Caterina.

But Caterina was no longer a child. She had grown into a beautiful young woman with the slender frame of a ballerina and brilliant peridot-green eyes flecked with gold that blazed with intelligence and curiosity.

And she has a baby.

Ava sank her face into her hands. How had she failed her? She had not protected her daughter as she should have. But why had Caterina acted so irresponsibly? What in heaven's name was being taught at the university? Ava patted her face, drying her cheeks.

At least the father wasn't Santo. Ava couldn't have borne that travesty. *Caterina must rise above the wounds inflicted on our family in Italy.*

But how? What would they do now?

7

The next morning, Caterina caught up with Ava in the vineyard after her early morning church services, which Caterina hadn't attended. She had far too much to confess, but then, so did her mother.

"Maman, wait up. We still need to talk." Besides Marisa, she had to know why Ava hadn't told her about her grandmother. Or had the investigator made a mistake? She hurried through the vineyard row, the sun already warm on her shoulders.

Ava turned and glared at Caterina. "You didn't find it necessary to talk to me about your baby."

"Her name is Marisa." Caterina braced herself for another argument. Stalling for a moment to order her thoughts, she plucked a grape from a well-manicured vine, inspected it, and popped it into her mouth. It wasn't ripe, but the flavors were intensifying. She brushed her hands on her dungarees. "I was scared and hurt. And afraid of what you'd think."

Ava arched a perfectly drawn eyebrow. "You were certainly right about that. If you'd told me, I would've seen that you went to a good maternity home, had decent care, and arranged an adoption. We could have taken care of this situation sooner."

"That's why I didn't tell you. I considered adoption, but I wanted to keep my baby. And I did have good care. I stayed with Faith and Patrick O'Connell in the city at their private home, not one of those dreadful penitentiary maternity homes."

"They take in girls like, like you? What kind of sinful people are they?"

Ava's voice was rising, and Caterina bit back the urge to match her tone. "They're good people. Faith is a midwife, so she delivered Marisa. And she was once a nun. She served at a Magdalene laundry in Ireland, but she left the order because of the cruel treatment of the girls, among other reasons."

"She's a fallen nun?" Her mother sniffed with disdain.

Caterina ignored her cutting remark. "I visited some of the maternity homes. They were awful. The girls there were desperate, and they were treated like prisoners, sinners, prostitutes."

"Because that's what they are."

"Or maybe they aren't. Maybe they're just like me."

Ava held up a hand and struggled to compose herself. "Be that as it may, I've decided you deserve another chance. This needn't ruin your life. Not if we act quickly."

"Marisa won't ruin my life. I love her."

Ava's expression softened a little. "Of course you do, but so will another family. One that can give her the stability a child needs. You must adopt her out." Ava smoothed a hand over her arm. Caterina thrust it away.

"No, I will not. I'll make the decisions about what's best for her. I'm her mother. And we have a stable family right here."

"Here?" Ava's eyes darted around. "Oh no, you can't bring her here. You'd ruin your chances at a good marriage."

"Honestly, I don't care if I ever get married. Look at you, you're fine. I can manage, too."

"It's hard to be alone. A widow with a child is acceptable, but an unwed mother with an illegitimate child is disgraceful. You're too young to make that decision; you don't know what you'd be missing." She grimaced as she considered her words. "Well, clearly you do. But is that what you want? A celibate life? If men look at you—and believe me, they will now—it will be for only one thing."

Caterina shook her head. "Sex isn't the dirty, disrespectful thing it's made out to be, Maman—that is, unless you think it is."

"Caterina, listen to me. You have no idea how hard I've worked to maintain our good reputation. You must give up this baby before it's too late. It's for the best, believe me."

"I'm not giving up Marisa, and I'm not asking you for help. I'm simply telling you how I plan to live my life now."

Ava's face contorted. For a moment, Caterina thought she would erupt in anger, but instead, she crumpled her face into her hands.

This was not the reaction Caterina had expected. She'd never seen her mother break down before. She hesitated before placing a hand on Ava's quivering shoulder.

After a few moments, Ava regained control. "Think for a moment. How will you care for a growing child?"

"I'll manage." Caterina leveled her gaze at her mother.

"You might have a child, but you're still a foolish girl, Caterina. Please understand what you'll have to deal with." Ava bowed her head. "Consider Marisa's future."

"I am." Frustrated by her inability to reach her mother and gain her understanding, Caterina kicked a rock with her boot and changed the subject to what she'd really come here to speak about. "There's something else. An investigator from New York was here yesterday. He gave me some documents and mentioned an inheritance. It's a house in Montalcino supposedly left to me by Papa's mother, who died earlier this year. Do you know anything about this?"

Ava's face grew pale, and her expression froze. After a long moment, she blinked. "No, I don't. I thought she'd died long ago. Before you were born."

Caterina cocked her head. "Then Papa lied to you?"

Ava licked her lips. "Well, I suppose he must have. But let's not speak ill of the dead. Your father was a good man."

"How strange." Caterina paused, thinking. None of this made sense. Why would her father tell her mother that? They were never returning to Italy. Didn't her father's mother write to him? What happened? Her mother's response raised more questions than it answered. Or was she concealing something? "Maybe I should have an attorney look at the documents and advise me. I could ask—"

"No, don't do that," Ava interjected. "I mean, it's a waste of money. If you inherited a house, simply tell the investigator you want to sell it right away. It's not as if you'll ever go there."

"I might. He said there's a provision to pay my travel expenses there. On an airplane." As Caterina thought of it, excitement coursed through her. It would be an adventure. Maybe her last one. "Look, I have a picture of it. It might even have a vineyard with it." She took out the old photo from her shirt pocket.

"I don't want to see it. That house is—" Ava stopped herself. "You shouldn't go."

"Why not? Maybe I have other family. I'd love to see Italy; I've heard so many stories from Raphael and—" Caterina stopped. "I'd just like to go," she added quietly.

"No. I forbid it," Ava said.

"I'll make my own decision." Caterina put a hand on her mother's shoulder. "That's my heritage. I have a right to know whatever you're keeping from me. I have family there, and I know nothing about them. We never even had family photos."

"I will not discuss it anymore. If you knew, you would thank me." Ava waved a hand in dismissal.

Caterina pressed on. "Do you know how much I missed having a grandmother? And you told me she'd died." Ava's face flushed and she quickly glanced away, but Caterina noticed her reaction. "You've lied to me, Maman. Why?"

"I had to." Ava narrowed her eyes. "It was dangerous."

"How dangerous could a little old lady be? Especially one who thought enough of me to include me in her will—never having met me or even having heard from me."

"There is nothing good there." Ava turned and continued walking.

"Why do you say that?" Caterina fell into step with her again. "The investigator told me he'd been here before and spoke to you. When were you going to tell me?"

"Let the past go." Ava paused at the end of a row. She took her daughter's hand and stroked it. *"Ma chérie,* trust me. Don't go to Italy."

"Tell me why I shouldn't."

Ava pressed her lips together and shook her head.

"Then I'm going. And I will find out, Maman, with or without you. I'm an adult, and I have a right to know about my family."

"You, an adult?" Ava said, expressing a puff of air between her lips. "You know so little of life. My father left me and my mother in Bordeaux to serve France in the Great War. Afterward, he was never the same. And my beautiful mother . . . influenza spared no class, and she succumbed within a fortnight. What I'd gone through by your age doesn't even compare—"

"I know it was difficult for you," Caterina said, interrupting her familiar ramble. "But I've experienced life, too. More than you realize."

"Don't interrupt me when I'm speaking to you." Ava's voice was rapidly rising to a shrill level. "You have no idea how I've tried to protect you. *None.* And this is the thanks I get?" She was yelling now. "And as for your life experiences, that's not something you should be proud of. And you lied about it all."

Caterina stiffened against Ava's tirade. "Just like you *lied* to me about my grandmother." Something was definitely amiss. She'd never known her mother to tell even a half truth. Or so she'd thought.

Ava stifled a sob, angrily brushing her eyes with the back of her hands.

She noticed Ava's trembling hands, her quivering lips. *Her fear.* There was more to this than her mother was telling her. Ava's angry resistance only made her more determined than ever. *What is she hiding?* "I want to meet my family. Why can't you even acknowledge them to me?" When Ava didn't respond, she said, "I'm not afraid."

A strangled sob choked from Ava's throat. "You'll find nothing but misery there, mark my words. Go ahead then. Go. But you'll regret it." Ava stalked away.

Though she'd tried to remain calm, Caterina was shaken by her mother's outburst. *Why would I regret it?*

8

Blazing with shame, Ava pinched the apricot silk organza fabric between her fingers and lifted the hem of her dress as she hurried across the crowded patio. It was a balmy Montalcino night with a million shimmering stars vying for brilliance, but the romance of the evening stopped there. All around her, the men were reliving the last war, speaking about atrocities she couldn't bear to hear again.

When she'd married Luca and moved here earlier in the year, she'd fallen in love with the sheer beauty of Tuscany. But now the charm of Montalcino had dimmed for her, and she found it growing more oppressive by the day. Her husband, Luca, was to blame, but what could she do?

She glanced behind her. The young Italian girls huddled at the far end of the stone-walled terrace were still laughing at her. Their insinuations about her husband's actions still rang in her ears. *Bambino bastardo.* A bastard baby.

Luca met her at the doorway. His eyes were glassy, and the sweet stench of grappa hung on his breath. "What's wrong now?" He blocked her path, mocking her, not allowing her to enter the villa.

Ava could hear the laughter growing louder, and she was dying of embarrassment. "You know what's wrong," she hissed. "Go back to Natalie. She's the one you want."

"Stop it, Ava. You're making a scene." Luca's steely blue eyes bore into hers.

"Me? They're saying she's carrying *your* child, not her husband's. Is it true?"

"What if it is?"

It was all Ava could do to keep from bursting into tears in a roomful of dignitaries. The laughter behind her blotted out all reason. When her husband stepped aside, she fled past him into the salon, racing for the staircase.

She knew Luca wouldn't follow her. He never did. He was obsessed with Natalie.

Glancing back, she saw her mother-in-law. Violetta was cutting through the crowd of dignitaries that had gathered to bestow a posthumous honor upon her husband, commemorating his service to Toscana. She must have witnessed the commotion and argument. Ava was mortified.

Violetta quickly intercepted her. Deep-purple Russian amethyst earrings that were family treasures dangled against her neck. Her hair was swept into an elaborate style befitting her station, and the subtle scent of violets perfumed her smooth skin. Though she was Italian, she spoke quietly in French to Ava. "Come with me, *chérie*. Let us go upstairs for a respite."

At just nineteen years old, Ava admired her mother-in-law's omnipresent dignity. Violetta Romagnoli Rosetta ran the villa and the surrounding vineyards with a firm, yet fair, hand. Some called her unorthodox—and worse—because she dared to rise above the women's gossip and do as she pleased. Since her husband's death just two years ago, she'd entered into business agreements with men in the wine industry, and from all accounts, she held her own against them.

When they reached Ava and Luca's suite on the second floor, Violetta pulled a cord to ring for the maid. "Don't listen to the rumors. You know what those girls are like."

"How can I not?" Ava wailed.

"Don't take them seriously. Luca is your husband. Collect yourself, and return to the party with a smile on your face to spite those wicked girls."

Ava plopped onto a chair.

"Luca is willful—he always has been." Violetta pursed her lips. "I'm the first to admit that my son is a difficult husband. But when you have children, you will have something else to occupy your time. And you will have their love."

A sob caught in Ava's throat. She'd lost Luca's child just a few months ago.

"Don't fret. The doctor assured us there will be more babies for you." She dabbed Ava's eyes with her violet-scented handkerchief. "Men have their own agenda, and we have ours. You must be the heart of your family." She shook her head. "And in my son's case, the head, too."

"Haven't you heard what people are saying about Luca and Natalie?" Tears spilled from Ava's eyes again, and she wished she could return home to France to her mother and father. But that was impossible. Her parents had died, and she had sold the château and vineyards in Bordeaux with the help of her elderly uncle and his lawyer. This was her life now.

"Ignore the gossip." Violetta pressed a handkerchief with the embroidered initials *VRR* into Ava's hand. She straightened, and her posture was as imperious as in the portrait of her that hung in the salon. "Have strength, Ava. You will need it in this life."

"I can't bear it, really I can't."

"Yes, you can. Now dry your eyes and put a cool cloth on your face. I'll return to our guests. You will return to the party, too— otherwise, those petty girls will have won. This is *our* house, Ava. Don't let that happen." Violetta turned, her voluminous skirts swishing regally behind her, and shut the door.

Ava huddled on the chaise longue. She wished she could speak to Violetta as she had her own mother. She admired her mother-in-law, but she couldn't unburden her heart to her.

Ava closed her eyes and thought about how she'd come to this point. She'd met Luca and his family when they'd visited friends who'd lived near her parents. Ava's father was an optimistic man who always saw the best in people. She could only imagine that he saw the best in Luca, too. At least, at first. One day, Luca left suddenly to return to Montalcino. Later, she wondered if her father might have sent him away.

After her father died of a heart attack, heartbroken over the loss of her mother, she'd received Luca's letter asking for her hand in marriage. A week later, she was on the train to Montalcino to stay at his family's villa.

Even now, she didn't know why she had opened the door to his midnight taps. She hadn't yet accepted Luca's marriage proposal; besides, her uncle must approve. And yet she'd let him into her room, willingly, giggling over their naughtiness. Was it her nervousness, her vanity, or her need for comfort?

His passion consumed her, and he forced himself upon her, although it was not yet their wedding day. When his hands quickly found her secret place, she realized her error, but it was too late. He was relentless, despite her pleas and cries. And when he was finished, he left her in a heap with a satisfied smirk on his face.

Stunned, she'd returned to France the next day, hating him. Was this the type of man she should be tied to for life?

She thought not.

But it wasn't long before her monthly cycle was late, and she was terrified. She was ruined, and worse, she was trapped. Women in a family such as hers simply did not have children out of wedlock. Her uncle, elderly though he was, would have threatened Luca's life. The only way out was to write to Luca and accept his proposal—if he would have her.

She could not shame her uncle; it would have been the death of him. As it was, he lasted just a few months more, but at least he died in peace, relieved that Ava was suitably married.

After their marriage, Luca insisted that she sell her family home and the surrounding vineyard and move to Montalcino. Their place was here, he reasoned. With a heavy heart, Ava packed her clothes and personal items and prepared the château for sale.

Before she left, she walked the vineyard one last time, remembering her parents' instructions on growing and harvesting the grapes and crafting their much-lauded wine. Overcome with emotion, she fell to her knees. With her bare hands, she clawed through the dirt and uprooted as many vines as she could that her father had planted. She packed the precious rootstock in a trunk to return to Montalcino. Upon her arrival, she'd planted the vines in a special place and personally tended them.

Ava passed a hand over her forehead. It wasn't long after they married that their lives began to unravel. She realized Luca had been in love with Natalie; he'd married her on the rebound after Natalie married Franco.

Luca's impulsive, reckless nature brought frequent trouble, and alcohol only made his behavior worse. He was drinking in the village with friends the night she had her miscarriage. Violetta had tended to her, nursing her through the worst of it.

Ava shook her head at the memory. What would she have done without Violetta?

The door swung open, and Ava looked up. It was Luca. A chill coursed through her.

"I hope you're satisfied," he said, tearing off his tie. "Natalie just left."

"What's the matter with you? I'm your wife. I'm the one who has been insulted. Everyone says you're having an affair with Natalie, and now she's pregnant."

Luca didn't respond.

"What about Natalie's husband? What about me?"

"She married him to spite me." Luca's face twisted into a grotesque, tormented mask. "I wouldn't have married you if you hadn't said you were pregnant."

"But you wrote to me. You proposed."

"And then you lied to me. You weren't pregnant." Fury blazed in Luca's eyes, and he clenched his fists, advancing upon her.

"But I was." Ava had never seen such a flash of anger in her husband. She pressed herself against the chaise longue.

He stood over her and lashed out, striking her across the cheek. She cried out, yet it only seemed to fuel his anger.

"Stop! Stop!" She raised her arms to protect her face.

"What's going on here?" Violetta's voice sliced through Luca's madness. She grabbed her son and shoved him from the room. "*Never* hit your wife. Your father would have been ashamed of you. Get out."

Ava curled into a ball, sobbing.

Violetta knelt beside her. "Are you hurt? Let me see your face."

When Ava dropped her hands from her face, Violetta sucked in her breath.

"Stay here." Violetta clucked her tongue. "You're in no condition to return to the party." She kissed her forehead. "My poor, poor girl."

9

AUGUST 1956 — NAPA VALLEY, CALIFORNIA

Caterina woke with an excruciating headache just as the dawning sun began to light the sky. Santo and Ava had intruded upon her dreams, and she'd had a restless night.

After yesterday's argument with her mother, she had spent the rest of the day with Juliana talking about Marisa and Italy and considering her options, which were few. While they chatted, they painted Juliana's room a soft shade of robin's-egg blue. They left the windows open to air the room, and Juliana decided to sleep in her old room in Nina's cottage. By the time they returned that evening, the windows of Mille Étoiles were dark, and Ava had gone to bed.

Caterina threw off her chenille blanket. Before she left, there was only one thing she wanted from Mille Étoiles. She didn't know how long it might be before she returned.

She changed into a white pullover top and slim pedal pushers, tied her tennis shoes, and hastily brushed her thick hair into a ponytail. She wound her way through leafy vineyards where vines were bowed with ripe cabernet grape clusters.

Pausing to catch her breath, Caterina gazed out over Napa Valley, which was bathed in tendrils of early morning light as the music of birdsong trilled in the air. Above her on the mountain, which soared to twenty-two hundred feet from sea level, rows of grape vines cascaded along the slopes. Here the delicate grapes were high above the fog that rolled in from the San Pablo Bay, protected from the threat of moisture that could ruin a crop in a few days. Vines planted above fourteen hundred feet were spared this hazard.

She wondered if Italy would have such perfect conditions, and a pang of loss shot through her.

She'd always loved being above the fog. The climate was different up here, and the grapes grown on these mountainous slopes reflected the terroir, the unique blend of soil and weather that produced some of the best wine grapes in the world.

Leaves rustled behind her, and Caterina turned. It was Vino, Santo's fluffy white sheepdog. "Hey, boy, are you following me?" She bent to scratch his neck. His eyes implored her to play.

"Not now, boy, but I'm going to miss you." After a moment, he scampered off, sniffing around, but something soon spooked him, and he began barking and darting around the hillside. Birds squawked overhead at his antics and circled around him.

Caterina glanced around and shivered. Despite the ruckus, the vineyard was eerily still; hardly a leaf fluttered in the clear-skied morning.

She strolled past winemaking equipment Ava had just purchased to modernize their method of processing grapes.

The heavy oak door to the wine cave had been left open for ventilation. She'd often taken solace here as a child. Blinking from the bright sunshine outside, she hesitated at the entrance to adjust to the dim light within.

She hugged her bare shoulders in the cool, humid air and breathed in the complex scents jostling for prominence: French oak barrels, aging wine, stone, and soil—the musty scents she loved. No matter how warm it was outside, it was always cool in the cave, the near-constant temperature sheltering the precious wine stored within.

The cave had been burrowed into the side of Howell Mountain decades ago. Gray stone walls led to a curved ceiling, and the cave splintered into branches. As a child, she used to slip away and hide there with her books and blankets, reading late into the evening until her mother or Raphael found her. The cave had been her refuge, but today something seemed off-kilter.

Just my nerves. Maybe it was because the cave sparked so many memories of Santo. She glanced around, thinking about how much she would miss it here.

Vino began howling outside.

She strolled past oak barrels stacked against the cellar walls, her tennis shoes slapping on the cool stone floor, admiring the smooth, precision-crafted French oak barrels, each one identified and marked. The markings on the barrelheads were called the cooperage. They identified where the wood came from, the barrel size, and the name of the cooper, or barrel-making company. The char, or firing rendered on the interior of the staves, which imparted flavor to the wine, was also included in these markings, among other details.

Allier, Vosges, Tronçais—each barrel was stamped with the name of the French forest where the trees were grown. The toasted oak imparted flavors of vanilla, clove, and other spices, which lent a unique signature to their wine. They were one of only a few wineries in California that insisted on such expensive barrels.

She passed the chardonnay—another one of their wine specialties—and turned into a different branch of the cave, where bottles were resting at the perfect incline for aging. Seeing no one, she turned back toward the cabernet barrels.

When her parents had immigrated to the United States, her mother had brought with her some of the coveted rootstock from her family's vineyard in Bordeaux. Caterina thought about how her mother had nursed the rootstock through her travels from France to Italy and across the Atlantic Ocean to America. Out of habit, Caterina knelt, checking the barrels, making sure there were no leaks. They were all full and dry.

"*Buongiorno,* Caterina."

Caterina yelped, startled at the sight of Santo. She caught her breath, trying to rein in her emotions. "You might have warned me," she managed to say. She thought he'd gone, but he must have been staying in Raphael's cottage at Mille Étoiles. She'd been with Juliana yesterday. *Why was he still here?*

"The lights were on." Santo hesitated. "It's been a long time," he said, his deep voice dropping another notch. "You look good, Cat."

She took a step back as if to avert the magnetism that always drew her toward him. Even in the dim light, Santo's vivid blue eyes shone like twin sapphires against his tanned skin, searing through the defenses to her heart as they always had. His cotton shirt and worn blue jeans hugged his body, which still looked firm and muscular beneath the cloth. She swallowed, instantly nervous. "Why are you here?"

"Raphael wanted to see me." He paused, taking in her face as if memorizing every feature. "And Juliana called, said I should come back for a vintner's reception." He moistened his full lips. "We don't have to talk if you don't want to, but I didn't think anyone would mind if I took a couple of bottles of wine. I wanted to get an early start on my way back to Davis."

Caterina couldn't think of how to respond.

She stared at the labels on the wine bottles he held in his hands. *Howell Mountain Cabernet, 1953.* "That's the wine we blended," she managed to say, touching a label. "That's what I came to get, too."

"Then you take these." He handed the bottles to her. "I want you to know, that was the best summer of my life."

Memories surged through her. *Then why didn't you return my calls?* She wanted to scream. Instead, she averted her gaze to conceal the hurt in her eyes. "Vino must have followed you. Guess that's why he was acting strangely."

Santo looked at her curiously and nodded. "I don't know what's gotten into him." He stooped to inspect a seam on a barrel.

Caterina's despair was so intense it was almost palpable. She wanted to flee—as she had at the party—but her feet remained rooted to the spot. She tilted her chin in defiance of her emotion, yet she couldn't deny her feelings for him. For nearly as long as she could remember, he had been an important part of her life.

Born in Montalcino, Santo had lost his parents when he was just a baby. As a small boy, he was passed from one of his father's relatives to another in Italy and then sent to New York to live with yet another. At the age of ten, he arrived at Mille Étoiles to live with his older cousin Raphael, who had become like a father to him.

From the moment she'd met Santo, Caterina had been intrigued by him. His independence, his soft Italian accent, the thick dark hair that curled around his collar. She'd taught him English; he'd taught her Italian. He'd once slain imaginary dragons alongside her here in this cave. Memories poured like salt into her reopened wounds as she recalled how close they had once been.

Until her mother had stepped in, calling her relationship with Santo improper. *You're growing into a young lady,* her mother had said. *Time to leave your childish ways and childhood friends behind.* By that, she knew her mother meant Santo, not Juliana. Santo, the farmhand, the boy without family. Unacceptable to her mother.

And now, so was she.

Satisfied with the seal on the barrel, Santo stood and trained his eyes, which were an arresting shade of lapis lazuli blue, on her. The silence between them was awkward.

"I would've thought you'd be married by now." Instantly, she regretted her words.

"Marriage is an important, lifelong commitment. Not one I take lightly, *cara.*"

69

Cara. Caterina remembered with a sinking feeling the last time he had used that term of endearment.

"And you? I saw you with Ted at the party." His expressive eyes didn't waver from hers, and she sensed sadness in his voice.

She shook her head. For some reason, she couldn't get her words out now. Everything she'd thought of saying to him over the past two years—all the angry tirades, admonitions, confessions—suddenly vanished. Instead, she simply drank in the nearness of him.

Santo reached out and trailed a finger along her cheek. "Can you ever forgive me for forcing myself on you?"

"But you didn't." Their desire had been mutual. Involuntarily, she pressed her cheek to the warmth of his hand. How many times had she yearned for his touch? For him? But he had denied her. Did she wish they'd never made love? At first, when she couldn't reach him, she'd often wished that, but after Marisa was born, she'd never regretted it, even though her challenges had multiplied. A lump formed in her throat, and she took a half step back. "I called you. I wrote to you. Many times."

Santo blinked hard. "I know."

"Then why didn't you answer or call me back?" *Why did you leave me?* Yet she knew the answer. If he'd ever loved her, he wouldn't have broken off their relationship. Even now, her heart was still raw.

"I'm truly sorry, Caterina." His voice sounded burdened.

What's done is done, she decided, steeling her mind. She was leaving for Italy soon. She cradled the wine he'd given her in her arm, angling her head from him to hide her anguish.

"Why did you run away from me at the party?"

A torrent of emotions rushed through her. Where should she begin? But the words lodged in her throat.

When she didn't respond, he said, "Then I guess this is good-bye." He turned to leave.

Caterina longed to call to him, to dash after him, to bare her soul to him and tell him about their baby. But her voice faltered, and her feet remained immoveable.

As she watched him walk away, she heard a low rumble that sounded like a subterranean train hurtling toward them.

Santo whirled around, and they stared at each other in fear for a split second before a sharp jolt knocked them to the ground. The wine bottles Caterina held crashed to the floor, and shards of glass projectiles shot through the air. Red wine splashed onto the stone floor.

The ground beneath them rippled like pudding, and Caterina screamed as she skidded across the vibrating stone floor. She stretched a hand to him. "Santo!"

Santo struggled to stand, but the ground continued to swell and shift beneath him. He clawed his way toward her.

The earth beneath her heaved upward, and the stone floor shifted with the motion, rolling like liquid lava.

The cave creaked on its ancient footings as ceiling stones loosened and fell around her. Behind her head, barrels shifted and gave way, careening through the cave, bouncing off walls. The barrels snapped and spilled their contents; wine sloshed around them. She blinked, rubbing dirt and wine from her face and eyes. Shifting with the rolling motion, Santo poised to leap toward her.

The magnitude intensified, and another jolt shot through the earth. An earsplitting roar erupted from the earth, and Caterina watched with horror as a crack in the stone floor widened beneath her legs. She scuffled back from it, her arms over her head, evading barrels. Any one of them could kill her. The gash widened, and Santo dove across the gap to her, darting through the rocks falling from the ceiling into the crevice. "Keep your head down!" he shouted.

With Santo holding her, she staggered to a wall, and she and

Santo pressed themselves against it. Caterina curled into herself, and Santo wrapped his arms around her, shielding her.

The lights overhead blinked, threatening extinction. The seismic shaking continued, and all around them, wooden barrels and glass bottles rattled and smashed to the ground.

The earth seemed to sway forever. They watched the scene, helpless to defend themselves against the destruction that unfolded around them as if in slow motion. The lightbulbs overhead popped, and Caterina and Santo were thrust into darkness, a terrifying complete blackness that blotted out everything but the screeching, crashing sounds surrounding them.

Caterina clung to Santo, and his grip on her tightened. She heard him whispering a prayer and realized her lips were moving along with his words. *Is this the end?* Squeezing her eyes shut, she sent up a fervent prayer for Marisa's safety. *Oh Lord, forgive me. I should have told Santo about her.*

And then, as suddenly as it had started, the earth ceased rumbling, and the cave was quiet, except for the steady dripping of wine.

After a moment, Santo rolled off her, and Caterina slumped against the wall.

"Are you okay?" he asked, feeling her limbs in the dark. "Anything broken?"

"I . . . I think I'm in one piece." She felt her wet scalp and found a tender spot. "I think I feel blood. Or wine."

He touched her head, examining the wound. "It's a small cut. Come on, we've got to get out of here," he said, helping her to her feet. "There's a lot of glass around us. Do you have your shoes on?"

She nodded and then realized he couldn't see her. "I do."

Santo gripped her around the waist. "Stay with me."

They fumbled through the dark, feeling their way in tiny steps. Santo brushed debris aside with his shoe before each step. It seemed to take forever before they crossed the crack in the floor, which was now littered with rocks. Caterina coughed on the dust swirling through the air.

Santo stopped. "Are you okay?" he asked.

She could hear the worry in his voice. She cleared her throat. "Keep going."

They made their way to the entrance but found the door had swung shut. Santo felt for the door handle. When he turned it, the massive oak door didn't budge. He shoved a strong shoulder into it, then the full force of his weight, but the door was jammed. "The hill must have slid," he said, slightly winded. "We're trapped."

"Shh, what's that?" On the other side of the door, rocks clattered amid a dog's mournful whines and plaintive howl.

"That's Vino!" Santo cried. "Here, boy! Come on, Vino, dig us out!"

A moment later, whimpers of pain replaced Vino's howls, and his digging stopped. Santo pressed his ear against the door. "He sounds hurt."

Caterina cupped her ear to the thick door. "Oh, poor baby."

They heard more whimpering. Then nothing.

"Is he still there?"

"Vino! Vino!" Santo shouted. The dog's anguished moan floated through the door. "He sounds hurt; I think he needs help. Vino!" They listened again and heard a few more cries.

Santo banged on the door. "Vino!" Silence. "He must be hurt pretty bad."

Caterina sucked in a breath. "Do you think—?"

"I don't know." He called to the dog, but there was no response.

"We might have died," Caterina said softly, and she touched his shoulder. Overwhelmed with emotion, she thought about Marisa. *Is she safe?* What about her mother and Raphael, Juliana and Nina, the O'Connell family?

"That was a big one," Santo said.

"There should be candles on the tasting table," Caterina said, turning in that direction. They had a long table and chairs set up in another branch of the cave for wine tastings with buyers and important clients. They felt along the cave wall, crunching over bits of glass, until at last Caterina knocked her shin against a table leg.

Rocks littered the tabletop. She felt her way through the wreckage, found a candle, and then picked her way to a spot where a cabinet should have been. She took another step and stumbled onto it. "There are matches in the cabinet, but it seems to have fallen over."

"Got it," Santo said, hefting the cabinet onto its side. "Here we are." He struck a match between them, illuminating their faces.

Santo's face was smudged, his hair was coated with dust, and his shirt was torn. His eyes—*Marisa's eyes*—were rimmed in red and shone with such concern for her that she felt like bursting into tears. She swallowed and realized she must be a mess, too. She smoothed strands of hair from her forehead and averted her gaze. "Here, light this candle."

He touched the flame to the wick, and the room flickered into view. Caterina found another candle. "Wait on that one," he said. "Might have to conserve our light."

She nodded and brushed away nervous tears. It would take time for someone to find them and then dig them out. She wished she'd never come here this weekend. She only wanted to be with Marisa and take her far, far away to someplace safe where no one would judge them.

She wished she could confide in Santo. He had already rejected her in favor of another woman—his soon-to-be wife, evidently—but she couldn't handle his rejection of Marisa, which she figured likely. She chewed her lip, tasting blood.

She thought of Juliana's words. *He has a right to know.* Santo had no idea what she was concealing, though she had no intention of telling him right now, not after her mother's dreadful reaction, and certainly not before she left for Italy.

"What else is here that we can use?" he asked, turning over a couple of chairs for them to sit on.

Caterina sank into a chair. "Besides wine?"

"Good idea." Santo whisked dirt from her bare shoulder, sending a charge through her heightened senses. He reached for a bottle of wine on the floor and then rummaged through the drawer for a bottle opener.

Caterina found two tasting goblets and a burlap pouch containing almonds on the floor. Fine silt covered everything now. She wiped the large wineglasses out with the edge of her shirt.

"This is *our* wine," Santo said, glancing at the label. He poured the deep-red wine with an unsteady hand. "Here's to surviving the big one," he said, raising his glass to her.

"We're not out yet," she said, her glass shaking in her hand— more from his proximity than the shock of the earthquake. "Careful," she said, her voice faltering. "The rims are chipped." She sipped the wine and tilted her head back, savoring the rich complexities of the Howell Mountain cabernet. She had to admit, it *was* good. Or was it just the setting? She blew out a breath.

Santo swirled the wine in his glass and inhaled the bouquet it released. "Now, that's a damned fine wine we brewed. Hell of a time to celebrate, huh?" He sipped the wine.

Caterina drew the wine into her mouth again and let it linger on various parts of her tongue, where different taste buds revealed a wine's true personality. The initial sip, the mid-palate, the back of the tongue. After she swallowed, a prickle of excitement quickened her heartbeat. She had an innate knowledge of excellence, and she was almost afraid of what she had just tasted. It was *that* good.

Or maybe anything tasted great after an earthquake when you

were thinking of leaving the only life you knew behind. "I haven't tried this in a long time. It's aged well."

Santo inhaled the bouquet. "Hasn't it?" His eyes met hers across the rims of their goblets.

Feeling his eyes on her, she lowered her glass and admired the color in the flicking candlelight. Silence grew between them, and a surge of memories swelled within her. Santo was intent on his wine, studying it. She sipped from her glass, remembering the last time she'd seen him.

It was here in this cave, two years ago at summer's end.

It was on a sweltering day, the kind of day without even a breeze to flutter the leaves. The coolness of the wine cave had beckoned to her.

Caterina closed her eyes, remembering.

She had been working all day in the wine cave, intent on blending a wine from their harvest and excited at the progress she'd made. She was reaching for perfection, and the blend was close. Yet something indefinable eluded her.

It was late in the day, and everyone who worked at the vineyard had already left. Except for Santo. They'd worked together all summer, but that day was special.

Santo strolled in. His white cotton shirt flapped open, revealing his muscular chest and a toned torso that dipped to a V into worn blue jeans slung low on his hips.

Caterina's neck grew warm at the sight of him.

"How's it going?" He leaned against the table and let his gaze linger on her shoulders, which were bare in the blush-pink, nipped-at-the-waist sundress she wore. His vibrant blue eyes seemed cool and endless, and when he raised his eyes to hers, she tumbled into their depths.

"Pretty good." She slid a glass across the plain oak table where she worked. She liked to work in a well-lit area, where she could judge the color, aroma, and taste without other sensory intervention. She'd spent hours testing different blends and searching for the best combination of their grapes, striving to enliven the aroma, balance the tannin level, and enhance the rich mineral flavors of the earth. "Try this."

As he reached for the goblet, she brushed his forearm, which still held the heat of the summer sun. His bronzed skin was smooth and taut across well-defined, veined muscles. Her pulse hammered in her ears.

Santo swirled the wine to aerate it. He sipped. She watched as he let the wine flow over his tongue, testing it on his palate before he swallowed.

He grew thoughtful, furrowing his dark brows. "The tannin level is good, but I'd still like an earthier taste. Which blocks of grapes are you using to blend today?" He leaned past her, lifting and smelling the vials and goblets she had labeled before her, his open shirt trailing against the table.

Caterina explained her process, and Santo studied the notes they'd made together in the notebook she held. He pulled a chair to the table and sat next to her. "Here, let's try this." He took her pencil and made some notes. With an exacting hand, he blended another sample and handed it to her.

She tilted the goblet against the light above, considering the dark bloodred color before lifting it to her nose and inhaling. As she opened her lips to the wine, she saw his gaze linger on her mouth. She lowered her eyelids and tasted. It was miraculous. She savored the wine, feeling the fullness of the blend. She opened her eyes. "This is definitely the direction."

"You've done most of the work." He tasted it, made another note, and blended another sample.

"We've worked together. Say, let's try this." Caterina reached for a glass beaker. They continued back and forth with suggestions, eager in their quest for a wine that seduced the palate and spoke to the soul. The effect of the wine was relaxing, yet Caterina felt a frisson of excitement growing between them.

A little while later, Santo lifted another glass to her. "Now see what you think."

She swirled the glass and drank, and as she did, one strap of her sundress slipped from her shoulder.

Santo watched the thin strap fall. After a moment, he pushed it back onto her shoulder, but he didn't remove his hand.

Suddenly, Caterina felt Santo's gaze on her. Brushing earthquake dust from her eyelashes, she opened her eyes and pushed aside her memories.

Candlelight flung shadows across Santo's face, highlighting worried creases on his brow.

She circled the rim of her glass with her finger, feeling for chips. "How long do you think can we last in here?"

"I don't know. As long as the oxygen holds out or the carbon dioxide doesn't overwhelm us." He took another sip and then wiped his eyes with a shirtsleeve. "Think there might be an ax in here?"

"I've never seen one." Caterina grew quiet, her thoughts turning to Marisa, her mother, Juliana, Nina, Raphael . . . their friends and family. Had they survived?

"Caterina, where are you?" After the earthquake subsided, Ava scrambled from her bed and raced upstairs to Caterina's bedroom. Her daughter's rumpled bed was empty. She called out again for her, but there was no answer. Wearing a thin silk nightgown, she sprinted barefoot through the house in the dim morning light searching for her daughter, but she was nowhere to be found. Adrenaline and terror flooded her.

The back door slammed, and she heard Nina and Raphael yelling for her. She ran back downstairs, sidestepping broken vases and windows in her path. A shard of glass cut her heel; she yanked it out and hurried on.

"*Dios mío,* are you okay?" Nina ran to Ava and hugged her, crying and praying in Spanish. Juliana trailed behind, her dark tangled hair tumbling around her shoulders, her eyes wide with fright. She hugged a pink terry cloth robe around her waist.

"I can't find Caterina," Ava said, catching her breath. "She's gone." The argument they'd had rushed back. Had Caterina already left?

"Her car is still in the driveway." Raphael had pulled on a pair of jeans and had mismatched leather slides on his feet. "You won't find her dressed like that. You need to put on some clothes and shoes. Careful, there's glass everywhere on the floor. Hang on." He lifted Ava and carried her to her room.

Ava clung to him, her arms encircling his bare, muscular chest.

The scent of a warm bed still clung to his skin, a musky male scent that Ava thought she'd forgotten about years ago.

Raphael put Ava down on her bed and retrieved a pair of thick-soled leather shoes from her closet. He knelt to slip her bare feet into each shoe. His hands felt sure and strong. "We'll start looking for Caterina while you get dressed. Watch where you step, even with your shoes on."

Ava watched him go, thankful that he was here. As she hurried to dress, she worried about Caterina. *What if she's hurt? Or worse?* She had tossed all night, reliving their argument. Even though she was trying to do what was best for Caterina, she regretted the way she'd handled it.

Ava flung her gown across the bed, thrust her arms into a navy-checked cotton shirt, and then slipped on a pair of dark cotton pants. She picked her way past a shattered mirror and left the room.

With the electricity off, the room was dim, though morning rays filtered through the highest windows. "We have flashlights in the kitchen," Ava said. They picked their way through a jumbled mess in the living room and into the kitchen.

Even in the dark, Nina knew her way around the kitchen. She rummaged through a drawer. "Here we are. Plenty of flashlights for everyone."

"I'll check the house and the cellar," Ava said.

"Juliana, you go with her," Raphael said, flicking on a flashlight. "Nina, look in the front of the house. I'll check the propane tanks and turn off the gas. We don't want this place blowing sky-high."

"Even the icebox overturned. What a mess." Nina stepped around the refrigerator, which had pitched forward onto its front. She picked up the telephone, jiggled the hook, and spun the dial to zero for the operator. "There's no dial tone." She replaced the receiver.

Raphael hitched up his jeans and then opened the door for Nina. "Santo's around somewhere; if you see him, let me know."

Ava stood with her feet fixed to the ground. A shiver coursed down her spine as she remembered when Santo had come to see her two years ago. She'd denied him her daughter. How angry he'd been. But she'd made the correct decision, the responsible decision. *Though now, look at what Caterina has done. A baby.* She'd failed her daughter.

"Come on, let's go." Juliana was impatient. "Cat might be hurt, or she might be unconscious, unable to hear us."

Ava hurried after her. "Caterina, are you here? Where are you?"

The two women strode through the large stone house, swinging beams of light into darkened rooms, exclaiming over the damage as they searched for Caterina. Two large windows had shattered, and bookcases had toppled onto other furniture. Lamps lay broken on the tile in the living room. In the dining room, china and crystal had smashed to the floor, though the wine bottles in the wrought-iron enclosure had survived.

Paintings hung askew, vases and picture frames were broken, and the stench of gas hung in the air. They climbed the stairs to the second level and checked it thoroughly, but Caterina wasn't there.

Ava and Juliana descended the stairs, opened the door to the cellar, and started down. Halfway down, the earth began to rumble again.

They pressed against the rock wall, terrified.

The vibration only lasted a few seconds and never reached the intensity of the last tremor.

"Are you okay?" Juliana asked.

"As well as can be expected," Ava replied. "That must have been an aftershock. We should expect quite a few of those." She picked her way down the stairs and looked around, but Caterina wasn't there. Except for the chandelier, which had crashed onto the top of the tasting table, not much had been disturbed. The wine racks in the cellar were secured to the walls, and all bottles were intact.

After the women emerged from the cellar, they heard scratching and whimpering at the rear door. Juliana rushed to open it. "It's Vino, poor boy. What's wrong, sweetie?"

Shaking, Vino held up a front leg.

"Maybe it's his paw," Juliana said, stroking Vino's thick fur.

Raphael appeared at the door.

"The gas is off now. Hey, what's the matter with Vino?" He knelt beside the dog. "Let me have a look."

Juliana ruffled the fur around the dog's neck while Raphael took the dog's front leg in his hand. As he did, Vino whimpered and pulled it back.

Raphael steadied the dog and scrutinized his injury. "Just bruised, nothing broken." Raphael released him.

Nina came in, winded, her hand pressed to her chest. "I looked everywhere in front and around the rear of the house, but I didn't see the kids. Anyone else see a sign of Caterina or Santo?"

Everyone looked at each other and then shook their heads. "Maybe they got up early to watch the sunrise," Nina said.

Ava pressed a hand to her mouth. Surely they weren't together. *They mustn't be.*

Vino stood up behind them, barking.

"Santo was leaving early to go home," Raphael said. "Both of their cars are parked in back of the house, so they're here somewhere on the property."

Vino began barking again. He hobbled to the door and tried to nose it open.

Raphael looked in the dog's direction. "I think Vino knows where they are."

Juliana opened the door. Clearly agitated, Vino limped out, barking at the mountain that rose behind them. He started off toward the cave.

"*Mon Dieu,* the cave," Ava said, turning to Raphael. "If Caterina couldn't sleep, she might have gone there."

They rushed outside, and as they did, they drew a collective gasp. The side of the mountain had given way in the earthquake. The entrance to the cave was buried under dirt, rocks, and debris.

Ava clutched Nina's trembling hand. Nina was murmuring prayers for Caterina and Santo.

She shot a worried look at Raphael and saw grave concern in his eyes. He put his arm around her shoulder, and she let it stay there, needing his comfort.

"We'll find them," he said. "Let's all start digging. I'll get some shovels."

I'm almost through the door." Santo was breathing heavily from the exertion. Perspiration beaded on the muscles lining his bare back and wrapping his torso. He had ripped a couple of iron bilge hoops from wine barrels and was using a piece of one to gouge through the thick oak door to the cave, chipping and stripping small pieces of wood from the sturdy planks with splintered, bloodied fingers.

Drenched in the blackness of the cave, they'd lost track of time. Santo was determined to free them.

"I wish you'd let me help you again," Caterina said. She sat at the table with the lone candle before her, resting her chin in her hand. Her white top was stained with dirt and blood. She had helped him dig through the door for a while, but he'd stopped her when he saw her hands were bleeding. Despite her protests, he'd bandaged her hands with strips torn from the bottom of his cotton shirt.

"Shouldn't be much longer. You're a stubborn woman, you know that?"

"Thank you. I'll take that as a compliment."

He scowled at her. "That's not the way I meant it."

"Then you probably meant . . . what, courageous? Indefatigable? Or insouciant?" The room seemed to crackle with tension between them.

"You learned some nice words in college."

"Like you didn't?"

Santo jabbed at the door again. "Fearless." He paused. "I remember when a pack of coyotes had threatened a new litter of puppies, you defended them with nothing but a wine stave clutched in your fist." He motioned to her, and she leaped to her feet to help him.

"We're not kids anymore, Caterina." Santo wiped perspiration from his forehead, and as he did, his gaze took her in from head to toe. "Something is different about you."

She straightened her spine. "Just older and wiser. No one takes advantage of me anymore."

"Is that what you thought?" He frowned and swung his head slowly.

"You never called."

"That wasn't my fault."

"It sure wasn't mine."

Santo drew in a breath, his powerful chest expanding, and then forced it out. "Did your mother ever tell you I called on her?"

"What are you talking about?"

"After we made love, you fell asleep. I showered and dressed and went to see Ava."

"About what?"

Santo drew his brows together. "I asked for her permission to marry you, of course."

Caterina's lips parted in astonishment. "Because we'd made love?" Was it an obligation he'd felt? "What did she say?" But even as the words left her mouth, she knew.

"Clearly I wasn't good enough for you." He quirked the side of his mouth in a wry expression.

"And you let that stop you?"

Santo put his fists on his hips. "She threatened Raphael's employment if I went against her."

Caterina felt as if the air had been punched from her chest. She would never have believed it, except that now, she knew Ava had lied about other important things, too. Her knees buckled, and she touched the stone wall for support.

"Are you okay?" Santo caught her in his arms.

"I don't know what to say." *Santo, you have a daughter.* No, not here, not like this. Instead, she asked, "Why didn't you tell me about seeing my mother before now?"

Santo shook his head with remorse. "I've asked myself that a thousand times. You and Ava were so close. If I came between you, if I forced you to choose me over your mother, I knew you wouldn't be happy."

"I understand." Caterina composed herself and picked up a piece of an iron bilge hoop. "Let's get this done and get out of here. We're wasting oxygen." When they got out, she would tell him. And if they didn't, there would still be time. She whacked the door.

Ava. If his story was accurate, what on earth had her mother been thinking? She hadn't even told her.

As Caterina worked beside Santo, breathing hard from exertion, she was achingly conscious of his sheer virility. She also caught him glancing at her exposed, suntanned shoulders. A moment later, she could've sworn his eyes rested for a split second on the curve of her breasts. Was there still something between her and Santo, or was it her imagination?

After a while, he stopped and rested a hand against the scarred door. "Is there anything besides wine to drink in here?"

"That's all we have in the cave."

"Let's take a break." They perched on the chairs, quenching their thirst with wine and sharing a brooding silence.

She watched the movement of his throat as he swallowed. She remembered running her hands across his throat as they made love. The touch of his skin, the smell of his hair, the sound of his deep whispers in the night. *I love you, cara. I love you.* One magical night she could never forget, no matter how she tried.

And it could have been forever. Her heart clenched at the loss.

She detected a glint in his eye—or was it the flicker of candle-light? Feeling self-conscious, she ran a hand across her wayward hair.

Her body was burning with heat, though not from exertion. She would never forget what it felt like to be in his arms. One moment they had been blending wine together in the cave, and then, in the blink of an eye, their lives changed.

Caterina drew a sip of wine, recalling the day that altered the course of their future.

They were in the cave testing wine. She had tasted a blended wine and let it flow over her tongue. "*This* is exactly what's been missing," she had said, her voice dropping a notch.

"It is, isn't it?" Santo had brought her hand up to his face.

She opened her palm to him, and he pressed his full lips against her soft skin. He moved on, dragging his lips across her shoulder, which was nearly bare in the sundress she wore.

"*Cara,* my Caterina. What a beautiful woman you've become."

Giving herself to the moment, Caterina arched her neck as he traveled across her exposed throat. When their lips finally met, their separate worlds ceased to exist.

Without a word, Santo stood and offered his hand. He guided her to the plush burgundy sofa that anchored the room; they sank into the cushions. Together they slipped free from the bondage of their thin cotton clothes, their warm bodies melding, while the desire that had simmered beneath the surface all summer exploded.

Caterina had never been intimate with a man. Somewhere, in the recesses of her mind, her mother's admonitions swirled, but she was powerless against the passion that inflamed her heart, her mind, her body.

At one point, Santo hesitated. He searched her eyes for confirmation before continuing their lovemaking, but Caterina pressed against him, her craving for him overwhelming her last vestiges of judgment. Santo's loving intensity matched the fullness in her heart.

Even now, as Caterina recalled their passion, she thought of how right it had felt between them. The love she and Santo had expressed for each other had brought her beloved Marisa into the world. How could that have been wrong?

Yet in the eyes of her mother, her faith, and society, it was.

The connection she felt with Santo was beyond anything her friends at school had ever whispered about. It was more than a lustful encounter; they had opened their hearts to each other.

And her mother had decimated their relationship before it ever had a chance to flourish.

Caterina drank in more wine to allay her thirst. Was it too late for all of them? Suddenly, she hated this place. She wanted nothing more than to get as far from Mille Étoiles as she could.

She thought of Marisa and wondered again if she was okay. Faith and Patrick were looking after her this weekend, but she ached to hold her little girl and know that she was safe. Had the earthquake affected San Francisco? Napa Valley was an hour away from the city. It had felt as if the earthquake had been centered right under them, but San Francisco was also at risk. She had to reach Marisa.

Santo put his glass down and stretched his shoulders. "We should get back to work."

They returned to the job at hand, and a few minutes later, Santo yelled, "I've got it!" He'd scraped against rock on the other side.

"Can you see anything?"

"A bunch of rocks and dirt." He cursed under his breath. "I'd hoped to see daylight through this rubble. It's a landslide, for sure."

"Can you tell how dense it is?"

He shook his head. "It might be a small amount, or it might be half the mountain. Let's keep going, *cara*."

That word, *cara,* slipped carelessly from his lips, breaking her heart yet again.

"How much longer can we survive in here?" How long would they have sufficient oxygen? Worse still, what about the rising carbon dioxide level, the deadly natural by-product of fermenting wine? The doors to the cave were always open when people were working to guard against carbon dioxide poisoning.

Santo looked grim. "There's no time to waste." He thrust the end of the iron hoop into the wood.

As they gouged and stripped away particles of wood, Caterina thought about the night they'd slept together—the only night—the night she'd replayed in her mind so many times. "Do you ever think about what might have been between us?"

A nerve above his eye twitched. "Of course I do." He reached through the hole he'd made in the door and swept dirt away. "But that was a long time ago." He gritted his teeth and gouged at the door again.

Caterina glanced at Santo and felt a stab of regret. *God must have it in for me.* Of all the men to be trapped in an earthquake with, why did it have to be him?

Suddenly, beams of light spilled through the hole they'd made through the door from outside. Raphael's voice boomed out. "Santo, Caterina, are you in there?"

Santo rushed to the door. "We're here," he called back. "But we can't open the door. Can you move the rocks?"

Caterina got up and stood behind Santo. The din increased, and she could make out other voices. Her mother, Nina, Juliana. The dog was howling with excitement.

Santo cried out, "Vino!" He turned to Caterina, relief spreading across his weary face.

Overcome with emotion, Caterina began to sob. After today, she might never see Santo again.

"Hey, we're safe now, *cara*," he said, putting his arm around her. His voice sounded thick. "We'll be free in a few minutes."

Crying harder, Caterina turned into his chest and felt the steady throb of his heart. She pressed her hands against his chest, logging into her memory the feel of his skin.

"Everything's okay now." Santo kissed her forehead and smiled. "At least we're talking again. If nothing else, this was worth it. I've missed you. Friends again?"

Friends? That was beyond her ability with him. He smiled down at her, his eyes sparking another sob that threatened to rack her body. Gripping her emotions, she turned her face to his. "Is that what you think?"

"Cat, come on, what more do you expect of me right now?"

"Hold on," Raphael called. "Almost there."

"What's wrong?" His smile disappeared, and he glared at her. "I thought things had changed between us."

"So had I." Caterina shook her head. *What good could come of this?* He was engaged; he had chosen another.

She was a mother; she had more important things to do with her time.

Ten minutes later, beams of light from flashlights and kerosene lamps flooded the cave, and they were freed. There were hugs and cries all around, though Caterina winced as Ava embraced her.

Raphael handed Caterina a kerosene lamp. She waited until the others walked ahead, and then she asked her mother the question burning in her mind. "Why didn't you tell me Santo had asked to marry me?"

Ava narrowed her eyes. "Is that what he told you?"

"Don't play this guessing game with me again. I know it's the truth."

"You don't know anything."

Caterina raised the lamp to illuminate her mother's face. "Maybe not, but mark my words, I'm going to find out everything." She pushed the lamp into her mother's hand and hurried to join Juliana.

As Caterina flung an arm around her dearest friend, Juliana whispered, "Everything okay between you and Santo?"

"Sure. Nothing happened in there." Technically that was true. But another one of her mother's lies had been unveiled, and her heart had been tested. She wondered if her feelings toward him would ever end. "What time is it?"

"Probably about four or five in the morning." Juliana swung her flashlight in front of them.

With Raphael and Nina leading the way, they picked their way through rocks and dirt, the night illuminated only by the glow of kerosene lamps.

"The electricity and telephone are out?" Caterina asked as they approached the darkened house.

"That's right, but we have plenty of kerosene, candles, and flashlights." Raphael opened the rear door to the main house. He stepped inside, swinging his flashlight around.

"I'll get more supplies." Nina pushed through the kitchen door.

Panic gripped Caterina. She *had* to know if Marisa was okay. With the phones out, her only option was to drive into the city to see how Marisa was.

"I have to go back to San Francisco right now." When everyone turned to look at her, Caterina realized too late how strange it must have sounded, but all she could think about was Marisa's safety. She turned to Santo. "Will you come with me?"

Santo looked suspiciously at her. "Why? It's late."

She crossed her arms. "Will you come or not?" She'd lost her chance to tell him about Marisa in the cave. He could drive her into San Francisco, and they could talk on the way. She didn't want to blurt out her secret about Marisa to him here, in front of everyone. They should be alone.

Ava spoke up. "Caterina, don't put Santo out. You're tired; you can leave when it's daylight." She slid a piercing peripheral gaze to Santo.

"Your mother's right," Raphael added. "The roads might be damaged—a bridge could be down. Wait until the sun is up."

Santo shoved a hand through his hair, shaking his head as if to verify what he'd told her in the cave. "I have to return to Davis anyway."

Davis. To see his fiancée, no doubt. Caterina swung her gaze from Ava to Santo and back again. Too much time had passed. Decisions had been made. She thought about the house in Montalcino. Gritting her teeth, she resolved to take Marisa there. If the vineyard came with the house, she could make wine to support them, just as Ava had done when her father had died. There she would be free of judgment, free to raise Marisa and live her life.

Raphael hitched up his trousers. "I need to check on the gas line again. Santo, I need your help." Raphael made his way to the door, and Santo followed him out without so much as a backward glance.

Ava went into the kitchen to check on Nina.

Juliana put a hand on her hip and looked at Caterina, her suspicions aroused. "What's going on, Cat?"

Caterina squeezed Juliana's hand. "I have to make sure Marisa is okay. Tell everyone I'm going to check on my apartment. I'll call you when I can." She hugged her friend.

Before Caterina could change her mind, she grabbed her purse from the table and her keys from the hook by the rear door. She tucked two bottles of wine Santo had brought from the cave under her arm and then flung open the door and raced to her car.

With one last tear-blurred look back at Mille Étoiles, she tapped on her bright lights and wheeled onto the pitch-dark road. Through the rubble she began the descent, swerving around rocks and fallen tree limbs.

When Caterina came to the main road, she saw the earthquake had buckled the asphalt and the road was closed, so she had to take a longer route to San Francisco.

Halfway there she stopped at a gas station to call the O'Connells, but the attendant told her their phone line was out. A few miles down the road, she pulled into a breakfast diner, but their phone lines were down, too.

Caterina pressed a hand against her pounding heart. She'd never been so worried in her life. She wouldn't rest until she saw Marisa.

There were so many cars snaking into the city that the usual hour drive took several hours. Even the soaring Golden Gate Bridge was jammed with creeping autos as she crossed the bay. Gazing across the city, she thought San Francisco looked relatively unharmed. She breathed a sigh of relief as she drove.

When Caterina rushed into the O'Connells' home, she called out, "Faith? Patrick?"

The family was in the kitchen getting ready for lunch. Marisa broke into a smile and squealed with glee when she saw her mother.

Caterina scooped her from her high chair and hugged her tightly to her chest, relief flooding her. "I'm so happy to see you, little one." Marisa's bright eyes—*Santo's eyes*—twinkled with happiness, oblivious to her mother's worries. She rocked her little girl in her arms. *I'll never let her go again.* She kissed Marisa's soft cheek, reaffirming her decision about their future. She might have lost her mother and Santo, but she would not lose Marisa.

"We heard the news this morning about Napa," Faith said. "We've been trying to reach you. Why, you put my heart crossways, I had such a fright."

"Everything is shut down," Caterina said. "I was trapped in our wine cave all day and most of the night."

"Fierce weather, indeed. Shook a bit here, but not much." Patrick rapped on the wall. "No damage, thank the Lord."

"I'll bet you haven't eaten." Faith added another place setting and insisted she sit down.

"Not really." Caterina swept a hand over her face and hair. "I must look a fright, too."

"Eat first. You can bathe later." Faith slid a serving of corned beef and cabbage onto Caterina's plate.

Never had food smelled so good. While Caterina ate, she fed Marisa, who was also hungry.

"How bad is the damage at the winery?" Patrick asked.

"We lost some wine, and the cave will have to be cleaned up and reinforced, but I think most of the equipment survived."

After Marisa's afternoon nap, playtime, and dinner, Caterina bathed her, changed her into her nightwear, and stroked her hair and back until she fell asleep. Satisfied that Marisa was sleeping soundly, Caterina tiptoed down the stairs to help Faith clear the table.

As they were washing dishes, Faith asked, "Did you have a chance to speak to your mother about Marisa?"

Caterina sighed. "We had a dreadful argument." Faith had so much confidence in the goodness of people that she hated to tell her the truth, but she did.

"Oh no!" Faith exclaimed, tears welling in her eyes. "I'd prayed so much for her acceptance of Marisa. What are you going to do?"

Caterina lifted a corner of her mouth. "Strangely enough, I just learned I've inherited a house in Italy. I've decided that Marisa and I are moving to Montalcino. We'll start fresh there." *No one will know about our past.*

As she spoke, her voice was filled with hope, but thoughts of separation slashed her heart. She would miss her family and friends,

Faith and Patrick, and all the good people she'd worked with in Napa and San Francisco. And Santo. Always Santo. As much as she hated to admit it.

"That's a timely gift from God, indeed it is." Faith nodded thoughtfully. "I'll pray you meet a good man there."

Caterina dried her hands and hugged her dear friend. Although Faith meant well, a man was the last thing on Caterina's mind now.

11

Early the next morning, Caterina managed to get a call through to Juliana at her mother's cottage on the vineyard. Juliana was helping Nina clean up, and she reported that none of the winemaking equipment had been damaged.

Caterina dressed in a slim-fitting taupe suit, secured her matching hat, and pulled on ivory three-quarter gloves. She kissed Marisa good-bye and reported to work at the St. Francis Hotel.

On her lunch break, she checked the documents in her purse. The date for the reading of the will in Montalcino was drawing near. She hurried to a private phone booth off the lobby. After she closed the glass door, she called the investigator, Anthony Martoni, who had visited her with news of her inheritance.

"Hello, Anthony. I'm calling to see if the offer for the flight to Montalcino is still available." She twirled the coiled telephone cord around her finger. "And I need a ticket for my baby," she added in a matter-of-fact manner. "Violetta Rosetta's great-granddaughter." She held her breath.

"Of course, Miss Rosetta, er, forgive me, Mrs.—"

She could hear the surprise in his voice. "You can still call me Caterina."

"Oh, uh, thank you. And will your husband be traveling with you as well?"

"No." At least that was true.

"I understand. My wife chastises me for working too much as well. Maybe he can get away with you next time. That's round trip, of course?"

"Why, yes." Caterina doubted she'd have need for return tickets, but she didn't want to explain, so she went along with his assumption.

"I'll make a note for my secretary. She'll also arrange your airport pickup and an inn for your stay." She could hear him rustling papers.

Caterina asked him a few questions about the house, and he assured her that the property in Montalcino was hers to live in or do with as she wished, although he suspected it would need repairs.

She wasn't afraid of hard work.

Anthony went on, "Heard on the news you had another earthquake out there. That was one of the most unnerving experiences I've ever had. Glad we don't have them in New York." He paused. "What did you say your husband does?"

Caterina winced. She was growing to hate her lies, but people didn't really want to know her truth. She could just imagine the feigned politeness, the whispers behind her back. *No, I'm not married. Never was. Knocked up? Oh yes, I was. That's right, pity he wouldn't marry me. But on we go* . . . She'd be branded a social pariah. And for what? Having sex? Giving birth? That was a normal part of life. The only thing missing was a marriage license. A damned piece of paper. She had to admit, her mother had been right about that. She dragged her attention back to the conversation.

"He's in the wine business, too. In fact, I forgot that I have to call him right away. Forgive me for being abrupt, Anthony, but I need to go. And thank you for the tickets."

"I'll have my secretary call you later with your travel itinerary." He hesitated. "Caterina?"

"Yes?"

"Your husband is one lucky man. If he ever changes his mind—"

"Why, thank you, Anthony." *The nerve of this man.* He was clearly emboldened by the distance, unlike the day he'd visited Mille Étoiles. "But for your wife's sake, I'll pretend I didn't hear that."

After she hung up, she shook her head. *Men.* Were they all alike? Maybe her mother was right. She opened the door of the phone booth and wove through throngs of hotel guests on her way back to her office.

She had so much to think about. She hadn't had a chance to read the entire legal document—besides, it was in Italian—but she trusted that everything was in order. Excitement sparked through her. *We're going to Italy.*

Her excitement was quickly replaced by a wave of trepidation. It would be a long journey for a baby, and she'd have to learn how to care for Marisa without Faith as her crutch.

Another thought struck her. After her father died, her mother had raised her. Ava had also been a mother alone in a foreign country. She had help from Nina around the house, but she'd also had the responsibility of running a business. Caterina considered the stress her mother must have been under, although it didn't negate the fact that Ava's temper had been out of control for years.

Nor that she thought Caterina should give up Marisa for adoption. How could Ava, of all people, suggest that?

Caterina turned her thoughts to the next item on her task list. Straightening her jacket, she marched into her boss's office to quit the job she'd fought so hard to get.

Over the next few days, Caterina split her time between caring for Marisa and preparing for their departure. She arranged her finances, and packed what she thought they might need for the trip.

Their journey was about to begin.

When the day of departure arrived, Caterina was filled with a mixture of elation and anxiety. A knock sounded at the door. "I'll get it—that's Juliana." Faith was in the kitchen, and Patrick was bringing her suitcases downstairs.

Caterina opened the door, and Juliana flung her arms around her. "Hello, world traveler! What an adventure you'll have. And how is my precious little girl?" She knelt to kiss Marisa, who was dressed in a navy-blue dress and jacket for traveling. "Marisa, you get prettier every day. Look at those gorgeous blue eyes."

Caterina smiled wistfully. "She has Santo's eyes, doesn't she? It was so difficult seeing him again." Glancing into the hallway mirror, she pinned on a small burgundy felt hat that matched her gray-and-burgundy traveling suit.

Behind her, Juliana dipped her head and cast her eyes down.

Caterina caught Juliana's reaction in the mirror. She swung around. "Jules, I know you called Santo."

Juliana sighed. "I'd hoped you might have a chance to talk to him. You and Santo have always had a thing for each other. I can see it in your eyes—and his. Whenever the three of us were together, every time you entered the room, Santo only looked at you."

Caterina was still hurt. "I specifically asked you not to tell him anything."

"And I didn't, but I couldn't stand to see you marry Ted. When my mother told me what Ava was planning, I panicked and called Santo."

Caterina put a hand on Juliana's arm. She couldn't be angry at her dearest friend, not now as she was leaving the country. "I understand why you did it, but nothing has changed between Santo and me. He's still engaged. You can't tell him anything. Promise me. I'll tell him when the time is right, but it's not now."

"I promise. I'm really sorry."

"And a shotgun wedding is the last thing I'd ever want." Caterina hugged her, and they both had tears in their eyes.

Juliana sighed longingly. "I'd love to go with you. I want to travel, see the world, live—*really* live. Once you get married, life changes." She blinked her large brown eyes. "Can I tell you a secret? I don't know if I *ever* want to get married. I like being free. Look at your mother. She's run Mille Étoiles for more than two decades. She could've remarried, but she didn't. Hell, when our moms were our age, they couldn't even vote." She managed a sad smile. "I'll miss you, Cat."

"You'll come see us."

Juliana nodded, her expression solemn. "Funny how life works out, huh?"

Caterina touched Juliana's shoulder. "Sure is. What if you visit and meet some amazing Italian man?"

"Even worse. You know how possessive they are."

"No. I don't." She spat out her words. Santo had left her without a word, even if it was at her mother's command.

"Sorry, I didn't mean—"

"Doesn't matter." Caterina waved it off, but her nerves were still raw. "It's time to go." They walked to the car. Marisa was taking tentative steps now. Caterina held both her hands, guiding her in front of her to the car.

"Walk, walk," Marisa said, though her new words sounded more like *wok-wok*. Caterina smiled and thought about the Italian words she might soon learn, too. Marisa didn't have many words yet, but she was certainly communicating with gusto.

Patrick carried her suitcases, along with the Mille Étoiles '53 cabernet bottles she'd grabbed on her way out. Faith and Patrick hugged her and wished her a safe flight, and Caterina saw tears in their eyes. They'd been so important to her this last year and a half. She promised them she'd write and send photos.

She got into Juliana's car, which was an older Chevrolet with wide bench seats. Caterina buckled her seat belt and held Marisa tightly on her lap. "They should make safer arrangements for babies and little children in cars."

"Probably will someday." Juliana steered through traffic. "I'm glad Raphael installed seat belts in all our cars. I really do feel safer." She inclined her head toward her purse. "If you look in the side pocket, you'll find my notes from Gilbert Waters about the wine competition in Paris. It's being held at the Ritz, and you should go if you can, even though you said you weren't going to enter Mille Étoiles wines."

Caterina scanned the notes that Juliana had prepared for her after her conversation with the magazine editor. She folded the paper and tucked it securely in her handbag. She wished she'd had time to prepare for the event, but she'd been so rushed since she'd decided to go to Italy.

They turned into the airport. Caterina hailed a porter to take their luggage, and then they made their way into the airport.

"Are you nervous?" Juliana asked. They stood inside the terminal waiting for Caterina's flight to be called. The rumble of airplanes landing and taking off filled the air, punctuated by loudspeaker announcements.

"I've gone way beyond that, Jules. I'm petrified." Caterina glanced at other well-dressed passengers, who seemed calm and sophisticated, and she tried to emulate their demeanor. The men wore suits, and the women looked like they'd stepped from the pages of *Vogue* magazine.

"I'm so jealous. I wish I could go with you." Juliana reached into her handbag and handed her a small leather-bound photo book. "Here, I made this for you. I thought you might want to share your American life with your new relatives."

Caterina flipped through the photographs. All the people she loved were there. Her mother, Juliana, Nina, Raphael . . . and Santo.

Even Vino. And Mille Étoiles, and their best wines. She said quietly, "We really did have a good life, didn't we?"

"We have a wonderful American family, even if we're not all related. Don't forget, I'm coming to visit you as soon as I can." Juliana hugged her again.

The two women clung to each other with tears in their eyes. Juliana brushed moisture from her cheek. "Want me to wait to see you off from the gate? I can park the car."

"No, you go ahead." Caterina didn't know how many more times she could say good-bye to those she loved. Except for her mother, who through Nina wasn't taking or returning her calls. Caterina regretted her mistakes, but she could only move forward now. She glanced at Marisa, who clasped her hand tightly. At least she wouldn't be saying good-bye to her daughter.

After Juliana left, Caterina lifted Marisa, shifted her onto her hip, and walked farther into the terminal. She sat near a large window where they could watch the planes taxi along the runway. She smoothed her light-gray twill traveling suit, which was edged in burgundy piping, and balanced Marisa on her lap. She checked her watch. Two minutes had passed since the last time she'd checked it.

A sleek airplane emblazoned with the logo for Pan American World Airways stretched before her. Four propellers shimmered in the morning sunlight. "What a beauty," she said to Marisa. "I wonder if that's our plane."

A dark-haired man seated in back of her turned toward her. "It is if you're going to Roma," he said with a slight Italian accent that reminded her of Santo's. "It's a Boeing 377 Stratocruiser. A real luxury aircraft. San Francisco, New York City, Roma. *Viaggio sicuro.*"

Caterina thanked him, and he tipped his hat. When an announcement crackled through the air a few minutes later, the man said, "That's our flight. Ready to board the Clipper?" He picked up a small leather cabin bag. "Shall I carry yours, too?"

"That's kind of you." A surge of nervous excitement sparked through her.

A smiling stewardess escorted them to their seats. The man sat down a few rows behind her. She settled into a plush seat, clutched Marisa on her lap, and peered out the window at the propellers.

The stewardess stopped by her aisle. "Champagne?"

"Oh, thank you," Caterina breathed.

The woman in the smart uniform handed her a glass. "First flight?" she whispered.

"Can you tell?" Caterina sipped from the glass. She raised her brow in approval. It was a fine French vintage.

"You're a little pale," the woman said kindly. "Relax. We'll be fine."

Caterina smiled back at her, but when the plane taxied and took off, her stomach did flip-flops. Marisa was curious, gazing at everything. As the plane climbed in the sky, Marisa began to whimper and cry.

Caterina rocked her in her lap to calm her. She took out a bottle of milk, and Marisa snuggled against her, sucking her bottle with trepidation, her eyes wide at the new experience of flight.

Feeling the vibration and hearing the roar of the engines, Caterina stared from the window. She watched San Francisco grow smaller in the distance.

She let out her breath. She'd done it. They were actually on their way. She had Marisa, and she'd left her troubles far behind. Or so she hoped.

They changed planes in New York, where Marisa threw a fit while they were waiting in the airport. She was wailing and screaming at the top of her lungs, and Caterina was so frustrated. It seemed there was nothing she could do to quiet her. What would Faith have done?

At last an older woman came to her rescue. "Mind if I say hello to her? I'm a grandmother of eight. Sometimes they like to see a new face." In a few minutes, the woman helped her calm Marisa by diverting her attention to the planes outside.

"I don't know why she's cranky." Caterina brushed wisps of hair from her flushed face. Their carefully pressed outfits were wrinkled, and Caterina's hat was askew. "She's usually better than this."

"Judging by the amount of drooling, she's probably teething," the gray-haired woman said.

"I don't know what to do." Caterina wished Faith were around.

"I can give you a little break. May I hold her?"

Caterina relinquished Marisa. This was more difficult than she'd imagined; she felt frustrated and overwhelmed. Had she made a mistake in bringing Marisa here and thinking that she could do this on her own?

The older woman took Marisa in her lap and rocked her while Caterina straightened her hat. "When you're at home, dear, give the child a cold washcloth to gnaw on; it will feel good on her gums. She'll probably like frozen banana slices, too."

As they chatted, the woman's gaze dropped to Caterina's left hand, and she frowned. "Aren't you married, dear?"

Caterina was too tired to argue. "Imagine, I lost my ring. My husband has another one waiting for me in Italy."

The woman looked skeptical. "Really? What's his name?"

"My husband's name? Why, it's . . . ah—"

"You're not married, are you?" The woman narrowed her eyes and scanned Caterina from head to toe, wrinkling her nose in disgust.

Caterina bristled. "Why should it matter to you?"

The woman's eyes widened. "I'm appalled you even have to ask. You've committed a grave sin. I can't be seen in public with someone like you. People know me." She held Marisa out as if she were dirty. "Take her back," she said tersely before she got up and stalked away.

Two other women standing in front of Caterina turned withering looks toward her. She rocked Marisa and stared straight ahead. She would not be intimidated by strangers.

Soon they were called to board their next flight. After the plane climbed to cruising altitude across the Atlantic Ocean, dinner was served and Caterina began to relax. Later, Marisa began fussing again. Caterina let her chew on a rubber bottle nipple until her daughter finally fell into an exhausted slumber in her lap.

Caterina didn't dare to jostle Marisa. Instead, she stared from the window over an endless sea below and thought about the day Santo had disappeared from her life. His actions had always baffled her and cut deep into her soul.

She had replayed that day countless times in her mind. Since Santo's revelation in the cave, it now made more sense. As she recalled, after they'd made love that fateful night, she had slept late the next day. But when she awoke, he was gone.

"Where's Santo?" she had asked Raphael.

"He's gone back to school."

Santo went to college in Davis, a town about an hour away. It might as well have been on the other side of the earth. She couldn't understand why he'd left so suddenly.

Later that day over dinner, her mother said, "We'll miss Santo, won't we? He probably raced back to be with his girlfriend. I heard him talking to one of the field hands before he left. Seems our Santo is engaged. Isn't that wonderful?"

Caterina struggled to conceal her shock. *It can't be,* she told herself, confused and hurt over what had transpired between them. Their lovemaking had bonded their bodies and souls; how could he possibly be in love with another?

After dinner she'd frantically tried to call him, but he didn't answer his telephone. That night she didn't sleep at all. She cried in agony until the sun pierced the curtains in her bedroom. When she rose, she splashed cold water on her burning face. She blinked at her reflection in the mirror. Her eyes were rimmed in red, and her face was splotchy. Unable to face the harsh light of day, she burrowed under her bedcovers and stayed in her room all day, feigning illness.

The following day, she returned to the university in San Francisco as planned to begin her final year. She tried to call Santo again, but there was still no answer. She'd committed the most heinous of sins, and he was her partner in this crime. Where was he?

She didn't regret that they'd made love. But how could he have left without a word?

She'd been utterly devastated.

Now, as Caterina stared out the window over the Atlantic Ocean, everything fell perfectly, horribly into place.

Ava had indeed denied Santo permission to marry Caterina.

Because of her mother's rigid moral stance, the only person Caterina could share her sad story with was Juliana, who was going through a tragedy of her own.

However, Santo seemed to bounce back quickly. Her mother might have squelched his plan, but by the time he left, he'd already decided to marry another. Probably the blond girl she'd seen him with once in Napa, she decided, disgusted and perturbed.

Was that the fickle sort of man she'd want to spend her life with? Thankful to have left the disaster behind, she closed her eyes and drifted off to the steady hum of the engines, though her sleep was troubled.

She and Marisa woke when the wheels scudded against the tarmac in Rome. Caterina waited until everyone else had disembarked.

After seeing others walk down the aisle, Marisa fussed over being carried, so Caterina held Marisa's hands in hers and let her walk in front of her for a little bit, taking care to maintain her little girl's balance. The stewardesses exclaimed over her child. Caterina was so proud; Marisa would be walking on her own soon. When Marisa grew tired, Caterina picked her up to continue. She walked out of the cabin and down the steps. A stewardess followed, carrying the wine she'd brought. "This must be good," the woman remarked.

"The best," Caterina replied, and she thanked her for her help.

They entered the terminal, where a driver in a dark suit met them. "Signora Rosetta? I'll take your luggage. Follow me, *per favore*."

Signora. This time, Caterina let him think she was married. They walked through the airport. They passed cafés, where pastries and steaming cups of cappuccino smelled absolutely wonderful.

She wished they had more time to spend in Rome, but she respected the time schedule the investigator's secretary had constructed for them. She slid into the car and asked, "How far is it to Montalcino?"

"Two hundred kilometers," the driver said. "About three hours, more or less. First time in Italy?" When she told him it was, the driver nodded. "I meet many Italians from America. We have time to drive past the Colosseum and a few other important sights if you'd like. Are you hungry? And the baby?"

It was as if he'd read her mind. "We have to eat, and I'd love a cappuccino," she said with a yawn. Though she'd slept on the airplane, it had been a light sleep, and she'd felt every bit of turbulence. The driver suggested a nearby café.

Caterina devoured a plate of pasta and vegetables, which she shared with Marisa, followed by cappuccino and biscotto. Marisa gnawed on the hard almond cookie. Caterina improvised and dipped the biscotto into a cup of tea for her. It seemed to soothe Marisa's sore gums. Caterina kissed Marisa, glad her little girl was feeling better.

Afterward, the driver drove past the Colosseum and the Spanish Steps and proudly pointed out a few of the best sights of Rome.

"I have precious cargo today," the driver said, smiling at her in the rearview mirror. "We Italians sometimes drive like maniacs, but for you and *la bambina,* I'll be very careful."

Caterina kissed Marisa and whispered to her, "We've really done it, kiddo. Welcome to our new life." She held Marisa in her arms, and the little girl dozed. It had been a taxing journey for both of them. Only time would tell if she had made the right decision to come here.

She glanced at the countryside, which looked so peaceful. Yet her mother's warnings about Italy clanged in her memory. So far it seemed like a good life with friendly people, excellent food, and incredible sights. What could possibly hurt them here?

12

MARCH 1929 — MONTALCINO, ITALY

Standing in a tiny shop tucked under a dwelling in the village, Ava ran her hand over the delicate ivory lace she'd selected. It would be just enough for a baby's christening dress.

She prayed that she and Luca would be blessed with a healthy child this time, although she hadn't confirmed her pregnancy or told him yet. Violetta had told her that children always changed men, making them more settled.

As she loosened her embroidered drawstring purse and fished out coins to pay, a commotion erupted behind her.

"Ignore them, they're imbeciles," the old shopkeeper said, counting Ava's coins on the wooden table.

Ava's face burned with embarrassment. Through the looking glass on the wall of the village shop, she could see three girls behind her, mocking her. They seemed to delight in following her wherever she went and whispering behind her back.

Her life in Tuscany had quickly become intolerable. Luca drank more than ever and ranted at the slightest perceived injustice visited upon him. She had learned to stay out of his way. She spent most of her days with Violetta, learning how to manage the bookkeeping for the wine business.

"*Grazie*," Ava said, hastily taking her purchase. She walked briskly from the shop, her calfskin ankle-strap button shoes clicking on the cobblestones. The girls followed her.

She looked for her cousin, who was to meet her in the square. Giovanna and her sister, Alma, were the only girls her age who had befriended her, though she had to admit that Natalie had been nice to her before the rumors began. They were all newly married, too, but they seemed much happier than she was.

Ava sat on a stone bench and angled her face from the girls, wishing her stylish cloche hat had a broader brim to hide beneath. The aromas of oregano, garlic, and basil wafted in the air, making her slightly nauseous.

All around her, birds were welcoming spring with cheerful song. The sprawling tree above the square was ablaze with tender green leaves. She should be thrilled at the possibility of another baby— one that might reach full term this time—but her heart was black with despair.

The closer Natalie came to giving birth, the more the gossip-mongers whispered their cruel stories, tittering every time they saw Ava. She couldn't go to the village market or a party or even church without stares and snickers from those she passed. She had been tried and condemned. And for what? Having a wayward husband? She had absolutely no control over Luca. Why were they blaming and torturing her?

Giovanna spied her and waved a gloved hand. She hurried to join Ava. Thankfully, when the girls saw Giovanna, they dispersed.

"What horrible creatures they are!" Giovanna exclaimed. She plopped onto the bench beside Ava, her full skirts billowing around her tiny waist.

"I don't pay any attention to them." Ava tried to act nonchalant. Italy was so different from her home in France. She was teased about her French accent, her fashionable dresses, the way she wore her hair, her customs, and her mispronunciations of Italian words. She didn't know if she was more ostracized for being French or for marrying Luca, one of their own.

"What are you going to do with that lace?" Giovanna asked, changing the subject. "It's beautiful."

"It's for a baby dress." Ava had been hand-stitching gowns for the babies she would have someday. She desperately wanted a child to occupy her time and fill her heart after the deaths of her parents. Perhaps it would make Luca happy, too, especially if she had a boy for him.

"They'll come soon enough." Giovanna fanned herself. "I just heard that Franco sent for a midwife last night. Natalie is in labor."

Ava jerked her head around. She wondered if the baby would look like Luca. If it did, there would be no end to the hateful rumors. "How is Natalie doing?"

Giovanna shook her head. "It's a hard labor."

After Giovanna and Ava returned to the villa, Violetta asked them to arrange flowers for a dinner party she was having. Giovanna continued chattering about childbirth, making Ava feel queasy.

Afterward, Ava changed into an emerald-green silk dress designed by a French couturier, Jean Patou. Her mother had bought it for her on a trip to Paris. It had a chic dropped waist, and the hemline hovered high on her shins, just beneath her knees. It bordered on scandalous in Montalcino, but tonight's guests were from France. They would appreciate her style.

Violetta's maid came in to dress her hair. The woman begrudgingly followed Ava's instructions and coaxed her hair into a new style that was all the rage in France. Ava hadn't bobbed her hair like so many of the young girls in Paris, but she had the latest finger waves. At least Violetta approved of her taste.

As the maid finished her coiffure, Luca rushed into their suite with a wild look in his eyes.

"That's lovely, thank you," Ava told the maid, quickly excusing her. She turned to Luca. "What's wrong?"

"It's Natalie," he said, winded. He threw off his jacket and paced the floor.

"Has she had the baby?"

"No," he snapped. "It's gone on too long, and the midwife is completely incompetent. Franco should have called a doctor hours ago. My mother just sent our doctor to the cottage."

Without a second thought, Ava brushed past him and raced down the stone steps. Violetta was standing by the wall-mounted telephone in the hall; she was speaking into the mouthpiece. Ava pressed a knuckle to her mouth. She hoped Natalie was all right. She didn't wish her any harm and thought the gossip had probably hurt her as well.

Violetta listened for a long moment and then shook her head. She said good-bye and hung up.

"How is Natalie?" Ava asked.

"She lost too much blood," Violetta began and then stopped to dab her eyes with a handkerchief. "Her baby is fine, but there was nothing the doctor could do for her."

Ava stared at her, terrified. She pressed a hand against her abdomen.

"Natalie gave her life for her child." Violetta held her arms out, and Ava fell into her embrace, trembling. "She was always an angel among us on earth."

Having a child was often a serious risk, especially if the child was overdue and had grown large, but Ava had never imagined Natalie might die.

"Natalie is dead?" Luca's angry voice boomed from the stairwell. His shirt hung open in disarray.

Violetta looked up at her son. "They did everything they could."

Luca scowled and disappeared down the hallway, returning a

minute later. "Franco knew she was in trouble. He did this to her, to ruin our plan. *Franco killed her.*" He spun on his heel, flung open the door, and stormed from the villa.

Rain was beginning to fall, but Luca was a man bent on a mission. Ava raced to the door. In the dusky twilight, she saw Luca run to the barn and then emerge on his horse. The driver had taken Violetta's car to the train station to pick up their dinner guests.

Luca kicked the horse and galloped up the lane, rain soaking his shirt to his skin. Ava called after him, but he didn't even look back.

"He's going to confront Franco!" Ava cried, suddenly fearful for Natalie's poor husband. *What did Luca mean about a plan?*

"*Dio mio,* I'll warn Franco." Violetta hurried to the telephone, cranked it, and waited for an operator. It seemed to take forever. Once the operator came on the line, Violetta waited again. "No answer," she said, her voice wavering. "Please keep trying." When there was still no answer, Violetta placed a call to one of Franco's uncles and asked him to look for Luca.

Ava sent up a prayer for Franco and Natalie and their poor little baby. What a tragedy it was. Franco was probably engulfed in grief.

They didn't have much time to grieve, as Violetta's distinguished guests were arriving soon. The driver returned, the guests joined them, and soon they were sitting down for dinner. Giovanna and her husband, Luca's cousin, had joined them, too.

Ava was worried about Luca, and she knew Violetta was, too. There had been no sign of him, and his chair at the table was conspicuously empty.

As the second course was being served, a loud knock sounded at the door. A short time later, one of the waitstaff whispered to Violetta. She excused herself and motioned for Ava to come with her. Giovanna and her husband could carry on the conversation at the table.

"Signora Rosetta." A uniformed police officer respectfully removed his hat as Violetta swept into the foyer.

"What is this about my son being arrested?"

Ava caught her breath. "Why? What has he done?" Whatever it was, Luca had gone too far this time.

13

As they wound through the rolling hills of the Tuscan countryside under a bright cerulean sky, Caterina was curiously drawn to the mountain vineyards they passed. This was the land of her ancestry. Marisa pressed her palms on the window as they drove, her head bobbing in excitement.

The driver pointed to a high mountaintop. "There's the village of Montalcino. Your destination is on the northeast slope. At the top is a medieval fortress. The first walls were built in 1361."

Caterina craned her neck to see it. The imposing stone structure was punctuated with Roman turrets overlooking the verdant valley below.

The driver wheeled into a long gravel driveway, at the end of which stood a large villa built in the Tuscan tradition. The stucco walls were washed in a soft rose color, and violet shutters framed tall windows. Flaming pink bougainvillea flowers cascaded against the wall, and potted cypress trees framed the arched front door. Olive trees swayed in the warm evening breeze. Two stucco cottages flanked the main home, and all the structures were crowned with terra-cotta tile roofs.

"*Buonasera*," a woman called out. She stood by the door and waved. She was casually dressed in an orange blouse and ruffled print skirt.

When the driver stopped, the woman hurried to the car. Caterina got out of the car, and the woman embraced her and Marisa.

"*Benvenuto,*" she said with a broad smile. Dark-blond hair fell around her shoulders. Caterina noticed splotches of flour on her soft cotton blouse. She spoke in Italian with animation, exclaiming over her and Marisa. Caterina caught a few words.

It had been several years since Caterina had spoken Italian with Santo, but she was fairly certain the woman thought they were related. "We're cousins?"

"Oh, sorry." The woman laughed and switched to English. "I am Giovanna. Your mother and I are cousins by marriage." She cooed to Marisa. "Ah, *la bambina dolce.*"

Caterina opened her mouth in surprise. Her mother had never said anything about a cousin. Caterina thought she was staying at an inn, not a relative's home.

Two young boys dashed from the side of the large house to retrieve their luggage.

"This is where Signora Violetta lived. Her instructions to the attorneys were for you to stay here as long as you wish. Of course, you're family. I'll have the boys put a baby crib in the room for you. Come with me." She motioned to her. "Many years ago, your mother lived here, too. It was right after she and Luca married, in the late 1920s. Did she tell you about it?"

"Not really." Caterina contained her astonishment. Balancing Marisa on her hip, she trailed after Giovanna, more intrigued than ever. This was her beloved father's home. How she wished she had known him.

Birds sang in the canopy of trees towering above them, gravel crunched beneath their feet, and lacy white jasmine flowers scented the air. They climbed worn stone steps to the entry. Caterina imagined little had changed since her mother had lived here.

When they stepped inside, Caterina took in the cool, welcoming interior. Dark wooden beams supported the high ceiling, smooth stone tiles gleamed underfoot, and a circular stone staircase wound to the second floor. Somewhere an operatic recording of Enrico Caruso in *Carmen* played, filling the air with rich, lyrical music.

Giovanna led them to their rooms on the second floor. "I'll have supper ready soon. Come down whenever you like. I know you must be tired after such a long journey. It's just us this evening. You'll meet the other heirs tomorrow, so you'll need a good night of rest."

Caterina saw a shadow cross Giovanna's face when she mentioned the heirs. Were these her relatives? Before she could ask about them, Giovanna opened a door to a guest room and waved her inside.

"Signora Violetta insisted on renovating the bedrooms in this old villa with en suite bathrooms. After her husband died in the war, she was lonely, so she rented rooms to honeymoon couples and retired people. Most of them became friends and visit often. It turned into a private inn, though no one else is here now. She became very selective. And I ran the house for *la signora*." She sighed. "I miss her so much."

"I wish I had known her, too," Caterina said. "Did she have other children?"

"No, she was not so fortunate. I was married to her brother-in-law's eldest son. I moved here to keep her company during the war. Living alone was not good then. Those were difficult years here in Toscana."

Caterina could hardly imagine what it must have been like during the war. She stepped inside the bedroom. Botanical artwork lined the walls, a stone fireplace anchored one corner, and fresh wildflowers filled a painted earthenware pitcher. The iron bed was covered in colorful cotton pillows. She couldn't have asked for a more enchanting room. "This is so lovely."

"This was once my room. It's one of my favorites." Giovanna smiled and left them to change into more casual clothes.

Marisa clambered onto the bed. Intrigued by the wildflowers in the pitcher, she yanked a cloth covering the nightstand in an effort to reach them, sending a lamp teetering to the edge.

"Marisa, no!" Caterina cried, diving for the lamp and catching it in midair. As she did, the pitcher overturned, flowers tumbled to the floor, and water seeped onto the cloth.

"Wa," Marisa said, slapping her tiny hands in the water.

She'd have to watch her more carefully, Caterina realized. What a godsend Faith had been. "That's right, water. But you mustn't touch it. Or the flowers."

Caterina picked up Marisa, grabbed a towel, and mopped up the water with her free hand. She moved the flowers to the top of the high bureau. Caterina was exhausted from the journey, but Marisa seemed recharged.

"Time for a change, little one." She changed Marisa's diaper and buttoned a fresh cotton dress on her. While Marisa was toddling around the room in new sandals, Caterina shed her gray traveling suit and pumps.

She kept an eye on Marisa while she splashed water onto her face and brushed her hair, and then she spied a small bottle of perfume in the bathroom. *Violetta di Parma.* It was the same perfume that sat untouched in her mother's bedroom. She had once asked her mother if she could try it, but Ava had told her it was a keepsake of remembrance. She dabbed the soft floral scent on her wrists and neck. Taking a cue from Giovanna, she dressed in a white cotton blouse, a print skirt, and woven espadrilles.

Gazing around the room, Caterina felt as if she had stepped back in time to a simpler way of life. She trailed her fingers along the snowy white, hand-sewn bed linens, the embroidered pillows, and crocheted throw. Everything in the room was handmade with expert craftsmanship.

Birdsong trilled from the open window. Caterina sat on the edge of the bed and swept Marisa into her arms. Unlike in San Francisco, there were no cars zipping past, no garbage trucks rumbling about. No trolley car bells clanging, no advertising crackling from radios. This was going to be a quiet, pastoral life for her and Marisa.

She couldn't wait to see the house she'd inherited and meet their relatives.

I brought something I thought you might like," Caterina said, placing the bag she'd carefully traveled with on the kitchen table. This was the wine that had survived the earthquake. She withdrew a bottle with a Mille Étoiles label and presented it to Giovanna and then slid onto a wooden stool with Marisa in her lap.

Caterina looked around the large kitchen, which was filled with well-used copper pots rubbed to a shine, carved wooden spoons, and handcrafted pottery painted with a riot of pretty images of olives, grapes, lemons, and animals. Colorful tiles covered the countertops. It was an Italian version of their kitchen at Mille Étoiles. She smiled at the comfort of it all, imagining her father as a little boy here.

"*Mille grazie.* What a beautiful label." Giovanna studied the artist's sketch of the imposing stone house on the front. "This looks like an old French château. Is this really in Napa?"

She nodded. "My mother built it according to the memory of her parents' home in Bordeaux."

"I remember how Ava used to speak of it. She loved it there. And she always had the best taste, even when she was young. We used to trade clothes when she lived here. I was lucky to have known her then. It's too bad we lost touch over the years. Somehow life intervened, and our letters became less frequent. How is she?"

"She's fine. Always busy." Caterina realized Giovanna must be about the same age as her mother, but she had such a youthful, happy disposition that she seemed younger than her years. How could they have been friends? Or had her mother changed over the years? "What was my mother like then?"

Giovanna inclined her head. "She was sad when she first came here. She'd lost her mother and father. Luca and I tried to make her laugh, and we did." Her smile faded, and she turned around.

"And what else?"

"Well, you know the rest, don't you?"

"My mother never spoke of her life in Italy. What can you tell me?"

"She never told you?" Giovanna's brows shot up in astonishment. She leaned on the counter and studied the wine bottle for a long moment.

"I'd like to learn more about my family here. And my father."

Giovanna dipped her head. "I'll save this wine for later, if you don't mind." She slipped the bottles into a hand-carved wine rack in one corner of the kitchen. "You're my guest, and I'd like to share our wines with you first."

"I'd like that very much." Why had Giovanna dodged her question? "Brunello di Montalcino wines are legendary."

Giovanna brought a wine bottle from the rack. "I think you'll like this vintage," she said, handing it to her. She inclined her head. "Americans eat earlier than Italians, don't they?"

Caterina laughed. "That's true," she said. "We ate in Rome, but I'm famished again. It must be the time difference."

Giovanna reached for an apron. "I'll start supper." She pulled a wooden high chair to the bar. "Here's a seat for Marisa."

Caterina lifted Marisa into the chair, and the little girl looked around her new surroundings with interest, babbling as she did. "Mmm, ma-ma-ma."

"She's such a happy baby." Giovanna handed Caterina a pair of antique clippers. "Would you mind cutting some herbs from the garden outside? Basil, parsley, and oregano, *per favore*. I'll watch Marisa."

Caterina stepped outside onto the stone terrace. A broad swath of hills waved beneath their hilltop perch, while mountains rose like whitecaps in the distance. Vineyards dotted the patchworked agricultural landscape below. Caterina peered over the terrace edge. A sprinkling of red and yellow wildflowers dotted the hillside. A smile spread on her face. She felt so free here. The shackles of her old life were loosening their grip.

She spied the raised herb garden and strolled toward it. Herbs grew in abundance under the hot Tuscan sun. She rubbed the bright-green basil leaves, releasing a brisk scent before snipping a couple of leafy stalks. The oregano leaves were small and powerful, and she cut several long strands, as well as ruffled parsley that danced in the mountain breeze. Had her parents clipped herbs from these gardens, too?

Caterina returned to the kitchen with bunches of aromatic herbs in her arms, inhaling the sweet, zesty freshness. The scent of sautéed garlic was rising in the air from a stovetop under a bricked archway. Giovanna was slicing vegetables for a salad and had several pots on the burners. It reminded her of Nina's kitchen, and she felt a pang of homesickness.

"We have salad, bread, capellini with Roma tomatoes, and veal Marsala." Giovanna placed a small plate of thinly sliced tomatoes and soft mozzarella cheese drizzled with olive oil and dusted with herbs before Marisa, who exclaimed gleefully.

Caterina laughed. "I think she likes Italian food." She sliced Marisa's food into small pieces and watched her eyes widen as she tasted the new treats.

"Let's open our wine now." Giovanna pulled the cork from the bottle with ease and poured a small amount into a glass for Caterina to taste, followed by a splash in her own glass. "It should air, of course, but you can taste it now."

Caterina swirled and inhaled. "*Magnifico.* I detect black cherry and black raspberry." She sniffed again. "Smells earthy, of leather and dark cocoa beans." This was a special wine, rare in the world of winemaking.

"It's our Brunello di Montalcino." Giovanna's voice rang with pride. "It has a touch of violet, too. Can you detect it?"

"I know it well. We served it at the St. Francis Hotel in San Francisco—when we could get it. I used to be the sommelier there." She paused with her glass in midair.

Caterina breathed in, savoring the wine's aroma. "This is made solely from *sangiovese grosso* grapes grown within the *commune,* isn't it? Every bottle is aged at least five to six years, if I'm not mistaken." She took a sip. What an amazing wine it was. She let the wine roll back on her tongue before swallowing. "Beautiful. The tannins are rich and smooth as suede."

"You're right. And we often age it as long as ten years—or more." Giovanna's smile broadened at Caterina's familiarity with their winemaking process. "The brunello, or *sangiovese grosso* grapes, are perfect for extended periods of aging. We don't blend our grapes with any other varieties."

Caterina listened intently. "How is the terroir and climate here for wine?"

"It's unique. It's fairly dry here, compared to the rest of Toscana. The northern slopes are cooler than the southern slopes, and the western slopes receive the most sun and sea winds. We have vineyards on all sides of the mountain so that we can blend the best wine using only our *sangiovese grosso.*" Giovanna poured the dark, fleshy red wine into their wine goblets.

"Excellent idea. I understand your soil, like ours in Napa, has volcanic material."

"It does. Clay and limestone, too, which adds complexity."

"I can't wait to learn more." Caterina raised her glass to Giovanna. "*Salute.*"

"*Salute.*" A genuine smile crinkled Giovanna's kind face. She clinked her glass with Caterina's. "It's so nice to meet someone who is knowledgeable and passionate about wine."

"Especially an American, no?" Caterina winked.

"And a woman, too." Giovanna laughed. "Especially after—what did you call it? Prohibit—"

"Prohibition." Caterina laughed along with Giovanna, and Marisa waved her arms and joined in the laughter, too.

"There aren't many of us who produce Brunello. You can count the wineries on two hands. Foreign clients are discovering this incredible wine, so every year, our sales grow a little. This is good, especially after the devastation of the war." She shook her head. "After Mussolini was arrested, so many died in Toscana at the hands of the Nazis. San Pancrazio, Civitella, Cornia." She frowned and averted her eyes. "So many from our families."

Caterina expressed her condolences, and Giovanna nodded her appreciation. "While we will never forget, we must move on and rebuild." She stirred a sauce on the stove. "We'll eat on the terrace; it's a lovely evening. Go on. I'll join you in a moment."

Caterina picked up Marisa and moved her high chair outside to the table. The sun had set, and stars were beginning to twinkle in the sky, reminding her of their panoramic view in Napa.

"Here we are." Giovanna placed a dish on the table. The two boys who had helped with the luggage followed her, carrying more food. "*Grazie,*" she said to them, adding a few words in Italian.

"Are they your sons?" Caterina asked.

"In a way. Their parents died in the war, so *la signora* took them in. They help here when they're not in school. They're good boys."

"Do you mind if I ask, are you married?" Caterina asked.

"I'm widowed. My first husband died of a rare heart condition not long after Ava and Luca left. My second husband died in the war before we could have children. There are many other women like me here. What can we do?" She shrugged and smiled after the boys. "Sometimes your true family is the one you create, not the one you're actually related to."

Giovanna's words reminded her of the ones she'd left behind at Mille Étoiles.

They sat down, and Giovanna explained how she made each dish. Caterina thought she'd never had such a delicious Italian meal before, and she complimented Giovanna.

"I love to cook," Giovanna replied. "And eat, of course," she added, patting her stomach. "That's what we do here—eat and drink and live a simple life." She sipped her wine. "So, how long do you plan to stay with us?"

"I plan to make it my home."

"Really?" Giovanna looked thoughtful.

"I can't wait to meet some of my father's relatives. Maybe you can tell me more about them."

"I'll try." Giovanna hesitated with her glass in midair. "I should warn you, though." She put her glass down and grew somber. "There might be . . . how do you say—" She paused and thrust her hands into the air. "*Explosions* tomorrow at the reading of the will."

"Explosions?" Caterina repeated, momentarily mystified. "Oh, do you mean fireworks?"

Giovanna laughed at her error. "That's right. We have explosive tempers. Some in your family have very clear ideas about what they think they should receive. And you're not from here."

"So we're outsiders," Caterina said, grasping the situation. She tore a piece of bread for Marisa, who eagerly gnawed the crust as she had the biscotto.

"Some people might be jealous. *La signora* had her own mind. She did what she wanted. And she wanted to provide for her grand-daughter, even though she'd never met you. Ava sent her photo-graphs of you when you were young. I'll show you Violetta's photograph album later. You might like to have some pictures."

"Yes, I would, thank you." Caterina was learning all sorts of new details about her family here. Why had her mother thought this would be so horrible?

Giovanna wound the capellini with a spoon and fork and ate, chewing thoughtfully. "You'll meet the attorneys tomorrow. They are driving here from Roma for the afternoon."

"I admit I'm a little nervous." Caterina sipped her wine. "What do you recall of my father?"

Giovanna hesitated and then smiled. "You know, you're nothing like your father."

Caterina was perplexed by her reply. "Did you know him?"

Giovanna nodded and looked ill at ease.

Caterina thought of the sweet memories of her father that her mother had shared. "I never knew my father. My mother told me he was handsome and charming, and he had the gift of persuasion. Can you tell me more about him?"

Giovanna shifted in her chair and seemed at a loss for words.

"My mother told me he was a good man, the best husband she could have asked for, and a wonderful father. I wish I'd known him longer before he died."

Giovanna began to choke on a mouthful. Her face darkened, and she took a large swallow of wine.

Caterina jumped up to help her, but Giovanna caught her breath. "No, I'm fine. I'm just . . . surprised."

"About what?"

Giovanna looked shocked; her face had paled, and her eyes darted from Caterina to the table and back again. "Oh, dear child, your father is—"

"Is what, Giovanna?" What on earth had so affected her?

"Alive. Oh my dear, your father is not dead at all."

Caterina could hardly believe what she'd heard. Every nerve in her body snapped to attention. "Are you *sure*?"

"*Assolutamente.*"

"How can that be? I've mourned his death all my life, and now you tell me he's still alive?" Her blood surged through her veins. What had her mother done?

Giovanna touched her hand. "I'm so sorry you had to find out this way. Ava did this to protect you when you were young. I warned her. But I thought she would have told you by now."

Her head swimming with fury, Caterina clenched her fists. "How could she have lied to me all these years? He was—is—my father. My *wonderful* father. I had a right to know." She paced in back of Marisa's chair, whose wide eyes followed her every move.

Frowning, Giovanna looked distressed. "Please sit down, Caterina. There's more you should know."

Caterina sank onto her chair. How could her mother have done such a thing? "She said my father had died in an automobile accident. I've got to see him. Where is he? Is he here in Italy?"

Giovanna took a sip of wine. "Perhaps your mother embellished the story for your benefit." She ran her hand over Caterina's. "Your father is a . . . difficult man. He has an evil side to him. This is why your mother protected you."

Caterina stared at Giovanna. Is this what her mother had warned her about? But why? He was her *father*. Surely he'd never hurt her.

Anger filled Caterina, numbing her reason. She was furious with her mother, even more now than before. Who *was* Ava Rosetta?

Giovanna rose from her chair and wrapped her arms around Caterina. "I didn't mean to hurt you."

"It's not your fault. How could you have known?" And how could Ava have kept this from her?

Marisa watched from her high chair, her lips quivering as she watched her mother. When she started to whimper, Caterina turned to cuddle her, assuring her that she loved her.

"You're such a good mother," Giovanna said.

"I'm trying, but she's tired," Caterina said. "And so am I." Thoughts of Juliana and Faith and Nina rushed to mind, and she choked up. She missed the people who had comforted her in the past. Now she was alone, except for Giovanna, whom she'd only known a few hours. Should she trust her story?

Giovanna rose from the table. "You should rest. Tomorrow will be an explosive day."

14

Ava woke to the sound of rattling windowpanes and paintings. Her heart beating wildly, she clung to the bed as the ground convulsed and several sharp jolts shook the house.

It wasn't long before Raphael burst through her bedroom door. "Are you okay?" He was panting from his sprint across the property.

"I am, but these morning wake-up calls have got to stop." Ava worked her feet into the slippers she now kept by her bed. She heard Nina call to her from the living room and assured her she was okay. "Let's get dressed and check on everything."

Nina poured juice for them while Raphael shut off the gas. After the last incident, she had secured the breakable items in the house. Raphael had started working with his crew on the cave and winery.

They'd all lived in California long enough to know that aftershocks could be as large as the original earthquake. And this one certainly had been.

Dressed in jeans and boots and cotton work shirts, Ava and Raphael started toward the winery. Dust was blowing on the morning wind. The smell of dry, raw earth assaulted her nose.

"*Mon Dieu!*" Ava cried, and she began running.

Boulders from the mountain were strewn across the property like tumbled dice, their new equipment smashed in the path of destruction. As Ava gazed around, her lips trembled, and she drew her brows together in defeat. Everything was ravaged, strewn with rocks and reddish-brown dirt and twisted beyond repair. Ava was so shocked that words escaped her. She glanced helplessly at Raphael.

Raphael caught up to her and held her in his arms. "It's only property, Ava; it can be replaced." As he spoke, he stroked her back.

"No, no, Raphael. God has turned against me." Ava buried her face in his chest.

"Ava, this is an act of nature, that's all."

Was it? Ava felt as if her heart were splitting. Everything she held dear was slipping from her grasp. Caterina, her vineyard. She sobbed into Raphael's shirt.

He turned her face up to his and ran his lips across her brow. "We'll manage. We always have." Gently, Raphael took her hand and led her through the rubble.

Ava picked her way through the rocks and ruin, coughing from the dust that had been kicked up. "Look at this place." Her entire life was in shambles, in every imaginable way.

"It looks bad, but maybe we can salvage something." Raphael squeezed her hand. "We've pulled through tough times before, Ava."

Ava looked up, inspecting the processing room outside the cave. To her dismay, boulders had punched through the roof, and the strong timbers had collapsed. Underneath it all, their equipment had been destroyed. The grape hopper, the crusher—now mangled beyond repair.

"It's going to cost a fortune to replace all this." Ava's shoulders slumped as they surveyed the extent of destruction. "We'll have to harvest soon. What are we going to do?"

Raphael placed his hands on Ava's arms and drew her to him, determination lining his face. "We'll find a way, and we'll rebuild better than before. You're going to blend a superb wine this year.

The best restaurants and hotels in the country will be clamoring for it. Mark my words, Ava."

Ava brushed her eyes. "Not this time," she murmured through her anguish. "I can't do this again. I simply don't have the strength anymore." *Not without Caterina.*

"You're the strongest woman I know." Raphael cupped her face in his hands. "And I'm here for you."

Feeling overwhelmed and defeated, Ava jerked away from Raphael and sank to her knees. She bowed her head, covering her face with her hands. "No, it's too much this time."

Raphael didn't know her financial situation. She had invested all the money she had and everything she could borrow into the new equipment. This was the first year of the grape harvest from the new fields she'd acquired, which were planted from grafts from her original French rootstock. She'd even sold their old equipment in order to purchase the new equipment. She had nothing left.

Raphael knelt beside her. "We can do it, Ava. I've seen you snatch the vineyard and winery from the brink of disaster more than once. Don't you remember the Depression?"

Ava choked upon hearing his words. Some years had been leaner than others, but never had their situation been so dire. Raphael smoothed his hands over her neck and shoulder, kneading the tension from her taut muscles. But it was too late.

She sobbed into her hands, the emotions of the last few days reaching a devastating crescendo. "This expansion was for Caterina and her inheritance. But she's gone—I drove her away." Caterina's plight had touched a deep nerve within Ava, and she'd lost her temper one too many times.

"Let's worry about this year's harvest right now. A lot of folks are depending on us, Ava."

As usual, Raphael had a calm head. She thought of Nina, the migrant workers, and other field hands. She was alone at the helm of a business that not only fed her family but also employed many people, a business subject to the vagaries of weather, commerce, and capital. And now she had a grandchild to consider. What was her name? *Marisa.* Such a pretty name. She choked at the thought and dried her eyes. "Maybe we could borrow equipment for harvest."

"We can try, though a lot of our neighbors are in trouble, too."

When the grapes were ready to harvest, everyone worked at once. "I'm not sure I can borrow more money. If I can, could we replace equipment in time? Otherwise, we'd have to drop the fruit." This was a last resort, and she knew it.

"That's costly, too."

Ava thought about all the work and money they'd already put in. *Will we lose it all?* One good harvest could return Mille Étoiles to profitability. She blinked, focusing her thoughts. She would forgive Caterina and beg for her forgiveness in return. Surely she would return with Marisa. All this would be theirs. Ava looked up. "Raphael, you're right. We must find a way. The grapes are special this year, like gold. It's our only chance. "

Raphael ran his hand along her back, and a corner of his mouth twitched up. "We'll need more money."

Ava's shoulders sagged. "I'll try to get it." There was another problem she hadn't told anyone about yet, not even Raphael.

The next day, Ava swung into her sedan. She flipped the visor down and checked her lipstick, nervously flicking a smidgen of red from the corner of her mouth.

She adjusted the collar of her white linen jacket and rearranged her paisley silk scarf, though it didn't need it. Nervousness churned within her. She was on her way to visit her banker in Napa, a good friend who'd always helped her in the past. Would he again? She needed another larger loan to replace their equipment before harvest. But there was more to it this time.

She released the emergency brake. When Caterina knew what a good harvest they'd had, she might return to help blend their wine. She squelched the doubt in the pit of her stomach and dragged her thoughts back to business.

The financial plan she and Raphael had prepared should be sufficient. Insurance would cover some but not all of what they needed. However, the bank had been acquired by a larger bank out of San Francisco, and she feared they would insist on documents she couldn't produce.

She turned the key in the ignition. When the car didn't start, she pumped the gas pedal a few times, her frustration growing.

Will my falsehoods cost me Mille Étoiles, too?

Pressing her lips together, Ava tried again. The engine roared to life. She started down the switchbacks of the sloping mountain road that lined Mille Étoiles and considered the challenges ahead.

This was the year she had to increase sales revenue for the expansion she'd embarked upon three years ago. Depending on the varietal, they aged their wines between twelve and twenty-six months before distributing to the fine restaurants, hotels, and wine shops that made up their client base.

Collectors also bought by the case to stock their personal cellars. Their Mille Étoiles red blend aged remarkably well. They counted many Hollywood actors, industrialists, and other discriminating collectors among their private clientele.

Winning awards had brought their wines to the attention of collectors and buyers. Since the earthquake had made international news, it was more important than ever to maintain their presence at events to keep skittish buyers calm. But to do all that, they had to salvage the harvest.

Ava slowed to steer into a hairpin turn, and as she did, saw a man standing on her land by the road, waving for help. It was probably one of the harvesters, surveying the maturing crop with Raphael.

This was her property; strangers seldom trespassed. She slowed to a halt and set the brake.

She cranked down the window. "What's wrong?" she called out.

"Raphael needs help now." The man had a raspy accented voice and a brimmed hat pulled low on his face. He walked toward the car. "Hurry."

Alarmed, she opened her car door. She stepped out, her smart taupe pumps clicking on the worn, cracked pavement. "What happened?"

In a flash, the man grabbed her arm, twisted it around, and shoved her chest against her car.

Ava screamed and struggled. "Stop it! What are you doing?" She couldn't see the assailant behind her, but his viselike grip and voice stirred a memory. She smashed her heel onto his boot and tried to jerk from his grasp.

The man laughed. "Steel-toe boots sure come in handy, don't they?"

At the sound of his normal voice, a shock bolted through Ava. *It can't be.* Though she shivered uncontrollably, she fought against the man, but he simply held her tighter and chuckled in her ear.

"Give up, my darling. I was always stronger than you."

"Luca." Ava spat out the word. The old fear she thought she'd never feel again seized her, and her thoughts spun wildly. *What's he doing here?* She hadn't seen him since Caterina was an infant. "I told you to never return," she hissed.

He laughed again and flipped her over, hovering in her face. "Not happy to see me?"

"You're dead to me." His breath smelled of cheap liquor and rotting teeth. He hadn't aged well. She tamped down her panic.

"I thought time might have softened your heart against me."

Hatred flared within her as vignettes of horror rushed through her mind. "*Never.* What you did was unforgivable, you sick bastard." She reared back to slap him across the face, but he caught her hand.

"Careful, you're going to have to confess those words to the good *padre.*"

"If you don't let go of me, I'll have to confess a lot more than that. I'll kill you, I swear I will." She spat in his face. *Nor will I cower.*

Momentarily surprised, a sinister glint gleamed in his eyes; he dragged a dirty sleeve across his face, wiping off her spittle. "What a shame. I thought you might have missed me," he said, taunting her. "Or at least declared me officially dead."

"Get off my property," she snapped. "I'm reporting you to the sheriff."

Luca let out a hearty guffaw and pressed himself against her. "Funny you should say that. I've been to the county records. You know, all this property is still in my name. You're not on the deed at all. Imagine that."

Ava exploded, pounding against his chest and clawing his face. "We bought this with *my* inheritance from *my* parents—it was *my* money,* Luca. You can't touch it. Besides, you were taken care of, though why your mother did is beyond me."

"She told you, did she? And did she tell you she refused to pay the money so I could return to Italy? I've had to live in Spain all these years. So now, I want what's rightfully mine." He laughed again. "Technically, you're trespassing on my property. And now I find you here all cozy with Raphael, the hired hand."

"You can't do this!" she screamed, struggling against him. "And leave Raphael out of this. He's nothing to you."

"Relax, my tigress. I'm not *doing* anything. It's been my property all along. I *let* you live here."

"*Let* me? How dare you show your face here again after what you did!" She still bore the physical and mental scars of his actions.

His lips curled into a sinister, tobacco-stained smile. With a sudden swift motion, Luca cracked her across the face with the back of his hand.

Ava screamed and slumped against the car, dazed by the blow. Her searing pain, her savage struggle, his blood and skin scraped under her nails—all this seemed to fuel his malicious pleasure.

He gripped her hair in his fist and shoved her face against the hot steel fender. "You know what that miserable old woman did?"

Ava squeezed her eyes shut and prayed someone would drive by. But she knew Raphael was working on the equipment, trying to salvage what he could. She'd left Nina in the kitchen. Luca could snap her neck in an instant and have no remorse. In fact, he'd enjoy it.

"You know, don't you?" he snarled in her ear.

"No, no, I don't!" she cried as pain pierced her resolve. She fought to keep her wits about her. *What can I do?*

"She wrote to me before she died to say she was cutting me out of her will, suspending my monthly allotment. Said it was time I made my own way, said that was her gift to me. And that damned house—where it all happened—she left that to *your daughter*." He tightened his hold on her. "So I got nothing. Now I'm here to collect what's rightfully mine."

"I'm not going anywhere. You'll die before you get your hands on Mille Étoiles." Ava worked a leg loose and kicked him, tearing her hosiery and losing a shoe in the scuffle.

"Strong words for such a pious bitch." His filthy hand crept along her neck, and his noxious breath enveloped her.

Ava glared at him in defiance. "Go ahead. They'll put you away for life this time."

He cuffed her ears. "You have two weeks to get out."

She winced against the burning blow and the ringing in her ears. "Or what, Luca? The sheriff will be looking for you."

He flicked open a large switchblade and flashed it past her eyes. "I'll be a wealthy widower." His once handsome face contorted into a monstrous mask. "If you don't leave, I'd rather torch the place. You'll be left with nothing but dead vines and burning embers." He stepped back, finished with her.

Ava scrambled into the car. She shoved it into gear and gunned the engine, aiming for Luca. He dove out of her path, and she swerved at the last moment, sobbing not because she was hurt but because she still couldn't bring herself to kill the bastard.

Her head throbbing, she peeled away. She was ashamed of the lies she'd told and infuriated over what her husband had done. As she whipped around the curves, her words from long ago still rang in her ears. *You're dead to me, Luca, and dead to Caterina. Get out, and never come back. Dead, do you hear? Dead!*

A part of her wished she had killed him that day. It would have been justice rightly served.

Even now, she could still taste the putrid dust of that searing Napa Valley afternoon in her mouth. Luca had taken the car and roared from the property, kicking up clouds of silt in his wake. After a few weeks, when she was certain he wouldn't return, she told everyone Luca had died in an automobile accident during a business trip.

Who would have believed her if she had told them the truth? Everyone liked Luca, thought he was a cheerful fellow, if a bit lazy. She'd had no one to protect her and her baby against her fiend of a husband. She'd *had* to protect Caterina; she would have died for her. A child shouldn't suffer the mistakes of the mother.

Tires squealing on the scorching pavement, Ava raced back to where Raphael was working. She jerked to a stop and stumbled from the car.

When Raphael saw her, he dropped what he was doing and ran to her in alarm. "Ava, you're hurt! What happened?"

She collapsed into his arms, and he held her gently, examining her bruised face as she cried. Only Raphael knew her secrets. She'd lied to everyone else, including her priest. *There must be a special category of hell for that.* She pressed her hand to her mouth and crumpled against him. Her tower of deceits was tumbling down, and her soul was shattering into a million pieces.

Now Raphael was in danger, too. If anything happened to him, she'd never forgive herself. She drew a ragged breath and between sobs choked out, "Luca's back."

"He did this?" Raphael kissed her bruised face.

She nodded, ashamed of her lies, though she had confided in him about Luca. She winced in pain. Luca had been right about one thing. Raphael meant a lot to her; he inhabited her dreams with increasing frequency. Her sins had mounted and multiplied, but she had not succumbed to adultery. According to her faith—and the law—she was still a married woman. Raphael understood and respected her boundaries, but it was growing harder for both of them.

Anger flared in his dark eyes. "Where the hell is he?"

"He was waiting for me at the bend in the road. He's probably gone by now."

Raphael drew his dark eyebrows together. "What does he want?"

"Everything. Mille Étoiles in still in his name. Since Luca hadn't really died, I couldn't produce a death certificate. I pled ignorance, and finally, the bank stopped asking for it. Douglas Lattimer knows me, and I've always paid the bank mortgage and property taxes. It got easier as time went on, but now the bank has a new owner." She bit her lip. "They want documentation now."

"You never told me that part of it, Ava. This is serious."

She raised her gaze to him. "Luca gave us two weeks to vacate and threatened to burn Mille Étoiles to the ground if we don't comply."

15

MONTALCINO, ITALY

Caterina woke to the aroma of fresh-baked bread and the sound of boys' laughter and wondered for a moment where she was. *Italy. Montalcino. With Marisa.*

She rolled out of bed and checked on Marisa, who was still sleeping soundly. Satisfied with her little girl's steady breathing, Caterina filled the deep claw-foot tub with water and eased into a sweet violet-scented bath in the en suite bathroom.

As she lay in the warm water, she thought about what Giovanna had said. The reading of the will was scheduled for the afternoon, and Giovanna was clearly anxious about it. Caterina was nearly impervious to volatile, screaming family members—few were in her mother's league, after all. However, it wasn't the loving family welcome she'd hoped for.

What really concerned her was what Giovanna had said about her father. *If I try to find him, will I be putting myself in danger?* She found it hard to believe. After all, Luca was her father.

But who is he? What had he done that was so terrible that Ava had been compelled to revise her daughter's childhood history?

After Caterina toweled off, she put on a soft cotton robe.

Questions gnawed at her while she woke Marisa and bathed her. She dressed her in a white eyelet cotton dress with white sandals and a blush-pink bow in her hair. "There you are, my pretty girl—a new summery outfit." Marisa flung her arms around her, and Caterina hugged her back.

Despite the news of her father, Caterina was still glad that she'd made the decision to move to Italy. She was tired of fighting with Ava and was looking forward to a fresh start.

"Oh, oh, oh!" Marisa exclaimed in a sweet singsong voice. With a wide-eyed expression of delight, she pointed to the fresh flowers, which Caterina had moved to the top of a high dresser.

Caterina smiled, relieved that Marisa was in good spirits this morning. The last few days had been trying. She had new respect for Faith and her skills with children.

While she kept an eye on Marisa, Caterina hurried to dress in a slim sleeveless dress of peach shantung silk. She draped the matching jacket over her shoulders and slipped her feet into a pair of beige patent leather pumps that elongated her legs even more. She fastened a pink coral beaded necklace around her neck and then brushed her dark brown hair until it shimmered in the sunlight filtering through the window. Marisa watched as Caterina pinned a matching pillbox to the crown of her head and waved her hair around it.

She added a splash of Violetta di Parma on her neck and décolletage. Marisa smiled with glee at the sweet aroma, so Caterina put a tiny dab on her wrist, too.

When she saw Giovanna downstairs, the woman kissed her on both cheeks. "*Bella, bella.*" Her face lit with happiness. "What a beautiful pair, mother and daughter. There's coffee on the terrace, along with fresh breads."

"Smells delicious." Caterina walked slowly with Marisa, holding her hand. She lifted her into the high chair and then sat at the table. The morning air was cool, and the fresh scent of dew-laden herbs perfumed the terrace. Caterina sipped her cappuccino and eyed the basket of assorted breads. "I'm in heaven."

"And I love to have people to bake for." Giovanna sat across from her. She turned to look out over the hillside and valley. "Our view is even more incredible during the day. See over there?" She pointed to a charming cottage hugging the hillside. "My friend Raphael lived there. He went to America and worked for your family in Napa."

Caterina held a slice of bread in midair. "And he still does."

"Really? He had a much younger cousin, Santo, who would be a little older than you. You must know him."

She glanced down and took care to sound nonchalant. "I haven't seen him in a long time." She didn't count their last disastrous meeting. "How well did you know Raphael?"

"We grew up together." A wistful expression crossed Giovanna's face. "Little Santo. Poor boy. *La signora* Violetta thought he would have better opportunities in America, so before the second war, she paid for his passage to New York to live with family. I'd heard that Raphael sent for him. So I guess you know the rest of the story."

Caterina nodded, taking in these details. She hadn't known the part about Violetta.

Giovanna went on. "Santo was a good boy. How did he turn out?"

It would seem strange if she didn't respond. "Fairly well, I guess. He went to the university and earned a doctorate degree. He has his own business, too. He's a viticulturist."

Giovanna's eyes twinkled with mischief. "And is he as handsome as Raphael was?"

Caterina was just sipping her cappuccino and sputtered over Giovanna's question. "Well, I suppose he's okay."

Giovanna looked amused. Caterina lifted her napkin. As she dabbed her mouth, she glanced around with fresh observance, appreciating where Santo had grown up. And now his daughter would have a similar childhood in this pastoral setting.

It seemed fitting.

And then it struck her. Now that her mother knew about Marisa, she would certainly share this with Raphael, and he would tell Santo. Caterina's eyes welled at the thought. She deeply regretted that she wouldn't be the one to tell Santo about Marisa—his daughter. She blinked rapidly, trying to conceal her emotion.

An American recording of Italian singer Mario Lanza drifted on the air, masking Caterina's silence.

"The explosions—the fireworks—will begin soon, I think." Giovanna poured a glass of wine for herself. "In preparation," she added, nodding to the wine. "Would you like a glass?"

Caterina declined, though she'd certainly accept the offer later. "How far is the other house—my house now, I guess—from here?"

"Not far. We'll have to see it before the sun sets. There's no electricity." Giovanna sipped her wine and studied her. "No one has lived there since . . ." She shuddered and crossed herself.

Caterina frowned. "What, Giovanna?" So far, this trip had raised more questions than answers.

Giovanna's expression saddened. "It's a long story. I'll explain later."

After lunch, Caterina rocked Marisa to sleep for her nap. Once she was asleep, Giovanna showed Caterina into the grand salon where the will was going to be formally read. "Let's sit where we can see everyone." Giovanna motioned to two high-backed chairs. Tapestry-covered sofas flanked a long, hand-hewn wooden table, around which stood carved wooden chairs.

Outside, the sound of crunching gravel and car doors heralded the arrival of the attorneys from Rome. Dressed in somber black suits and starched white shirts, the two men greeted them with courtesy, their faces expressionless.

"This way," Giovanna said. The attorneys followed her to the salon and snapped open their briefcases on the table. As they were organizing their documents and carbon copies, more people began to arrive and file into the room.

Caterina smiled and nodded at other attendees, but curiously, no one acknowledged her. She stole glances at each person, wondering who might be related to her. She stared at an impeccably attired older woman who had stately carriage. *Is she my great-aunt?* There was a younger woman with her, casually dressed, who kept looking in Caterina's direction. *A cousin?* On the other side of the table, she saw a couple with two girls and two boys, perhaps eight to fourteen years old. Were they distant cousins?

A middle-aged man dressed in work clothes greeted Giovanna with warmth. By the time everyone was settled, about twenty people filled the room. They all seemed to know each other. Caterina felt the glare of eyes on her, the stranger in the room.

Once everyone was seated, the attorneys opened their files, and the older gentleman began to read the last will and testament of Violetta Maria Romagnoli Rosetta, resident of Montalcino and matriarch of the Rosetta family. He read the document in Italian, and while Caterina understood quite a bit, she had difficulty understanding everything that was said. Giovanna's name was mentioned, and she seemed pleased and relieved.

At one point, the older woman whispered to her companion and then turned an icy stare in Caterina's direction, lifted her chin, and glared down her nose at her. What did *that* mean?

The attorney read one section, and the couple with four children smiled and embraced. Another line was read, and the man who had greeted Giovanna said, "*Grazie, la signora,*" and smiled heavenward.

The reading continued, and all heads swiveled toward the older woman, who remained stone-faced. The younger woman clasped her hand, but the older woman shook her off.

"Santo Casini."

Caterina snapped her head up, surprised. As the attorney spoke,

Caterina heard him say *vigneto,* which was Italian for vineyard. Santo must have received notice, too.

"Caterina Rosetta, daughter of Luca Rosetta, granddaughter of Violetta Maria Romagnoli Rosetta." Silence filled the air, and all heads turned in her direction. Caterina's heart pounded.

"La Casa di Romagnoli." The attorney went on, but Caterina had a hard time following the legal terms in Italian.

Just as Caterina uttered *grazie,* the imperious older woman stood and strode across the room. Giovanna clutched Caterina's hand.

The woman halted in front of her and began to rant in Italian, gesturing with both hands.

"But I had nothing to do with this," Caterina said, rising to defend herself and her honor.

Giovanna sprang to her feet, speaking rapidly to the woman and trying to calm her.

The woman turned and spat on the floor in front of Caterina and shook her hand in front of her face. "You thief! You . . . your papà . . . not welcome here. Leave!" She flicked her hands, turned on her heel, and stalked from the salon.

The younger woman raced after her, yelling at Caterina, "That should be mine! You have no right to do this!"

"I've done nothing," Caterina said, incensed. What was she talking about?

The room burst with chatter. Everyone seemed to be speaking at once, pointing to her and then gesturing and shaking their heads.

This is Giovanna's explosion. Caterina's first thought was to flee, but then she squared her shoulders and glared at everyone. "I . . . will . . . *not* . . . leave. I am your relative, but did any of you come to introduce yourself? To welcome me? *No.* Only Giovanna. And I never knew my father." She put her hands on her hips. "Now, I'm going to see the house my grandmother, *mia nonna,* wanted me to have."

She could hear people gasp, and the babbling began again.

"Oh, for heaven's sake!" Caterina swung around to face the at-torneys. "Do you need me anymore today?" When the men shook their heads, Caterina spun back to the other attendees. "I didn't come here to steal anything from anyone, and I will not be treated like I did. I don't deserve such rudeness."

Caterina marched from the room with Giovanna close behind her. She was shaking with fury and shame. The burnish was off the pastoral existence she'd imagined for herself and Marisa. Reality had abruptly set in. *Will my father's reputation haunt us here?* She slammed the door behind them.

16

NAPA VALLEY, CALIFORNIA

The bank president steepled his hands behind his massive oak desk, his expression dour. "I understand your position, and I'm sorry, Ava. You know I hold you in high esteem, but the bank has a new owner. I'll be honest; it'll be tough to get this request through the loan committee."

Ava had been afraid of this, but still, she couldn't believe what she was hearing. She'd known Douglas Lattimer for years, and he'd always personally approved her loans for seasonal working capital. She pressed her damp palms against the skirt of her celadon-green linen dress.

"Douglas, Mille Étoiles has been a good customer. Doesn't that count for anything?"

He removed his horn-rims and rubbed them with a cloth. "In the past week, almost every vineyard owner has been here asking for a loan, Ava. I'm afraid we can't handle them all." He put his glasses on and flipped through her file. "We're also missing a number of documents in your file. We need Luca's death certificate. Beg your pardon, but he's still on the deed."

"Didn't I give that to you already? I'm sure I did years ago." Ava put a pleasant smile on her face, though she was trembling inside.

"Maybe it was misplaced. But I'll need to have that before presenting your request."

"Honestly, I'm not sure I can find it, Douglas."

He closed her file. "Ava, you need that. You can get another copy from the records office."

Flushed with anger and embarrassment, Ava gathered her document folder, fumbled for her purse, and stood. "I must say, Douglas. I've never been treated with such disrespect. And from you, of all people."

"Look, Ava—"

"You gave Clyde Henderson twice what I'm asking for to replace his equipment. His wine isn't half as good as ours, and you told me yourself he's always late on his payments." Ava remembered what he'd shared with her at the last winemaker's dinner she'd had. *The secrets a good bottle of wine could uncork. Wine loosens the tongue of even the most ardent soul.* "Why, Douglas?"

His face reddened, and he lowered his voice. "Look, Ava, if you had a cosigner, maybe I could push it through."

"Did Clyde have a cosigner?"

"No, but that was different."

"How?"

When he didn't answer, Ava spun around. It was a boys' club, and she would always be considered an interloper. She saw a sea of male heads swivel as she strode through the bank. She stepped outside, squinting against the bright summer sun. The grapes would be ripe soon. They were no closer to replacing equipment. Soon they'd have to decide whether to harvest or drop the fruit. She fought a surge of panic.

She started for her car, her heels striking the pavement with vengeance. As she turned the corner into the parking area, she bumped into a young woman, dislodging the hat she'd chosen with such care that morning.

"Ava, are you okay?"

Ava pushed her hat back into place. "Oh, Juliana, I'm just so angry right now."

"What happened?"

Ava expressed a puff of air between her lips. "Douglas Lattimer. Why, the nerve of that man! We've repaid every cent we've ever borrowed. Imagine the money that bank has made from Mille Étoiles." Huffing, she waved a hand in resentment. "He's of no help now, and we must replace our equipment before harvest."

Juliana hesitated for a moment. "Aren't there other banks you could try?"

Ava lifted her chin. "There sure are." But would other bankers also sit in judgment of her? She peered at Juliana. Like Caterina, she had also matured into a young woman seemingly overnight. Where had the years gone? She fiddled with her white cotton gloves. "Have you heard from Caterina?"

"She called to say she'd arrived."

"I see." Her heart sank; Caterina had not called her. "Is she staying at . . . her house?" Those words felt strange on her tongue.

"Not yet. She said something about a private villa. I'm really not sure."

Ava took this in. "I have to ask. Did you know about . . . ?" She had trouble articulating her words. *Caterina's daughter. My granddaughter.* She'd always looked forward to being a grandmother, though she hadn't imagined it would be like this.

"Marisa?" Juliana spoke softly. "Yes, I did."

Checking her anger, Ava cleared her throat. "I'm glad Caterina had someone to talk to. I just wish it had been me."

"I know. She asked me to keep her secret, and I did." Juliana reached out and squeezed her hand.

Ava appreciated Juliana's understanding, but it was little comfort to a mother's broken heart. After she left Juliana, she slipped on a pair of dark sunglasses to conceal her despair. Her principles had deprived her of her only child. She'd never dreamed Caterina would move to Italy.

Has she met Giovanna? Had it not been for her cousin, Ava wouldn't have survived the shame of her marriage there. Giovanna had been married to the eldest son of Luca's father's brother. They were so close that Ava had once entrusted her deepest secret to Giovanna.

After Ava left Italy, they'd drifted apart, their letters becoming more infrequent as the years passed. She and Giovanna had completely lost touch during the Second World War. She missed her dear friend but knew she'd never see her again. It was the price she'd had to pay for obscuring the truth.

She wished Caterina had heeded her warning. Would she ever see her daughter again?

MONTALCINO, ITALY

After she stormed out of the salon where the will had been read, Caterina climbed the stairs to check on Marisa, who was still napping. Caterina drew her fingers across Marisa's downy cheek. *She's an angel.*

Marisa slept on her stomach with her head turned to one side, her knees drawn up under her, and her diaper-clad bottom hunched in the air like a little frog. Securing her peach pillbox, Caterina leaned over and kissed Marisa's forehead. She opened a window for fresh air and left the door ajar so she could hear Marisa when she woke. She tiptoed from the bedroom.

When Caterina returned downstairs, Giovanna was waiting.

"The relatives are gone now," Giovanna said. "Come, I have something to show you."

Caterina followed her, still seething over the scene at the reading of the will. Her father's family wanted nothing to do with her. How dare they insinuate she had somehow stolen the home Violetta had bequeathed to her? How could they have thought that of her?

They walked through the salon, and Giovanna motioned to a

grouping of old photographs in polished silver frames. Caterina sucked in a breath. "That's me when I was little. And my mother."

"Violetta always cared about you." Giovanna turned to a full-length portrait of a striking woman painted with broad, dramatic brush strokes. Her dark hair was pulled back from her face, which was framed with deep amethyst earrings that matched the intense color of her eyes.

"This was your grandmother," Giovanna said. "Violetta was a stunning beauty in her time and was painted by the most popular portraitists of her day. This one is by Giovanni Boldini, known as the master of swish. You might know his *Portrait of Madame X—* scandalous it was, at the time." Giovanna waved a hand around the large room.

The ceiling soared overhead with redbrick archways, which framed an array of tastefully arranged paintings, including exquisite landscapes and artfully draped nudes. Small spotlights had been mounted above each painting.

Giovanna went on, "Violetta was an art collector. She even painted some, too."

"Really?" Caterina leaned in for a closer look at the Boldini canvas. She found her grandmother's high cheekbones and the heart shape of her face eerily familiar. It was almost like gazing into a mirror.

"That was Violetta," Giovanna said, pride evident in her voice. "As a young woman in her first year of marriage."

"She's breathtaking." Caterina admired the resolute tilt of her chin and the unflinching expression in her eyes.

"You certainly favor her. When you stepped from the car, I was shocked. It was like rolling back time. Maybe that's why your relatives reacted so vehemently to you. She was strong-minded; she always made her own decisions. Not everyone agreed with her ideas. Even the Nazis cowered before her. She commanded respect."

Hearing that, Caterina felt a little better. She stood rooted to the spot, staring at her grandmother. This was Luca's mother. The grandmother she wished she'd known. Was she really like her? "Her eyes were amazing. Mine aren't anything like that."

"She was named for her eyes." Giovanna turned to her. "You have beautiful eyes, too. Your husband is a lucky man. Is he joining you here soon?"

A wave of shame and discomfort washed through her. The question she'd feared was before her now, suspended in space, waiting to be answered. She thought of the stories she had fabricated and the one she was prepared to tell here in Montalcino. *My husband, oh yes, he was a wonderful man, but he died quite suddenly not long ago. . . .*

A shudder raced through her. That sounded eerily familiar now. It was similar to the tale her mother had told her about Luca. Was history repeating itself? But no, her mother hadn't been pregnant out of wedlock. She couldn't possibly understand.

Giovanna had a pleasant smile of expectation on her face, waiting to hear about her undoubtedly magnificent husband. Caterina turned to face her, painfully aware of how disappointed Giovanna would be in her. But it was time to tell the truth. If Giovanna spurned her, like her mother had, it would be a shame, but she and Marisa would survive.

"I'm not married. I have no husband."

"Oh, I'm so sorry," Giovanna said with sympathy. "You are like me, yes—a widow?"

"No, I've never been married."

Giovanna's eyebrows shot up. "Oh, *Dio mio.*"

Caterina was becoming accustomed to myriad responses from people. Anger from her mother, sympathy and support from Juliana, moral conclusions from strangers. And now shock from Giovanna. She braced herself. Would Giovanna ask them to leave? Her San Francisco landlord evicted women for such a crime.

Giovanna was visibly startled, but she composed herself. "I admit I'm surprised. But it's not my place to judge. You're brave to be a mother alone."

"I don't know how brave I am. I didn't set out to campaign for a change in societal attitudes toward unwed mothers."

"I'm sure you've suffered rejection. But you have a beautiful daughter. God will forgive you, even if society and your relatives won't." Giovanna glanced at Violetta's painting. "You really are like her."

Caterina followed her gaze. Violetta's expressive eyes also held courage and compassion, and Caterina found it comforting.

"You inherited the will of Violetta Rosetta. No one could tell her what to do—not even her husband. She honored him as she vowed, but she spoke her mind and did what she thought was correct." She lowered her voice, even though they were alone. "That's one reason everyone was afraid of her. Violetta refused to be part of their petty social games and narrow views. This is a small community with a long memory."

"It's like that at home, too." The relatives' reaction made more sense to Caterina now.

"You came to Montalcino to escape persecution?"

Caterina hesitated. If she hadn't had the good fortune of meeting Faith and Patrick O'Connell, she might have ended up in one of the oppressive maternity homes she had seen for wayward women—society's manifestation of attitudes toward women who had done nothing more than what nature intended, though the men were seldom chastised or held accountable. "I also came to find my family."

A thought occurred to Caterina. Why should she be concerned about the acceptance of a faceless, collective society or now-distant family? *The only acceptance that matters is self-acceptance.* As for her own values, she had acknowledged her failings. *Life must allow mistakes.*

Otherwise, how would anyone ever learn, improve, or teach others? With distance, she saw her life more clearly.

A phrase formed in her mind. *Out of mistakes grows wisdom.* She shook her head. Was that a whisper from Violetta?

Giovanna placed her hand on Caterina's arm. "I will keep your secret. Most people here—even your family—will not understand."

Would her honesty harm their acceptance in the small community? Would they be ostracized, along with Giovanna? "Judging from today's explosive reaction, maybe it's better for now." Caterina blinked back regret. She could shoulder rejection, but she should not force it onto Giovanna and Marisa.

Giovanna patted her hand and then inclined her head toward the terrace. "Let's have a glass of wine. We'll sit in the sun."

Giovanna left Caterina sitting at a small round table, which was covered with brilliant hand-painted tiles. A few minutes later, Giovanna reappeared carrying a bottle of white wine and a tray of almonds, cheese, olives, and bread.

"This wine is Vernaccia di San Gimignano." Giovanna poured wine into two glasses. "It's made from the Vernaccia grape in the region around San Gimignano. And *pane con le olive* and *focaccia al pomodoro,*" she added, motioning to the savory breads studded with olives and crowned with tomatoes.

The aroma reminded Caterina of how hungry she was. She tore a hunk of bread and moistened it with green olive oil. *Delicious.* She nibbled on a few nuts and sampled the wine.

"This is quite good." Caterina tilted her glass against the sunlight to admire the golden color. She drank, and as the wine flowed over her tongue, she noted an impression of dry earthiness tinged with sweet honey.

Caterina shrugged out of her peach shantung silk jacket and then reached up to remove the bobby pins from her matching pillbox, shaking her hair after she freed it. The afternoon sun was warm on her shoulders, and she slipped off her pumps under the table. Her nerves were dissipating. "There's so much I don't know about my family, Giovanna. Can you tell me more?"

"I hardly know where to start."

"Tell me about my father. Why is he so hated?"

Giovanna sipped her wine. "You should hear the story from your mother. Ava can explain it best."

"But she's not talking to me anymore." Caterina gazed out over the valley that unfurled beneath them. Sections of vines and cultivated crops formed a variegated green patchwork quilt of nature's bounty. Here and there stood mounds of old rubble, destruction left in the path of war. Her mother's admonitions still roared in her ears. "When I told her about Marisa, she insisted I give her up for adoption."

Giovanna sat up and looked horrified. "No, no, not that sweet child! How could Ava say such a thing? Didn't she support you?"

Caterina glanced away, acutely embarrassed over the secretive way she had handled her pregnancy. "It was my fault; I was away at college, and I hid my pregnancy. And then I hid Marisa. I was living in San Francisco away from Mille Étoiles."

Memories flooded her mind. *I was a coward. I was angry and ashamed, feeling jilted and wronged.* Now that she was here—away from home—she was beginning to see her life and her choices with greater clarity. Was it the brilliant sunlight that seemed to envelop the mountaintop of Montalcino in a halo of enlightenment? Or was it the distance across the Atlantic Ocean that helped separate fact from fallacy?

Giovanna listened and nodded thoughtfully. "You have come to Italy. And now you are like Violetta. You have endured great pain, and you have taken courageous steps."

Caterina sipped her wine and made a vow. Someday she would

live up to her grandmother's legacy. "About my father. Please tell me about him."

Giovanna stifled a yawn. "It's been such a long day. Let's talk about him another time."

Caterina could wait, but she couldn't help but wonder. What was Giovanna keeping from her?

17

Had Ava heard the police officer correctly? Every nerve in her body sprang to alert. *Luca, what have you done?* Ava clutched Violetta's arm as if she could absorb some of her mother-in-law's indomitable strength.

In the presence of the stately Violetta, the officer at their front door averted his eyes. "Signora, we have arrested your son for the murder of Franco Casini."

Ava struggled to maintain her composure. What had possessed her husband? How could he have murdered a man, especially one as kind as Franco? A cry erupted from her throat, and Violetta crushed her to her side.

"*Grazie.* We will follow you to police headquarters." Violetta closed the door behind him and sent a housemaid for Giovanna's husband, who was at the dining table with their guests from France. After she explained the situation to him, Violetta and Ava climbed into the car with the driver.

When they arrived at the small police station, the presiding officer told them what they had found. Deranged with grief and blaming Franco for Natalie's death, Luca had taken a pistol from his father's study, confronted Franco, and shot him through the heart. Franco had died instantly.

Ava pressed a handkerchief to her face, but nothing could stem the tide of tears that streaked her face. *Franco and Natalie, both dead.* Only their newborn child had survived.

Luca was being held in a cell. Ava was so ashamed of his actions that she declined to see him. Violetta went in to see him but returned after only a few minutes. In the presence of the *polizia,* her face was inscrutable, devoid of emotion.

Violetta remained stoic at the police headquarters, but on the way home in the backseat of the car, Ava saw her mother-in-law's eyes welling. Violetta's iron will was crumbling. And later that night, Ava heard soft, heartbreaking sobs coming from Violetta's suite.

A man was dead by her husband's hand. As long as Ava lived, she would never forget that dreadful night.

The ensuing trial was a nightmare, and Ava found herself completely ostracized from the community. Through seemingly endless days, Violetta remained devoted to Luca, who had been released on bail. Every day she rose and dressed in somber shades and appeared in court to support her son. Ava tried to emulate her, but inside she was devastated. She merely went through the motions, numb to the ordeal.

As a consequence of that terrible evening, Luca was found guilty and imprisoned. Utterly distraught, Ava cloistered herself in the villa, refusing to go out, growing weaker every day. Only Giovanna and Alma continued to visit her. Finally, Violetta sent a doctor to examine her. It was confirmed; Ava was pregnant.

Through it all, Violetta seemed to have an infinite reservoir of strength. She appealed to a government official on Luca's behalf. After a month of anguished conversations behind closed doors, a judge reexamined the case and made a surprise determination. It was decided that Luca had acted out of extreme grief, and his sentence was reduced to time served.

The day before Luca was to be released from prison, Violetta called Ava into the salon. "Sit down, *ma chérie,*" she said.

Ava sat across from her on a ruby velvet settee, surrounded by statues and paintings that Violetta had collected from her travels across Europe. She was so nervous she could hardly speak. The man who would be returning to her tomorrow was not the man she had married. "What is it?"

"I must tell you of an important condition of Luca's release." Violetta's voice was firm, but her deep amethyst eyes held a mother's sorrow. "He has been allowed two days to gather his belongings and leave the country."

Ava sucked in a breath. "Leave Italy? But why?"

"It was a compromise." Violetta looked down at her hands clasped in her lap. "It was the best we could do."

"Where will we go?" Ava's heart was pounding against her rib cage.

"I have booked passage for you both to America. My son can start over there. It's far enough away that he will not be tempted to return."

Ava panicked. She was half-frightened of her husband now. "But it's so far from my home. I'll never see France again."

"Perhaps not," Violetta said, her voice breaking with compassion. "I am sorry."

Ava drew her brows together. "No, I won't go. No one can make me go, can they?"

"While that is your prerogative, you should accept that your place is beside your husband now. You were married in the church, and your child will need a father." Violetta touched her heart as she spoke. "Bear in mind that I will probably never see my son again. Or meet my grandchildren."

"This can't be," Ava said, pressing a hand against her abdomen. How could she leave? She loved Violetta; what would she do without her guidance? She sat back, stunned at the development and overwhelmed by thoughts of their future.

"I assure you. There is no other choice. My son is on his own now; he must become a man." Violetta rose abruptly, but not before Ava saw a single tear spill from Violetta's eye. "My maid will help you pack, and I will arrange the transfer of your funds to a bank in America." She embraced Ava and then left the salon.

For the first time ever, Violetta felt frail in Ava's arms, and Ava realized how much weight her mother-in-law had lost. Ava watched her climb the stairs. And then she understood. She and Luca could begin life anew in America, far from gossip and hatred. No one there need ever know of their past. But Luca's sins would haunt Violetta for the rest of her life in Tuscany.

That evening, Ava cried long into the night, not for herself or Luca, but for Violetta.

Two days after Luca's release from prison, Ava clutched the railing on a ship bound for America. The ocean breeze whisked stinging tears from her eyes. She gathered her collar around her neck, shivering alone in the salted mist of the sea. Luca was sleeping off a hangover in their stateroom.

At nineteen years of age, she was facing a new world essentially by herself.

Ava thought her heart would shatter into a thousand pieces. She was deeply ashamed of her husband. Never again would she visit France or her friends in Bordeaux.

Before she left, Ava learned from Giovanna that speculation was running rampant about how much Luca's freedom might have cost Violetta or what favors she might have called in, but Violetta never spoke of it.

Ava brushed a tear from her eye. She resolved to conduct herself as Violetta would, with strength and integrity.

She carried just two trunks on this journey, one packed with clothes and mementos, and the other filled with the cherished grapevines she'd once dug from her parents' fertile soil in Bordeaux, now nestled in folds of burlap.

Clutching her cloche hat to her head, Ava blinked against the wind. She hoped the precious vines would survive the voyage. Along with the beloved child developing in her womb, it was all she cared about anymore.

18

Caterina had put Marisa to bed early for the night—her little girl was feeling the effects of the time difference—and now she sat next to the telephone in Giovanna's office, waiting for the international operator to put her call through to California and ring her back.

She'd promised to check in with Juliana. She had called right after landing in Italy, but they hadn't spoken very long. It was early in California, and she hoped she could catch Juliana before she started her workday.

The telephone trilled, and Caterina leaped to her feet and answered it. *"Pronto? Pronto?"* It was the operator, who promptly put her through to the American operator. After a few moments, she could hear the line ringing.

Juliana answered, sounding sleepy.

"Juliana, it's me, Caterina." She clutched the phone, pleased to hear her friend. "I needed to hear your voice. What's going on back there?"

There was an awkward moment of silence on the phone before Juliana spoke, as if she were weighing her words, which wasn't like Juliana at all. *Must be the connection delay.*

"Earthquake," crackled down the line, and the fine hairs on Caterina's neck bristled.

"What?" she shouted.

"There's been another earthquake, Caterina. Mille Étoiles was hit pretty hard."

Caterina drew her teeth across her lower lip. "Is everyone okay?"

"We're all fine, but the equipment has been damaged. It's bad. Ava's trying to borrow money to replace it."

"I'm sure the bank will help her."

Another long pause ensued. "There's a complication. It's about your father."

Caterina twisted the phone cord. "I know. I discovered he's still alive. I met a distant cousin of my mother."

"Cat, he's *here*. Luca attacked your mother, threatened her, and roughed her up. The sheriff is looking for him."

She clutched the phone. "Is she hurt?"

"A few bruises, that's all. But she's defiant. Refuses to back down."

"Is Raphael with her?"

"He never leaves her side. He's been sleeping in the main house. Raphael and Nina insisted."

"Good." She was glad Raphael was there. Her mother wasn't the type to ask for help.

Caterina squeezed her eyes shut. A week ago she'd had a deceased father who had been a wonderful husband and father. Now he was alive and wreaking havoc.

An avalanche of emotions crashed through her. For years she had wished her father were alive. She'd dreamed of the things they might have done together; how comforting it would have been to have had a father to confide in. She'd deeply missed his presence in her life. She pressed a hand against her mouth, stifling a sob against the receiver.

"Are you still there, Cat?" Juliana's concerned voice crackled across the telephone wire.

"I am," Caterina said, sniffing. "It's a lot to take in."

"He's not quite the dad you had imagined, is he?"

Though tears wet her lashes, she managed a strangled laugh. "No, we thought he was Prince Charming." Quivering with a mixture of shock and anger and disappointment, she wiped her eyes with the back of her hand. She was through mourning the father she'd thought she'd had. It was time to face reality.

"I'm really sorry, Cat. At least we knew my dad was a real jerk." Juliana paused. "There's more. Your mother called a meeting with all of us. Luca wants Mille Étoiles. His name is still on the deed for the house and vineyards."

"He can't do that. We've lived there for years."

"The attorney said it doesn't matter. Luca can take the house and the land."

Caterina was stunned. As much as she despised her mother for rejecting Marisa, she was devastated to think Ava might lose their home and the business they'd built up over more than two decades. Her anger toward her mother dissipated. How could she help?

She thought quickly. Caterina had worked alongside her mother while she was in high school and during her summer holidays from college. She couldn't remember seeing any paperwork about the ownership of the real estate. Her mother had always told her that her family inheritance had paid for the land that became Mille Étoiles, and she had no reason to disbelieve that. But she *had* seen the incorporation documents for the business. She thought back to the business law courses she'd taken in college. *What if* . . .

"Juliana, my father's name might be on the property deed, but I'm fairly certain it's not on the business. The vineyard is actually a separate entity from the winemaking and sales business that is Mille Étoiles Wines. I know they have separate bank accounts, and I'm pretty sure the dates were well after my father left."

"You might have something there."

"Tell my mother to have her attorney look at it." Caterina fell silent. This was a disaster. What if they lost the vineyards?

How would they carry on with their winemaking business?

She wrapped the phone cord tighter around her finger, thinking. They had achieved a coveted reputation for excellence among those in the wine industry in America—including those who knew wines on an international level. How could they use that? *What advantage do we have?* A thought occurred to her. If they could acquire equivalent—or better—quality grapes, the Mille Étoiles Wine label might survive even if they lost the vineyards. A plan began to take shape in her mind.

"Cat, are you still there?"

"Listen, Juliana, I have an idea. Find something to write with."

She quickly outlined a plan to Juliana and then hung up the telephone receiver.

Caterina went outside onto the terrace. The starlit sky reminded her of the view from Mille Étoiles. She and her mother might have their differences, but Ava was still her mother, and they shared a passion for winemaking.

Though she thought she had left that part of her life far behind, there was nothing she wouldn't do to save Mille Étoiles and the business they'd worked so hard to build. Everyone depended on it—her mother, Raphael, Nina, the fieldworkers. If there was something within her power she could do to help, she would.

And there was.

As she stood staring into the vast star-studded night, a plan percolated in her mind.

The next day, Giovanna drove Caterina and Marisa to see the home Violetta had left to them.

Caterina positioned Marisa on one hip and gazed at the stone cottage that stood before them, excited to explore inside. She had an important favor to ask of Giovanna today, but it could wait until later.

The tile-roofed house was perched on a plateau that clung to the sloping hillside. Tall, bedraggled cypress trees delineated the property lines. Years of dirt caked the windows, and the wooden sills were cracked and dried from the sun. Climbing vines had grown wild, ensnaring the brick wall that lined the front of the house.

Marisa pointed to the cottage and babbled happily.

Caterina smiled at Giovanna. "I think she likes it. We're home, little girl. What do you think?"

Giovanna stood with her hands on her hips and surveyed the property. "It needs a lot of work. It's been closed for years."

"We can manage, can't we, Marisa?" Caterina had fallen in love with the house from the old photo the investigator had given her in San Francisco. Although the house was more aged than she'd realized it would be, she was certain she could restore it.

They walked up the leaf-strewn path to the large wooden front door. She put Marisa down and withdrew a key from the pocket of her yellow seersucker sundress. Giovanna took Marisa's hand while Caterina fit the key into the keyhole and tried to open the door.

"I can't turn it." Caterina couldn't wait to go inside and take inventory of the furnishings and repairs. She jiggled the lock and tried to turn the key the other way. "Now it's stuck."

"Here, let me try it," Giovanna said. "These old locks are temperamental."

"O-pen," Marisa intoned, and banged her tiny fist on the door.

Caterina stepped aside and took Marisa's hand while Giovanna tried to coax open the door.

"I can't budge it." Giovanna stepped back. "Maybe it's a sign," she mumbled.

Caterina barely caught her words. "A sign?"

Giovanna shrugged. "This house needs new life. You and Marisa will do that." She nodded emphatically. "There's a locksmith in town. We can go to his shop today."

Disappointed, Caterina picked up Marisa and walked to the side of the house. She rubbed dirt and grime from a window and peeked inside. "Oh, look, there's furniture in here!" she exclaimed. "There's a large wooden chest and chairs in the living room."

Her spirits soared. "I see wood beams in the ceiling, and there's a brick archway leading into what's probably a dining area or kitchen." Caterina loved what she could make out and couldn't wait to get inside. She'd start by cleaning and airing the house, painting the walls, and preparing a room just for Marisa. Ideas swirled in her mind. She wanted it to be a happy home with bright colors and lots of sun streaming through the windows.

Yet a memory nagged at her. Her mother knew something about this cottage, but she wouldn't say what had happened here. *What mystery did these walls hold?*

"It was a pretty little place inside, as I recall."

"Why has it been vacant so long?" Caterina hoisted Marisa higher on her hip and started off for the vineyard. What had Giovanna meant by "a sign"? she wondered.

Giovanna hesitated, biting her lip. "Violetta didn't want to rent it out again."

"Why not?"

"And here's the best part," Giovanna said, ignoring her question. She stopped at the edge of the property, smiling with pride. "Your vineyard." Giovanna pointed out the boundaries.

Caterina gazed over rows of impeccably maintained vines stretching across the hillside. Despite her questions, she was growing even more ecstatic over what she saw. "Someone is taking care of the vineyard. Looks like the grapes will be ready for harvest soon." She inspected some of the tight grape clusters supported on sturdy, gnarled trunks. Bluish-black grapes shone to perfection in the morning sunlight.

"Violetta leased the land to a winemaker. You can continue to do that."

"I plan to make my own wine." Caterina had been hoping the vineyard went with the house and was overjoyed to discover it did.

Caterina was thrilled at the prospect of starting her own vineyard. She'd been thinking about the equipment she'd need, the label she'd design, and a thousand other details. She couldn't wait to start this step of her plan.

This is our new life. Caterina gazed out over the property, letting this knowledge sink in. The vineyard was all she'd dreamed it would be. The house and gardens around it would require more work than she'd anticipated, but that didn't dampen her enthusiasm.

This was her first home—hers and Marisa's—and she was utterly elated. She hugged Marisa to her chest, and then twirled around with her. "This will be our fresh start," she said, happiness welling within her.

As if she understood, Marisa laughed and flung her arms around Caterina's neck.

Giovanna laughed with them, and Caterina pecked her on the cheek. Although the relatives on her father's side had spurned her, Caterina was so happy to have found a friend in Giovanna, who promised to help her learn her way around Montalcino and Tuscany.

They decided to visit the locksmith right away, so Caterina followed Giovanna back to the Fiat automobile she drove. As Giovanna started the car, Caterina said, "I didn't have room to bring many clothes, and I'd like to get some summer things for Marisa, too."

"After we meet with the locksmith, there are several little shops we can visit," Giovanna replied.

They drove into the village, and Caterina marveled at the narrow cobblestone streets that curved along the hillside. Stone structures covered with sturdy tile roofs stood joined as if supporting each other as they clung to the hilltop. Giovanna parked alongside a nondescript faded redbrick arched doorway, and they went inside. Giovanna greeted a wizened old man who was surrounded by piles of ancient doorknobs, locks, and skeleton keys. After she explained the situation, the old man shook his head vehemently.

He turned his shaggy gray head toward Caterina. "You are the American?"

Word got around fast in the tiny town. Caterina smiled pleasantly, clutching Marisa to her side. "That's right."

He motioned emphatically as he spoke, punctuating his words. "That house is bad luck. The lock is keeping you out. It's for your own good."

Giovanna cut him off, unleashing a tirade of reprimands and gestures. Caterina wondered, is this what had concerned her mother? She wondered again, *What took place there?*

The locksmith looked indignant at first and then became sheepish under Giovanna's continued admonitions.

"*Basta, basta,*" he muttered, waving his hands.

Giovanna turned to Caterina. "The locksmith will find time next week to repair the lock," she announced, shooting him a stern look before they left.

"He seemed awfully superstitious." Caterina didn't know whether to be annoyed or concerned.

"We move at a different pace here than in America," Giovanna replied, ignoring Caterina's comment. "Would you like to walk through the fortress, and then we can do a little shopping for you and *la bambina*?"

Caterina wished she could have gotten into the house today, but she was beginning to learn that here in Tuscany, time had an easy fluidity and was meant to be enjoyed. No one rushed about like those in San Francisco. Still, the old locksmith's strange behavior lodged in her mind.

They left the car and walked along narrow medieval lanes. Caterina marveled at the stone walls of the fortress, which Giovanna called *la Rocca*. They climbed high onto the ancient ramparts, taking turns carrying Marisa until their thigh muscles burned from the effort. Once there, it was worth it; the panoramic view of the undulating Tuscan countryside was astounding.

"Look over there." Giovanna gestured toward another mountain. "That's Monte Amiata." As they walked around the fortification, Giovanna pointed out the regions of Val d'Orcia and Maremma. "And there, across the Crete, is Siena."

Afterward they threaded their way back through stone-flanked streets and past the picturesque clock tower, whose bell tolled on the hour.

Alongside a pretty piazza, Giovanna took Caterina to a little shop festooned with red awnings where she found several dresses and play clothes for Marisa. Next they went to another tiny, ivy-covered boutique that sold the sort of colorful, casual sundresses and skirts that Giovanna wore and Caterina had admired.

Caterina selected a few skirts, added some bright sashes, and then chose a pair of slim-tapered cotton slacks, a casual white shirt, and a turquoise shirtdress.

Giovanna held Marisa while Caterina tried on her clothes. Caterina emerged when she was finished and saw Giovanna hugging Marisa to her chest, singing a song to her. If only Ava had accepted Marisa as Giovanna had.

Giovanna looked up and smiled. "If I'd had a child, I would have wanted her to be just like Marisa. She's a sweet, precious girl. Surely Ava will change her mind."

"I hope so." Caterina sat beside her and took her hand. She trusted this woman who had been her mother's dearest friend. "Would you like to look after Marisa for a couple of days?"

Giovanna's face lit with excitement. "I'd love to. You'd trust me?"

"You're part of my family, Giovanna." Caterina squeezed her hand. She thought of the notes that Juliana had given her on the way to the airport, detailing the information that Bessie Waters, the editor's wife, had relayed to her. "I have important business in Paris for Mille Étoiles, and you'd be doing me a huge favor."

"What will you do in Paris?"

"There's a competition for wine, and I plan to enter ours from Mille Étoiles. If we can win, or even place, it will boost our sales." And help save their winemaking business, even if they lost the property to Luca. She and Ava might not be speaking, but that wouldn't stop her from doing what she could when her mother was threatened. The wine competition had been on her mind, and she'd read Juliana's notes several times since boarding the plane to Italy. "However, I have to ask you for the bottles I brought."

After they left the boutique, they sat at a shaded table under a gnarled olive tree outside of a café. Red, pink, and white geraniums spilled from colorful painted pottery. Giovanna ordered wine and an antipasto platter of meats and cheeses.

"Everything sounds delicious, especially the *ragù* sauce." Caterina read the handwritten menu.

"It's good, but mine is better," Giovanna said with a sniff. "Try the *tagliatelle alla boscaiola*—that's fresh pasta with porcini mushrooms. It's a traditional dish here in Toscana."

The owner, a jovial white-aproned man who smelled of garlic and oregano, brought them a carafe of red wine and a bottle of green extra-virgin olive oil from his farm. Giovanna poured a little into a fragrant puddle on a plate. "This is a specialty of the region, too." She reached for a hunk of crusty bread.

Marisa loved the farfalle pasta, and the owner brought her soft roasted red peppers, green beans, and sweet oranges.

"This is absolutely delicious," Caterina said. "I'll have to buy a larger dress size in no time."

Giovanna smiled. "It's how we always eat. Don't worry about gaining weight; you'll work it off once you begin renovating the cottage. Eat, relax, enjoy. This is how we live."

And that's how it should be, Caterina thought, relaxing. The sun warmed her shoulders, and a light breeze flicked wisps of hair from her forehead. From where they sat, the view across the hillsides and valley was spectacular. In the distance, mountain peaks spiked the horizon. Caterina smiled and sipped her wine. *What could be better?* A thought crept into her mind. *Sharing it with someone you love.*

After the main meal, Giovanna asked for cappuccino and *cantuccini,* a twice-baked oblong cookie with almonds and pistachios that Caterina knew as biscotto.

As they ate, Caterina asked about her father, but Giovanna swiftly changed the subject. Caterina was disturbed that Giovanna wouldn't share more with her, but she decided not to press her. Maybe she didn't think it was her place, or perhaps the time wasn't right.

They languished and chatted for a long time. Giovanna talked about some of Caterina's relatives. Two of her young uncles had died in the war, an aunt had died in childbirth, and one cousin was living in Austria.

"Do you think they'll ever welcome me?"

Giovanna lowered her voice. "If they know Marisa is illegitimate, they will shun you. Our priest will not even baptize children born out of wedlock."

Caterina sat back, stunned. The simple life she'd imagined here vanished like smoke. "Marisa was baptized in San Francisco," she said indignantly. "I'm tired of lying, Giovanna."

"Think of Marisa. Would you want her to go through life with the stigma of illegitimacy? Deprived of opportunities? No. Better to say your husband died in America." She dipped her chin to make her point. "God will forgive your lie."

"Ma-ma-ma," Marisa said, waving her hands.

Caterina caught her tiny hand and kissed it. Maybe Giovanna was right. She might stand on principle, but she'd also vowed that no one would ever hurt her daughter. Though she hated to, she'd have to construct another fantasy if they were to live here. Regardless of where she went, she realized she'd have to live with her transgressions and conceal the past to start anew.

After they returned to the villa, Caterina climbed the curved staircase with Marisa and put her in the crib for a nap. Marisa drifted off immediately, and Caterina quietly hung up her new clothes. She sorted through what she'd brought from home that would be suitable for Paris.

Caterina was relieved Giovanna hadn't opened the wine she'd brought from Mille Étoiles. She and Santo had blended a world-class wine. The tasting would be blind—none of the judges would know the origin of the wines. *Will the French judges recognize a California wine?* Nevertheless, she was determined to gain entry into the most important wine competition in Paris.

A win would be an important step toward saving the Mille Étoiles wine business. It could also help her build a reputation here in Italy for her own wine.

Caterina selected the most sophisticated outfits she'd brought with her—a black Christian Dior suit and a peach silk shantung dress and jacket. She packed her high-heeled pumps and rolled her strand of pearls in a silk jewelry bag to carry in her purse. When she was ready, she glanced around, making sure she hadn't forgotten anything.

Marisa was still sleeping. Caterina folded her new sashes and opened a bureau drawer. Handmade linens filled the drawer, so she shifted them to make room. As she did, she felt a paper stuck in the rear of the drawer. She tugged it free.

It was a thin envelope, yellowed with age. She placed it on top of the dresser, meaning to give it to Giovanna. But when she turned it

over, there was something familiar about the handwriting. The letter *n* in Giovanna's name had a little point on it, and the *i* in *Italia*
had a large upper loop.

Her mother wrote like that.

Caterina looked closer. The postmark read *New York City, 1929.*
Twenty-seven years ago.

Curious, she lifted the flap. The paper crinkled with a faint musty
odor. The letter inside was covered in spidery faded ink. She looked
at the signature.

Ava.

Caterina smoothed the sharp creases as if she could brush away
time—the years as well as the intolerance and misunderstandings that
separated her and her mother.

*What was she like when she was my age? 1929. No, younger than I am
now. And just married.* Surely she had been full of hope and happiness
then.

She began to read, translating as she went.

> *Dearest Giovanna,*
>
> *My dear cousin, I'm writing to you from the stateroom of our ship
> crossing the Atlantic Ocean. The sea is endless; never could I have
> imagined its sheer vastness.*
>
> *The relentless motion has added to my nausea. I have
> prayed to every saint I could think of—St. Rita, St. Anne,
> St. Gerard—and asked for the blessing and health of the tiny life
> I carry. I pray Violetta is right, that a child will complete us,
> make us a family.*
>
> *Long ago I forgave Luca for forcing himself on me before our
> marriage—or did I somehow invite his ardor? Even so, I cherished
> the child we conceived from that sinful union. If my miscarriage was
> God's punishment, then I fear another one now.*

My heart aches at the thought of all that has transpired these last few months. Every day I pray for the souls of Natalie and Franco.

How can I ever thank you for your kindness? Without you and Alma, I could not have survived the tragedy and Luca's incarceration.

I've tried to be brave about this journey, but alone in my stateroom I weep every night at the thought that I might never see my beloved France or Italy again. I understand and accept these terms that gained Luca's release from prison—but my freedom has been curtailed as well.

Nevertheless, I am committed to making the best of our exile. In the eyes of God, he is my husband, and I am bound to him until death.

It pains me to confess this, but as soon as we set foot on the ship, Luca began to cavort with a group of Russian aristocrats. I scarcely see him; when I do, he is far from sober. My only consolation is that the sale of alcohol is prohibited in America, except for religious and medicinal purposes. I never imagined that I would celebrate such a restriction, but in Luca's case, it seems warranted. Nevertheless, I shall miss my wine with dinner—unless we find a way to make our own, I suppose.

It's nearly four o'clock in the morning now, and Luca still has not returned to our bed. He returns only to bathe and dress. My bruises serve as a reminder to not question his whereabouts anymore.

I should not complain; I am grateful at least to have the money from my family's estate. What would we have done otherwise?

My warmest embrace to you,

Ava

Shocked by what she'd read, Caterina lowered the pages. The solid ground of the family she thought she knew shifted beneath her once again. She had never dreamed that her mother's marriage was fraught with such difficulties.

Ava's letter also raised more questions than it answered.

What had her father done for which he was incarcerated? Why was he released?

It was hard to understand everything without knowing what had transpired before, but one passage struck a chord and she read it again.

Ava was pregnant before she married.

Caterina ran a weary hand over her face. The half-truths and out-right lies were mounting on both sides of the divide between her and her mother. More than ever, she had to find answers to her past. Then a thought struck her. Were they more alike than different, after all?

19

The next morning after breakfast, fueled by her desire to find more letters from her mother, Caterina searched the guest room where she and Marisa were staying. When they'd first arrived, Giovanna had mentioned that at one time the room had been hers.

While Marisa played near her with her painted blocks from San Francisco, Caterina pulled out drawers, crawled under the bed, and looked behind furniture. But she found nothing. Marisa clapped as she watched. She wore one of the new pink rompers they'd bought in the village, and Caterina had dressed in a turquoise sundress.

Caterina sat next to Marisa and hugged her. "I wish you could help me, sweetie."

Where would Giovanna have hidden Ava's letters? If she kept them at all. Caterina thought of asking Giovanna, but her host had been so resistant to sharing details about Luca or her cottage that she thought better of it.

Her eyes traveled up the tall armoire. It had four long, narrow doors painted with vines and a mirror in the center. Caterina kicked off her espadrilles and climbed onto a chair. She opened the doors and ran a hand over a high shelf inside.

Nothing.

She reached down, snagged a coat hanger, and swung it until she hit the rear of the armoire. Still nothing.

Caterina worked her way along the top shelf, pausing to drag the chair from one door to the next. She made it to the last door and had nearly given up when the wooden hanger thudded against something. Coaxing the item forth with the hanger, she guided it toward the ledge. As it came into view, she saw it was an inlaid cigar box. She lifted it out and sat on the bed.

When Caterina opened the wooden box, a faint scent of tobacco wafted to her nose. There lay several letters bound with a narrow lavender ribbon tied in a neat bow. The postmark on the top letter was dated 1929. She fanned the envelopes. The handwriting on a couple of them belonged to Ava.

A knock sounded on the door. Startled, Caterina shoved the box behind the pillows.

"Caterina, I've made your train reservation to Paris." It was Giovanna.

Marisa toddled toward the door, and Caterina jumped from the bed to open it. "Thank you, Giovanna," she said, catching her breath.

"I reserved a couchette, a sleeper berth, for you. It will be a full day and night of travel. It's quite a beautiful journey." Giovanna gathered the folds of her full floral skirt in one hand and leaned over to greet Marisa. "We'll have so much fun together while your mother is away."

"This means so much to me," Caterina said. "Are you sure you can manage? Marisa can be a handful."

"You are not to worry. My sister is coming to stay while you're gone. We'll be fine. And Marisa will be completely spoiled by the time you return."

Marisa began chattering to Giovanna. "Fru" meant fruit juice, and "wa" was water.

Caterina stroked Marisa's dark curls. "I think she's thirsty."

"Then let's go downstairs." Giovanna held out her hand to Marisa, who tentatively took it.

Marisa swiveled around, hesitant to let her mother out of her sight.

"She wants you to come with us," Giovanna said, beckoning to her. "And I promised I'd show you more of Violetta's artwork."

"Sure," Caterina said, taking Marisa's other hand. She wished she could read the letters she'd found, but that would have to wait.

You'll be a good girl, won't you?" Shifting the narrow skirt of her traveling suit, Caterina knelt to hug Marisa and kiss her cheek.

Although it was early in the morning, Marisa was bright-eyed and inquisitive. She'd tried to pull loose from her mother in the train station, but Caterina kept a firm grip on her hand.

Giovanna and her sister Alma—who looked so much like Giovanna—waited on the small train platform. All around them, people were boarding the railcars. Giovanna had insisted on driving Caterina to the station in nearby Siena.

After hugging the sisters and Marisa again, Caterina stepped onto the train. Excitement sparked through her. She would only be gone a couple of days, but it would be a whirlwind business trip.

She heard a commotion, and when she glanced behind her, she saw two stylishly dressed women who were about Giovanna's and Alma's ages greeting them. They wore felt hats trimmed with netting, belted jackets, and leather pumps.

Caterina watched as they exclaimed over Marisa, and she strained to listen, but others were climbing the train steps behind her.

Once aboard, Caterina waved good-bye from a window. Marisa mimicked her, swaying her little hand. Her huge blue eyes were round with wonder, taking in all the new sights. Fortunately, there were no tears of separation in Marisa's eyes, only in Caterina's.

Caterina turned from the window and spied the two women who had greeted Giovanna and Alma on the platform boarding her railcar. Caterina wondered who they were. Had they known Luca and Ava? She made a note to speak to them.

"*Mi scusi.*" Caterina jostled though the crowded aisle and found her seat.

Snippets of Italian and French and Spanish floated through the train car, and Caterina trained her ear on nearby conversations, appreciating the rhythmic melody of Romance languages so different from English.

Caterina had always longed to see Paris—this was another dream come true. She reminded herself that she had an important job to do there, but still, it was Paris. She thought about the paintings and photos she'd seen in San Francisco at the museums. The Eiffel Tower, the Seine, the museums, the boutiques. She could hardly wait.

Caterina settled into her seat and wedged her bag with its precious wine next to her for protection. The long train gained speed as it clattered across the rolling hills, its whistle blaring its right of way.

Giovanna had reserved a couchette so Caterina could sleep overnight as the train sped through Florence, Milan, Turin, and Lyon en route to Paris.

Outside Caterina's window, vineyards rose and fell from sight as the express train hurtled through the wine country, whizzing by tiny country train platforms, grapevine-covered pergolas, and skyward-pointing cypress trees that swayed majestically at their passage.

She removed her short kid gloves and laid them on her lap. Instead of gazing from the window, she eagerly lifted the flap on her leather handbag. The old letters she'd found were nestled inside, and she'd been dying to read them.

Caterina brought out the first letter and lifted it to her nose. The scent of stale tobacco from its resting place permeated the yellowed paper. She settled back to read.

> *My darling Giovanna,*
> *It is with great sadness that I write to you today. I have spent the last few days in the ship's infirmary recovering from a miscarriage. Do*

you know that Luca refused to visit me? The doctor sent for him, but I was told that he was so upset that he could not visit. Upset? I think not. Inebriated was more likely his condition. Alas, I am only a wife. What can I say to my husband that I have not said before?

At least I can recover in peace and solitude. We are yet a few days from New York City. Perhaps the change will do us good. I pray that Luca and I can begin a new life in America. If not, what is my alternative? To divorce my husband, never to remarry or have children? To leave the church and live apart from my faith? No, I cannot imagine a life without the family I've always dreamed of.

I pray when we reach New York City the dark clouds will lift from our life. If not for his mother's intervention, Luca would have spent the remainder of his days in prison, and yet, he refuses to be grateful. Indeed, his resentment seems to grow with each passing day.

How did Violetta manage it? I wonder. Did she call in every favor, pay off every official? It must have cost a fortune.

America is our second chance. Perhaps the man I thought I married will reemerge, and we can put this horrible period behind us. Pray for me, dear cousin, as I do for you.

I wish I could say that I'll see you soon, but I fear we might never see one another again.

With kisses,

Ava

Stunned, Caterina rested the letter in her lap. She couldn't imagine going through such turmoil in a marriage. Her heart swelled with sorrow for her mother. Even though she had forged her own way in America and now ran her own business—and in that regard was more modern than many of Caterina's friends' mothers—Ava was still a woman from the old country.

Now that Caterina was here, she understood her mother's frame of reference far better than before. Giovanna's warning about Marisa's illegitimacy sprang to mind.

Caterina folded the letter and returned it to the envelope. She was beginning to understand Giovanna's reticence in telling her about her father and Ava's concealment of the truth.

Wasn't she planning a similar course of lies for Marisa?

She opened another letter her mother had written to Giovanna from the Plaza Hotel in New York. Ava was on her way to Napa. As Caterina read through it, she was shocked at what her mother had endured and awed by the actions she'd taken of her own accord. She bit her lower lip, oblivious now to the beauty of the countryside hurtling past.

A uniformed male attendant interrupted her reverie to direct her to the dining car. While she was gone, he explained, they would prepare the sleeping berths.

Caterina returned the letters to the safety of her purse. She stood to make her way to the dining car, touching the seats for balance as she walked through the aisle of the rumbling train.

As she thought about her mother, she wondered, would their lies further divide them, or eventually reunite them?

PARIS, FRANCE

As light crept through the edges of the shaded train windows, Caterina stirred. The swaying motion had rocked her to sleep the night before. Opening her eyes, she stretched in her couchette and threw off her thin blanket. The two Italian women she'd seen speaking to Giovanna and Alma—Susana and Imelda—were already awake and whispering in the adjoining berths.

Caterina had sought out the pair not long after the train had left the Siena station. They'd dined together and then stayed up late watching the scenery, chatting, and sharing a bottle of wine. She wanted to learn as much as possible about the region she now called home. She thought about asking if they knew of Luca and Ava, but the conversation veered into another direction as the wine flowed.

Caterina rubbed her eyes and then checked on the precious wine. She'd slept with it to make sure it didn't disappear during the night. With Luca threatening to take over the vineyard, she had hoped these two bottles could help lay a new foundation for the Mille Étoiles Wine label. She slid open the canvas drapery.

"Good morning," Susana said. Her bright green eyes were friendly. "Did you sleep well?"

"I did, even in this hard bunk." Caterina sat up and swept her hair from her face. "Where are we?"

"We're in France. We crossed the frontier during the night."

Caterina peered from a window. The mountains and vineyards had given way to farms with row crops and dairy cows. *France*. Her mother's birthplace. Unlike Italy, Ava had told her many stories of France. "How much longer?"

"Two or three hours," Imelda said. As she spoke, she wound her black hair shot with gray into a neat bun. "We'll have breakfast first, and then we arrive in Paris." The two women shared a conspiratorial look. "As soon as we arrive, we're going shopping. Where did you say you were staying?"

"I'm booked into a small hotel in Le Marais." Giovanna had made the reservation for her, saying she would enjoy this area of Paris.

"Why, we're in Le Marais, too," Susana said. "Would you like to join us?"

Caterina had several hours before the judging was scheduled to begin. The women seemed nice, so she agreed. She excused herself to freshen up.

Before long, the train pulled into the Gare de Lyon. A grand archway soared overhead, its metal rafters a lacy ode to industrialism. Light filtered through glass panes lining the top of the terminal walls. All around, chatter in her mother's native tongue rose and fell like starlings at dawn. A smile spread across her face.

She was in Paris.

Inside the station, large schedule boards held destinations from Caterina's books and dreams: Nice, Marseille, Avignon, Venice, Barcelona, Geneva, Lausanne. She was so excited, and she could hardly believe she was here.

She collected her purse and suitcase and took special care with the bag containing the wine. As she made her way through the station with the two women, she passed a sign that read Buffet de la Gare de Lyon. She'd read about the shimmering golden salons of this beautiful Belle Époque restaurant, where Coco Chanel, Salvador Dalí, and Jean Cocteau often dined.

As if reading her mind, Imelda said, "You should go there on your return visit. Save room for the rum baba; it's to die for."

Outside, arched palladium windows, an imposing clock tower, and a stone façade festooned with garlands, nudes, and cherubs soared above her. The bustling city of Paris stretched out before her.

"Let's share a taxi," Imelda said.

They joined the queue of travelers, and within minutes their luggage was loaded, and they were transported into another world of tree-lined boulevards flanked by rows of gabled Haussmann architectural gems.

Caterina was in awe.

They agreed to meet again after they checked into their hotels. Caterina stepped out of the taxi in front of a little twenty-room, ivy-covered hotel, which was tucked into a narrow, cobblestoned side street in an old section of Le Marais.

She walked in. The interior was a riot of faded floral patterns of voluptuous cabbage roses, curling jasmine tendrils, and elegant orchids. The sensual aroma of potpourri conjured antique roses, silky amber, and sweet spices of the ancient Orient trade routes. At once she was reminded of her mother's boudoir.

A woman in a fuchsia silk jacket and enameled butterflies in her sleek gray coiffure sat at an ornate reception desk.

Caterina put down her traveling case. "Madame Robert?"

"*Oui?* How may I help you?"

"I am Mademoiselle Rosetta. Madame Rosetta made a reservation for me here."

At the mention of Giovanna's name, the woman sprang into action, greeting her like a long-lost relative. Caterina learned that Giovanna and Madame Robert had been referring travelers to one another for years, and when Madame Robert found out Caterina was Giovanna's cousin—even by marriage—she couldn't do enough for her.

Caterina thanked her, took the key to her room, and climbed

the stairs. Once inside her room, it was as if she'd entered an Art Nouveau music box. The gilded walls bore paintings, the bed was covered in silk, and mirrored armoire doors reflected sunlight spilling in from the terrace. She couldn't imagine a prettier room.

She unpacked and hung up her suit, hoping the wrinkles would fall out by the afternoon. When she returned downstairs, the Italian sisters were waiting for her.

"We're only a block away," Imelda said.

The three of them strolled along the cobblestoned streets of the Marais, stopping to go into interesting boutiques. Imelda and Susana bought a few things, but Caterina was saving her money for something special. When they passed a lingerie shop, Caterina paused in front of the window. Even in San Francisco, she'd never seen such exquisite silk robes. "I'd like to stop here."

"You'll love French lingerie, and you have a beautiful figure," Imelda said. "When we were young, we bought it for our wedding nights, before we lost our figures to our children. You should put some aside."

The proprietor showed her several sets of brassieres and panties trimmed in lace and a bustier and silk stockings. They were exquisitely feminine and arranged from sultry midnight black to a rainbow of colors.

"I'll take these," Caterina decided, making her selections. The sales clerk wrapped the silk pieces in tissue, and soon the trio was on their way to lunch.

They settled on a brasserie near their hotels. Caterina ordered a light plate of salad and bread. She was growing excited over the wine competition that afternoon and didn't want to eat too much beforehand. She believed the wine they'd produced was among the best in the world. She could only hope the judges would agree.

While they waited for their food, Caterina asked, "Do you come to Paris often?"

"We take an annual trip," Susana said. "Except during the war, it's been our tradition. Sometimes our mother and aunts join us, too. Do you have relatives other than Giovanna here?"

Caterina had been waiting for the right moment to ask about Luca and Ava. She had wanted to gain their trust first. "My father is Luca Rosetta."

At the mention of his name, smiles slipped from the women's faces. "I haven't heard that name in years," Imelda said, attempting a recovery.

Susana spoke up. "He married a French woman, your mother, yes?"

"My mother's name is Ava; she's from Bordeaux." When Caterina told them she'd never known her father, they seemed more at ease.

"I met Ava through Giovanna." Susana threw a glance at her sister. "That was a long time ago. I'm glad she and Luca separated. She was lovely, and he was trouble. When we were girls, our father wouldn't let him call on us."

"He always had eyes for Natalie, anyway," Imelda added. "But Franco married her."

Both sisters fell silent. The tension between them was palpable.

Caterina recognized the names from her mother's letter. *Who was Natalie? Who was Franco?* "I know so little about my family. I'd like to hear more."

Imelda arched a brow. "You should ask your mother, really."

Caterina had heard that before from Giovanna. This time, she was determined to learn more. "My mother won't speak of her life in Italy, so I'd appreciate anything you can tell me. What was my father like?"

Susana nodded to her. "If her mother won't tell her—"

"Should we?" Imelda looked worried.

"It happened so long ago." Susana frowned. She touched Caterina's hand. "You're such a lovely young woman. Does it really matter now?"

Caterina felt her cheeks redden. "If people are whispering behind my back about my father, I'd like to know why. You would be doing me a great service."

"She has a point," Susana said. "If I were her, I'd want to know."

Imelda seemed even more uncomfortable. "We shouldn't repeat rumors."

"They weren't rumors. There was a trial."

Caterina held her breath and waited, willing Susana to elaborate.

Susana raised her chin to the waiter and ordered a carafe of wine. "Please don't tell your mother we told you."

"I promise I won't." As Caterina sipped a mineral water, Susana began her story.

"Luca, Natalie, Franco—we all grew up together. Natalie Sorabella was the prettiest girl in our class; all the boys liked her. Her eyes were the most brilliant shade of blue you've ever seen, as deep and rich as the Mediterranean Sea. She wasn't like some pretty, but vain, girls. She was a real friend, kind and loyal and sweet."

Imelda placed her hand on Susana's and interjected, "But Natalie's father was poor; she had no dowry for a good marriage. Luca adored her, but Violetta sent him away; that's when he met your mother in France. By the time he returned, Natalie had already married. Luca was devastated and proposed to your mother shortly thereafter. We remember when Ava arrived. What a sweet, sad girl she was. Her mother and father had died, so it was a good marriage for Luca because she had a fine dowry from her parents' estate."

Caterina listened intently. A window to a new world was opening before her. "Then what happened?"

"Luca was still drawn to Natalie like a bee to a flower. Poor Ava. She suffered a miscarriage, and some said it was because of Luca."

Caterina could tell they were holding back. "And Franco?"

The sisters exchanged another doubtful look. "The ugliness began when Natalie became pregnant," Susana said. "Luca became even more obsessed with her. He doted on her so much that many suspected he was the true father. Then, when our dear Natalie died in childbirth, Luca went crazy. He blamed her husband. He claimed Franco let her die to spite him."

"And did he?"

"No. Franco loved his wife. But the baby was much larger than anyone imagined, and Natalie was weak from a prolonged labor."

Caterina thought about the references in her mother's letter to Giovanna. The puzzle was taking shape in a terrible manner.

"Luca had his father's pistol." Imelda sighed. "He was convicted of murdering Franco and was sent to prison. I'm so sorry to have to tell you."

"I needed to know." Caterina sat back, trying to temper her shock. "But he and my mother went to America."

"Luca's mother, Violetta, petitioned the judge, and it was decided that the offense was committed during extreme grief, so Luca was released. Your parents left for America right away. I think they had to."

Ava's letter made more sense to Caterina now. They continued talking through the rest of lunch, but Caterina's heart ached for the misery Ava and Violetta must have endured. This explained why Ava had concealed the truth. How does a mother tell a child that her father is a murderer?

After lunch, Imelda and Susana left Caterina at her hotel to change clothes for the afternoon event. Caterina took a short bath and brushed her hair.

She opened her package and put on her new lingerie, a black bustier and silky hose. As she slithered into the lacy silk ensemble, she felt very feminine, very French. She slipped her feet into her favorite heels, which elongated her legs. She stood tall as she assessed her new look.

Feeling daring, she sat at the vanity and applied vibrant red lipstick. She'd bought a new Max Factor color in San Francisco called Red Contrast, which was supposed to illuminate the lips and provide high contrast in the face. She pressed her lips together and glanced at herself in the antique mirror. A sensual smile curved back at her. She felt emboldened.

Her heels clicking across the wooden floor, Caterina strode to the bathroom and brushed the last wrinkles from the chic ebony suit she'd purchased from I. Magnin's, her favorite department store, located on Union Square near the St. Francis Hotel. The local residents had dubbed it the "White Marble Palace," and Caterina felt special just walking in. The slim-fitting, nipped-waist dress and three-quarter-sleeve jacket had been designed by Christian Dior and imported from France. It was perfect for today.

She was relieved she could fit into the snug waistline again. For summer, she wore it with matinee-length pearls, six-button white gloves, and her favorite black hat, which was trimmed with a white ribbon and flashed a leopard print facing under the brim. Growing up at the vineyard in Napa Valley, she had dressed more casually, but she'd always loved beautiful clothes. She'd inherited that from Ava, who always looked stylish, even in her pressed cotton shirts and dungarees at the vineyard.

As Caterina finished dressing, she reflected on Ava's struggles, contemplating the courage she must have had to survive. Knowing this, she was even more determined to make a success of their entry in the wine competition.

Her gaze lingered on her mother's yellowed letters she'd left on the dresser. Until now, Caterina had never given much thought as to how her mother had coped or how she had felt. The letters she'd read sounded like they were from a friend rather than the stern mother she'd known. Still, there were so many unanswered questions.

As Caterina secured her hat with a hatpin and pulled on her gloves, she couldn't help but wonder what had ultimately transpired between Ava and Luca. Why had Luca left? Or did Ava banish him?

Pieces of the puzzle were still missing.

21

Seated at the Queen Anne writing desk at the Plaza Hotel, Ava gazed at the telegraph that had just arrived. Her grandfather's friend from France, who now lived in Napa, California, had wired the banking information she'd asked him for.

Did she dare put her plan in motion? Luca couldn't be bothered about the future; he was living the high life with his new friends here in New York. Their cash reserves were dwindling with his lavish lifestyle.

The truth was that she simply couldn't bear living in a hotel a moment longer with a madman she feared. But was she up to traveling across a vast, unknown country alone? And taking the chance that Luca might not join her later?

Part of her hoped he wouldn't follow her. But she knew he would. He'd follow her money. Violetta had informed him she'd spent his inheritance to gain his freedom. He would have to work or start a business.

Ava raised her head and stared at herself in the gilt-edged mirror. Though her face was smooth, she felt old, much older than her years.

Ava secured her waves with a platinum clip and trailed a subtle lilac perfume on her wrists and behind her ears. As she did, she thought of Violetta and all that she had left behind in Montalcino. She would make Violetta proud, she resolved.

She rose and chose one of her best dresses from the cherrywood armoire, smoothing the lavender silk Jean Patou design over her satin slip. She'd lost so much weight on the voyage after her miscarriage that the dress hung loosely on her. She arranged a matching felt cloche hat over her neatly coiled hair and then clasped her T-strap shoes. She called the bell desk for a taxi.

Before she could leave, Luca burst through the door. "Where you goin'?" His speech was slurred, and it was only two o'clock in the afternoon. He flopped on his back onto the bed, his broad chest heaving from the mere exertion of walking to their suite. His long legs dangled onto the Persian carpet.

"Shopping." Ava slipped the telegram into her purse.

Luca stretched a hand toward her. "Come to papa, baby."

He stank of alcohol. Ava suppressed a shudder. "I will not. You're drunk again."

"I'm celebrating."

Ava pulled on a pair of white cotton gloves and picked up her purse.

"Don't you want to know what?" He paused to belch. "It's Tuesday," he said, pulling his shirt free and unzipping his pants. "Let's celebrate together."

Ava had once been seduced by his charming manner and dimpled cheeks, but she had finally had enough. "Don't let me stop you," she said in a cold voice. "Aren't your friends waiting for you somewhere?"

Luca scowled at her and zipped his pants. "Is that the way you want it now?"

"I want you to stop playing with your friends and plan a future for us. For the family we both want. You destroyed our life in Italy; don't do it here, too." Ava turned away before he could reach her, and she slammed the door to their suite behind her.

When she arrived at her destination, Ava gazed up at the grand edifice. She paid the driver, gathered her purse, and marched into the New York City bank that held her inheritance. Her heart was pounding so she was certain it could be seen and heard in that hushed haven of money. She sniffed. The bank even smelled like money.

She approached a man in a dark suit. "How might I help you, young lady?" He smoothed his thinning hair.

Ava sat down, crossed her legs demurely at the ankle, and introduced herself. "I'd like to transfer money to my bank in San Francisco." She was thankful her parents had insisted she study English in school.

"Is your father"—his gaze dropped to the diamond ring on her left hand—"or husband here with you today?"

"My husband? Why, no. Should he be?" Ava gave him a sweet smile.

"One moment, please." The man looked up her account and frowned. "His name is noted on the account. Why don't you bring him with you tomorrow? We'll be happy to help you then." The man started to rise.

"But the account is in my name only." Violetta had insisted on that. Why should that matter? It was *her* money.

"Maybe they do things differently in France, but you're in America now." The banker gave her a condescending smile. "He really should be with you. That's a mighty large sum of money for one as young as you."

Did he think her incapable of making decisions? Ava glanced at his nameplate on the desk, thinking fast. She *had* to make the transfer. "Monsieur Richard Halifax," she began, giving his name her fullest French pronunciation. She blinked, widening her eyes. "That's impossible."

Preening under attention, Mr. Halifax lowered himself into his chair again. "Why is that, madam?"

"You see, my husband is waiting for me in San Francisco, and I am on my way to meet him." She remembered her dear mother, how she playfully flirted with her father, even after years of marriage. "Sometimes you must use your womanly wiles," her mother had told her, laughing. Though it might be demeaning in this case, she was desperate. Demands would get her nowhere. Ava sniffed and fluttered her lashes.

Mr. Halifax looked uncomfortable. He took a pressed handkerchief and handed it to her. "Please don't fret; I'll see what I can do for you."

"That's so kind of you." She pressed the fine cloth to the corner of her eye. "Here's the telephone number you can call to verify the account. And make the transfer." She slid the telegram across the desk. She thought of Violetta and her iron will. She would not leave until the transfer was made. And she would call Violetta if she had to.

The banker made the call, and while he spoke, Ava continued to dab her eyes with his handkerchief for effect. *How dare he insist I return with Luca!* She was incensed.

Mr. Halifax hung up the telephone. "Your banker in San Francisco confirmed your account." He drummed his fingers on the desk.

Ava leaned forward. "Monsieur Halifax, I am eternally indebted to you. *Merci.*" Another smile, another flutter of the lashes.

A moment later, he nodded his assent, acquiescing to her will. "Well, seeing as how you're in a bind, and your husband is expecting you, I'll make an exception."

An *exception* to transfer money from her own account? She signed the documents he slid before her, and when the transfer paperwork was complete, she clenched her jaw and thanked him.

As Ava walked out, she heard him mutter something about independent-minded Frenchwomen corrupting the gentlewomen of America and its way of life. She smiled in triumph and hurried from the building.

My sins are certainly multiplying in America. She walked straight to a nearby church and confessed her sin of lying. Yet she felt entirely justified. What else could she have done? She couldn't live the life of a quiet, compliant wife with a man such as Luca. Before Ava had left Italy, Violetta had counseled her to be decisive and strong in America.

The next day while Luca was out, Ava packed her clothes and boarded a train for San Francisco. She left a letter for him, knowing it was cowardly, but she feared his violent reaction and reprisal.

Luca's actions were completely foreign to her. Her mother had never been subjected to such cruelty or brutality from her kind father. This was not the sort of marriage she wanted. But she and Luca had been married in the Catholic Church. In her religion, marriage was for life.

The train pulled from the station, and Ava felt as if she were breaking free from the past. A frisson of excitement bubbled to the surface of her mind. She was on her way in a new country. The 1900s had been the beginning of a new modern century. Women in America even had the right to vote in national elections. France and Italy could not be far behind, she imagined. *Maybe Violetta was right to send us here.*

Despite Prohibition, she'd heard vintners were having good harvests in California. Nevertheless, her vision expanded with every mile that rambled behind her.

As she sat on the train watching the sprawling landscape blur past her window, she prayed Luca would find sobriety and make his way to her. She'd left him a little money, but he would have to make a decision soon. And if he didn't, she was prepared to forge her own path. This was America, the land of opportunity.

As the steel locomotive powered across the vast country, Ava's burdens fell by the wayside. This was the first time she had felt truly independent.

She bobbed her hair into a short, sassy style as the train climbed the Rocky Mountains, loosened her corset as they crossed the California state line, and decided she'd buy a new wardrobe with skirts that climbed high to her knees when she saw the azure waters of the Pacific Ocean. By the time the train eased into the San Francisco station, Ava stepped onto the platform a new woman.

The buzz on the platform left her light-headed with excitement. She giggled at the slang words she heard people toss like confetti in the air—*the bee's knees, the cat's meow,* and *the heebie-jeebies.* She hailed a porter and took a taxi to a grand hotel on Union Square a fellow passenger had recommended.

"The St. Francis, please." Ava settled back. The glittering city by the bay sprang around her, and she loved it.

The next day, she visited her bank and confirmed her funds, checked on her beloved grapevines in her trunk, and then went shopping for appropriate clothes for city and country living. Finally, she contacted her grandfather's friend Charles Valois and arranged to meet him in Napa.

The older man picked her up in Napa at the train station. He wore the casual tweed clothes of a gentleman farmer. He was French, and he still had his standards.

Ava greeted him with a kiss on each cheek, and they spoke in their native language. He drove her to his home, which was situated on a higher elevation. His wife, Ines, had prepared lunch for them on the terrace overlooking the valley. Charles opened two bottles of their best wines for her to taste.

"I'm impressed," Ava said when she tasted the wine. She arched a newly thinned eyebrow in surprise. The robust red was nearly as good as what she'd tasted in Bordeaux and Montalcino.

"It's the climatic conditions," Charles explained. "The weather, the soil, the rainfall, and the heat—everything here conspires to make wines that rival the best wines in Europe."

"I'd like to continue our family tradition," Ava said, sipping the wine. She added that Luca would be joining her soon.

"The only drawback right now is the Volstead Act, which bans the sale of alcoholic beverages, including wine. President Wilson vetoed the bill, but Congress overrode his veto."

"You're still growing grapes and making wine. How do you manage?" she asked.

"We provide sacramental wine for priests and rabbis," Charles said. "We also sell grapes for home winemaking use, which is allowed in limited quantities. In addition, we can produce and store wine in our cellars for personal consumption. Prohibition won't last forever. Those who know say it mightn't last more than a few more years."

Ava listened carefully, savoring the magnificent wine. *How silly that only the devout and infirm can enjoy wine.* She had the money to wait it out, and if she gained contracts for sacramental or medicinal wine, she could last longer. "Do you know of any vineyards or land I might purchase?"

Charles and Ines traded a look. "As a matter of fact, I do. There's an old vineyard on Howell Mountain. Would you like to see it?"

After lunch, the three of them piled into a farm truck, and Charles wound up a narrow mountain lane. "This vineyard dates to the last century. The entry is through these tall cypress trees."

Charles parked the truck, and the three of them got out to walk the property. Charles showed her the original vineyard with its gnarled grapevines and abundance of sun.

"It's perfect." The back of Ava's neck tingled with excitement.

"I can show you a couple of more places, but in my opinion, this one is the best," Charles said. They'd been there so long that the sun was setting. Charles lifted lanterns from the truck, lit them, and handed one to Ava. "The sunset from the far vantage point is splendid. Monet would covet such a view—it's nature's masterpiece."

He was right. The setting sun burnished the sky with incredible brilliance. Blazing hues splashed the sky with glorious kaleidoscope

colors of turquoise, orange, gold, and pink. Ava stood at the upper
edge of the property and gazed across the land. It was one of the
most beautiful natural pieces of property for a vineyard that she'd
ever seen. And to think that it was here, in America. It seemed as if
God had answered her prayers. Violetta had indeed done her a favor,
after all.

She arched her neck back and lifted her eyes to the heavens. Above
her, a thousand stars dotted the sky, brightening as night encroached.
Ava caught her breath, mesmerized by the diamond-pricked blanket flung high above.

"Mille étoiles," Ava murmured. *A thousand stars.* With or without
her husband, she was home.

22

SEPTEMBER 1956 — PARIS, FRANCE

"Merci, monsieur," Caterina said. She paid the taxi driver and stepped out, taking care with her ebony suit and high heels. She peered up at the eighteenth-century, town house–style hotel. Its discreet canopied entry was flanked by a small army of bellhops in gold braid–trimmed uniforms and smart caps. The palatial Hôtel Ritz was the centerpiece of the Place Vendôme, an octagonal expanse in the 1st arrondissement of Paris.

Any other time, Caterina would have been excited to visit the legendary hotel, but today she was on a mission. Gripping her precious cargo close to her, she entered the hotel and followed the directions she'd been given to the salon where the judging was to take place.

Anxiety welled within her. She shook off thoughts of old letters, her father, and the past to focus on the competition. If their wine placed or won, it could mean the difference between the continuance or demise of the Mille Étoiles wine label.

To her left was a bar decorated in the Victorian style with red velvet armchairs and dark polished wood. The Ritz Bar teemed with a collection of interesting-looking people. There were handsome businessmen in dark suits and starched white shirts and stunning women in slim suits, wearing gloves, stiletto heels, and veiled hats.

The scene was elegant and lively. As Caterina hurried past, she recalled the St. Francis Hotel in San Francisco. She missed her old friends, but this was her life now. She pressed the brass elevator button with determination.

The gilded lift seemed to take forever to arrive. Nervous at the thought of the event, she chewed a corner of her lip until she realized she was destroying the makeup she'd applied so carefully in her hotel room. The door slid open, and an attendant opened the ornate accordion gate for her.

A minute later, she stepped from the elevator and hurried to the lavish powder room to repair her matte red lipstick. Thick carpet muffled her footsteps, and gilt-edged mirrors sparkled with her reflection. She breathed out, regained her composure, and compulsively checked the wine in her bag again.

After a last glance in the mirror, she was on her way. She found the meeting place and opened the door.

She paused at the entry. The salon was full of the crème de la crème of the European wine industry. She recognized a French couple who had visited Mille Étoiles a few years ago while on tour in California. The woman was impossibly thin and smoked a cigarette in a slim gold cigarette holder. The portly, swarthy man seated next to her glared at Caterina. *The Morels.* They had been rude, Caterina recalled, lifting her chin. They'd belittled their wine and winemaking methods at Mille Étoiles. Ava had sworn she'd never let them back on the property.

Caterina swung her gaze away from them and nodded to a man seated at the reception desk.

"*Bonjour, mademoiselle,*" the host said. He was a man of medium height with dark-framed glasses, and he exuded an air of restrained sophistication. Bottles with familiar labels stood on tables, while people greeted one another with familiarity.

"*Bonjour.*" Caterina introduced herself.

"*Enchanté,* Mademoiselle Rosetta of Napa, California." A few people turned to look, curious about the intruder from California. The man pressed his lips into a thin line. "On holiday, are you?"

"No, I live in Montalcino now." The Morels were smirking, sliding their gaze in her direction and talking to other people at their table. She ignored them. "I'm here to see Victor Devereaux."

A bushy eyebrow shot up at the mention of the event organizer's name. "He's quite, ah, *occupied.*" Other people in the room cast surreptitious glances in her direction. It was as if she had shouted a vulgarity during High Mass.

Caterina would not be deterred. She took advantage of her height; with her high heels, she towered above him by a head. She pursed her red lips and glared down at him through half-lidded eyes. "I'll wait."

"*Impossible,* I'm afraid." He gave a dismissive flick of his wrist. "His schedule is full."

"He is expecting me. I'm from Mille Étoiles winery in Napa."

"A *California* winery?" His tone indicated that such a thing was preposterous. More disapproving heads swiveled in her direction.

"*Oui.*" Caterina remained immoveable.

"*Non, non, non,*" the man said, touching the arm of his glasses as if an adjustment in his eyeglasses were surely required, for he couldn't believe the oddity before him. "He has important business today." The host turned his back to her.

"Indeed he does. *I'm* here." Caterina quickly determined she had nothing to lose by matching his impudence. She noticed a trim, handsome man at a far table staring at her, a smile flickering on his lips. *I hope they're all enjoying this.* She also hoped her face wasn't flushing, and then she decided she didn't care if it was.

The host expressed a puff of air and turned back to her, dropping his voice to a harsh whisper. "This event is for serious winemakers, not schoolgirls dabbling in grape juice. Please leave at once, *mademoiselle.*"

The future of the heritage she cherished hinged on her ability in this moment. She swallowed her fear. Caterina raised her brow in a slight, haughty movement she'd often seen her mother do.

"I have an invitation to see Victor Devereaux," she began, speaking in English and then switching to perfect, rapid-fire French, her voice rising just as her mother's did. "And I will not be deterred. If you do not present me to him, then I will visit him at his home this evening to explain why I am interrupting his private time with his family. I am sure he will not be pleased by your insolence, which is clear evidence of your fear of the quality of our wine. Reserve your judging for the wine, *monsieur.*"

The Morels laughed out loud. The host's face reddened, and the distinguished man from the back of the room broke out in laughter. He began clapping slowly and made his way to the front of the salon. "Bravo," he said, now standing in front of her. "What a performance."

Caterina maintained her composure. If she was going to be thrown out, she'd do it with style. "And you are . . . ?"

"Victor Devereaux," he replied with a slight bow, his eyes twinkling. He had the golden tan of a man who spent idle time in Deauville, and the upper-crust manners of a Parisian. "My wife's family is from Bordeaux. I recognized your accent." To the other man, he said, "Pierre, you may be excused. Mademoiselle Rosetta and I have business to discuss."

Caterina caught her breath, hardly daring to believe that she'd pierced the inner circle. Inclining her head, she said, "I'm glad I amused you."

"This way," Victor said amiably, indicating a nearby table. "I'm curious to know what brings you so far from home. Please, have a seat."

Caterina eased into a chair, gently placing her bag next to her. She turned her back to the Morels. "I've come to enter our wine from Mille Étoiles." She took care to speak clearly, even though he had switched to English. "We have won several important contests in North America."

A smile played on his face. "And how did you learn of our competition?"

Caterina told him about the editor of *Wine Appreciation* magazine. "Gilbert Waters thought we should enter."

"Really? I know him quite well." He leaned across the table and spoke earnestly. "You understand this is a blind judgment, yes? If your wine is not of sufficient quality—no disrespect intended, *mademoiselle*—then it might prove disastrous for your business." He slanted his head over one shoulder toward a small throng of men and women. "We have members of the press here."

"*Je comprends.*" Caterina knew the risk involved.

"Well, then, let's see your wine."

Caterina reached into her bag and handed a bottle to him.

As he studied the label, a flicker of recognition crossed his face. "This château, I've seen it." He looked up at her. "This is the estate of Alexandre-Xavier de Laurette, a marquis."

"My mother says our home in Napa is modeled after her childhood home in the village of Pauillac." Ava had told her about the village, which was situated in the much-heralded wine-producing Médoc region northwest of Bordeaux.

"The property was sold some time ago." Victor looked interested. "Was Monsieur le Marquis your grandfather?"

Caterina shrugged. After what she'd been through in Italy, being marked as a murderer's daughter and shunned by his family, she was hesitant to admit to any relatives. "My mother left France when she was young. She and my father came from winemaking families in France and Italy."

"I see. Well, I'll have to taste before entry is allowed, you understand?" After Caterina nodded, he motioned to a young woman, who hurried to the table. "Odette, have this bottle opened so I can sample it."

While the woman was gone, Victor asked Caterina several questions about their vineyards in Napa. He seemed quite interested in California and its climate, soil, and wine industry. They discussed the terroir, and Caterina mentioned the recent earthquake.

"*Un tremblement de terre?*" he intoned, and he shuddered. "Years ago I was in a large earthquake in Argentina while I was visiting friends. Earthquakes are God's way of getting our attention, but wine is our way of coping with the aftershocks." The woman returned with a crystal wine goblet.

Caterina held her breath. This was the moment she'd dreaded.

Victor swirled the wine, inspected the color in the light cast by chandeliers above, and inhaled the bouquet. He stared at her above the rim of the crystal.

Caterina lowered her eyelids, trying not to appear too eager, and waited for his opinion.

He said nothing. He drank a small measure of wine, letting it flow over his tongue, his expression grave and thoughtful. At last, he gave an almost indiscernible shake of his head.

She caught it and released the breath she'd been holding. The answer was *non*. It wasn't the answer she wanted, but she had to accept it. He was the final authority on entry. Arguing for a place on the ballot would not serve her well in the future.

"*Merci,*" she murmured. A hot flush of embarrassment encircled her neck. She could hear Madame Morel's dismissive comments behind her. She reached for her bag.

"*D'accord,* we will accept this wine," he said, his manner pleasant but noncommittal. "Please wait outside the salon, and the verdict will be given later today. Odette will escort you and notify you of final judging." He stood up, signaling the end of their meeting. "*Merci, mademoiselle—bonne chance.*"

For a moment, Caterina thought she saw a pleasant expression flicker in his eyes as he wished her luck. "*Merci, monsieur.*"

As she sauntered from the room, she felt all eyes on her. She tilted her chin and shot a look of triumph at the Morels. She might not be welcome, but she knew Mille Étoiles made a damn fine wine. It was a beautiful reflection of the terroir and was aging superbly. They had achieved a high degree of excellence.

She and Santo. And the family they had created in America. With berries that Raphael had painstakingly grown and harvested; on land to which Ava had devoted her life; from vines her mother had brought from Bordeaux, through Montalcino.

More than that, the love she'd always had for Santo was manifested in their wine. After this vintage, there would never be another wine of its quality from Mille Étoiles. In her heart, she knew it was synergy between them that had created the magic of this vintage.

The decision was up to the judges now. With the frosty welcome she'd received, she was relieved the identity of the wines would be concealed during judging.

Odette ushered Caterina to a public lounge area before returning to the salon. Caterina walked to a chair upholstered in red velvet and rested her fingertips on the silky fabric. She smelled cigarette smoke behind her.

"So you are here to steal more secrets from us?"

Caterina swung around, nose to nose with the despicable woman. "Madame Morel. As I recall, you were the one asking questions of us."

Monsieur Morel came to the defense of his wife. "Doesn't matter. Your land, your climate, your methods—it is all inferior. It shows in your wine." He waved a hand in dismissal.

Caterina bristled. "We shall see, won't we?"

Madame Morel blew smoke in Caterina's direction. "You're wasting your time here."

"Only with you, Madame." Seething, Caterina whirled around, anxious to get away from the venomous pair.

Other vintners milled about, masking their anxiety with small talk. Caterina cut through the crowd and strode to the open-air courtyard. She sat on a stone bench under the cool, leafy canopy of a flowering tree, composing herself. Surrounded by potted calla lilies and topiaries, she breathed in the calming scents of nature. She settled in for a long wait.

A couple of hours later, Caterina noticed a familiar masculine profile—thick hair, strong cheekbones, broad shoulders—belonging to a man in a trim dark suit wedging his way through a crowd near the doorway. She blinked. Surely her nerves were playing havoc with her imagination.

It can't be.

But it was. Santo angled through the swarm of tourists. He was walking straight toward her, his gait charged with determination, gravel crunching beneath his polished shoes. Her senses went on high alert. One didn't just fly halfway around the world on a whim. Her hand flew to her chest, and her pulse raced. *Has something happened at home?*

"Santo, you're here. What's *wrong*?" she demanded, rising. "Is it my mother?" Her thoughts raced to Luca. *Had he hurt her? No, no . . .*

Santo placed his hands on her shoulders and kissed her on the cheeks. "Relax, *cara*, I came to help."

"All that way?" She plopped down and expelled a breath. How dare he worry her like that.

Santo executed a brief, facetious bow. "And a good afternoon to you, too, *mademoiselle*."

"I don't need your help." She tilted her chin but slid a long glance at him. She'd never seen him in a suit before. *Why does he have to look so handsome?* So . . . she searched for a word. Aristocratic, even.

"I'm well aware of that." A dark brow shot up. "This is a significant competition."

"How did you know I was here?"

"Juliana called me."

She loved her dear friend, but Juliana was pushing the boundaries of their friendship again. "I can't believe she did that," she muttered, crossing her arms. What was she going to do with Santo here?

"Don't be angry at her. Juliana told everyone. She's a publicist; that's her job."

She narrowed her eyes. "I'm handling this just fine. I don't need you barging in, acting like a hero."

"I see your point, but I promised Raphael I'd look after the entry. It's vitally important—*financially* important—to everyone at Mille Étoiles." He joined her on the bench. "At any rate, I thought you might like to have some company. That wine is our baby—yours and mine. I want it to win as much as you do."

Caterina cringed when he used the word *baby*. She tapped a heel on the ground. "They're judging now."

"So they told me. Seems you made quite an entrance. Madame Morel had some choice words about you."

Caterina made a face. "She and her husband came to Mille Étoiles. They were so insulting my mother asked them to leave."

"Figures." He laughed. "Any idea what the competition is like?"

"The best from Bordeaux, of course. There are five *premier cru* red wines—the first growth—they're all here."

"From Médoc?"

She nodded, worrying the ends of her hair in an old nervous habit. "And Château Haut-Brion, I saw them, too. I recognized the winemakers from photos. All the important houses from France are here. A few from other countries, too. I've seen others waiting and heard them talking."

Santo rested his hand on hers; she didn't resist. "We have an excellent wine, Caterina. It deserves to be among this company. It can only improve, you know."

As she looked at him, his intense, lapis lazuli blue eyes sparkled in the slanting afternoon sun, weakening her resolve.

He traced a circle on the back of her hand. "Listen, I've been thinking about how we might handle this situation if we don't win."

"No!" she cried, removing her hand from his. "Don't jinx it."

Santo chuckled, and she remembered how she used to say that when they were children. And that was the trouble with this situation, she realized. Nearly every happy childhood memory she had was tied to Santo Casini.

He cleared his throat to speak—his voice sounded a little hoarse, but it was sensual, too. *Why did he have to come here?*

Before he could respond, a young woman approached them. "Mademoiselle, Monsieur Devereaux requests your presence in the salon," she said. "The judging is complete."

23

When Caterina and Santo walked into the ivory-and-gold-mirrored salon where the judges and winemakers were gathered, Caterina felt stares of ridicule and heard whispers. *How dare an American winemaker enter such a prestigious contest? Who does she think she is?*

Santo heard the comments, too, but he didn't understand French as well as she did. "There are the Morels. What are they saying?" He bent his head close to hers. "Whatever it is doesn't sound good."

"It's not." She translated the remarks. "As you heard, my entrance wasn't particularly well received." Though her words were edged with bitterness, she was warming to the fact that he was here. At least she wasn't alone. But it didn't mean she had to fall for him again. "Our wine gained entry into the competition, and that's all that matters."

Santo touched her elbow. "Let's sit in the back. If we have to make a fast exit, we'll be in position."

Caterina stepped away from him to compose herself. "What can they do to us?" She shrugged. She'd already suffered unkind remarks. Only Victor Devereaux had accepted her as a worthy competitor. An unsettling thought struck her. Perhaps he wanted to make an example of her, show the world how loathsome American wines really were. Was there another side to Victor Devereaux?

"Besides skewer you in the international press?" The Morels were talking to a man who was taking notes. They looked in their direction and laughed.

"We should stay and mingle with the reporters." Caterina fidgeted with the handles on a small black purse she'd bought in Rome. "This is a good opportunity to put Mille Étoiles on the international map."

He winked at her. "Especially if we have to salvage your reputation and that of California winemakers."

"I'm ready to do whatever it takes." Santo was right, and she knew it. She thought of her mother and Raphael and Nina and all the other workers who depended on Mille Étoiles for their livelihood. She brushed her hair over her shoulder. A win might also accelerate her reputation as a winemaker in Europe.

No matter what the judges' decision was with regard to their wine, she would do what she could while she was here.

A dozen stern-faced judges were seated in the front of the room at a long banquet table draped with fine peach-tinted linens. A podium anchored the center. A few judges were checking their lists and making final notes, while others who had completed their voting chatted among themselves. Rows of chairs were arranged for the announcement of the winners.

Around the room, newspaper and magazine writers were speaking to other winemakers, and photographers were snapping photographs of prestigious winemakers and their wines.

As they walked through the crowded room, Caterina caught a glimpse in the mirror, pleasantly surprised by the stylish image she and Santo conveyed. She thought of how they'd grown up together in dungarees.

Santo's handsome face was tanned from the summer sun, his dark hair glinted with copper highlights. She touched her leopard print–brimmed hat and stood straighter in her chic ebony suit. At least they looked the part of successful winemakers.

Feeling confident, Caterina approached a group of reporters. "*Bonjour.*" She introduced herself and Santo. "We're from Mille

Étoiles, a winery in Napa, California. We've entered our red caber-net wine."

The reporters traded uncomfortable looks, and the group quickly dispersed, with only one Italian reporter murmuring her apology. "I'd promised to speak to another winemaker, please understand."

Caterina turned to Santo. "So much for that idea."

Santo looked worried. "You've made quite an impression."

"Yeah, like a bad case of measles."

He put his arm around her and drew her close to his side. "That's why I came."

"For the measles?"

"No, silly, to support you." He glanced at the crowd. "This is a vicious group."

"Or just set in their ways." She sighed. "Let's find chairs and sit down. No one will talk to us, anyway."

"So what? We'll let our wine speak for us."

They shared a smile, like a secret between them.

Monsieur Morel sat in the front, gloating, while his wife perched her thin frame next to him and toyed with her cigarette holder, smirking at them.

Caterina ignored them. "Let's go to the back." While they made their way to the back of the room, she thought about Santo and how hard he'd studied and worked.

He'd built quite a lucrative consulting practice in the interven-ing years. He'd once shared with her his dream of building a world-class winery. *He deserves this, too.*

Santo had paid his dues. Just as Caterina had, he'd also grown up learning all the fine points of viticulture from Raphael, a fourth-generation viticulturist, and winemaking from Ava, a fifth-generation winemaker. He'd combined this experience with his university education in viticulture, his sense for business, and his natural cre-ativity.

Santo had earned the right to receive credit for his accomplishments, too. Caterina sustained the unwelcome comments and glares; she understood the reticence of her fellow male winemakers to allow a woman entry into their rarified circle. But Santo had so much to offer.

"How's this?" Santo gestured to a pair of chairs. "A straight exit to the door in case the natives turn hostile."

"Good idea." Caterina eased into a chair and crossed her legs. Her leg touched his, and a jolt of electricity shot through her. Averting her eyes, she adjusted her leg away from him. From the corner of her eye, she could've sworn she saw a look of amusement cross his face.

Victor Devereaux approached the podium and called for attention. The votes had been tallied.

The winemakers took their seats while reporters and photographers scurried into position. Working backward, Victor began to call out the names of the winners in the white wine categories. Congratulatory comments and polite applause followed the announcement of each finalist as they waited for the grand winner in each category. They listened to the parade of riesling, pinot gris, sauvignon blanc, gewürztraminer, chenin blanc, and chardonnay, among others, along with blended varieties from important regions in France, as well as other countries.

Next came the red wines, with entries of pinot noir, sangiovese, tempranillo, grenache, zinfandel, merlot, syrah, cabernet sauvignon, and other blended wines. The great wines of Burgundy and Bordeaux, the Pomerol and Margaux and Saint-Émilion, wines from Italy and Argentina—all were represented in this prestigious contest. Santo and Caterina clapped loudly when a Brunello di Montalcino from the property Giovanna oversaw won its category.

Santo took Caterina's hand and squeezed it tightly. Desperately wanting to win, yet knowing it was nearly futile, Caterina held her breath before each finalist was announced. Their wine was passed over each time, while the Morels accepted an award for their wine.

"We can leave after this," Santo said, leaning toward her.

Caterina knew he saw the torment in her eyes.

When Victor came to the final contestant in their category, he paused and peered closer at the paper he held. Covering the microphone, he consulted with Odette, his assistant. She nodded emphatically to him. He returned to the microphone and cleared his voice. The Morels smiled haughtily and prepared to rise to accept the honor.

"Ladies and gentlemen, we have a surprise winner." He gazed around the room and cleared his throat. "Mille Étoiles, of Napa, California, is our grand winner in this category, for a wine blended by Caterina Rosetta and Santo Casini."

Caterina sat stunned, hardly daring to believe what she had just heard. Santo let out a yelp and hugged her. Instead of the congratulatory comments and applause, the room was hushed. Everyone seemed astonished at the vote. Monsieur Morel huffed, and a wave of dissonance surged through the room. Victor Devereux, obviously sensing the growing discord, quickly moved on to the final awards, the grand prize winners for the competition.

The overall winner for white wine was announced, and the room erupted with congratulations and camera flashes. The beaming winemakers poised for photographs.

"And now," Victor said, "the grand prize winner for red wine." He cleared his throat and looked directly at Caterina. "Mille Étoiles."

"We've won!" Caterina cried, feeling as if she would explode with happiness.

"We did it!" Santo jumped to his feet. "Our baby won!" He hugged her and whirled her around, laughing with joy.

"I always knew it was special." Caterina laughed with him until tears sparkled on her lashes. She hardly noticed the controversy erupting in the room.

One of the judges demanded, "Who chose that?"

Odette showed the judge his ballot, and then several others insisted upon reviewing theirs, too.

"This is preposterous," Monsieur Morel said. "There must be a mistake. Their American wine will never measure up to our standards."

"Yes, a mistake *must* have been made," Madame Morel added, flicking an ash. "They are inferior."

Another judge said, "That's impossible. I must change my vote."

"Something is wrong," the person in front of them said. "They should be disqualified."

As the tide of sentiment surged against them, Caterina threw a desperate look at Santo. Would they lose what they had worked so hard to achieve?

24

Watching the outburst among the wine judges, Caterina hardly dared move.

Victor Devereaux was exasperated. He pounded on the podium, demanding attention. "All decisions are final," he said, raising his voice. "You had time to make your decisions."

"*Il n'est pas possible,*" someone from the audience said. "An American wine has never earned such accolades. There must be an error or miscalculation."

Caterina clutched Santo's hand. She and Santo had earned this.

"*Non, non, non,*" Odette insisted. "These entries were carefully concealed and tracked, and all votes verified. There is no mistake."

Victor held up his hands to quiet the crowd. "Let us welcome a pair of fine young winemakers into our club."

"But they're novices," Monsieur Morel said, flinging his hands up. "Unbelievable."

"A travesty."

"I suggest you try their wine for yourself." Victor motioned to Caterina to approach the podium.

"How can you even propose that?" Madame Morel stood, incensed, and tugged on her husband's arm.

Amid the grumbles of the crowd, Caterina and Santo made their way to the front. When they passed the Morels, Caterina couldn't help but smile in triumph.

Santo winked at them and leaned in to the husband. "Guess you should've paid more attention when you visited Mille Étoiles."

Madame Morel stubbed out her cigarette with a vengeance. Her husband took her by the arm, and they stalked out, muttering their displeasure.

Caterina suppressed a laugh, and they turned to Victor, who welcomed them with a broad smile and open arms. They accepted a small trophy and posed with him for a photograph, and then he kissed them on each cheek.

"Well done." Victor seemed genuinely happy for them. "Don't let a few of your more vocal competitors dissuade you from your art. I look forward to following your work."

Caterina and Santo thanked him, and then the meeting ended. A lone reporter approached them.

"Hi there," the young woman said. She glanced around. "I thought there'd be a line waiting to interview you."

"Hardly," Santo said. "If there were a line forming, it would be to flog us. You're an American?"

"Yeah. Guess we're not too popular right now." The woman laughed. "I write about European culture for *The New York Times*. I'd like to ask you a few questions."

Caterina and Santo spent a few minutes speaking to the woman and then posed for a photograph with their wine.

After that, a couple of winemakers approached them and offered congratulations. Caterina was truly appreciative of their sentiments. She thanked them and invited them to visit Mille Étoiles if they ever came to California.

When the crowd dissolved, Santo offered her his arm. "You were perfect, and amazingly, no one got hurt. For a moment I thought we had a riot on our hands. Care to join me for a glass of celebratory champagne?"

"Absolutely."

A few minutes later, they toasted their success in the Ritz Bar.

"Now the real work begins," Caterina said. "Juliana is going to send out press releases, and we—or my mother, that is—will contact buyers to share the good news with them."

"And sell more cases," Santo added, finishing her thought.

"With high pre-sales, my mother can borrow against the purchase orders rather than the property to make equipment repairs before harvest. I can't wait to call Juliana. And tell them about the Morels." She was giddy with joy, the champagne contributing to her light-headedness. This was the break they needed. Mille Étoiles Wines had been recognized on the world stage.

"Let's call Juliana now," Santo said. They went to the hotel concierge, who placed the call for them.

It was still quite early in the morning in California. Juliana answered on the first ring, and Caterina figured she'd been waiting for her call. "Did I wake you?"

"Are you kidding? I haven't slept all night. I hope you have great news."

"We do. Juliana, we won!"

"In which category?" Juliana asked.

"The grand prize." Caterina let out a small squeal. "Mille Étoiles was voted best red wine of the competition."

Juliana whistled. "Congratulations, this is a huge deal. I'll get right on it. You've probably saved the Mille Étoiles wine business." She hesitated. "Did Santo make it there?"

"Yes, he's here with me." Caterina glanced up at Santo. Now wasn't the time to chastise her friend; besides, she had to admit it was nice celebrating their win together.

Juliana promised she'd call Ava and Raphael right away.

After they hung up, they decided to find a casual brasserie for dinner. They were both tired from the stress-filled day, although it had ended better than either of them had imagined. Santo wanted to drop his luggage at his hotel first.

"Where are you staying?" Caterina asked as they stepped into a taxi to go back to their hotels.

"At a little hotel a friend of mine in Italy suggested." Santo gave the driver the address, and Caterina looked at him quizzically.

"That's where I'm staying. Who's your friend?"

"Giovanna Rosetta. She used to watch me when I was little. A few weeks ago, an investigator visited me in Davis and told me I had inherited property in Montalcino."

Caterina closed her eyes, remembering that she'd heard his name called during the reading of the will. *Our lives are far too intertwined.* And then another thought struck her. "You're not going to Montalcino, are you?"

"Well, I might now." A teasing smile touched his lips, his vivid blue eyes taunting her.

"Why didn't you say anything before I left?"

"You left in the middle of the night to drive to San Francisco, remember?"

She could hear the sarcasm in his voice. *Damn him.* She slipped on a pair of large, dark sunglasses she'd bought for the trip. "How did you get in that will? Don't tell me you're related to my grandmother."

"My mother's sister married Violetta's best friend's son. It's a small town. I knew Violetta when I was a kid. I used to visit her before I moved to America. She knew my parents and thought highly of them, so she paid for my passage to New York. She thought it would be a good opportunity for me." His cocky smile faded. "You never met her, did you?"

Caterina shook her head. "I didn't even know I *had* a grandmother."

"If it's any consolation, I didn't realize she was your grandmother.

Your last name is fairly common there. Raphael and Ava never really connected things for us."

Caterina was silent for a moment. "What was Violetta like?"

"She had a great laugh, incredible violet eyes, and thick white hair piled on top of her head, always secured with jeweled combs. She baked the most amazing bread, and her cannelloni was the best I've ever had. She was a woman who had strong opinions, but she always had the best of intentions." He motioned toward her. "Sort of like you. And she always smelled of violets."

"Violetta di Parma," Caterina said, remembering. She glanced at Santo under her lashes. "How long do you plan to be here?"

"A few days," he said. "I've never been to Paris. Why don't you stay, too?"

"Maybe. I'll have to make a telephone call." She wondered if she could ask Giovanna and her sister to look after Marisa for another day or two. She hated to be apart from her baby girl, but she really needed to speak to Santo, and she had to do it just right.

When they arrived at the hotel, Caterina asked Madame Robert to put in a call to Giovanna. The only telephone was downstairs in the office. Santo left to put his bag in his room and freshen up.

"Marisa is an absolute angel," Giovanna said on the telephone. "Alma and I love looking after her. You and Santo enjoy Paris."

"I'll still miss her." Caterina was thankful for Giovanna. "Kiss Marisa for me, and I'll see you soon." She hung up the receiver, delighted at the thought of spending a few extra days in Paris with Santo, away from curious eyes.

Madame Robert suggested a restaurant nearby. It was a lovely summer evening, so Caterina and Santo decided to stroll along the Rue des Archives and explore the side streets.

It was still early for supper. A *boulangerie* they passed smelled heavenly. They stopped at the Jewish bakery and Caterina and Santo shared raspberry rugelach and candied fruit stollen. They proclaimed the pastries the best they'd ever had.

Caterina loved the cobblestoned streets of Le Marais, one of the oldest districts in Paris. "Madame Robert told me that Victor Hugo once lived here in the Marais."

Santo looked interested. "Do you still read like you used to?"

"Not as much, but I still love a good book." Between work and Marisa, she had little time. "Look, there's a bookstore. Let's go inside."

They browsed for a few minutes, and when Santo tapped her on the shoulder, he held up a pair of Hugo's novels, *Les Misérables* and *Notre-Dame de Paris*. She loved that they were in French, and he bought both books for her before she could protest.

Continuing along, they peeked into boutiques that had the most elegant clothes. Santo bought perfume for her from one of the shops. L'Heure Bleue, an enchanting perfume from Guerlain, reminded her of iris, rose, and jasmine, flowers that grew at Mille Étoiles and Montalcino. It had a warm, ambery *sillage*.

Santo nuzzled his nose to her wrist. "That's marvelously mysterious on you."

"And you must have this one." Caterina held up a bottle she'd chosen for him.

He closed his eyes to inhale. "That's sensational, what is it?"

"Eau de Fleurs de Cédrat. Reminds me of Napa in the spring, when the citrus trees bloom."

"You have a good nose, mademoiselle," the salesclerk said before she wrapped up both perfumes for them. The woman took her time to prepare their package and added several small vials for them to try later.

When they arrived at the brasserie, Santo suggested they sit outside in a tiny courtyard to one side of the red-canopied restaurant.

They sat next to each other at a small table by a stone wall covered in pink climbing roses.

Caterina removed her jacket, revealing her slim-fitting dress.

"I didn't realize you had that on underneath." Santo trailed a finger along her bare arm. "You've grown up to be a beautiful woman, Caterina Rosetta." He tapped her temple. "And a damned smart one, too. What you pulled off at that competition was incredible. Who would have thought to do that but you?"

Caterina gazed at him from under the brim of her hat and laughed. "I believe those are the nicest compliments you've given me. And the books and perfume, why, I feel utterly spoiled."

"You deserve to be," he said, his deep voice dropping a notch. "Besides, we're celebrating. How often do we do that?"

White lights twinkled above them. From their vantage point, they could observe other couples strolling by. Caterina rested her chin on her hand, watching the stylish women of Paris parade past in their creative ensembles and fashionable hats.

"I thought you said you were starving," Santo said, snapping her out of her trance.

"I am." The pastries hadn't alleviated her hunger. She looked at the menu. Everything sounded delicious. "How can I decide?"

"Let's try a few things." Santo squeezed her hand.

"How about *l'assiette de charcuterie,*" she said. "With country pâté, duck prosciutto, caramelized onions, and cornichons."

"I thought you'd order the escargot." He winked at her.

"Absolutely, with herbed butter. Oh, and the *huîtres chaudes,* too."

"Oysters?"

"*Oui, avec des épinards et une sauce à la crème de Champagne.*" She laughed. "With spinach and champagne cream sauce."

For the main course, Santo ordered *filet au poivre,* a steak with peppercorn and cognac sauce. Caterina decided on a small Niçoise salad and *cuisses de grenouille à la Provençale.*

"Is that what I think it is?" He made a face.

"It's one of my mother's favorite dishes. Very hard to find in America." She leaned forward. "And the *soufflé au chocolat* for dessert."

"Just in case we're still hungry," he said, laughing.

Caterina ordered for them, and they settled back to enjoy a bottle of Bordeaux wine that neither of them had ever tried. Strains of jazz floated through the air from a window above. Caterina fixed the scene in her mind to recall later. The only missing part was Marisa. In a perfect world, they should be laughing and talking about their little girl, too.

Before they parted for good, she would tell him about his daughter.

"You look like you're a thousand miles away," Santo said, interrupting her thoughts. He raised his glass to her. "Here's to the continuance of Mille Étoiles Wines. And to us."

She sipped her wine, wondering if he'd meant anything else by that. When they'd made the telephone calls from the Hôtel Ritz, he hadn't called his fiancée.

He smiled at her with Marisa's eyes, and she felt their old kindred spirits emerge. This was the first time they'd been alone—on their own—for as long as she could remember. No Mille Étoiles, no family, no friends. She reached under the table and twined her fingers with his. A connection sparked between them. He might hate her in a few days, but tonight—and the next couple of days—she planned to cherish.

It was a welcome respite from tough decisions, financial pressures, and family ghosts.

They enjoyed everything they ordered, but they were sure to leave room for the luscious *soufflé au chocolat,* which was served with crème anglaise. They sipped *café pressé* and watched people walk by, laughing as they recalled childhood escapades.

"And do you remember the time the three of us dressed up for Halloween as Dracula," Caterina said, "and scared Nina and Raphael to death?"

"It was a long time before I lived that one down." Santo chuckled. "Raphael thought the ketchup we drizzled on the ground was blood from one of his dogs."

"Oh, no, I'd forgotten that part. We screamed, and Nina thought one of us was hurt. I think Juliana was grounded for that." The smile slipped from Caterina's face.

"What's wrong?" Santo took her hand. His eyes were twin pools of vibrating, electric blue. Caterina had to look away. It was as if he could see all her secrets. "So many memories," she murmured.

"And most of them good. Come on, you must admit that."

"Thanks to you. It would have been awfully lonely at Mille Étoiles without you."

"You had Juliana. She's like a sister to you."

"But you were the one who always found trouble."

"Me? Ha! You were the instigator," Santo said. "I'll never forget when you led the expedition to search out secret tunnels in the mountains. Those old, neglected wine caves from Prohibition were pretty spooky."

Caterina lifted a corner of her mouth. "Do you remember the ghost wineries?"

"I was convinced those abandoned wineries were haunted."

"I think some of them were. Remember how we scared Juliana one night, dressing in sheets and brandishing flashlights?" She laughed again.

"Yeah, I think *I* was grounded for that one."

"Well, if Juliana hadn't broken her arm when she jumped . . ."

"Poor little thing." Santo pushed out his lower lip. "She put on such a brave face that day."

"The way you splinted it, I thought you'd be a doctor someday." Caterina looked at him with admiration. He'd always acted quickly under pressure. Her gaze dropped to his mouth, to the full lips that curved so easily into hers.

As if reading her mind, Santo slid his hand around the back of her neck. He pulled her toward him; a moment later, his mouth was on hers.

Caterina sank into the moist warmth of his kiss.

He dragged his lips to her throat, and she tilted her head back. It seemed like the most natural thing in the world to do here in Paris— the city of lovers—on a warm summer evening. She met his lips again, and all her worries evaporated. His mouth tasted of dark chocolate, rich coffee, and dry Bordeaux wine.

"Ready to go?" His voice sounded husky.

Caterina nodded. They strolled through the streets, their arms wound around one another. With her high heels on, she was nearly as tall as he was, and he stood a few inches over six feet. Even though they'd never had the chance to walk together like this—sharing one another's company in the open—it felt natural to her.

They'd spent most of their young lives together, but never like this. If it weren't for his fiancée, would their relationship have developed in their real world?

They wandered into a couple of art galleries that were open late, and before long, they found themselves at the Place de Vosges, a pretty square in Le Marais surrounded by elegant redbrick townhomes and anchored with a rippling, tiered stone fountain in the center. Lovers lingered around sepia edges of golden light that spilled into the grassy, tree-lined area and footpaths. Murmured endearments floated in the sultry night air.

Santo stopped by the fountain, reached into his trouser pocket, and flipped a shiny franc into the water.

"What's your wish?" Caterina asked. She pressed her hands against his chest, enjoying the feel of his muscular body. The moon bathed them in a soft glow, and Caterina felt as if they were alone in a world of their own.

Santo cradled her face in his hands. "Caterina, don't act like you don't know."

25

When Caterina and Santo returned to the inn, Madame Robert was still at her desk. After they greeted her, she murmured, *"L'amour, l'amour . . . l'amour n'est pas mort,"* and kissed the photo of a man on her worn, gold-leafed Louis XV registry desk. *Love is not dead.*

Caterina paused before climbing the stairs. "Your husband?"

Madame Robert, wrinkled as a raisin, pursed her lips and winked again. *"Non, non,* Jacques was my lover. If I'd ever married him, it would have ruined our relationship." She brushed her hands together. "My husband had his affairs; I had mine." She delivered this intimate information without remorse, as cheerful and casual as if Caterina were inquiring about the weather.

"Sure are different attitudes in France and America," Santo said, chuckling.

Caterina elbowed him.

"What? Sex is healthy between two people in love."

"Good night, Madame Robert." Caterina clasped Santo's hand behind her back and slinked up the stairs ahead of him. His passionate kisses at the Place de Vosges had aroused her long-dormant ardor.

"Nice stockings," he said, drawing a finger down the rear seam of her silk hosiery.

Caterina paused at a landing near the top and gave him a small half smile before she continued up the last flight, putting a little extra sway in her hips.

She hesitated at the top of the stairs. Santo encircled her with his arms. Sliding her hands down his chest, she could feel the sensuality that flowed through his veins like velvety wine into a decanter, breathing oxygen into her soul.

She'd never met another man like Santo Casini. Did she dare steal him away from the life he'd planned?

His heartbeat matched the rapid rhythm of hers. An antique wall sconce illuminated his strong forehead and cheekbones.

His eyes held a question for her.

A slight lift of her brow and a dip of her chin was all the confirmation he seemed to need. He opened the door to his suite and then locked it behind them.

His room was as beautiful as hers. Santo nuzzled her neck as he helped her remove her jacket. Slowly she peeled off her gloves and then removed her hat, shaking out her hair. Turning into him, she touched his lips, tracing them as if to memorize the curves and fullness.

With a lingering glance, she crossed to the balcony and flung open the tall doors, flooding the room with moonlight. The sounds of Paris drifted in. From a nightclub across the street came a pianist's tune of longing, while bells tolled the hour and the laughter of lovers bubbled from the sidewalk. Here and there, taxis beeped their warnings.

A pair of crystal balloon snifters sparkled on a low table, and Santo poured a measure of cognac from a decanter for them. "Nightcap?"

"*Merci, monsieur.*" She brought the glass to her nose and breathed in the bouquet of the golden elixir. She raised her eyes to him. "Cognac is the perfume of wine, a salve to the senses."

He brought his face to hers and kissed her with such passion that she was stirred to her core. Any trace of reticence she might have had instantly evaporated.

Caterina reclined on a chaise longue by the open doors. A balmy breeze ruffled the soft fabric of her dress, and the moon highlighted her skin. She stretched her long legs to the end of the chaise longue.

Santo trailed his hand along the length of her legs, admiring the sheen of her silk hosiery. "Hypnotic," he murmured.

His breath quickening, Santo loosened his tie and then removed it, along with his jacket. Resting a hand on the chaise longue, he paused to savor every curve of her magnificence. "This is quite different from our first time in the cave."

A throaty laugh rumbled in her chest. "We were children then, weren't we?"

"We still knew what we wanted."

Lowering her eyes, she murmured, "Much has changed since then."

"Has it really?" Santo skimmed the length of her bare arm.

As Caterina responded to his touch, he inched closer. She pulled him to her. His lips were warm and moist and sweet with the taste of cognac.

After a few minutes, she turned her back to him and lifted her hair, piling it onto her head. Beginning at the neckline, Santo lowered her zipper, revealing her new lacy black bustier and a matching garter belt.

He let out a low whistle. "Were you expecting me?"

She stood and let her dress fall to the floor. "I went shopping this morning. I wanted to feel the romance of Paris from the inside out." She gave him a mischievous smile—the smile of a woman, not the girl she had been before she'd taken control of her life.

Santo took her hands in his and stepped back to admire her. "I'd like to enjoy this for a while. But not too long."

He left her to shed his clothes and retrieve robes from the armoire. When he returned to her, Caterina laughed. He was wearing a pale silk robe.

"They're both pink." He draped the other one around her shoulders. "Another drop of cognac?"

"*Oui, merci.*" She strolled outside onto the balcony, her heels tapping the floor.

Caterina leaned against the stone balustrade and gazed out over the city spread before her, its lights shimmering like diamonds. She'd dreamed of Paris for years. When she'd planned this trip, she'd thought she'd be alone. She glanced over her shoulder, hardly believing that Santo was here with her.

This man—he was a new version of the Santo she'd known; he seemed wiser and more experienced. He even carried himself differently—a new air of confidence cloaked him, and it fit him well. She remembered how they had played together as children, exploring and laughing and teasing one another.

It is so different now?

She didn't know what future awaited them, but tonight was a night she would treasure forever.

The sky rumbled, and a flash of lightning lit the sky. Sensing the energy in the air, she turned her back to the rail and slid her hands wide against it, angling a leg and arching her back. "What do you think?" she asked playfully.

"I think you're the most gorgeous creature I've ever seen." Santo paused in the doorway as a clap of thunder split the night. "Even the gods are applauding." He pushed the cognac aside, stepped outside, and whisked her into his arms. His mouth crushed against her lips as a light rain dampened their faces.

Caterina matched the intensity of his kiss. Minutes later, momentarily sated, she turned her face to the sky, catching raindrops in her mouth. "Look, the angels are crying with joy for us," she said, laughing, as they clung together, relishing the sensation of one another, rain soaking through their thin robes.

They raced inside and tumbled to the floor, their bodies entwined with passion. Santo threw a blanket to the floor, and her fervor for him heightened. As before, once aroused, there was no turning back, and Caterina and Santo were swept into a private world of ecstasy.

Afraid of becoming pregnant again, she'd asked him to be careful, and he complied with her wishes, though it was excruciating for both of them. She hoped they'd been careful enough.

After they'd made love, Caterina swept her hands over the length of his nude body, remembering the first time they'd been together and marveling at how he'd changed. His chest and legs were muscular, firmly developed from exercise. She touched his throat and chest with her lips until he groaned again with pleasure.

Curled into the crook of his arm, she felt his hands exploring her skin, which was damp with perspiration. When he touched a mark on her hip, she stiffened and rolled over, shifting her body away from him. A slight stretch mark from her pregnancy flanked both hips. She'd quickly lost weight, returning to the size she had been before Marisa was born, but a woman's body often bore the telltale signs of childbirth. *Does he recognize what they are?*

"Hey, where're you going?" Santo threw a weary arm across her. "Stay with me. I love you, *cara*."

"I love you, too," she murmured. A few moments later, he drifted off, and Caterina molded her body to his. She thought about finding a sheet to cover herself, but with the fresh, rain-cooled air placating their warm, spent bodies, she quickly fell into a deep slumber.

The lilies smell so sweet," Caterina said. She stooped to smell a brilliant bouquet of white blossoms at a street vendor's stand. She brushed a strand of hair back from her face and tucked it into a bright, printed silk twill scarf she'd bought the first day she arrived in Paris. She had tied the scarf at the nape of her neck. She added the flowers to an armful of creamy ivory and soft pink roses she'd already selected. A brief sunrise shower had misted the flowers, enhancing their aroma with a veil of fresh moisture.

"Be careful that the orange lily stamens don't stain your white sundress," the vendor said as she wrapped the flowers for Caterina.

After she left the flower stand, Caterina strolled through the narrow stone streets of the Marais district on her way back to the hotel. It was such a beautiful morning. *I haven't felt this happy in years.* She hated to see it end so soon.

"*Bonjour,*" she said to the hotel manager. Madame Robert hadn't minded when she gave up her room and moved into Santo's suite the next morning. They hadn't left the room at all the next day, and they were famished when they'd finally dressed and gone out for dinner.

The woman was singing to herself in a low, sultry tone as she wrote in her record-keeping log.

"What's that song?" Caterina thought the tune sounded familiar, but she couldn't place it.

A slow smile curved on the woman's lips. "It's called '*La Vie en Rose,*'" she replied. "Édith Piaf wrote it. You might like Marlene Dietrich's version, too."

"It's a haunting melody."

"And one of my favorites. It's a love song about a woman who sees the world in rosy hues when she's with her lover."

Caterina plucked a pink rose from her bouquet and gave it to her, kissing the woman's lined face. "I know exactly how she feels. I'll have to find that record before I leave."

"*Merci.*" Madame Robert lifted the flower to her nose. "Go upstairs, your man is waiting for you. Enjoy him." With a knowing look, she placed the rose beside her lover's framed photo.

Caterina started up the stairs. Never had she imagined that her visit to Paris would be as wonderful as this. Today she simply wanted to enjoy Santo and Paris, a small slice of the sweet life that might never come again.

When she reached the room, Santo had arranged a pot of coffee with pastries on a little tile mosaic-topped table on the balcony.

"Darling, I'm back," she called.

Santo emerged from the bathroom, towel-drying his dark, curly hair. He had another towel wrapped around his waist, and his chest was bare. Caterina caught her breath at the sight of him. With his water-dappled bronze skin gleaming against the white towel, he could have been a god of ancient Rome.

He paused, admiration evident on his face, too. "Just look at you, *cara,* you're the picture of summer in Paris. I want to remember you like this, always." He took the flowers from her and placed them into a vase and then slipped a strap from her sundress. "We'll add water later," he said, lifting her onto the tangled, unmade bed.

She tossed his towel aside, enjoying the sight of him, now fully aroused. She shed her dress, and they made love again as the sounds of Paris filtered through the open doors.

"We're so decadent," she murmured as he flung himself onto the rumpled white sheet beside her, breathing hard.

"And why not?" He raised himself on one elbow and gazed at her with hooded eyes. Slits of azure blue were framed with dark lashes.

What a beautiful man he's become. He still took her breath away. "I only wish it could last," she said before she could catch herself. She hadn't planned on talking about their future. Not now, not yet.

"I don't see why it can't," he said lazily. He trailed a finger from her nose, past her mouth, between her breasts, and down her stomach, sending chills through her. "This is real, *cara.* It always has been."

He sealed his lips over hers, drawing out his kiss with slow, passionate intensity. Finally, he dragged his mouth from hers and pulled back, his eyes blazing with emotion. "Marry me," he said, his words sounding so certain. "Come back with me."

If only it were that simple. Then again, why not? This is what she wanted, not just in Paris for a few stolen day, but forever. Regardless of what her mother might think, this was the man she wanted to spend her life with. This is how she wanted to wake every day until she died—which might be sooner rather than later once he discovered her secret. Every fiber of her being screamed *yes, yes, yes,* but she couldn't say that. Not yet, not until she told him about Marisa.

"I love you, Santo, and I want nothing more than to spend our lives together."

"Is that a yes?" He tilted her chin and kissed her.

She teased his lips with her tongue. "I can't give you my answer yet."

"Even after this?" he asked playfully, rubbing his nude leg alongside of hers.

Caterina tousled his hair, dying to ask him the question that had nagged her for so long. "What about your fiancée?"

"What fiancée?"

She smacked him with a pillow. "You lied to me?"

Turning serious, Santo caught her gaze. "No, your mother told you that, remember?"

He was right; after their first night together, they hadn't spoken again. Caterina dropped the pillow, curious. "Why didn't you set the record straight?"

He lifted a shoulder with a half shrug. "Didn't think it mattered. Maybe it helped me get over you at the time." He fixed her face between his hands. "I'm asking you again. Say yes, *cara*." His deep voice reverberated in his chest.

It would be so easy. But not yet. "You'll understand soon, I promise."

"Please don't tell me you want me to ask your mother for her approval." He sat up, shaking his head. "I've already tried that once."

She stared at him. "So you were telling the truth."

A sad smile crossed his face, and he nodded. "It was right after we'd made love the first time. But Ava set me straight; she told me I had nothing to offer you."

"And she really threatened Raphael's employment?"

"She was dead serious. I couldn't endanger his livelihood. Forgive me."

Caterina knew her mother's wrath all too well. Now she understood why Santo hadn't returned her calls.

He drew up a corner of his mouth in a wry expression. "But I'm not asking her. I'm asking you. Will you marry me?"

"Know that I want to, darling." She kissed him softly. She pulled away and gazed into his eyes. "But first, will you come back to Montalcino with me? I have something to show you."

Can you imagine hiding something so valuable for so long?" Santo said, staring at the small, exquisite painting. They were at the Musée du Louvre now, having spent the day strolling around Paris sightseeing.

Marisa immediately sprang to Caterina's mind, and she began choking at his words.

"Are you okay?" He patted her on the back.

Caterina nodded, catching her breath. "There are so many stories about this painting." They talked about how the *Mona Lisa* painting had been stolen from the Louvre by a worker. The painting remained missing for more than two years.

They'd had such a pleasant day shopping at boutiques and stopping for coffee or a glass of wine and enjoying the sights for which Paris was famous. Caterina had been pleased that Santo had wanted to visit the Louvre as much as she did.

Caterina went on, recalling lessons from her art history class. "The *Mona Lisa* also went missing again during the second war. Nazis looted the Louvre, crated up the *Mona Lisa,* and stored her in the dark dungeons of the Altaussee salt mine in the Austrian Alps. They stole more than eighty wagonloads of art from here, as well as from the Uffizi Palace in Florence, and thousands of other works from private collectors."

"Terrible place for such a lady." Santo squeezed her hand.

Caterina inclined her head, studying Leonardo da Vinci's famous work. "But there's another mystery surrounding her. Some say a copy was sent to Altaussee instead. I've heard the Louvre managed to send her to the Château de Chambord in the Loire Valley with other art before the Nazi invasion. Some say she was transported to Chauvigny in a sealed ambulance."

"That was creative." Santo looked closer at the painting.

"No kidding. From there, it's said she was moved to Montauban, then Montal, and finally, she was returned here." She shook her head, thinking about what her parents had lived through during the first war and the more recent ravages of the second war. "Just imagine what it was like here then."

"Dark days, indeed, and not that long ago. My relatives in Tuscany suffered a lot." Santo slid his arm around her and pulled her close to his side. "So who was Mona Lisa? She has such a mysterious little smile."

"Good question. The painting is also called *La Gioconda.* Most believe she was Lisa del Giocondo, the wife of a wealthy man from Florence, but opinions differ. She was painted in the early 1500s. Time has a way of misting the truth." Nervously, she lowered her gaze. They were leaving tomorrow morning. Her own truth would soon be revealed.

"Ah, a Tuscan woman." He winked at her. "Maybe a distant relative."

She responded with a mysterious little smile of her own.

After they left the Louvre, they strolled through the nearby

Jardin des Tuileries, stopping in the gardens to watch a young boy and his little sister playing with sailboats at a pond. When one of the masts on the toy broke, Santo knelt and helped the boy repair it with a length of string.

He gave it back to the boy and mussed his hair. When the girl flung her arms around Santo's neck in gratitude, Caterina transposed Marisa's face over the girl's and felt as if her heart would burst. Seeing him with children made her love him even more.

At the end of the Tuileries, Santo hailed a taxi to take them from the Place de la Concorde to Pont Neuf. "We have to walk across the oldest bridge in Paris to visit the Île de la Cité," he insisted.

Caterina was happy to explore the little island in the middle of the river Seine with him. She'd always wanted to see the Notre-Dame de Paris. Santo was curious about everything, and she loved that about him. Yet even as they explored, Caterina felt an internal clock counting down the minutes to the inevitable appointment she had with the truth.

The sun was setting as they strolled across the bridge, stopping here and there to watch the array of colorful boats that plied the narrow river.

Santo pulled Caterina into a semicircular stone alcove built into the bridge, where they had a stunning vantage point of the Louvre on one side and the Eiffel Tower on the other. He pulled her close to him, and they sat watching the city, enjoying the moment.

"We have so much to celebrate," Santo said. "Winning the competition, but most of all, finding each other again."

"That's the best part," she replied, nestling into him. She'd become addicted to the feel of his body next to hers.

He kissed her on the nose. "This might be our last night in Paris, but I don't want our relationship to end here."

"It won't," Caterina promised. And it never would, not once he met Marisa. But would he accept his daughter or shun her? She gazed at his strong profile, which was silhouetted against flickering evening lights. Their meeting would be a true measure of the man he was.

Santo leaned in to kiss her, and she felt herself falling under his spell again. "Why must I wait until we return to Montalcino for an answer, Caterina?"

She smiled to hide her anxiety. "You'll see."

He leaned back and draped his arm around her. "Whatever your reason, it won't change my feelings for you. I lost you once, I can't lose you again."

26

After a long journey from Paris, Santo and Caterina arrived at the train station in Siena and saw Giovanna waving from the platform. Caterina had called her from the hotel to tell her that Santo would be returning with her. She'd asked Giovanna not to speak about Marisa in front of him.

Giovanna threw her arms around Santo as soon as he stepped onto the platform. "Santo, it's been so many years. What a handsome man you've become."

"And you haven't changed a bit, Giovanna," he said, hugging her.

"Nonsense, but I'm glad you're back." Giovanna kissed him on both cheeks. "With the two of you here, the villa is becoming such a happy place again."

They chatted as Giovanna drove to the villa. After they arrived, Caterina led Giovanna into the salon, calling back to Santo, "Wait there, we'll just be a moment."

Caterina dropped her voice to a whisper. "How is Marisa?"

"She's been such a sweet baby." Giovanna smiled. "And no trouble at all. She's upstairs taking her nap. My sister Alma is with her now."

Caterina's heart pounded at the thought of Santo and Marisa under the same roof. It wouldn't be long before she'd know where she stood with him. But whatever happened, he'd know about Marisa at last. "Giovanna, I have to tell you something," Caterina said, pressing her lips together before she continued. "Santo is Marisa's father, but he doesn't know yet."

"I suspected that when you called." A sad smile spread across her face, along with a worried, pained expression. "She has his eyes, of course. Santo is a good man. He'll do the right thing for both of you."

Caterina was surprised at the strange emotion etched on Giovanna's face, but she hurried on before Santo could overhear them. "I didn't want him to marry me out of duty. And I want to have Marisa there when I tell him so he can see her."

"Wait until she wakes up so she'll be in a good mood. She went to sleep right before I left. She'll probably sleep another hour, maybe two."

Caterina exhaled. "I've waited so long to tell him, what's another couple of hours?" Shivering with anticipation, she hugged Giovanna. "Thank you for everything you've done."

"No need to thank me." Giovanna kissed her cheek. "You're all family."

They walked back to the entryway, where Santo was just closing the front door. He held up two keys in his hand. "A man just dropped these off for you, Giovanna. He said the work at the house was done."

"Those are the keys to the house I inherited," Caterina said. "We couldn't get in before because the lock was stuck."

Santo jingled the keys. "Then let's go see it now."

"Now?" Giovanna shot a glance at Caterina.

"We have some time," Caterina said.

Santo had already opened the door. "Come on, I'd like to see it, too."

"Are you sure?" Giovanna touched her temple with seeming uncertainty.

"I'll be right back," Caterina said, sensing reluctance from

Giovanna, though she didn't understand her hesitation. "I have to freshen up. I'll only be a moment." She ran upstairs. She opened a door, careful not to make a sound, and tiptoed across the room to the crib.

As Marisa slept, her pink lips moved in a suckling motion, and she tugged her knees under her belly, thrusting her diaper-clad bottom into the air. Caterina stifled a giggle. She whispered to Alma, and then kissed Marisa on the cheek. She'd let Marisa have her nap. It wouldn't be long before she met her father.

Caterina went downstairs, still wearing the peach-colored dress and jacket she'd worn from Paris on the train back. It wasn't exactly what she should be wearing to look at the dusty old cottage, but they were only going to be there a short time.

A rush of excitement spiraled down Caterina's spine as Santo slid the key into the front door of the stone cottage that was now her property. The wooden door creaked open under her hand, and a musty smell assaulted her nose. Particles of dust floated in the air, highlighted by long shafts of summer sun slanting through windows scored with streaks of rain-speckled dirt.

When Caterina stepped through the door, it was as if the decades fell away.

"Nothing has been touched in years," Giovanna said to Caterina and Santo, who followed her inside. "*La signora* inherited it from her family, and she always rented it furnished, so most of the furniture you need should be here. I haven't seen it in a long time." Santo held a kerosene lantern, which Giovanna had insisted they bring. "Years ago, I motored over some boxes and papers to store, though Violetta wouldn't let me go inside. Said she was rearranging things." She flicked dust from a chest. "Needs a good cleaning."

Caterina wrinkled her nose at the musty odor. "And a good airing out."

"Signora Violetta is the only one who has been in the house since—" Giovanna stopped, her attention riveted on a large window in the main living area. Her hand flew to her mouth, and she began to back away.

"Since when?" Caterina rested her hand on Giovanna's arm and followed her gaze. The sun's rays outlined a series of handprints on the window. A torn, bedraggled drapery framed the window, and rustic furniture was shoved against the wall, which showed signs of damage. Someone had hastily straightened the scene, perhaps many years ago. *What happened here?*

Giovanna's wide eyes swung from Santo to Caterina. "Since a good man and his wife died here." She clutched Santo's arm. "Some people say their spirits still live here."

"Why do they think that?" Caterina asked. People often died at home in their beds, surround by loved ones.

Giovanna didn't answer. Instead, she made the sign of the cross. "I'll wait outside," she said, her voice trembling.

"It's all right, Giovanna." Santo rubbed her shoulders in an effort to put her at ease.

Giovanna shuddered and hurried from the house, glancing back at them with a brave smile. "You'll be fine," she said, as if to reassure herself.

"Wonder what happened to them." Caterina took a few more steps, waving cobwebs from the air as she did. She wished she'd changed clothes—her dress would likely become soiled from the accumulated grime that covered every surface.

"Let me go first." Santo edged closer to her, brushing cobwebs from her dress and hair. "This house has been closed for a long time."

"Giovanna is acting strangely." As excited as she was to see the cottage, Caterina felt an odd undercurrent, an uneasiness she couldn't quite place. "Think the place is haunted?"

Santo hesitated, his eyes roaming into every corner. "I don't believe in ghosts, if that's what you mean. But something doesn't feel right here."

A scratching noise in the dining room made them both jump. "What's that?" Caterina exclaimed.

Santo pushed a hutch aside, and a rat scurried across the wood plank floor for cover.

"How did he get in here?" Caterina pressed a hand against her chest.

"Relax, it's just a rodent. He's more frightened than we are." He peered around a corner. "Come on, follow me."

The kitchen wasn't much to see, although the old-fashioned stove was charming in an antique sort of way. "Guess I'll have to make do with that," Caterina said.

"Did you plan to live here?"

She hesitated. He'd asked her to marry him, but what would he think of Marisa when she told him? "I can fix it up, maybe rent it out. The vineyard is in great shape; wait until you see that."

Santo stared at her for a long moment. "Let's see the rest of it," he said, his voice subdued.

They turned into a darkened hallway.

"Hold up while I light this lamp." Santo struck a match. He adjusted the flame, and the hallway came into view. Slits of daylight shone from under three closed doors.

Caterina wrinkled her nose. The scent of sulfur was almost a welcome diversion from the dust. Santo led the way with the lamp, so she stayed close behind him. She slid her hand through the crook of his elbow.

Their footsteps thudded in the hall, the sound echoing against the walls. They stopped at the first door, and Santo opened it. A bed with a once-white embroidered coverlet stood ready to receive guests. A layer of dust and cobwebs covered the furniture. The room was a scene mired in the past. Santo turned to her. "Let's keep going."

Caterina nodded. Every nerve ending was on high alert. They walked on to the next door and opened it. She gasped. "Why, it's a nursery. Look at the toys, the little crib."

A wooden crib stood in the center of the room, and a few toys were neatly arranged as if waiting for the baby. Santo stepped inside, raising the lamp to get a better view. A pastoral meadow scene had been painted on one wall. Little brown rabbits were nestled among blades of grass, and bluebirds and robins perched in a lemon tree. Pink hydrangeas and vining roses covered a stone wall, over which a white-maned pony hung its head.

"Someone was quite an artist. They must have loved this baby very much." Caterina crossed the room and pushed a closed drapery aside to let more light into the room. Marisa would love it. With the draperies closed for many years, the painting had retained its bright colors. Santo lowered the flame.

He picked up a wooden toy giraffe, its paint peeling with age, and inspected it. A string with a tag was looped around the neck. "These toys were never used. They still have handwritten price tags." He glanced around. "This room feels odd—I'm getting a sense of déjà vu." He spoke in a hushed tone.

"Maybe you had toys like that when you were young. They're probably common here."

"Guess so."

Caterina touched the detail work on the crib's railing, which was covered with fine dust grit. She lifted a neatly folded blanket in the crib to brush her hands off. A tin sat beside it. She shook it, and sweet powder sprinkled into the air. "Look, powder for the baby." She turned to Santo. "I wonder who lived here."

Santo scooped up a carved toy truck that just fit in the palm of his hand. The wheels spun on a wire axle. He pocketed the truck and shook his head, sadness filling his eyes. "That poor child lost his parents here. Or maybe he died, too." Their eyes met in mutual understanding. "I can't stay in here. Let's move on." He increased the flame as he went back into the darkened hallway.

Caterina clung to his arm. Her heart beat faster as they approached the last door.

He pushed it open and waved the lantern to and fro. "What's that?"

A dressmaker's form stood near a window, and a dingy white flowing dress covered the padded form. "She must have been making a dress." Caterina walked over to it. Steel pins still protruded from the fabric.

"You're about the same size." Santo stepped into the bedroom.

A sliver of daylight beamed through a partly open drapery, throwing shadows across the room. "Spooky. This is what people have been seeing through the window. Not a ghost." Caterina glanced around. A rose-colored marble fireplace anchored the room, undoubtedly vital in the cold winter months at this elevation. Pillows rested on the rumpled bed, and a door to an armoire stood ajar. Next to the fireplace was a writing desk with candles and a lantern. Italian newspapers and clipped articles were stacked to one side, and a thick folder rested next to them. Boxes were stacked to one side.

Caterina glanced at the papers. "Giovanna said she'd helped Violetta bring some boxes and papers here. That must be them."

The light from the open window was growing dim as the sun edged closer to the horizon. "Santo, bring the lamp closer." Caterina brushed years of dust from the paper on the top. There was a photograph of a house—*this* house—on the front page. It was well kept, but unmistakable. As she read the text beneath it, she pressed her hand against her mouth. *Oh, dear God.* A chill settled on her. No wonder the locksmith had acted as he did. "Santo, you need to see this."

"What is it?" Santo put his hand on her shoulder and peered over. "*Omicidio.*" He looked up.

"Homicide, isn't it?" Caterina met his eyes. Her nerves tingled.

"That's right." He repositioned the lamp to continue reading. "A man was murdered in his home. And his wife preceded him in death. She died in childbirth. Their names were—" He sucked in a shocked breath, and his grip on her shoulder tightened.

"Franco and Natalie." Caterina nodded as she spoke, shifting under his sudden clutch. *Why the reaction?* she wondered. His hand began shaking.

"My father was . . . *murdered*?" Santo drew his hands over his face and blinked in disbelief. He turned her to him, his face ashen. "You *knew* about this?"

Caterina blinked. *His* father? Santo was clearly confused. *Wasn't he?* "I met some women on the train who live in Montalcino. They told me the story of Franco and Natalie Sorabella."

"No, you mean Casini. My mother's maiden name was Sorabella."

Caterina's lips parted in astonishment. Natalie had died in childbirth. She'd assumed the child had died, too. "They were *your* parents?" She felt weak, and the room seemed to waver around her.

Santo put the lantern down on the desk and sank onto the edge of the bed, its springs squeaking under his weight. Obviously distressed, he shook his head sharply. "I was told they died in an accident. This is like a kick in the gut." He took the newspaper from her.

"Then that was meant to be your nursery," Caterina said, stunned. Questions swirled through her mind. Santo's face was turning a deep shade of crimson as he fought to control his raging emotions.

He read on. "They were renting a house from the Rosetta family." He drew his dark eyebrows together in consternation. "Luca Rosetta was charged with the murder of my father. It happened here, in this house."

Caterina slumped next to him on the bed. She swallowed hard, trying to sort it out. What had Susana said on the train? "The ugliness began when Natalie became pregnant," Susana had told her. "Luca became even more obsessed with her. He doted on her so much that many suspected he was the true father."

Tears welled in her eyes and her face crumpled as an unspeakable realization set in. *Could Luca be Santo's real father?*

Ava was right. This was horrific, and a thousand times worse than she'd ever imagined. A wave of misery crashed over Caterina, and she felt sick to her stomach.

Santo scrubbed his hands over his face. "This is crazy."

"I had no idea." She took his hand in hers. His hand was ice cold, and he wore an expression of shock. And he didn't know the half of it. "My mother never said anything."

Santo shook his head. "Her husband—*your father*—murdered my father." At a loss for words, he stared at Caterina.

She tightened her grip on his hand for strength. Her father had killed Santo's father? She shook her head in bewilderment, trying to piece the parts together. *No, that isn't exactly right, is it?* She had trouble drawing in a breath. "Raphael never said anything to you?"

Struggling through his feelings, Santo blinked hard. "He always told me that my father died in an accident."

"I guess they didn't want to hurt us." Caterina's head pounded. The gruesome puzzle was coming together, and the picture was un-fathomable.

She felt dazed as the ghastly events took shape in her mind. If Luca was *his* father, too . . . *oh God, no.* Alarm seized her as the revelation settled into her bones, numbing her limbs. Now she understood why Ava had so vehemently denied Santo when he'd asked for permis-sion to marry her daughter. Her mother's words flooded back to her. Ava didn't loathe Santo; she desperately feared the outcome if they fell in love and wanted to marry. Caterina squeezed her eyes shut. *And that's exactly what happened.*

When she opened her eyes, the room seemed to swim before her.

Santo's gaze fixed on a spot as he tried to process this information. "Growing up with one parent is enormously different from not having parents at all." His voice was edged with pain long suppressed. "I never had a home; I never belonged anywhere. I was passed from one relative to another whenever they tired of me. You have no idea how I suffered as a child."

"But you're no longer a child, Santo." Caterina tamped down the hysteria coiled within her, ready to burst. "You're a successful, grown man who will soon start his own family."

"And now we know the truth Ava and Raphael were concealing." He rubbed his brow in confusion. "Not that it changes anything between us, *cara*. But this is a shock."

"A shock," she echoed, stupefied. Remorse crushed the breath from her, and she dragged a hand over her face. Once, a long time ago, they had confided everything to each other. Now she was keeping secrets of such magnitude from him that he might never forgive her once he knew.

"Look at all this." Santo reached for another news article with a later date and continued reading. "Luca Rosetta was released from prison after it was determined to be an accident caused by mental duress." He thumbed through a stack of correspondence. "These are letters between your grandmother and the attorneys and judges. Pleading for his life. What about my *father's* life?" A vein throbbed in his temple.

Caterina caught her breath. *Had it been an accident?* Giovanna had warned her about Luca. The fact remained; the father she'd grown up idolizing had killed a man. He was a murderer. And yet, as atrocious and abominable as that thought was, it diminished in comparison to the dilemma that loomed before them.

"That explains why Violetta paid for my passage to America. And why she left me a vineyard in her will."

Reeling from the discovery of facts she'd never imagined,

Caterina clutched her throat, mortified. Feeling trapped, she sprang from the bed, pacing, her heels making sharp clicking sounds on the hardwood floor. From the moment she and her mother, terrified of societal and familial ostracism, decided to conceal the truth, their lives had been destined for ruination.

The weight of their deception crushed her soul, and Caterina swayed on her feet. Recasting the past had met with grievous consequences. She swung around. The walls seemed to close in on her, threatening to extinguish their lives. "I've got to get out of here!" she cried, racing to the door, panic engulfing her.

What will Santo say when I tell him about Marisa? About us?

27

NAPA VALLEY, CALIFORNIA

As soon as Ava hung up the phone, she raced from the house to find Raphael. She spied him at the top of a rise and ran toward him, kicking up dirt behind her. Vino trailed her, barking in her wake at the excitement. When she reached Raphael, she flung her arms around him with glee. "We've won, we've won! Caterina and Santo did it!"

Raphael gave a victory yelp and flung his straw hat in the air. He caught Ava in his arms and whirled her around, her pink skirt flaring in ripples around her bare legs. They fell against one another, laughing with relief. Vino joined in, jumping and barking at the celebration.

"Now we have a chance," Ava said, pushing her loose hair from her forehead and clasping a hand to her chest. "They spoke with a reporter from *The New York Times*. Our clients are bound to read about it."

"This is the break we needed." Raphael set her on her feet and stood with his arms on her shoulders. "Did the kids call you?"

"No, Juliana called. She said they'd telephoned from Paris." Still winded, Ava looked into Raphael's eyes. "I wish Caterina had called me."

"You and Caterina need to talk." Raphael rested his arm across her shoulder and pulled her close to him. They strolled along the ridge of the mountain, with Vino trotting behind them.

Ava had told Raphael and Nina about Caterina and her baby. She threw a glance at Raphael. "I don't know how to reach her."

"Call Giovanna. She's probably still staying at Violetta's villa. Even if she isn't, Montalcino is a small village. Caterina wouldn't go unnoticed."

Ava was ashamed of how she'd treated Caterina. She'd had time to think about her reaction to Caterina's announcement. When her daughter needed her the most, Ava had shunned her.

She had made her own mistakes when she was young.

Ava remembered when she'd met Luca. He was dashing and spontaneous and so much fun. *And I had been so vain, so sure of my loveliness, an innocent girl who knew nothing of the cruelties of men or of life or of the payment that would be extracted from me for having such feelings.*

That was the truth. La vérité. *If I had only known it then.* She'd deeply regretted her mistakes and had tried to make sure Caterina wouldn't make the same errors.

Ava bent to scratch Vino behind the ears. "I wish she'd confided in me when she was pregnant. I'd always thought we were so close."

"She feared your reaction," Raphael said gently. "You lied to her, too."

"You weren't entirely truthful with Santo."

"No, and I regret that. We were shielding them. Perhaps too much," Raphael added.

"Caterina wants to know about her family." As she thought of all the love and memories she'd deprived her daughter of, her shame grew. Ava had also felt the loss of her friendship with Giovanna and the love that Violetta had had for her. There would have been letters and photographs and telephone calls exchanged. Christmas and birthday gifts for Caterina and maybe even a visit from Giovanna. She shook her head. "How could I have told Caterina her father was a *murderer*?"

"Did you have to paint him in such a glowing light?"

"I only wanted her to be happy. It started out innocently enough. She was a little girl and began asking questions when she went to school."

"You have a grandchild now. What are you going to do about that?"

Ava grew quiet, thinking about Marisa. She'd missed the first year of her life. How scared Caterina must have been going through pregnancy and labor without her mother. She remembered how she'd felt.

"It's time I found forgiveness in my heart. We've just won a wonderful accolade. We should be celebrating now as a family." Ava made a resolution to forgive Caterina, but would her daughter forgive her, too?

MONTALCINO, ITALY

Caterina stepped out of the car, feeling light-headed as she walked to the front door of the villa. Giovanna hurried ahead of them to speak to her sister Alma, who was still at the villa looking after Marisa.

Caterina was relieved to return to the villa. She'd missed Marisa so much the past few days in Paris. And she'd thought of little else since the discovery of her family history in the cottage. She was particularly worried about how Santo would react to meeting her. But a larger dilemma now gnawed at her. Was he *really* her half sibling?

And could they risk the chance? The church would never condone their marriage, and their children would be ostracized. She didn't know of any priest who would baptize children of incest. More than that, close marriages within families heightened the risk of deformities. She could not, in good conscience, willfully inflict physical or mental impairments upon children she might have. Though if she had such a child, she would love it all the same.

A thought struck her. *Has Marisa been affected?* Caterina quickened her step.

"Slow down," Santo said, encircling her waist with his arm. "I've been thinking—the vineyard Violetta left me is next to yours. Despite what happened at the cottage, we could renovate it together, and bottle our own Brunello for export."

Caterina caught her lower lip between her teeth. That was a beautiful dream, but most likely that's all it would ever be. As each day passed, that vision crumbled a little more. A life together had been within their grasp, but fate had intervened.

As they approached the front door, Santo went on, "*Cara,* I refuse to hide our relationship anymore. When we return to Mille Étoiles, let's tell your mother and Raphael about our love. And there's no reason we can't be married soon." He reached for her hand and brought it to his lips, caressing her skin.

At his tender movement, she sank against him, drawing strength. "Santo, whatever happens, I want you to know how much I love you."

A smile lit his face. "Caterina, don't be so bleak. There's nothing we can't overcome together."

What a quaint thought. Yesterday she would have agreed.

Giovanna reappeared at the front door and held it open for them. "I love having the two of you here. Santo, I hope we see more of you."

As Caterina walked inside, Giovanna surreptitiously pressed a hand against Caterina's forearm.

"That's entirely probable." Santo beamed. "You see, I've asked Caterina to marry me." He took Caterina's hand in his.

"Why, that's wonderful! Congratulations!" Giovanna exclaimed, eyes darting between them as if in question. "We'll celebrate this evening. As for now, why don't you both change out of your traveling clothes. Santo, I have a room ready for you. Have a good hot bath and relax."

"I could think of nothing better right now," Santo said, rubbing his neck. It had been a long overnight journey from Paris.

Caterina kissed him on the cheek. "Let's meet in the salon later. I have something I must tell you."

She hurried upstairs and lifted Marisa from her crib, kissing her face and hugging her to her breast. "My little darling, I missed you so much."

"Mama," Marisa said, her eyes brightening. She laughed and flung her little arms around her mother's neck.

Knowing what she did now—that Marisa might be a child of an incestuous relationship—Caterina rushed her dear child to the window, where sunlight illuminated her face.

Cradling Marisa in her arms, she hurriedly examined the sweet face she knew so well and the strong limbs that propelled her child forward with such glee. Lively intelligence shone in her eyes.

She let out a tiny breath of relief, though she would have to scrutinize her daughter from now on for any sign of physical or mental impairment or symptoms of illness. The history books were full of references to serious illnesses of those who were the product of close family relations. But Marisa looked happy and healthy in every way that Caterina could see.

Giovanna and Alma tapped on the door.

"Come in."

"We want you to know that Marisa has been such an angel." Giovanna's face was lit with joy. "We've enjoyed looking after her. We gave her a bath and washed her hair last night. She had such fun in our big cast-iron tub."

Caterina stared at the sisters. *What did they know about Luca and Natalie?* Although she dreaded doing so, she had to ask them before she spoke to Santo again.

"I met a pair of women on the train to Paris." Caterina told them about the story that Imelda and Susana had relayed to her. "Did Luca and Natalie have an affair?"

Giovanna and Alma traded uncomfortable glances, but neither of them said a word.

"You know something, don't you?"

Lifting her shoulders, Alma spread her hands. "Everyone knew Luca was in love with her."

Caterina tried again. "Do you think Santo is Luca's son?"

Alma started to speak again, but Giovanna shot her a withering look.

"Ladies, I have to know."

"Who knows anything for certain?" Giovanna flushed. "There was talk, but how can anything be proved? Santo is a wonderful young man, he's Marisa's father, and you're in love. Maybe it was only gossip."

Caterina stared at her. "How could we bring more children into a possibly incestuous relationship?"

Giovanna passed a hand over her brow. "It would be wrong," she agreed, frowning with despair. "I suppose there's a chance that Luca could be Santo's father."

"What's the probability?" Caterina steeled herself. This was surreal. She usually spoke of probability and percentages in winemaking.

Alma chewed a fingernail, while Giovanna shifted on her feet.

Marisa complained, so Caterina put her down and kneeled beside her. "Would either of *you* risk it?"

Giovanna sighed and shared a sorrowful look with Alma. Both women shook their heads. *No.* Giovanna drew a handkerchief from her pocket and dabbed the corners of her eyes. "What a terrible shame."

At last, all the disparate pieces shifted into an agonizing picture. Caterina's darkest fear had been confirmed. She smoothed Marisa's silky dark cap of hair with a quivering hand. "This is why my mother was against our marriage, why she discouraged even our friendship." Squeezing her eyes against hot tears, she hugged Marisa to her breast.

Heartbroken, Caterina thanked them for their honesty and asked them to look after Marisa while she spoke first to Santo. It was imperative that Santo meet Marisa today. *As for the rest . . .* She struggled to rise from the floor, her legs nearly buckling from the weight of the truth.

After the two women left, Caterina put Marisa back in the crib with her toys while she got ready for the most important day of her life. "This is your special day," she said to Marisa, her voice cracking. "You're going to meet your father."

Easing into the warm, sudsy water, Caterina thought a bath had never felt so good, though it did little to cleanse her sins. She washed her hair and then slicked it into a thick bun at the nape of her neck. Though her heart was heavy, she applied the perfume they'd bought in Paris, put on a new white sundress and espadrilles she'd found in the boutique in Montalcino, and then clipped on peridot-and-gold filigreed earrings that dangled against her neck and accentuated her eyes, disguising the raging storm within her.

As she thought of their predicament, she ached for Ava, too, for the monumental secret she'd kept all these years in an effort to shelter her daughter. *Would I have done the same?* She couldn't say, but her anger toward her softened.

"It's your turn, Marisa. Time to change." With shaking hands, Caterina changed Marisa's diaper and then brushed Marisa's dark hair to the side, clipping her curls with a blue barrette that matched her eyes. She chose a cornflower-blue smock dress with white piping and grosgrain bows.

"There, you look so sweet. This is a day we shall never forget." She kissed Marisa, signaled for Giovanna to watch her, and started downstairs, her heart pounding.

Santo was sitting at a table having coffee when she entered the salon. He was studying the little blue toy truck they'd found in the
cottage. His hair was freshly washed, too, and he'd changed into a
pale yellow shirt and white linen pants—very Italian-style, Caterina
noted. She detected the scent she'd chosen for him in Paris, too. He
looked so handsome, relaxed, and happy. She hesitated for a moment,
fixing the scene in her mind like a snapshot. *Santo, in Italy. Before I
break his heart.*

Caterina walked toward him. She drew an unsteady breath. Their
relationship would never be the same again. Santo rose when he saw
her walk into the room.

Violetta's portrait gazed down upon her, and Caterina shivered,
discomfited. "Santo, let's talk on the terrace."

"Sure." With a puzzled frown, he took her hand and led her
outside across the stone pavers. The aromas of cypress and olive
trees, fresh orange blossoms, and ripening grapes wafted through the
air, and Caterina thought she would never forget the scents of
Montalcino this day. They sat on a stone bench overlooking the verdant valley and rolling hills of Tuscany. Birds trilled in trees that
arched overhead.

"What a view. I'd never tire of this." Santo draped his arm around
her. "You look beautiful, *cara*. Now what is it you want to talk
about?"

Caterina clasped his hand, hardly knowing where to begin. *First,
Marisa.* She moistened her lips. "Remember when I told you that
I'd been trying to reach you?"

"You mean, after we'd made love?" His eyes filled with sorrow.
Caterina nodded.

"It was wrong for me to have taken your virtue and left you. I
know I hurt you, and I pray you'll forgive me. I was honoring your
mother and her wishes, but as a man, I should have followed my
heart and my conscience. In your mother's defense, she didn't know

that we'd been together, that we'd made love. If she had, it might have made a difference." Santo smoothed a thumb along her cheek. "I apologize, and I promise I'll never leave you again." He brought her hand to his lips and kissed it. "Or dodge your phone calls."

She clutched his hand for strength and realized she was trembling. "I was calling for a very important reason."

Santo furrowed his brow. "Tell me, *cara.*" His deep voice resonated with love and compassion. "I'm listening."

She glanced away, preparing to utter the words she'd endlessly rehearsed. The hills in the distance wavered before her eyes. Blinking, she dragged her gaze back to him. "I was pregnant."

A range of emotions—shock, hurt, anguish—washed across his face as he struggled to assimilate her words. "And the baby? Did you lose it?"

"No." Caterina's breath was shallow with anticipation. Her head felt light.

"You . . . you had a *baby*?" Santo's gaze fell to her abdomen, and he pressed his hand against her flat belly.

"A little girl." The facts hung in the air, immutable now. Her mouth felt suddenly dry.

Wincing with remorse, he thrust his hands through his thick, damp hair. "I'm so, so sorry, Caterina. I never imagined that . . ." His voice trailed off, and then he gripped her hands in alarm. "Where is she? You didn't adopt her out, did you?"

"She's upstairs." Caterina gave him a tentative smile. "Her name is Marisa. She's beautiful, and she can't wait to meet her father." *There. I've said it.*

"*Marisa, Marisa, una bella bambina!*" Santo wrapped his arms around her, his heart throbbing against her chest, overwhelming her with the intensity of his reaction. "*Dio mio,* I can't imagine what you must have gone through. I *should* have been there with you. We should have been together." He showered her face with kisses before rising and offering her his hand. "Lead me to my daughter, *cara*," he said, his voice husky.

Caterina's breath caught in her throat. She turned her face up to his, not caring that her cheeks were damp with tears, and brushed her lips against his. This was the response she'd ached for.

She slipped her hand into his, and he clutched her hand to his chest, kissing her through his own tears. Together they walked up-stairs, supporting each other.

Caterina opened the door to her suite. Giovanna and Alma were with Marisa, though the two women were more subdued than they had been.

Santo's eyes lit with joy, and he pressed his hand to his heart. When Marisa turned to him, he sucked in a breath. With her vivid blue eyes, rimmed with dark lashes, there was no denying she was his daughter.

Caterina picked up Marisa, smoothed her blue smock, and brought her to Santo. "It's high time the two of you met."

Marisa cooed, and Santo reached for her. "May I hold her?" His eyes glistened with happiness.

Caterina handed Marisa to Santo, her heart bursting with love at seeing them together. Marisa looked so small in his strong arms. Ca-terina pressed her hands to her mouth, watching as they explored each other's faces, swooning when Santo kissed Marisa on the cheek and murmured endearments in Italian. It was all she'd ever hoped for, though their future together was bleak.

"*Una dolce bambina*." Santo stared at Marisa in awe. "She's the most perfect, beautiful little girl I've ever seen," he said, his voice hoarse with emotion.

Seeing his joyful reaction brought tears to her eyes, too, and Ca-terina was so thankful she'd not gone through with the adoption. *Imagine if I had.* This was the best possible scenario for her daughter. She swallowed against a knot in her throat. Marisa would have her natural mother and father who dearly loved her, even though they might not ever live together as a traditional family.

And then she wondered how she could possibly endure the pain of seeing Santo but not being with him as a lover and mate. Her heart seemed to wither within her at the thought.

She would treasure their time in Paris as a rare jewel. At that time, she had not known their actions were sinful. She'd only known that she loved him as she would never love another. Myriad emotions coursed through her, each an intense wave breaking against the foundation of her soul. Caterina drew a weary hand across her brow, determined to suspend time—and further revelations.

They spent the rest of the day together as a family, and Caterina cherished every moment, framing them in her mind like treasured photographs. They ate lunch on the terrace with Giovanna and Alma, and Santo wanted to know everything about Marisa.

"What does she like to eat? What does she like to play with?"

Caterina forced a smile as he went on, enjoying this simple time together, though sadness permeated every fiber of her being. Santo wanted to know what Marisa's first words were, did she have teeth yet, what day was she born, how much did she weigh, and so many other details, drunk with the sheer delight of being a father. It was all she could have asked for and more than she'd ever imagined.

Or had a right to. Was God giving her a brief respite before the final punishment?

Santo gave Marisa the little blue truck he'd brought home from his old nursery, and they played on the terrace. He held her hand as she tottered through the house, supporting her when she stumbled. That evening, he helped give her a bath and told her a story before putting her to sleep in her crib. With eyes glistening with love, he watched over her until she fell asleep.

Santo's reaction was all Caterina had ever dreamed of. As she sat beside him next to Marisa's crib, he clasped her hand and brought it to his lips.

"We can't change the past," he said. "But we can create our future."

Can we? A wave of sadness coursed through her. She dreaded telling him what their future might really hold.

Caterina and Santo left Marisa and sat at the table on the terrace. Stars blazed in the ebony sky, and the nighttime song of the cicadas echoed through the valley below. He lifted a bottle of red wine that Giovanna had left for them and poured it into two glasses. The wine shimmered in the sepia glow of flickering candles. Caterina gazed into the flames, wondering how to tell Santo of their possible close relationship.

"To our future," Santo said, clinking her glass with his.

"Whatever that might be." She lowered her eyes and sipped.

Santo cocked his head. "Caterina, I have no doubts. I want us to be married. I'd like to spend a few days here in Montalcino—I have some relatives to visit—and then we can return to California."

"But I gave up my apartment, and I can't go back to Mille Étoiles. My mother and I argued about Marisa. She wanted me to give her up."

After swirling and sipping, Santo took her hand and caressed it against his cheek. "I'm so glad you didn't. Then come to Davis with me. I have a small garage apartment. It's not much, but I've been saving a lot of money. We can find a larger place. In fact, I've had my eye on something. We can be married as soon as we arrive."

Caterina studied the wine in her glass for a long moment. "Santo, I need some time." *Time to discover the truth.*

"What do you mean?" He encircled her with his arm.

Caterina wished she could wipe clean the slate of the past, but her father's ill deeds seemed destined to haunt her unless she could prove otherwise. Santo wore such an expression of love; she couldn't bear to share such potentially devastating news until she knew for certain they were related. *Or not.*

"As long as I'm here, I want to learn more about my family. Why don't you go ahead without us, and we'll follow when we can." She'd been thinking about who she could talk to who might have information about Luca and Natalie. Doctors, priests, family members, friends. *Who might know?*

He groaned in disappointment. "I'll hate leaving without you, but it will give me time to make preparations." He touched his lips to hers. "I'll miss you. I wish we could share a bed tonight, my love."

"You know we can't do that in Giovanna's home." She smiled. "It's not proper, especially with *your* daughter beside us. You have a lot to learn about being a father."

"I think it will come naturally." He pulled her to his side, and she rested her head on his shoulder as they watched the night sky, hesitant to return to their separate rooms.

Caterina ached in the depths of her being. Was the story Imelda and Susana told her true? How would she ever know for certain?

Worse, whichever path she chose, if she were wrong, she would ruin their lives.

28

Caterina leaned against Santo as he laughed and talked with his cousins, aunts, and uncles, enjoying the lively banter. They were visiting Santo's aunt Rosa, his mother's younger sister, in her modest Tuscan villa, which was nestled into the hillside and offered vast panoramic views. Unlike Caterina's own relatives, Santo's extended family had welcomed her into the family fold. Santo had lived with several of them before he'd been sent to America just before the war to live with another branch of the family. Although he was so young he didn't remember much about his relatives, they had quickly embraced him.

All of Santo's relatives were in good spirits and happy to see him again. The red wine was flowing, the phonograph was blaring Italian love songs, and everyone was eager to hear about Santo's life in America.

Rosa touched Caterina on the shoulder. "Come with me," she said, smiling broadly. "I have something very special to show you."

Santo winked at Caterina as she left the kitchen, where he lingered behind, talking and laughing with his cousins. Caterina followed his aunt into a bedroom.

Rosa creaked open the door to an antique armoire, which was inlaid with an intricate pattern of blond and dark woods. The aroma of dried violets and lavender wafted from the interior. Reaching far into the wardrobe, Rosa drew out a long ivory dress of silk and lace with care. The design was simple and flowing but obviously made with an expert hand.

At once, Caterina knew what it was. "Natalie's wedding dress?"

Rosa nodded, her eyes brimming with cherished memories. "She was a lovely bride. Angelic, innocent, happy. I miss her sweet smile, her quick laughter." A wistful expression creased her face. She lifted the dress to Caterina's shoulders and the dress grazed the floor. "Please, try it on. For me. It would make me so, so happy." Her face bloomed with anticipation.

Caterina couldn't refuse her hostess. She unzipped her white eyelet shift dress and stepped out of it. While she lifted her arms, Rosa held the dress over Caterina's head and let it fall over her slip. The older woman let out a cry and clasped her hands to her ample bosom.

Caterina turned to face the age-mottled, mirrored doors of the armoire. She sucked in her breath at her reflection. All at once, she was transported to the 1920s. The silk rippled around her calves and puddled on the wooden planked floor. With heels, it would be perfect.

Caterina stroked the smooth, well-preserved silk. Was Santo conceived the night Natalie shed this dress and made love to her husband? Or, if the gossip was true, was she already with child?

"You should have this dress," Rosa said, her eyes dancing with delight. "Maybe you'll wear it for your marriage to Natalie's son. It would be poetic, yes?"

"I would be so honored." Caterina was in awe of Rosa's offer.

Rosa framed Caterina's face in her hands and kissed her on each cheek. "I know you'll make a warm, loving home for Natalie's handsome boy and her grandchildren. She would have loved you so much."

If only it can be so.

An idea clicked in Caterina's mind. "Do you have any of her letters or writings?"

Rosa pursed her lips in thought. "I don't know."

Caterina clasped her hands. "It would mean so much to Santo, and to me, to read anything she might have written. Even a diary or journal." *Especially that.*

"I'll look, but it was so long ago."

Caterina hesitated. Did she dare ask Rosa about Luca? It might be considered rude, but she was desperate for information. "Rosa, did you ever hear a rumor about Natalie and Luca Rosetta?"

The smile slipped from Rosa's face. "It was gossip, that's all it was. We don't talk about that in this house. It couldn't have been true."

However, Rosa's physical reaction belied her words. Caterina clutched Rosa's hands, pleading with her. "Please, if you know anything, tell me. It's vitally important to us."

Rosa's face paled, and she waved a hand in resignation. "Luca boasted of an incident before Natalie and Franco married. Our father was livid. He threatened Luca's life."

Caterina closed her eyes. "What reason did he have?"

"No, I can't speak of it." Rosa spoke with vehemence. "It was a tragedy."

"Tell me if I'm right. It had to do with Luca and Natalie?" When Rosa nodded, Caterina pressed on. "I hate to ask, but we must know the truth. Did he compromise her before her wedding?"

Rosa's eyes misted. As memories filled her thoughts, she touched the fine lace on the dress Caterina still wore. "Natalie denied it, but she wasn't the type to cause trouble. She was afraid for her papa and for her fiancé. Franco would've had to avenge her honor."

"But *you* believe Luca took advantage of her, don't you?"

"I don't know." Rosa pressed a hand against her finely lined forehead. "That was such a long time ago. Let it go, *tesoro.*"

Caterina embraced her. But now she was more determined than ever to know the truth.

The summer cry of crickets chirped across the Tuscan hillsides, filling the air with pastoral song. Caterina placed Marisa in a wooden high chair and pulled her to the dining table on the terrace. Marisa had been fussy ever since Santo had left to return to California.

They'd had a few wonderful days visiting his family and taking in the sights of Tuscany. Santo showered Marisa with love, and she was immediately drawn to him as if she knew he was her father. Now, understandably, she missed her daddy, as did her mother.

Caterina sat down to dinner with Giovanna and Alma. Giovanna had prepared crostini, followed by pappardelle with porcini mushrooms and artichokes, salad, and *pollo alla cacciatore*. Caterina complimented Giovanna on the pasta and chicken.

She diced pasta and vegetables for Marisa, who was feeding herself fairly well with her hands and usually managed to get most of her food in her mouth. Even with a bib, she still needed a good wipe-down after mealtimes, though. Caterina couldn't help smiling at the pasta stuck to Marisa's nose.

"It's so quiet without Santo now." Giovanna slid an inquisitive look toward Caterina. "You didn't tell him about Luca and Natalie, did you?"

"Not yet. I must know for certain." Would she ever know for sure? She felt sick just thinking about that, but there *had* to be someone who would know. "I spoke to his aunt Rosa, but she couldn't tell me much—at least nothing I could verify. She promised not to say anything to Santo yet. Who in the village might help me discover true Santo's parentage?"

"We can make some discreet inquiries in town," Giovanna replied.

Alma fidgeted with her food and arched a brow. "I don't normally listen to gossip, but there's a lot of talk."

"Have you heard anything about *him*?" Caterina picked a mushroom from Marisa's lap. She hated to acknowledge Luca as her father now. If she ever found him, would he tell her the truth about his relationship with Natalie?

Visibly uncomfortable, Giovanna shot a look at Alma and then took a long sip of wine.

"Nothing new," Alma said. "The old women are dredging up ancient gossip. Some things never change."

Changing the subject, Giovanna said, "I'd love for you to stay and help with our grape harvest. We could create wine tastings for guests. You just won a major wine competition, so people will trust your opinion. You can work with us."

Alma added, "And I can watch Marisa, dear. I often look after my grandchildren. One more is no trouble."

Caterina sucked in a breath. "Do you really mean that?"

"We insist," Giovanna said. "You're family, my dear. You and Marisa are welcome to stay here as long as you'd like. You'll need time to make the cottage fit to live in and get on your feet."

"You have no idea how grateful I am," Caterina said, relief flooding her. It was almost the best outcome she could hope for, besides a future with Santo. Her eyes glistening, she hugged the two women. She couldn't help but wish she had such an easy relationship with her own mother.

Their offers were generous, and Caterina was deeply touched. If she confirmed that she and Santo were half siblings—and she'd never rest until she knew—she would remain in Montalcino. She couldn't bear to live near him in California. How could they possibly see each other and yet never express their love in the most intimate way as they had before? To live that way would break their hearts. Just thinking about it caused a hard lump to form in her throat.

And then there was Marisa. Though her little girl would miss her father, he could visit her.

Still, she could save money and start her own wine label. Although fate had not been kind, she could make Montalcino their home. But what if people here discovered Marisa's heritage? Would Marisa's illegitimate status be received here? If the word got out, it might be even worse than in America. Only Giovanna and Alma understood. Was there anywhere they could go to be accepted? She heaved a ragged sigh. *Once people find out . . .* She shook her head. She already knew the answer to that.

Caterina pulled closer to the table, scraping her chair against the stone floor. "Giovanna, I have a confession to make. In my room, I found some old letters from my mother addressed to you. I read up to the point where my mother was on her way to San Francisco and Napa, and I was appalled by Luca's treatment of her."

Alma nodded. "We all were."

"Did you ever hear from her again?"

Giovanna looked thoughtful. "Ava wrote after you were born and often sent photos, but we lost touch during the war."

"You knew she and Luca split up. Didn't she write to you about that?"

"Some history deserves to remain buried." Giovanna's voice was tinged with warning.

"I can't get my mother's letters out of my mind. I need to know what happened next. Were we ever a family? Why did Luca leave?"

Giovanna shot a look at Alma. "Let the past be past, Caterina. Luca is out of your life. Be thankful for that." Giovanna touched Caterina's shoulder with compassion. "Leave your father alone, dear."

But Caterina had many questions, and she couldn't get Luca and Natalie out of her mind. *Was it only a rumor, or was there truth to it?* Caterina felt sick to her stomach just thinking about it.

"If you're going to be up for a while, I'll go up and put Marisa to bed," Alma said.

"I'd appreciate that." Caterina cleaned Marisa's hands and face with her napkin and then kissed her good night.

The two sisters left with Marisa to retire to their rooms. Caterina sat alone on the stone patio gazing dully over rolling hills and distant mountains. The sun had dipped beneath the horizon, and scattered pinholes of light pierced the darkness beneath her as hearths were illuminated and terraces lit. The night was young for summer in Italy, but Caterina felt as old as the mountains.

She wished she could confront her father and vent her anger toward him. Why couldn't he have been the father she needed? Instead, his irresponsible actions may have decimated her life and the lives of those she loved the most.

Caterina stood and paced the length of the terrace. She wrapped her arms around her torso, aching at Santo's absence. An owl called out, and she turned. Through the open doors, a shaft of moonlight caught her eye, illuminating Violetta's portrait. Her grandmother's vibrant eyes seemed to bore into Caterina, willing her on.

Over the next few days, Caterina tried to learn more details of the relationship between Luca and Natalie. She visited the elderly doctor who had arrived too late to save Natalie, but he could not shed any light on who the father might have been, other than Franco. In fact, he was indignant that she might believe the gossip that had been circulating.

She also tracked down a priest who remembered Luca and Natalie and Franco. He patiently explained that he could not divulge details from private confessions. Caterina couldn't tell him why she was asking, because she didn't want Marisa to be ostracized in the event they remained in Italy.

She called on one of Santo's cousins she'd met, but again, the woman offered little enlightenment other than she'd heard the rumors, too. In the end, no one could confirm or deny her suspicion.

After her last visit to the village, Caterina decided to pay her respects to the grandmother she wished she'd known. She carried Marisa and walked to the ancient Rosetta family cemetery down the lane from the villa. Clouds dotted the sky, and a warm wind whipped across the face of the hillside, tangling her full skirt around her legs and spinning dry dust into the air.

Caterina opened an iron gate, which squeaked on its rusted hinges. Blackbirds squawked from the stone walls surrounding the patch of land. Olive trees swayed overhead, and purple iris quivered on their stalks. She found the fresh grave of Violetta Romagnoli Rosetta and stood behind the stone.

"Here is your great-granddaughter," Caterina said, smoothing Marisa's hair. Her little girl smiled brightly and reached out to touch the shiny marble headstone.

Holding Marisa's hand, Caterina knelt on the ground by Violetta's grave site and thought about the tragedy of the murder. A good man died, Violetta lost a son, Ava banished a husband, and Caterina never knew her father. Now she understood why Ava had severed all ties in Italy.

For Caterina, understanding the past was an important step on her journey. She had come to Italy to learn more about her murky ancestry, and she had accomplished that. Though she hadn't found the warm, welcoming family she'd hoped for, Giovanna and Alma had filled the void. She felt as close to them as if they were family. She'd also discovered more of the truth. A few parts were still lacking, but she'd find no more answers here.

A phrase that had passed through her mind when she'd first seen Violetta's painting floated to her consciousness again. *Out of mistakes grows wisdom.* Perhaps Violetta was speaking to her again.

She bowed her head and said a prayer for Violetta. She thanked her for her bequest to her for the cottage and for the vineyard that still flourished, and then she rose and kissed the polished headstone.

Marisa watched her with a curious gaze. When Caterina turned to her, Marisa held her arms out and uttered a single new word, "Hug?"

"Oh, yes, hugs, hugs, hugs, my precious girl. I love you so much,"

Caterina said, embracing her little girl until she thought her heart would burst. There was nothing she wouldn't do for her daughter.

She was a Rosetta, and family was as important to her as it had been to Violetta. As much as she'd grown to love Italy and knew she'd return, she suddenly realized her home—and especially Marisa's—was in the vineyards of California.

Caterina had grown up without a father, and she'd desperately missed his presence. However, she was still determined to find answers. If she did, and the worst occurred, she would shutter her heart to allow Marisa to have a relationship with Santo. She *must* give her daughter the gift of a father, especially one who so loved and adored her.

As Caterina turned over the conundrum of Santo's parentage, she realized only one person remained who might confirm or deny the rumors.

Caterina clutched the telephone in Giovanna's study, waiting for the international operator to put her through to Napa.

"Are you sure this is what you want?" Giovanna said, frowning.

Caterina nodded. "I'm sure. But I don't know if I'll be welcome."

"Try her. Ava might surprise you." Giovanna patted her shoulder. "But if not, you're welcome to stay."

The line was ringing now. She hoped her mother would answer.

"Remember, Ava had good intentions. Life isn't perfect; we merely try to make the best decisions we can at the moment." Giovanna kissed her forehead. "I've loved having you and Marisa here, and I hope you'll return soon," she added before she left the room.

Caterina would miss Giovanna and Alma and all that she'd grown to love in Italy. The line clicked several times, and Caterina held her breath. *Out of mistakes grows wisdom,* she repeated to herself.

But had enough time passed for such seeds to sprout?

"Hello, Mille Étoiles." Ava's strained voice sounded like it emanated from the bottom of an empty vat.

Caterina sat on the edge of her chair and sucked in a nervous breath before she spoke. "Maman, it's Caterina."

A seemingly interminable pause ensued as the telephone line clicked, carrying her voice across the sea, the plains, the mountains. Her heart pounded in wait.

"*Ma chérie!*" Ava exclaimed, her voice thick with emotion. "I'm so happy you called."

Caterina clasped the receiver with white knuckles. She could hear her mother choking up on the other end of the line, and her eyes misted, too.

Caterina found her voice. "We've had our disagreements, and I love Italy, but I've been thinking—"

"Please come home, *chérie*. I've missed you . . . and I'd like to get to know my granddaughter."

"Oh yes, Maman, yes, I'd like that very much." She sniffed through her own tears. When she assured her they would be home soon, Ava sobbed with happiness. *This will be a fresh beginning for all of us.*

"Maman, there's one more thing I must know before we arrive. Is Luca still around?" The line was so quiet Caterina thought it might be dead.

Finally, Ava spoke. "I believe so. You'll need to be careful, Caterina."

Caterina hung up the phone. Luca was the last person in the world she cared to confront, but there was no other way to find the truth. Only then could she and Santo determine the course of their lives.

NAPA, CALIFORNIA

The next day, Ava woke to a flurry of telephone calls.

She'd been taking calls all day in her office overlooking the vineyards of Mille Étoiles. She balanced the receiver on her shoulder as she spoke. "The wine was blended by my daughter, Caterina Rosetta, and Santo Casini." After a few minutes, she finished the sales call and hung up. She made a note in a file and added it to a stack of other folders.

She'd been so relieved and excited that Caterina had called. *And she's coming home with Marisa.* She had so much to do, but the phone rang yet again.

"Hello, Mille Étoiles Wines. How may I help you?" She picked up her pen to make notes or write a purchase order as she spoke.

Evidently, an article in *The New York Times* had announced that their wine won highest honors in the exclusive Paris competition. Buyers and collectors had immediately started to call.

She was thrilled that Caterina had achieved such a victory. She was so proud of her.

Juliana was also working hard to publicize the big win, and Ava appreciated her help. The vineyard, the winery, the sales—Mille Étoiles was a lot for her to handle.

They had to borrow or generate funds before harvest. Because of a string of warm days, the grapes were ripening ahead of schedule this year.

"*Merci.* We appreciate your order. Good-bye." Ava leaned back in her chair. She couldn't remember a busier day.

Before she closed the office for the evening, she glanced around, making sure she had tended to everything. She straightened a vase of fresh white daisies near the windows.

As she did, movement in the vineyard below caught her eye. It was dusk, so it was hard to see clearly. She peered from the window. Someone was in the vineyard; she could see a tall man wearing a dark jacket and cap scurrying between rows.

"That's odd." It wasn't Raphael, and the workers started early in the morning. No one was supposed to be in the vineyard now. She sucked her breath in, instantly nervous. *Is it Luca?*

On second thought, it was probably a transient worker who had forgotten one of his tools. The incident with Luca had put her on edge. Nevertheless, she made a mental note to mention this to Raphael.

Her attorney had told her that it was a simple fact that Luca's name was on the deed, no matter how long he had been gone. Nor did it matter that it was her money—her inheritance—that had bought the property.

She shook her head. She might have to say good-bye to her beloved home at Mille Étoiles, but if enough purchase orders came in, they might be able to salvage their livelihood.

Suddenly, the window in front of her exploded in a shower of glass, and something burst against a painting across the room with a thud. Ava screamed and flattened herself against the wall. *What's happening?*

A man's malicious laugh spiraled up through the broken window.

Luca. Ava crawled across the floor, taking care to avoid glass splinters. She lifted the painting, spied a brick on the floor, and stretched toward it. A note was wrapped around it with twine.

She peeled the note off and opened it.

Your time is up, it read.

The next morning, a knock sounded on the door. Ava adjusted her full-skirted navy dress trimmed in white piping and opened the door to an attorney she knew from the village. "Good morning, Russell. What a pleasant surprise. What brings you here so early?"

Russell Glenhall removed his hat and held it to his chest. "May I come in, Ava?" He passed a hand over his thinning gray hair.

"Of course. Would you care for coffee?"

"I'd like that, ma'am."

Ava turned, her low-heeled navy pumps clicking across the wooden floor, and made her way into the dining room, where she often entertained wine buyers and press. The portly attorney followed her.

She poured coffee from a silver pot into thin china cups, sat down at the long, polished table, and folded her hands. "What can I help you with today, Russell?"

One eye twitched, and he rubbed it in irritation. For a moment, he stared at the pink roses in the center of the table before taking a swig of coffee and clearing his throat. "Unfortunately, this is not a pleasant visit, Ava. Luca has retained me and plans to file an eviction notice against you to regain control of his property."

"Eviction?"

"He wants Mille Étoiles. You must vacate the premises."

"I'm not leaving, Russell. This is my home and my business."

He let out a long sigh. "I was afraid that's what you would say." He opened his suit jacket and removed a sheaf of papers from his breast pocket and held them out to her. "In that case, here's Luca's demand." When she didn't move to accept the documents, he hesitated and then placed them on the table before her. "You should have a lawyer look at those, Ava."

"I can read," she snapped, her blood pressure rising. "How dare you intrude upon my goodwill and hospitality to serve me with legal documents. You, sir, are a man without manners."

Frowning in discomfort, he replied, "Ava, I honestly wish it hadn't come to this. Please have an attorney review these and advise you. Luca means business. He thought he was going to receive an inheritance from his mother, or at least a continuance of support from the estate, but he did not. His own mother passed him over in favor of your daughter."

"That's because Violetta was a wise woman. Caterina is more deserving. She won't squander her inheritance." At the thought of her daughter, Ava's despair deepened.

Russell wiped beads of perspiration from his upper lip. "Surely you can understand and be reasonable."

"No. I cannot." Her heart pounding with anger and indignation, Ava drew herself up from her chair. "What I understand is that Luca nearly killed me. Everyone in town saw my bruises, but no one offered to help me then, including you. I found this property, and the money that my father and mother and their ancestors toiled for went to its purchase. Furthermore, I have spent the last two decades building it to what it is today. What did Luca do in the interim years? Clearly, nothing."

Russell struggled wearily to his feet. "Ava, he's still your husband. Maybe I can negotiate a settlement. You can sell Mille Étoiles and divide the profits. I think I can get him to be reasonable."

She gave a bitter laugh. "After he throws bricks through my windows and accosts me on the street? No, I will not negotiate with a man who deals in intimidation. Nor his representative. The answer is no."

Ava walked to the front door and opened it. "Luca will never set foot on Mille Étoiles, and that's final. Good day, Russell."

Later that evening, Ava and Raphael sat down to supper on the patio overlooking the vineyards. The evening breeze brought cool ocean air. Nina had prepared a supper of tomato basil soup, pasta, salad, and baguettes for them before she left to see Juliana.

Raphael poured olive oil onto a plate and sprinkled fresh oregano on it. "Did you speak to your lawyer today?" He broke the bread and dipped it into the oil and then served it to Ava.

"I did." She'd told him about Russell's visit that morning before leaving for Napa. She filled his wineglass with one of their red wines. "Since I won't settle, the case will go to trial."

"Can't imagine folks wouldn't be on your side, Ava."

"It's nice to think that, but the deed is still in Luca's name. As angry as I am, the law is quite clear. My lawyer imparted the facts to me this afternoon. As much as I argued, even I could see that the scales of justice are not tipped in my favor."

"Is there any chance a ruling might go in your favor?"

She cast her eyes down, stricken with despair. "I'm told the best I can hope for is that the property will be sold and divided."

Raphael asked, "How long until the trial?"

"My lawyer said it would be soon." Ava gazed over the vineyard that might be lost to her forever. She knew the property like a mother knows her child. Her eyelids grew heavy with fatigue. Even with her eyes closed, she could conjure every gnarled vine, every hillside slope, every slanting ray of sun, every path of the evening breeze.

With difficulty, she raised her face to Raphael and tried to appear stronger than she was. The thought of starting again, even with Raphael by her side, was utterly overwhelming.

She cleared her throat to speak. "This is my home, my life. *Our life*. Raphael, I don't want to leave Mille Étoiles."

Raphael tilted her chin up and dabbed her glistening eyes with his handkerchief. "If it comes to that, we'll find another property and start over together."

She met his warm brown eyes and smiled through her anguish. Reaching a trembling hand to her wine, she swirled and sipped, thinking about the night she and Luca had fought. "*Merci, mon amour.*" She kissed Raphael on the cheek. *What a good, kind man he is.* And so much more.

Without hesitation, Raphael turned in to meet her lips and drew a hand along her cheek. When they finally drew apart, Ava could hardly catch her breath. For years she'd wondered what it would be like to kiss him. *What a fool I've been to wait.* In just a moment, the darkness of her world was splintered with a ray of hope. With aching need unreleased, she ran her hands through his hair and pulled him to her again.

"Mmm," Raphael murmured. "Do you know how long I've waited for this, *amore mio?*"

"As long as I have. And it was far too long."

An unspoken vow passed between them. He held her in his arms, offering his comfort and love without reserve and caressing her skin with utmost tenderness. "*Sei la mia anima gemella.*"

She touched his forehead with her own. Never had she felt such a connection. Certainly not with Luca. "And you're my soul mate, too."

29

SAN FRANCISCO, CALIFORNIA

Juliana's eyes flashed with excitement as the red-capped airport porter hoisted Caterina's luggage into her trunk. "Tell me all about your trip before we get to Mille Étoiles. I can't wait to hear more about the wine competition."

Caterina hugged her friend. She'd called Juliana instead of Santo to meet her at the airport because she wanted to speak to her mother before she determined how to proceed with Santo.

She tipped the porter and slid into the front seat with Marisa, who was rubbing her eyes from her long nap on the airplane. It had been an arduous journey on the Boeing 377 Stratocruiser, first from Rome to New York and then from New York to San Francisco. Though it had been strenuous—Marisa was cranky much of the way until she mercifully fell asleep—the most stressful part was yet to come. Would Ava truly welcome them home?

"I'm glad we have a long drive to Napa to talk." Caterina wore her gray traveling suit and had dressed Marisa in a pink-and-green seersucker dress she'd bought at a children's shop in Paris. She wanted her little girl to look special for her first meeting with her grandmother. She brushed wrinkles from Marisa's pretty cotton dress.

Juliana started the engine. "I want to hear everything." As she pulled into traffic, Marisa bobbed her head at the window, wide-eyed at the other cars whizzing past.

Caterina told Juliana about Giovanna and the reading of the will. "And then I went to Paris for the competition." Her time in Paris had been like a precious dream she would hold in her heart forever, but one that might dissipate in the stark light of day if examined too closely.

"And?" Juliana arched an eyebrow and looked as if she would burst.

"Santo and I had a wonderful time, but we have a lot of things to work out first." She couldn't bring herself to tell Juliana about the possibility that Luca might have fathered Santo until she knew more. And obtaining that information would be dangerous. "I didn't realize how much I would miss him after he left." Without Santo, it was as if her soul had withered.

Juliana slid a sharp look toward Caterina. "How do you think your mom will take the little one this time?"

"She sounded different on the phone. I found some letters she'd written years ago. Those letters revealed a chilling past I never knew existed. Whatever she did, she did with good intentions." Caterina told her about what she'd learned about her father.

"That's incredible. I'm so sorry, Cat." Juliana shook her head. "But I have good news. While you were trotting around the globe and winning awards, your mother and I have been working hard."

"Doing what?"

"You have no idea what happened, do you?" Juliana laughed. "If it's any consolation, the last few days have been unbelievable. When you called me from Paris, you told me you met a reporter for *The New York Times* at the competition. Well, guess what? She immediately wrote an article about the event for the newspaper highlighting the Mille Étoiles win, and holy cow, the phone started ringing. Your mom and I have been on the phone nonstop."

"*What?*"

"That's right." Juliana winked at her. "Your plan worked. Mille Étoiles ain't dead yet. And neither are you."

"That's wonderful. I'm so relieved. It's a beginning, at least." A speck of hope warmed Caterina's chest. She glanced at Juliana, who was blushing and fidgeting. "Okay, Jules, what else do you have to report?"

"I met someone." Juliana wiggled in her seat with excitement. "His name is Henry, and he has a vineyard up valley."

"Really? What's he like?"

"He's such a sweetheart." She shot a look at Caterina. "He's a widow with two little children. But he's not Mexican, so he'll really have to work to win over my mother."

"Then it's serious?"

"I really like him a lot. He's not Al, but he's pretty special." Juliana raised her brow. "But I still don't know about this whole marriage thing."

"Have you told your mom anything?"

"Are you kidding? That can wait."

Caterina laughed. She could just imagine what Nina would have to say.

Juliana turned into the long entry to Mille Étoiles and drove past the gate that bore the star-studded grapevine logo. Having just returned from France and Italy, Caterina was struck anew by the appearance of Mille Étoiles. The architecture really did resemble some of the châteaux she'd seen traveling through France to Paris.

Her mother had tried to re-create the life she'd once known and loved. Caterina now understood her penchant for pâté over hot dogs, brioche over biscuits. As they neared the front entrance, Caterina spotted Ava. Her hair was swept from her face, and she wore her vineyard work clothes—pressed blue dungarees cuffed at the ankle and a crisp white cotton shirt. She looked chic with a red bandanna tied around her neck at a jaunty angle. Only Ava could make ordinary work clothes look so stylish.

Juliana eased her large Chevrolet sedan to a stop in front of the house. "I'll go around the back and find my mother. I want to keep out of the line of fire, just in case."

"Chicken," Caterina said, teasing her.

Juliana laughed. "She's your mother, not mine. Mine's bad enough. Now that she knows about Marisa, she's been pestering me about babies."

Caterina straightened Marisa's pink hair ribbon and scooped the little girl into her arms. She could feel Marisa's little heartbeat pounding like a hummingbird's in her chest; her own heart mirrored the rapid rhythm. Ava might have approved of her return, but it didn't mean she wouldn't have tough questions.

"Welcome back, *ma chérie,*" Ava called out. She tented a hand against the high summer sun to shade her eyes.

"Hello, Maman."

Ava took a tentative step toward her.

As Caterina approached, she could see turmoil etched on Ava's face. A moment later she stood face-to-face with her mother, though Ava said not a word. Marisa reached out and touched Ava's bright red bandanna and cooed with curiosity.

At that, Ava burst out sobbing and flung her arms around the two of them, and soon Caterina was crying with relief, too.

When they finally went into the house, Ava sank onto the sofa in the living room and patted a spot beside her. "You should have told me sooner, *chérie.*"

"I knew how you'd react," Caterina said, clutching Marisa as she sat down. "And I was ashamed to tell you."

Ava shook her head with sorrow. "Forgive me for being unapproachable."

"I do, but I wish I'd known about my father."

"That's fair. I should have told you sooner. But he's such an evil man, Caterina. I didn't want to hurt you, and I didn't know if you would understand."

"I do now. I found some letters you wrote years ago to Giovanna. You went through so much with him. You did what you had to do."

Ava gulped a breath. "I decided it was better to lie to you, to construct a story of a loving father who'd died in an accident, than to tell you the truth—or worse, to let him have any contact with you. I became overprotective, determined that you would not make the same mistakes I had. I admit it was wrong of me, but at the time, it made sense."

Caterina pressed a hand against her forehead and then wiped her hand against her gray skirt as if to rub off the memory of her father. "I'm glad I know now, Maman."

Caterina fell silent, remembering the stories her mother had told over the years. She thought of how her mother had reacted to the news of her inheritance. The mysteries of her childhood and her mother's actions made more sense to her now.

Ava stroked Marisa's fine curls. "May I hold her?" Caterina handed Marisa to her, and Ava hugged the little girl to her breast as Marisa smiled up at her. "She's an angel," Ava murmured. "What beautiful eyes she has." She inclined her head, as if trying to recall a memory.

Caterina held her breath. Could she see Santo in Marisa's eyes?

Ava shook her head and went on, "For years I was worried you'd have the same difficulty conceiving that I did. I never wanted you to go through that." As Ava gazed down at Marisa, her lashes were feathered with moisture, and a smile lit her face.

Questions still burned in Caterina's mind. She had to know more. "What happened to your first child, Maman?"

"Oh, my poor baby." Ava cast her eyes heavenward and sighed. "Luca came home drunk one hot summer evening in Italy, and I asked him where he had been. It angered him, and he hit me."

Caterina rubbed her temples. "Were you injured?"

"I suffered a head injury, and I lost the baby. I was devastated. Luca stormed off, so Violetta nursed me through that agonizing evening. Later, Luca never believed I had lost the baby. He actually convinced himself I wasn't pregnant and I had tricked him into marriage."

Her mother had never shared this part of her life before. Imagining her as a frightened teenager in a foreign country made Caterina's heart go out to her. She had to ask, "Why did you stay with him?"

"By being pregnant before marriage, I had already committed one grave sin. I was determined to make the marriage work. In the beginning, I was in love—or thought I was. If I divorced, I couldn't marry in the church again. I'd always dreamed of having a large family." Marisa grasped Ava's finger, and she smiled at the little girl. "I had a long talk with the priest about it."

Caterina listened, wondering what she would have done. It was easy to think of oneself as being brave in a situation as long as the troubles belong to another. Here she was, a mother who had hid her child for fear of what? Being disowned? Being judged? It hardly compared to the terror her mother had lived through.

"I know about Natalie and Franco. Santo's parents."

Ava asked softly, "Do you know how they died?"

"I do."

"Natalie was beautiful, but she was frail of health." Ava's eyes held a faraway look, and she rocked Marisa in her arms. "I didn't know it when I married your father, but Luca had always been in love with Natalie."

"Mama, Mama, Mama," Marisa said, waving her hands.

Caterina leaned back, a single question burning in her mind. Did her mother know the truth of Santo's parentage? Or had she only heard the rumors? Caterina passed a hand over her face. Only Luca could answer that question.

Ava seemed relieved to have unburdened herself of her long-buried secrets. She looked up at Caterina and smiled sadly—a good, true smile that Caterina had seldom seen growing up. But there was more in her mother's eyes; it was the strange calm of forgiveness Caterina had once thought alien to Ava's constitution. She had truly accepted Marisa.

They were a family again. Caterina placed a hand over her mother's, but she was surprised to feel her quivering. It wasn't just their conversation that had upset Ava; Caterina detected something more. She pressed on. "Have you heard from Luca again?"

Fear flashed in Ava's eyes.

Caterina's heart beat faster. "Has he tried to hurt you again?"

"He threw a brick with a note attached to it through the window." Ava squeezed Caterina's hand. "It was a warning to leave Mille Étoiles."

Caterina widened her eyes. "We're not going to, are we?" When Ava didn't respond, she gazed around the room. This was their home.

"He has filed suit to take over Mille Étoiles. But we will not leave without a fight. Raphael has men guarding the property."

"How did this happen?"

Ava furrowed her brow. "The short version? Luca's name is on the deed, not mine. But it was my money, and we've made Mille Étoiles the success it is today. Not him. But should we lose, we'll have a chance to rebuild elsewhere, thanks to your win in Paris." Ava managed a brave smile.

Caterina saw worry on her mother's face. Luca wanted vengeance, and he'd stop at nothing. Which did he care more about—claiming Mille Étoiles or seeing Ava suffer? He was much more dangerous than she'd thought.

A chilling portent seized Caterina.

30

Ava parked her car around the corner from a children's shop in Napa, glancing nervously around her for signs of Luca as she hurried into the boutique.

Raphael had found Caterina's old baby crib in the attic, and Caterina had brought a few outfits and toys with her, but Ava knew her new granddaughter needed so much more. She purchased several sets of bedding, a half dozen summer outfits, and a few toys and stuffed animals she couldn't resist. *And why not?* she thought proudly, forcing her thoughts from Luca. *I'm her grandmother.*

While the clerk wrapped her purchases, Ava strolled around the shop. She stopped in front of a mirror to adjust the narrow belt on the full-skirted ivory linen sundress she wore. When she'd bought it in San Francisco, the salesclerk had assured her it didn't look too young for her. She loved it, but she didn't want to look ridiculous.

Especially now that she was a grandmother.

For a woman in her forties, Ava knew she still looked fairly good. The physical work in the vineyard kept her trim. She touched a diamond-studded brooch she'd pinned to the lapel on the matching jacket. The brooch was a cascading spray of sparkling stars. Her heart quickened as she thought of the day, not so long ago, that she'd received this most precious gift. *Not for Mille Étoiles,* Raphael had said, *but for the stars in your eyes.* She'd never known such a kind man.

Ava was pleased and relieved that Caterina had returned with her baby. She'd been shocked when Caterina had first told her, but her daughter had already suffered enough because of her stubborn attitude, and Ava had missed out on the joy of witnessing the birth of her first grandchild. *If God forgives mistakes,* she thought, *so should I.*

Ava checked her watch. She didn't want to be late; she'd been looking forward to her lunch date today. Her religion might forbid remarriage in the church, but it couldn't govern the emotions of the heart. Not for Caterina, and not for her.

Waiting for her packages, she felt a hand on her shoulder and jumped with fright.

"I didn't mean to scare you," Raphael said, his dark eyes twinkling. "I saw your car outside."

Ava was glad to see him. "I've bought the prettiest things for little Marisa—wait until you see them."

"Then I'm just in time." Raphael hooked the bags over his arm, picked up the boxes, and opened the door for Ava. "You look worried. What's wrong?"

"Ever since Luca reappeared, I've been on edge. I jump at the slightest noise now."

She opened the trunk, and Raphael deposited the packages. He shut the lid and turned to her, sunlight framing his face. His white shirt was neatly pressed, and he smelled of citrus and woods. She'd bought a bottle of Acqua di Parma Colonia for him the last time she'd been shopping in San Francisco; the fragrance always reminded her of Italy. Raphael brushed her arm, and a spark of electricity snapped along her nerve endings. "Where would you like to go today?"

"Remember that pretty little lake high in the mountains near Sonoma?"

Ava nodded. "I'd like that." She slipped into his truck beside him.

He fired the engine and turned onto a street that led through the old downtown section of Napa. No one in the village thought anything about seeing the two of them together. Everyone knew they ran Mille Étoiles together and had for many years.

At first, after Luca had gone, there had been supposition about their relationship, but Ava made sure that she was the most pious, principled woman in town. The gossip soon ceased. Furthermore, nothing was happening between them at the time.

Now, no one suspected them anymore—or if they did, no one cared.

Once, Ava had wondered why Raphael stayed. He was an attractive man, and he could've had any number of women who'd been interested in him over the years. He seemed settled at Mille Étoiles, satisfied with the relationship she had once dictated. Lately, though, something had shifted within her. She was no longer content with . the status quo.

Raphael glanced at her as he drove through the countryside. "So has little Marisa stolen your heart?"

"Completely," she said simply. "I regret having treated Caterina as I did." They climbed in elevation, and the temperature dropped. She shook her hair in the cool breeze from the open window.

"And what's different now?"

"While she was in Italy, I had a lot of time to think about my mistakes and how I'd hurt people because of them."

"Caterina will forgive you." Raphael touched her hand. "But you've missed out on life, too."

After bumping over a dirt path, they arrived at the lake and stepped from the truck. A variety of indigenous trees—oak, maple, and laurel—surrounded the clear azure lake. Their branches rustled with remnants of Pacific Ocean breezes that wafted across the mountains and valleys.

Raphael helped Ava from the truck. He tucked a plaid blanket and a bottle of wine under his arm and picked up a brown paper grocery bag filled with hard salami, parmesan cheese, and sourdough bread.

Glancing around to make sure they were alone, Ava spread the blanket near the water's edge. She arranged their lunch on plates she'd brought while Raphael opened the wine and poured two glasses. They stretched out on the blanket, eating together in comfortable silence and watching the forest wildlife. They did this every couple of weeks, as long as the weather was pleasant. They got away, spent time together, and talked about the vineyard, harvests, and wine.

A glossy green-headed mallard duck paddled through the water, and Raphael tossed bread crumbs to him. The drake bobbed and gulped the crusty bread. "So you had a few revelations, did you?" Raphael threw another bit for the drake's brown hen.

Ava hesitated for a few moments. "I regret being so strict with Caterina."

"She grew up to be a fine young lady, though. She had you to thank for that."

"My temper was quick. I was harsh, often without justification. I wanted a better life for her. Not just better than what I had; I wanted her to have the very best. She was always a good girl, always tried to do the right thing."

"Smart, too."

"So is Santo. You did well by him."

"He's doing well for himself. Building quite a business in Davis. Don't see him much anymore—he travels a lot." He tossed more crumbs to the pair of mallards. "Know who the father is?"

"She still hasn't said. It's someone from school. The name will come out in time. I'll be patient." *As long as it isn't Santo.* Surely Caterina would have told her if he were the father. And if he were, how would she ever tell Caterina the truth? And yet, Marisa's eyes were so like Santo's. But plenty of people had vivid blue eyes, didn't they?

Raphael scattered the remaining crumbs on the water's surface. "What else is in your book of regrets?"

Ava sipped her wine. One of her deepest regrets was sitting right beside her. Instead of lamenting her shortcomings, she lifted her chin with defiance. "I definitely regret not shooting Luca."

He laughed and shooed a fly from her food. "You told me that gun wasn't loaded."

"It wasn't, but he didn't know that." She smirked with satisfaction. "That's the only reason he left." She glanced around, still nervous that he was in the vicinity.

Raphael sliced off a few slivers of salami and cheese for her. "Wish I'd known more then. Could've done a better job of protecting you."

"It wasn't your place at the time." She shaded her face from the sun and gazed into his eyes. "But I'm glad you're here now."

Raphael shifted to block the sun from her eyes. "We'll face Luca together this time." He poured another splash of wine into her glass.

Ava swirled her wine and slanted her glass toward the sunlight, inspecting it out of habit. There were so many things she wanted to say to Caterina and Raphael. Even Santo. "Know what else I regret?"

Raphael tossed a few more crumbs in the water. "What?"

"Us. Why didn't we follow our hearts a long time ago?"

"You know why." Raphael frowned. "Even if you'd divorced Luca, we couldn't have married in the church. That's important to you."

That was true, she thought sadly. "Except for Santo, I always thought you missed having children of your own. Look at how much we denied ourselves. Do you really think God would have minded that much?"

He smiled down at her. "I came to terms with the restrictions on our relationship many years ago. You know how I feel about you, and that's all that matters. I made a promise to you long ago. I'll never leave you, Ava."

She slid a hand around his neck and pulled him closer to her. His breath was warm on her face. Closing her eyes, she kissed him on the lips and felt a connection flame between them.

A few minutes later, Raphael pulled away. "We should get back," he said, his voice husky.

Nina, I'm home," Caterina called out when she returned to Mille Étoiles. Nina had been watching Marisa that morning while she was in the city meeting with Elsa Williams, president of the Women's Commercial Bank, by referral from the First Lady of California, for whom she'd planned a dinner at the St. Francis Hotel before she'd left for Italy.

Ava had asked her to call for help. Fortunately, Caterina had been able to meet with the banker right away. The meeting had gone well, and to her relief, Elsa had asked for more details about their wine operation. The bank was one of the few options for women in business, since most other banks required a man's co-signature.

The air was rich with the aroma of Nina's fresh-baked bread. The scent reminded her of Giovanna and of the delicious bakeries she and Santo had found in Paris. Since her return, her heart had been heavy with memories of their time together. As far as she knew, Santo didn't know she'd returned; he was away on a business trip. She had a few days before she had to face him. How could she continue a relationship with him until she knew the truth?

She still needed to talk to her mother. Tonight, if she could.

Caterina wound her way into the kitchen and picked up Marisa. "How's my baby girl?"

"Marisa was such a sweetheart." Nina was clearly pleased to have

Marisa there. In fact, having Marisa in the house seemed to lift everyone's spirits.

Caterina held her wiggly young child on her lap and squeezed her tightly with love. Marisa giggled. "Mama hugs, mama hugs."

Nina wiped her floured hands on her apron and poured a glass of iced tea for her. "How about a tuna salad for lunch? I have fresh garden greens in the refrigerator."

"Sounds delicious." Caterina pressed the cool glass of tea to her lips. The heat of the summer was becoming oppressive. "Raphael says that if this heat holds out, we'll be ahead of schedule for the harvest."

Ava walked through the kitchen door, smiling. "Even more reason for you to be here."

Since Caterina had returned to Mille Étoiles with Marisa, Ava and Nina had been bustling about preparing the home for a toddler. Before she arrived, Raphael had put a fresh coat of white paint on her old baby crib and trimmed it with pink accents.

"Where'd you go this morning?" Caterina asked, noticing Ava's pink cheeks. "You got some sun."

"I did some shopping in Napa for Marisa. I bought sheets for the crib and some new toys and outfits for her. I wanted to surprise you."

Ava and Nina were both excited over Marisa, who was toddling around the house now, touching furniture for support as she tore through the rooms.

"Nina and I will finish decorating Marisa's room today," Ava said.

"I just love looking after her." Nina placed a salad in front of Caterina and then resumed her bread-making. She punched down a mound of bread dough. "I don't know if Juliana will ever have children, that stubborn girl." She punched the bread again.

Ava sat next to Caterina. "Tell me about your trip to the city today."

"I met with Elsa Williams at the Women's Commercial Bank. I thought the visit went well. She asked for more detailed projections."

"I know of her, *ma chérie*. She's quite demanding and only accepts the crème de la crème, the best clients to represent. That's why she's successful. I'm glad you met with her." Ava took Marisa and rocked her on her lap. "I can really use your help here. It's important we follow up with wine buyers, too."

Caterina nodded. "And I'll follow up with Elsa Williams. I think she might be willing to lend against our orders for the equipment we need for harvest."

"That would be our salvation," Ava said. "We need to pounce on the news of the Paris win while we can. In a few weeks, we'll be old news. We have to write orders now."

Caterina stabbed a cherry tomato and took a bite of her salad, nodding in agreement.

"Juliana is continuing her press efforts. Every day she calls with a new request for an interview." Ava hesitated. "I'd rather you took that over, Caterina. You should be the new face of Mille Étoiles."

"But you've always been the head of Mille Étoiles."

Ava shook her head. "I can't do it alone anymore. I'm tired. I've been doing this all my life. I love it, but I'd like to live more."

Caterina cocked her head. "What do you mean?"

"I want to do something besides tend grapes before I die." Ava ruffled Marisa's fine dark hair as she spoke. "While you were gone, I realized I haven't really lived."

"How can you say that? You've accomplished more than any other woman in the wine industry," Caterina said, incredulous. "You've helped put California wine on the world map."

"You're young and ambitious, much like I was when I first arrived here. But it was difficult fulfilling the roles of both mother and father, as well as growing a business that's tied to Mother Nature's fickleness. Without a husband, you're going to find that, too."

Caterina bristled at her words. "Times have changed, Maman. You did it, and so can I. I don't need a man by my side any more than you did." Even as she said these bold words, her heart faltered. She'd give anything to have Santo by her side.

"No, you don't." Ava's eyes held a faraway look. "But sometimes, wouldn't it be nice?"

In back of them, Nina huffed. "Overrated, if you ask me."

"We only live once." Ava rested her chin in her hand. "There's something I've been afraid to do. I'm going to correct that."

Caterina threw a look at her mother. Something in her voice sounded strange; she couldn't place it. And then she thought of how she'd felt in Paris—and how she still felt—and in an instant she recognized the quality in Ava's voice.

All her life, she'd never known her mother to be in love.

Did Ava have someone in her life? Did her mother have more secrets?

As Caterina was contemplating this, Raphael opened the door. Caterina glanced up at Raphael, who also had a ruddy tint to his cheeks. She looked back at her mother. A thought flashed across her mind.

Caterina took her plate to the sink. "Delicious lunch, Nina, thank you." She turned and took Marisa from Ava. She paused, gauging her mother's mood, relieved that Ava was happy today. It was imperative she speak to her mother about Luca and Natalie before Santo returned.

"Maman, while Marisa is napping this afternoon, I'd like to talk with you about something important."

31

After Marisa had drifted to sleep for her afternoon nap, Caterina changed into light trousers and a thin shirt for protection against the summer sun. She and Ava set off for a walk through the vineyard. Caterina listened to Ava's updates about the state of the vineyard, waiting for an opportunity to ask her mother about the past.

Raphael had mentioned that Santo was returning soon from working with clients in Southern California. Caterina needed a resolution to their dilemma. Were they half siblings? The mere consideration of it filled her with anxiety. On reflection she wondered, *What if my mother doesn't have a definitive answer?*

"You haven't asked me much about Italy." Caterina plucked a nearly ripe grape and tasted it. Sweetness burst in her mouth. All around them, the scent of ripening fruit permeated the air.

Ava angled her straw hat. "Much of it I'd rather forget. But I miss Giovanna. How is she?"

Caterina told Ava all about Giovanna and Alma and how kind they had been to her and Marisa.

"I'm glad you met them. I was always so fond of them. We used to write with plans of visiting each other, but as the years passed, it wasn't possible. And now, with the trial at hand, they might never see any of this."

Caterina slid a sideways gaze at her mother, assessing her temperament. She had so many questions for Ava she hardly knew where to start. But only one would change the course of her life.

Soon she'd have to talk to Santo. He'd called for her, but she'd been away each time. "Why does Luca hate us so much?" Caterina asked.

Ava kicked a patch of dirt with the heel of her boot. "What does it matter now?"

"I have to know why he is trying to destroy us." Caterina pressed on. This time, she would not be deterred. "He's my father. I need to know everything, Maman."

Her mother paused in a clearing and gazed over the valley below, which was ribboned with row crops and vineyards. "I suppose it's time to unburden my heart. I hope you'll forgive me. My attorney tells me much of this might also come out in the trial, so I'd rather you heard it from me first."

Anguish washed across Ava's face as she stared into the distance, prying open a rusty-hinged door to her memories. "You were the child I had prayed for—you were a precious baby girl, my Caterina Marguerite Rosetta. You were an eternal delight, and I don't know what I would have done without you, *ma chérie.*"

Caterina needed more from her mother. "In your last letter to Giovanna, you were planning to go to San Francisco alone. What happened after you arrived?"

Coming out of her trance-like stare, Ava brushed windblown rose petals from her white cotton blouse and nodded to herself. "First, I set out to Napa—it was a tiny village then—to meet my grandfather's friend. I told him exactly what I was looking for, and he showed me a parcel of land that would be superb for cultivating grapes for wine."

"This land."

"Yes, it was. When I saw how the land rolled across mountainous slopes so high above the fog line, much like Montalcino, I felt such an immediate, strong affinity toward this property. I arranged to purchase it right away. With the old vineyard and land for expansion, it was perfect. That day I spent so long walking the property that the sun set, and soon a thousand stars blanketed the sky—for that reason, I christened it Mille Étoiles."

Caterina touched her mother's hand. She'd heard part of this story before, except in the prior version, Ava and Luca had found the property together. "When did Luca join you?"

"Within a few weeks. His money ran out, and he left New York City to find me. The day he arrived, I was terribly ill with influenza and expected at the attorney's office to finalize the documents for the purchase of the property. Of course, I was shivering with fever and couldn't move from my sickbed, so I gave Luca a power of attorney to sign the documents in my name."

"But he didn't do that, did he?"

Ava shook her head. "Later, when I found out, I wanted my name added to the documents, but he refused to do so. No one would help me. It was 1929; I was nineteen and a foreigner in this country. It was simply the way things were done."

Even today. After having felt like an outsider in Italy, Caterina could easily imagine her mother's situation.

"When I felt better, I began to sketch a smaller version of my parents' château in Bordeaux for the architect. Our first vintage from the old vines was a success. We were fortunate; Luca charmed everyone he met, and soon we gained contracts to supply wine to churches and synagogues during Prohibition. Not everyone was as lucky; a neighbor of ours, a woman whose husband died of a weak heart, made deliveries of her special cosmetic creams and ointments to the fashionable ladies of San Francisco every week. I suspect her delivery truck contained more wine than creams, but with Prohibition winding down, no one seemed to care."

"How was Luca then?"

"Better. We were happy for a time. I loved my baby, I had a beautiful home, and I was confident that I was doing what I was put here on earth to do. Winemaking was my art."

"When did things change between you and Luca, Maman?"

Ava shrugged a shoulder. "Our tranquil life didn't last long. Luca quickly lost interest in the vineyard. I completed the planting of the vineyards, as well as the construction of the house. I tried to provide balance and calm in our lives. But Luca drank a lot of our first harvest. When he was drunk, he became cruel, and the more he drank, the more his behavior changed, even when he was sober. I confided his increasingly hateful behavior to my priest and my doctor, but they made me feel like I had somehow failed in my duty. They told me to try harder."

Caterina bit back a comment. That advice was still doled out today. *When would it change?*

Ava cast her eyes down as she went on, "One night he perched—naked as a newborn—from a high window ledge in the château, firing a pistol into the night, shouting obscenities about an imagined assailant. Fortunately, only a few defenseless grape clusters were lost in his murderous rage, but his behavior swiftly worsened. I often feared an accident."

Caterina listened, imagining her mother as a young bride in a foreign country with a heavy load of responsibility.

Ava's shoulders drooped as she relived the past. "Once, I told the doctor my broken nose and bruised cheeks and limbs were the result of a fall. No one really believed me, but no one offered help either. Men didn't become involved with other men's affairs."

Caterina caught Ava's hand and squeezed it. She couldn't imagine living with such a man.

"And then the unimaginable happened. One night Luca returned home late. I awoke from the deepest slumber with a knife pressed to my throat. He was drunk, ranting about how you were not his child but a child of another man who would lay claim to Mille Étoiles. Even today it hurts me to repeat these words. How could such thoughts have entered his mind? His eyes held a wild, evil look that I'd never seen before."

Ava touched her neck as she spoke, and Caterina's heart went out to her.

"He had the advantage." Ava's voice was strained as she relived the event. "I knew a struggle would end my life. I held my body still as stone, my breath constricted in my chest. I dared not move, even as the tip of his blade drew blood." Ava touched a small scar on her neck and held Caterina's gaze. "You slept in the bassinet next to my bed."

Caterina sucked in a breath, imagining herself in such a situation with Marisa by her side. It was unfathomable.

"I prayed Luca wouldn't notice you. I thought, would your mother be murdered as you slept? Would he turn his blade upon you? Horror gripped my soul, blinding my reason."

Ava's eyes misted. "At that moment, you rustled in the innocence of your sleep. Luca released his clutch about my throat and turned his wild-eyed attention to you, but before he could move toward you, a savage fury overtook me. I didn't know myself capable of such actions. I clawed his eyes with my nails and crushed his throat with my elbow. Finally, as his knife clattered to the floor, I dove after it and thrust it upon him.

"As I inflicted the wound upon his skin—how disconcertingly easy it was to lay open the bare skin of his arm—a look of shock glazed his face, and he seemed to awaken from his demonic possession. A pious woman might have dropped the knife and forgiven her husband, but I was no longer that kind of woman. I advanced on him and drove him from the house, a knife in one hand, a gun from my lingerie drawer in the other, even as your wails pierced the night.

"'Go from here!' I screamed. 'You are dead to me and dead to my child!' I threatened to kill him. God forgive me, but I meant it. That night I banished him from our home and our lives forever.

"Raphael found me shivering on the stone steps, a gun in my lap, blood oozing from my neck. He led me upstairs, cleaned my wound, and rocked you back to sleep. I was so shaken I couldn't sleep for several nights, fearful he might return."

Caterina ached in her bones for her mother, feeling as old as the gnarled vines surrounding her. Sniffing, she wrapped her arms around Ava in a protective embrace. The sordid story was almost unbearable; the details were worse than she'd ever imagined. "He might have killed you. And I might have died, too."

Ava rested a moment in her daughter's arms and then pulled away to continue. "There's more. A devoted wife might have searched for her husband. Did he need medical help? I didn't know, and I didn't care. He was dead to me. I concocted a story and told everyone he had left on a business trip. A month later, he sent a letter. I returned it unopened and sent a letter warning him against contacting us again. Then I told everyone he had died in an auto accident during his trip. No one questioned my story. Raphael was the only one I confided in, and only for his protection."

"You could have divorced him."

"Actually, I prayed he would die and leave me a widow, however improper that might have been. If I were a divorcée, I couldn't re-marry in the church, and I simply couldn't subject you to gossip and speculation. Better that your father was dead, I thought. The daughter of a widow is not shunned in society as is the daughter of a divor-cée. This is America, land of the free, but prejudices remain. I was determined that you would have a brilliant marriage someday—unlike my own travesty."

Caterina squeezed her mother's hand. Since having Marisa, she understood what lengths a mother would go to in order to protect her child. *"Je comprends, Maman."*

They walked on through the vineyard, Vino still by their side.

"Merci, ma chérie, but I cry at what a wicked, deceitful woman

I became. I never mustered the courage to share this with you. I am ashamed of my actions, yet I would do it again to protect you."

"Your secret was a heavy burden to carry."

Ava nodded. "It has been. From that day on, sleep eluded me; my nerves were constantly on edge. I began to rant at the slightest provocation. I didn't know if I would ever be myself again. And I didn't have the heart to write to Violetta and tell her everything that had happened, only that he was gone. Violetta knew what her son was capable of, but I could not bear to write of such things to her at the time. The years swiftly passed, and the war cut off communication. I pray she forgave me for my lack of contact."

Caterina draped her arm around her mother. "I'm sure she did." Her head was swirling with emotion, even though the events her mother spoke about had happened a quarter of a century ago. Luca had terrorized her mother then and continued to do so today. She blinked, trying to clear the image of the heinous scene in Ava's bedroom. "It wasn't your fault that Luca was a tormented soul. You were young when you married. You did the best you could under great duress." Maybe Ava hadn't always been truthful, but she'd made her decisions from a place of love.

"Thank you for saying that. I tried, *chérie*." Ava sighed. "If only that gun had been loaded, we wouldn't have Luca to deal with now."

They walked on in silence as Caterina let her mother's story sink in. She thought of Santo and how different he was from Luca.

Caterina had to ask the vital question that burned within her, though in her soul she feared confirmation. Giovanna and Alma had told her what they recalled and what they'd heard, but she needed to know the truth from her mother. *If she knew.*

"Maman, about Franco and Natalie."

Ava's jaw flexed. "Santo's parents were a lovely couple."

Everyone she'd met in Italy had agreed. She forged on. "Luca was in love with Natalie, wasn't he?"

Her mother's eyes glazed over. "Yes." Ava's voice was barely above a whisper.

Caterina's tongue felt thick. She rolled the despicable words around her mouth before sending them out, never to be retrieved. "Do you think Luca is Santo's real father?"

Ava nodded and hung her head. She placed a hand on Caterina's shoulder, her frame heaving with emotion. "I'm so sorry I never told you." Tears slipped from her eyes as she released her deepest secret.

Caterina screamed denial in her mind. *No, no, no!* "Are you absolutely certain?" She clung to a frayed thread of hope.

"That's what he told me," Ava murmured. "How I wish it were not so."

The bright, hopeful core of Caterina's soul dimmed against her father's deed. She gasped for breath, feeling as if she'd been jerked from life's placid surface into hell's raging fury below.

Ava sobbed against Caterina's shoulder. "At one time, Santo was in love with you, *ma chérie.*"

How could life be so cruel? The solid floor of her reality split as her world pitched and heaved on the quake of veracity. Nausea careened through her.

"He came to me and asked for your hand in marriage, but I sent him away. It could never be. I broke the poor boy's heart."

And mine. Caterina raked her teeth across her lower lip. How would she ever tell Santo?

Ava framed Caterina's face in her hands. "I'm so sorry, but see how much worse it might have been?"

A fresh pain knifed through Caterina's heart. At once, she understood why her mother had kept so much from her. To inflict sorrow upon one you loved was infinitely more painful than shouldering the burden alone.

Which is why Caterina couldn't tell Ava her beautiful little granddaughter was Santo's child.

32

Seated beside her attorney in the small, stifling courtroom, Ava clenched her jaw and swung her gaze to the witness box, where her nemesis had been facing her all morning.

Luca sat near the judge, preening in the spotlight and confidently answering questions in a deep, mellifluous voice—the same honeyed Italian cadence that had turned her head as a young girl—put forth by his attorney, Russell Glenhall. He'd cleaned up, too. Wearing a charcoal suit and a white starched shirt, Luca was the picture of a successful, responsible businessman.

Ava knew better. She still bore the scars to prove it.

Behind Ava in the first wooden pew sat Caterina, Raphael, and Nina. Fellow winemakers and friends filled the courtroom.

"Mr. Rosetta, please tell the court why you did not return to Mille Étoiles after Mrs. Rosetta banned you from the house."

"I desperately wanted to, but my wife threatened me if I returned." Luca cast a cool look in Ava's direction, challenging her to prove him wrong.

More lies. Ava scrawled a note on a notepad for her lawyer, Walter Bren, a seasoned attorney in Napa whom she'd known for years.

Luca had been on the stand for two hours, and he'd spun a sparkling tale of decency and good works. Ava had been the evil perpetrator, depriving him of his beloved daughter and squandering vineyard profits to sustain a lavish lifestyle of servants and San Francisco shopping trips.

Ava ached for Caterina that she should have to endure these lies from the man who was her father in name only. Did Caterina believe any of it? Did the judge or jurors?

When Luca trained his eyes on Caterina, it was all Ava could do to maintain control. She glanced back at her daughter, whose lips were set in a thin line, her eyes narrowed. Ava fumed in silence.

After her attorney conducted cross-examination, which Luca smoothly lied his way through, the court broke for a small recess and then resumed. A parade of witnesses attested to Ava's good character and business history, and then it was Ava's turn in the witness box.

"State your full name for the court record, please." Walter Bren regarded Ava with an expression of pleasant confidence.

"Ava de Laurette Rosetta." She sat erect in her navy linen suit, crossed her legs at the ankles, and slid her pumps to one side. Being in a courtroom shouldn't make her uneasy; after all, she knew most of the men on the jury from Napa.

In the front row of the jury box sat the local dry goods storekeeper, a plumber, and a postal clerk. There were her fellow vintners and farmers, men who had been slow to welcome her into the fold but who, over the years, had come to respect her winemaking abilities. She'd lent them equipment when they needed it. They'd commiserated together in inclement weather and celebrated successful harvests. They were her neighbors; she knew their wives and children. But would they support her now?

Like her, everyone was dressed formally today; gone were their casual daily work clothes. Every man wore a suit to enter the solemn court of the Honorable J. Quincy Thurston. Pews of gray and black formed solemn lines, as if any moment they would rise for a funeral procession.

Walter continued his questions. "When did you arrive in the United States?"

"In 1929." A memory of the bitter March voyage across the Atlantic sprang to mind, and Ava shivered despite the heat in the courtroom. She'd lost a child on that journey, and the husband who sat across from her had been too inebriated—or heartless—to even visit her in the infirmary.

She reined in her emotions. Her lawyer continued his line of questioning, and she gave succinct answers, just as he'd instructed her to do during the past week.

Under oath, Ava was truthful about the past. She looked at Caterina as she recounted incidents she'd finally shared with her daughter. Walter rested his hand on the witness stand beside her. "And did you lie about your husband's death?"

This was the question they'd rehearsed, but that didn't make it any easier to admit her guilt. "Yes." Her voice sounded thin and hollow to her ears. She was under oath; she'd sworn on a Bible to tell the truth.

"Why, Mrs. Rosetta?"

She drew air into her lungs, fortifying her resolve. "I was afraid of him. And divorce is not condoned in my faith." Walter continued his questions. With an unwavering gaze at Luca, she answered, telling of the abuse and injuries she'd sustained at his hands and the financial hardships she'd endured. She told the court about Luca's imprisonment and subsequent banishment from Italy. When asked about the difficulties of running the vineyard, she turned and spoke to the jury. And when questioned about the difficulties of raising her child alone, she spoke from her heart to Caterina.

Her attorney did not ask about her husband's infidelities. She said nothing of Natalie or the other women she suspected Luca had been with.

Russell Glenhall cross-examined her, and Ava struggled to keep her anger in check. Yes, she had lied about Luca's disappearance and death. *How many ways will he ask that question?* Russell droned on, pinpointing details, while Walter made notes. She refuted most of Luca's statements.

After Ava concluded her testimony, some of the men in the courtroom audience were shaking their heads. *Do they believe me now?* She had lied to everyone about Luca's death for so many years. Her former banker, Douglas Lattimer, stared straight ahead, refusing to make eye contact with her as she made her way back to her attorney's side. No one else returned her gaze. Not her postman, not her plumber, not her fellow farmers and winemakers.

Nevertheless, Ava kept her expression stoic. She had admitted her mistakes and told the truth, which was more than Luca had done. All the ugliness of her past life was now laid bare, dutifully recorded for posterity and public consumption by the court reporter. It was as if she had been stripped naked, and she felt vulnerable. Of course, she had regrets. But she would do it all over again to protect her daughter.

Over the next hour, the lawyers presented their closing statements, and Judge Thurston excused the jury for deliberations. The men filed out. None of them looked back at Ava.

With a smug smile, Luca sauntered through the courtroom with his attorney. Like a lioness protecting her cub, Ava glared at him as he approached Caterina.

"*Buongiorno, principessa.*" Luca held his hands out to his daughter.

Ava's heart thudded with anger, and she could have vaulted across the room in a blinding attack, but Walter pressed a hand on her arm. "Don't do it, Ava. Not here."

Caterina glared at Luca. "Don't speak to me," she snapped, gesturing. "You weren't worthy of my mother's affection. You are no father to me."

Hatred blazed in Caterina's eyes. Ava opened her mouth to add something, but Raphael cut her off.

"Go on, Luca," Raphael interjected. "Keep your distance from Ava and Caterina."

"And who are *you* to care about them?" Luca whipped the back of his fingers from under his chin in a vulgar movement toward Raphael.

"More than you ever were." Raphael put his hands on his hips and stood his ground.

"Come with me, Mr. Rosetta." Russell cut in and steered his client from the courtroom.

After Luca left, Raphael was at Ava's side in a moment, along with Caterina and Nina and Juliana, who had joined them, too. Caterina flung her arms around her mother, and Ava could feel her trembling, not with fear but outrage.

"Caterina, I wish you'd never had to meet your father."

"What a horrible, malicious man. How can he be my father?"

Raphael scowled. "He was better off dead."

Ava pressed her hand against Caterina's smooth cheek. "My darling, he is no reflection on you. You carry my blood in you, not his."

Ava hugged each of them in turn. Only Santo was missing from their little family. Raphael had told her that he was still with his clients in Southern California.

She'd never told Raphael of their exchange of words when Santo asked for Caterina's hand in marriage. That seemed so long ago now, yet after revealing most of her deepest secrets on the witness stand today, she decided she should finally purge her conscience and tell Raphael about it after the trial. He would be disappointed in her, but she prayed he'd understand. At the time, she'd used the only leverage she had to contain the awful truth.

Ava turned to Walter. "How do you think it went? Will we lose our home?"

Her attorney pressed his lips together and nodded toward the door where the jury was ensconced in discussion. "I couldn't tell which side their sentiments are on. Couple of them took notes, but as I warned you, Ava, you are at a disadvantage."

"How long will it take for them to decide?" Nina asked. Ava noticed she'd worn her best Sunday summer dress today, a floral cotton shirtdress that looked more comfortable than her own stuffy suit. The windows were open, and the overhead fans were spinning, but she was sweltering in the indoor heat.

"Hard to say," Walter replied. "Could be a couple of hours or more."

They waited in the courtroom, but as it neared the end of the day, the judge sent them home without a verdict.

That evening as the night air grew cool, Ava listened to the crickets outside, and when the birds chirped with the sunrise, she was still awake.

The jurors continued their deliberations the next day while Ava waited with Caterina, Nina, and Raphael. Late in the afternoon, Judge Thurston summoned them into the courtroom.

The jury had reached a verdict.

Russell Glenhall called Luca, who was staying at a nearby boardinghouse. Walter Bren took his place beside Ava.

Luca entered the courtroom, a self-satisfied sneer chiseled on his face. When he nodded to Caterina, Ava nearly lost control again.

"All rise."

The judge entered and took his place, and then the jurors returned to the courtroom. Ava grappled with her emotions. In a few minutes, she would know whether she had won the battle, or lost her home and livelihood. She looked at the jury, but no one met her gaze. The men wore tired expressions, but they seemed resolute.

Ava watched as the judge and attorneys went through their actions. At Walter's motion, she rose and pressed her fingertips against the table for support. In the heat, she felt faint, but she steeled herself. She would not succumb to her body's natural defenses.

The jury foreman stepped forward, and the judge reviewed the jury's decision.

Judge Thurston nodded at the attorneys, Luca, and finally, Ava. He folded his hands, surveyed the courtroom, and asked the foreman to state the jury's decision.

When the decision was read, Ava's knees nearly buckled with relief. The jury had deliberated and found in favor of Ava.

Mille Étoiles belonged to her.

She turned to the twelve men who comprised the jury, pressed her hands to her heart, and mouthed the words *thank you*. Her attorney nodded his appreciation as well. She angled her head from Luca, who was glowering at her across the room. Russell was whispering to his client, but Luca's face only grew darker with anger.

Caterina, Raphael, and Nina let out exclamations of joy and relief and rushed toward her, crushing her in their enthusiastic embraces.

"This is remarkable!" Walter exclaimed with pride. "No matter how much evidence we had on our side, for the jury to go against your husband and recognize your claim as a woman is a sign that the times are changing indeed. Well done, Ava." He shook her hand and slapped Raphael on the back.

Despite the celebratory mood, Caterina frowned. "Why shouldn't we have the same rights as men?"

"My three daughters put forth the same question, young lady." Walter beamed at her. "Someday women will change the world."

Juliana came into the courtroom holding Marisa, who had been fussy earlier. She'd been waiting outside with her and was overjoyed when Nina told her the verdict. Caterina took Marisa in her arms, and Ava embraced them both. "This is for your future, and Marisa's, too," Ava said.

Luca brushed his attorney's hand from his shoulder and stood. As the men on the jury filed from the courtroom, he glared with menace at each one of them, as if to burn their faces into his brain.

As Ava watched him, a wave of apprehension surged through her.

She'd seen that expression before, on the night Natalie had died and he'd gone to confront her husband.

Ignoring his counsel's protests, Luca whirled around and stormed toward Ava. She might have won the court case, but Luca wasn't ready to concede defeat. Her heart thudded against her chest with each step he took. A vision of the night he'd nearly killed her clouded her vision.

Raphael and Walter saw Luca approaching and stepped in front of Ava.

"Out of my way!" Luca bellowed, gesturing. "This is between me and my wife now."

"The court's decision has been made," Walter said, motioning to Russell and the bailiff for assistance. The other two men hurried across the room and surrounded Luca.

From a nearby window, a shadow from the slanting afternoon sun fell over Luca. Though the room was stifling in the summer heat, a chill coursed through Ava.

Stymied, Luca trained an intense scowl on Ava. "This is your fault, Ava."

Walter cut in. "You brought the lawsuit, Luca. And now a decision has been made. Respect that, please."

Luca would not be deterred. "You will pay for this, Ava. You lied to me about being pregnant. I should have been with Natalie. I deserve to have Mille Étoiles." His raspy voice emanated from the black depths of his troubled soul. "Everyone at Mille Étoiles will pay for this." His upper lip curled back from his teeth, and his scarred hands drew into hardened fists by his side.

Ava drew herself up against Luca's fierce conviction. This was the expression she'd feared on his face so many years ago, but she was no longer under his dominance. "Leave us, Luca," she said, summoning her reserves. "It's over." Raphael puffed out his chest, ready to protect her.

"You won't get away with this." Luca spun on his heel and marched from the courtroom.

Later, Ava would barely recall the words Judge Thurston uttered, but she would never forget the reek of evil that permeated the room in Luca's wake, or that Raphael caught her in his arms before she fainted from the combination of heat and anxiety.

Ava's eyes fluttered open, and she found herself in the first pew, the worn wood smooth beneath her. Raphael cradled her head. All that mattered to her was that Luca had no claim to Mille Étoiles. She had saved it for Caterina and Marisa.

"Maman, drink this." Caterina pressed a cool glass of water to Ava's lips.

Ava rose up, gathering her strength. Nina was fanning her with a newspaper.

After she drank, she fell back against Raphael. Luca's malicious words had lodged in her mind. She knew her husband all too well.

And she knew it wasn't over between them. He would try to exact his revenge.

33

"Caterina, how I've missed you," Santo murmured, his deep voice reverberating in his chest and echoing off the cool walls of the wine cave. He threaded his fingers through her hair and pulled her close.

She had asked Santo to meet her in the cave where she knew they could have a few moments alone, far from curious glances or prying eyes. She had ached for him—longed to feel his muscular arms around her, loving her, desiring her, just once more. Santo was the light in her soul. Without him, her world would soon dim.

She succumbed to the warmth of his skin on hers and the ardor in his vibrant eyes, which blazed with love for her. He teased her lips with his tongue, and she responded, her heart breaking as she recalled their interlude in Paris.

Once she revealed their blood relationship—and she must—he would never touch her this way again. *How could he?* It might be wrong of her, but she needed his touch just once more, a small, covetous sin to savor and recall through the lonely years that surely lay ahead.

"Two crystal glasses, a bottle of our wine, and a beautiful woman by my side. What more could a man want?" Santo tucked a blanket and bottle under one arm and encircled Caterina's waist with the other.

They left the cave and cut through the vineyard toward the sloping mountainside path. A ripe, earthy, green scent hung in the air; sunshine diffused the aroma of leaves and fruit.

The sun hovered above the ocean's rim, etching elongated shadows in its wake and illuminating the land that stretched before them.

Caterina folded her hand above her eyes. "We can just make it to the top of the ridge by sunset."

They climbed from the vineyard toward a high promontory that jutted out over the agricultural valley below. Pine, eucalyptus, and redwood trees flanked the trail, and the sun cast a golden glow as it dipped toward the azure waters of the Pacific Ocean.

"How is Marisa doing?" Santo's eyes sparkled as his daughter's name rolled off his tongue with the sweetness of song. "And how soon can I see her?"

Caterina thrilled to his utterance of their daughter's name; the love and pride in his voice elevated three short syllables to poetry.

Taking her time, she told him about their return trip and the new words Marisa was learning. "Would you like to see her tomorrow? Nina and my mother are giving Marisa her supper and putting her to bed soon." She lowered her lashes and slid her gaze toward him. "Can you blame me for wanting you to myself first?"

"I admit, I felt the same." Santo ran his hand along her arm, his thumb circling her skin, the pressure mounting slightly with each rotation. "But I can't wait to see Marisa again. And I don't care what people in the valley might say."

As they climbed higher, Santo told her about his trip to Southern California vineyards in San Diego and Temecula. "The climate is warmer, but they're making good wine. We can visit the sandy beaches there. Has Marisa ever seen the ocean?"

"Only from a bridge in a car." Santo's enthusiasm for their daughter was what Caterina had yearned for. Her prayers had been answered, but not exactly as she'd hoped.

At the edge of the mountain, redwood trees spiked high above a secluded cradle, their lower branches forming a thatched roof and framing a stunning ocean view in the distance. They spread the blanket, uncorked the bottle, and raised their glasses against the shimmering sunset.

"To us," Santo said. Slanting rays burnished his dark, gleaming hair and bronzed his skin, while his eyes shimmered with love. "And to our future together."

"To our Marisa," Caterina replied, fervently wishing a future together could be theirs. Delaying the inevitable moment, she leaned against him, raising the wine they'd blended against the sun's vivid rays, illuminating the dark, fleshy red with fiery brilliance.

Santo swirled, sniffed, and lifted the glass to his lips. "We didn't need an award to know this is one damned fine wine."

"Wine, like perfume, is an extravagant gift of nature." Caterina sipped the wine, counting their precious moments like the rarest of pearls. Time was suspended as she watched him drink, the liquid flowing over his lips, longing flaring within her.

"Imagine what we can do next, *cara*." He nuzzled her neck. "Together we're magic. Just look at our little girl. I'm bursting to tell Raphael, but we should announce our plans together."

"Our plans?"

"Our wedding." A slow smile lit his face, and his eyes crinkled with joy. "*Luce dei miei occhi*. You're the light of my eyes."

A wedding that can never be, she thought, based on their grave sin of incest. A lump formed in her throat, and she drank again, fortifying herself for the abhorrent blow she had to deliver to her beloved.

Santo drew his hand along her cheek. "I have so many ideas for us and our future, Caterina. The circumstances were a shock at first, but I've never been happier. This is what I've always wanted, even though the sequence of events was somewhat out of order."

Caterina's eyes fluttered with pain; each of his words was a skewer to her heart. She clenched the stem to still her trembling hand. "Santo, we're from such a small region of Italy, aren't we?"

"Where many marriages are still arranged. And yet, here we are, in America, free to do as we please."

She swallowed against the panic that threatened to silence her voice. "There's something I must tell you, but know it's the last thing I should ever want to say."

"Why the serious look on your face, *cara*? What's wrong?"

Caterina took in the fullness of his lower lip, the cheekbones that framed his face, the dark curls that sprang loose from their dressing. He was a gorgeous specimen of a man, but her love for him was so much more than physical attraction. She loved him to the very depths of his soul as she had never loved another. And never would.

She bit the tip of her tongue, reluctant to send the first arrow into his soul. "About your parents . . ."

"They would have loved you."

"No, that's not it." She choked on her words.

"Then what is it?" Drawing his dark eyebrows in concern, Santo bolted upright when he saw her face. "Caterina, you've gone pale. Do you feel all right?" He pressed his hand against her forehead.

She lowered her eyelids. "I'm not sure you know your correct origin."

"Origin?" he echoed, perplexed, the corners of his mouth flattening. "What do you mean?"

She raised her gaze to his, regretting what she had to say. "When I was in Italy, I made an appalling, horrendous discovery." She hesitated. She could stop now before she crossed the ugly line of truth, live in blissful sin with him, and take this secret to her grave.

"What could be so awful, *cara*? Nothing can change the love we have for each other."

Caterina blinked several times, willing herself to do what was morally right. What if their next child was physically or mentally defective because of their close blood relation? How could she inflict such a life sentence upon an innocent child? *Santo's child.* As far as she knew, Marisa was healthy. But who were they to tempt God's ire?

Anxiety tightened like a vise around her midsection, inhibiting her breath, squeezing her diaphragm until she forced out the words. She gasped against the burdened contraction. "Franco was not your real father. It was . . . Luca."

Santo's frozen expression was a snapshot in her mind. *Before. After.*

"It's the awful truth," she whispered. "Luca was in love with your mother."

"That's crazy, and absolutely impossible. Raphael would have told me." Disbelief shone on his face, but it would not alter the truth.

"That's what I thought, too. But the entire village knew about them. Giovanna, Alma. My mother confirmed it." And Luca, in his way. She'd almost asked him in the courtroom, before Raphael cut in, but she really didn't have to. She knew the answer. *What a contemptible man.*

"Then we're . . ." Santo's voice trailed off, and his face paled in shock. His eyes blurred with the heartbreak of realization. "No! This can't be true!" Santo thrust their glasses aside and gripped Caterina's face between his hands. "Caterina, I *love* you."

His brilliant eyes burned with the intensity of impending loss, and Caterina trembled in his arms. "And I love you, but we can't do this anymore, not now!" she cried as he raked his lips in anguish across her forehead. She collapsed on the blanket, the swaying boughs of the trees overhead compounding her unsteadiness.

"To hell with Luca—this is *our* life. We have a daughter."

"Nothing will stop us from being her parents, *amore mio.*" Caterina ran a hand over his chest as if her touch could lessen the agony of his cracking heart. "But we're committing . . . incest."

"No! I would know it; I would *feel* it." Santo gritted his teeth, but when she didn't respond, he crumpled against her, his body heaving with grief.

"We can't risk the consequences," she said, sobbing through her words. She drew her lips across his hair and face, felt his cheeks dampened with their tears. "What if our next child is born deformed or deranged because of us and our wanton disregard for the laws of nature? How could we live with that? And the church will never recognize our union."

"No, I will not accept this." Santo smashed the ground with his fist, uttering a string of Italian expletives. "How can our love be wrong? Every child, every soul, is brought into this world for a reason. We would love and care for our children, no matter what." He clenched her in an embrace, his mouth searching and finding hers, his urgent aching need for comfort demanding, overwhelming.

Though she agreed in principle, Caterina couldn't find the breath to tell him his words were futile. They had as much chance of harnessing the setting sun as achieving the life they'd dreamed of in this world.

Santo's torment was palpable; Caterina could feel waves of sorrow emanating from him, crashing into her. She absorbed his grief as penance, her own heart shattering along with his.

After a while, Santo rolled onto his back and drew her to his chest. "Does Raphael know?"

"He must." Caterina shivered in the waning light. "But he's loved you like a father. Forgive him, Santo."

"And your mother knew. That's why she wouldn't let us marry." He spat out another Italian phrase damning Luca to hell for all eternity. "Raphael and Ava were trying to protect us. What an awful burden this was for them."

The evening chorus of crickets rose in the undergrowth around them. Santo's liquid blue eyes held the most sorrowful expression she'd ever seen. He grasped her hand, clenching it firmly to his breastbone. His hand was clammy, his breathing labored. "Tell me how you found out."

It was natural for Santo to want details, so she summoned the strength to tell him. "I first heard the story on the train to Paris from two women who lived in Siena. They spoke of Franco and of Natalie Sorabella, of their grand love and tragedy. I didn't know your parents' first names. I didn't piece it together until the day we found the articles in the cottage, and you told me Sorabella was your mother's maiden name."

"I remember how ill you looked. Why did you keep this from me in Italy?" he asked, his eyes moist. His face was a mask of misery and confusion.

"I had to be sure, Santo. How could I break our hearts unless I was certain?"

"I understand. The fault lies with Luca." Santo stroked Caterina's long, loose hair. She leaned deeper into him, and he pulled her closer. "But this will never change how I feel about you, Caterina."

His heart beat wildly against her skin, and she couldn't imagine living without his touch, his kisses. A fresh torrent of tears welled in her eyes. Yet the fact remained; Marisa was the child of an incestuous relationship, however unknowing they had been. She could not perpetuate the relationship. Waves of anguish swept through her; her heart was breaking from the tidal force. "I will always love you, Santo. You are Marisa's father. But we cannot do this; you know that."

Santo lifted her chin, cradling her face between strong, capable hands that had stroked her with tenderness and coaxed passion from her body. "I respect that, Caterina, but being apart doesn't feel right to me either." His brilliant eyes were rimmed with red, and his voice cracked as he spoke. "If you were truly my half sister, I honestly believe I would know in my heart. How can I ever accept this?"

"We must." The pain within her was so excruciating, it was as if her heart were being ripped from her flesh. "Marisa can't help what we've done."

"In my heart, I don't believe this, *cara.* I know you do, and so do others. But I swear to you, I will find the truth and dispel this absurdity."

Hot tears pooled in her eyes, and she clutched his shirt, shaking her head in despair. "And if this is the only truth you find?"

Flexing his jaw, Santo raised anguished eyes to the dark, inky sky above. "Then, God, I implore you, please kill me now."

34

The aroma of simmering peach preserves wafted through the kitchen. Caterina scooped Marisa from her high chair. Her daughter's beautiful, vivid eyes taunted her now, an aching omnipresent reminder of the love forbidden to her. Santo had visited Marisa the next day while Ava was out. Though their lips curved into smiles for Marisa, their eyes were glazed from torture and lack of sleep.

Rest had eluded her again last night, but the demands of life would not spare her. She moved sluggishly through the days. The busy harvest time was well under way now, and early reports from across the valley were as optimistic as their own results.

If only her future were as hopeful.

Sitting across from her at the kitchen table was Ava. Caterina thought her mother looked better today than she had in several days, though worry was still etched in the faint creases around her eyes. The trial had taken its toll on her. And none of them could forget the threat Luca had issued before he'd stormed from the courtroom. *Everyone at Mille Étoiles will pay for this.*

Caterina pressed a hand to her heart. God had no mercy for their crimes. Not for her, not for Santo, not for Ava. Her sins weighed on her conscience; it was time to confess.

The rear screen door squeaked open, and Raphael stepped inside. "Have to oil those noisy springs again," Nina said, stirring a pot of simmering peaches. Sterilized jars stood ready to receive the peach preserves.

"I'll see to it, Nina." Raphael pushed his straw hat back on his head and deposited a stack of envelopes on the kitchen table. "Here's your mail, Ava."

Caterina saw her mother's eyes brighten when Raphael walked into the kitchen. They were good for each other, and she was glad Raphael so obviously cared for her mother. The way Raphael had watched over Ava at the trial endeared him to her even more. At least someone had found love in their midst.

"Thank you, Raphael." Ava's gaze lingered on Raphael as they exchanged weary smiles.

They had started work long before dawn. All through the valley, the harvest was in full swing. Despite damage from the earthquake, vineyard owners had pulled together, assisting those whose equipment had been damaged. The grapes were in rare, exquisite form this year. A festive mood filled the region, from Sonoma to Napa to St. Helena. At Mille Étoiles, they had already started harvesting some of their younger blocks of vines.

Caterina stifled a yawn. Marisa wasn't accustomed to the new time schedule yet, so she wasn't ready for her nap. Nina looked after Marisa while Caterina worked alongside Ava and Raphael, overseeing the harvest and testing the grapes.

Ava picked up the mail and thumbed through the letters. She hesitated when she came to a scrawled letter. "Strange . . . what's this?" She picked up a knife and slit the envelope open.

Caterina squinted at it. "Looks like an angry hand."

Ava withdrew a letter, opened it, and gasped.

"What's wrong, Maman?" Caterina held Marisa and looked over Ava's shoulder at the paper her mother had dropped like a hot ember.

"It's another threat." Ava's eyes flashed with anger.

Raphael placed a hand on Ava's shoulder. "From Luca?"

"He didn't sign his name, but I know his handwriting."

Caterina shot a glance at Raphael, whose mouth was pressed in a determined line.

Ava read quickly, her expression turning to horror as she did. "*Mon Dieu,* our vines have been poisoned."

"What?" Outrage seized Caterina. Harvest was in progress; they couldn't harvest poisoned fruit.

Ava and Raphael traded a worried look.

"Despite the verdict, Luca still wants Mille Étoiles," Ava said. "I know him. If he doesn't get it, he will destroy it. And us along with it."

"Poisoning the vines?" Caterina clamped a hand to her forehead in disbelief. "What kind of a person would do such a thing?" She pressed Marisa to her chest as if to shield her from peril.

A dry, hot breeze blew through the open kitchen window, lifting the yellow curtains and carrying with it an ominous air of danger. Caterina huddled around the table with Ava, Nina, and Raphael.

"Luca can't be serious." Raphael splayed his fingers across the letter they'd just received. As he read it again, he mumbled a curse in Italian.

Ava dabbed her face with the corner of a napkin. "This is not to be taken lightly. He warned us. And I know exactly what he's capable of."

Will Luca ever leave us alone? Caterina met her mother's gaze, and for the first time in her life, she caught a glimpse of fear in Ava's eyes.

Nina stirred her peach preserves. She peered out the window at the vineyards. "He could be out there now. We need to call the sheriff right away."

Ava unfolded another piece of paper. "Wait. Here's a map." She studied the rows for a moment. "It's the vineyard—the old, original block of vines." She tapped near the center of the map where three plants had been circled. "We need to test these vines right away."

"Those are some of our best vines." A chill spiraled up Caterina's spine. "But why would he include a map? Why would he even tell us?"

"He's gloating, egging us on." Raphael shook his head. "A man like that enjoys torturing people. He wants to watch us suffer. And we will. We'll have to test *all* the vines. And possibly destroy them."

Caterina sucked in a breath. "How can we possibly test them all?"

"Santo has access to testing equipment. Luca won't get away with this." Raphael started for the telephone. Santo could use the sophisticated technology at the University of California in Davis, his alma mater.

Caterina felt her world shift on its axis. "Hasn't Luca done enough damage to us?"

Ava leaped to her feet and grasped Raphael's arm, finding strength. "This is a threat against our livelihood. If the vines are poisoned, people could die."

Caterina listened to the calls. There was nothing more they could do until the vines were tested. She left the kitchen with Marisa and climbed the stairs.

Cradling her daughter against her shoulder, Caterina rocked her to sleep in Ava's old rocking chair—the same pine rocker her mother had once soothed her in. She gazed at Marisa. They needed Santo's expertise now, but his daughter would need him in her life.

Her mother had struggled to keep the vineyard alive through droughts, Prohibition, and economic depression. And now, her father might be the ruin of it. A hateful lump formed in her throat. He'd ruined her life.

Caterina squeezed her eyes shut. Marisa's tiny heart tapped against her chest. She heard the telephone ring and then heard Nina call to her while climbing the stairs. Marisa was asleep, so she put her in the crib for her nap and met Nina at the door.

"Raphael and Ava went to meet the sheriff. They won't be long, but Santo's secretary is on the line. Will you speak to her?"

Caterina followed her downstairs and picked up the receiver. "Hello?"

Santo's secretary told her that Santo was away from the office.

Clutching the phone, she said, "It's urgent that we reach him. Do you know where he is?" Caterina listened. "Thank you. I'll find him." She turned to Nina. "Santo is nearby. He's at the old winery above us. I'll go. Can you please check on Marisa while I'm out?"

Caterina grabbed her purse and keys and raced to her car. Pressing the accelerator in her Chevrolet, Caterina whipped up the mountain roads. Her heart thudded at the thought of seeing him again.

What was he doing at the neighboring vineyard? It had been for sale for years. Did he have a client for it?

As she turned into a curve, an oncoming truck crossed the center line and headed straight for her. Startled, Caterina jerked the steering wheel to the side, barely managing to keep the tires on the mountain road's edge as her wheels kicked rocks down a sheer drop beneath her.

"Get over!" she yelled, her frustration spilling out. The other driver yanked back his truck, scraping the side of the mountain as he overcorrected. Caterina peered into the window as the two cars whooshed by. A brimmed hat obscured the man's face. "Someone's been hitting the wine early," she muttered, and then a thought struck her. *Could that have been Luca?*

She stopped her car in front of an old winery up the hill from Mille Étoiles. She stepped from the car, the dry earth dusting her soft-soled shoes. Santo's Roman-red Corvette roadster and a white Cadillac were parked in front.

Built in the late 1800s, the property had fallen into disrepair and had been vacated during Prohibition. The property was known as a ghost winery. Not that it was haunted—*though it could be,* she thought, judging from the look of it.

Ava had once tried to buy the vineyard, but the owner was a

crafty, chauvinistic old man who refused to sell it to a woman. He'd priced it so high that Ava couldn't afford it. Other serious vintners were so incensed they boycotted him. Stories of cursed, haunted grounds grew, and soon, no one would touch the property. The owner lowered the price repeatedly, but the damage was done. With the price so low, everyone suspected the ghost stories were true.

By then, Ava refused to give the old man a cent.

The stone structure soared three stories high into the clear blue sky, much like Mille Étoiles. At the top of the peak, she glanced over her shoulder. The Pacific Ocean sparkled with diamond brilliance in the distance, its constant waves reassuring. She turned back to the house. Gaping windows yawned before her as if in slumber. Though it was run-down, she had such fond memories of the property. She and Santo and Juliana had played here when they were young.

Squirrels chattered to one side, scampering around, gathering their nut supply for the winter months ahead. At this elevation, the property would be blanketed under a layer of snow in the winter, the old vines dormant. The stress of the cold winter months was essential for the best grapes.

The more stress nature heaped upon the vines, the more flavorful the wine. The grapes, or berries, grew small and dense at this elevation. Less water in the fruit meant a higher ratio of skin to fruit within, and more skin meant more tannin, which imparted intense flavor to the wine. This was prime property.

Caterina swung on her heel, squinting against the sun. Old vines stretched before her, and acres of land ripe for new farming flanked the original vineyard. Her heart leaped at the thought.

She hurried toward the looming house. The front door stood ajar. She started to push it open but stopped. She could hear voices inside. She peered through the narrow opening and saw Santo. Instantly her body betrayed her, aching for the touch of Santo's hand and the feel of his arms around her.

Santo and a woman stood in the middle of the room. The woman's blond hair was swinging around her shoulders and gleaming in sunlight beaming through open windows. They were talking and leaning close to each other. Santo said something, and the woman flashed a blindingly white smile.

Caterina could smell the woman's perfume from here, beckoning to Santo like a siren's song. She had seemingly endless legs and a curvy figure.

A chill crept over her. This was no ghostly apparition, but her heart still lurched in alarm.

"When this was built," the woman was saying, "it must have been one of the most beautiful homes and wineries in the valley. You'll have to spend quite a lot of money to bring it back to its original splendor, but it'll be worth it."

The woman was right. Between rats and the passage of time, the house was rough. Caterina recalled the antiquated kitchen, which was probably unusable. The bathrooms were equally despicable, and the wallpaper was faded and torn. But the only thing the narrow oak floor needed was a good sanding and refinishing to bring it back to life.

Was this the plan Santo had mentioned before she'd confided her dreadful secret? Caterina edged closer to the door, straining to hear. How could she endure the agony if he lived so close?

Santo brushed a thick layer of dust from the moldings in the living room. "These were clearly the work of a fine European craftsperson."

At the sound of his deep baritone voice, Caterina's heartbeat escalated. She listened intently, hardly daring to breathe.

The woman stood near Santo, a hand on her hip. "The Mille Étoiles winery abuts this property; it's just below." When he didn't respond, she said, "There are other properties we can look at that don't need nearly as much work."

"No, I like this one." He sat on his haunches to inspect the wood floors. "Looks like red oak. Once restored, this house will be a real beauty."

"Do you plan to do the work yourself?"

"Some of it," he said. "I can get a lot done while the vines are sleeping."

The woman smiled again; her sunny disposition was dazzling. "I'd love to decorate this. Could be awfully cozy up here in the winter with this incredible fireplace," she said, her voice dropping a notch in a clear invitation. She leaned against a carved stone fireplace so large that a child could stand in it.

Caterina's heart sank. The woman was gorgeous. What man could resist her? But Caterina had no right to Santo now. She leaned against the stone wall, grief-stricken.

Santo looked up with interest. "I'll think about it. Lots of work to do first."

The woman placed a hand on his shoulder. "What do you see in this house? It's so dilapidated."

"I like its location," Santo replied.

Caterina watched him run his broad hands over the oak floors— the same hands that had caressed her in Paris. She still ached with desire for him, though she knew her feelings violated everything she held sacred.

Caterina had played with Santo and Juliana on these grounds when they were young. They had even fantasized about living here. Years ago Santo told her that his goal was to buy this old stone winery and bring it back to its former glory. The elevation was ideal for cabernet grapes. Once she had even imagined their children roaming the adjoining properties.

Santo stood up and brushed his hands off against his denim jeans. "We could begin work on it as soon as harvest is over."

The woman slid her hand down her tight skirt. "Why don't we talk more over dinner?"

Santo put his hands on his hips. "Sure, let's have dinner in town. I have a favorite place for good Italian food."

"I'd like that."

Just then, the woman's expression changed. She'd seen Caterina. Santo turned and saw her at the entrance.

Caterina sucked in her breath and opened the door. She stared at the blond woman and then slowly swung her gaze to Santo, struggling to maintain her composure. "I saw your car outside. Raphael has been trying to reach you. We received a letter, Mille Étoiles is under—" She stopped short and shot a look at the blond woman, who seemed to radiate sunshine and sex. "You need to see him right away. Now. It's urgent."

Visibly unsettled, Santo's eyes bored into her. "Caterina, what's going on?" His face was masked with desire and anguish.

Caterina's eyes burned with despair; just seeing him was excruciating.

"You're Caterina Rosetta?" A smile played on the woman's lips. "Your mother owns Mille Étoiles, right?"

Caterina shot her a cursory look. "Yes."

The woman placed her hand on Santo's arm in a familiar manner. "I'm Marilyn Mueller," the woman said, extending her hand to her. "I'm a real estate agent."

Caterina spun around. It wasn't like her to be rude, but seeing Santo again, especially with this woman, was more than she could handle. What could she do? *Nothing.* Their family's history would never allow them to be together.

A sad smile flickered on Santo's face. "I wanted to surprise you, *cara.* This vineyard, this old house we always loved, this is for us, for our future. We can make our own life up here." He lowered his voice. "I don't care what people think."

Caterina's lips parted in astonishment. *This is even worse.* This was the dream they'd once shared and the life she'd desperately yearned for, but now, in light of her father's probable actions, it could never come to fruition.

Waves of agony and guilt swept through her, and she cried out in pain as she backed through the door. They were ruined in the eyes of God, their family, their neighbors. Couldn't he see that? Their beautiful dream crumbled before her eyes. She squeezed her eyes against her torturous vision and whirled around.

"Wait, *cara,* wait!" Santo cried, covering the floor in long strides. "I must talk to you."

Blinded by tears, she raced to her car.

"Caterina!" Santo caught up with her and clutched her to his chest. "I can't imagine living without you. I'm not giving you up. We have to fight together, *cara.*"

"No, we can't do this!" she cried, backing away from him. "But for God's sake, you've got to see Raphael right away. We're under attack, and our vines might have been poisoned!" After she got into her car, she sped from the driveway, kicking up a cloud of dust as the wheels spun in haste.

35

Caterina stood by a tall window in her mother's office overlooking the vineyards of Mille Étoiles. Heat radiated from the glass pane, though a breeze circulated the warm summer air in the office. She'd been on the telephone most of the day assisting Ava, negotiating with buyers who had heard about their award in Paris.

After she'd seen Santo at the old ghost winery, he had arrived the next day to test the vines with Raphael. Her emotions were raw, and she'd managed to avoid him, but she'd give anything to hear from him now.

Had their best vines been poisoned?

And how long would her heart continue to beat without Santo?

Feeling on edge, she clomped downstairs, hurried outside, and trudged up the hillside to one of their higher blocks of vines, which was slated for harvest soon.

The punishing burn in her thigh muscles pumped oxygen into her blood, though it did little to clear her mind. She paused to check a cluster of grapes.

The leaves and grapes had taken on rich color in a natural process known as *véraison,* which signaled the onset of ripening. Small and tightly clustered, the thick-skinned, tannin-rich grapes were powerfully concentrated.

Their harvest was on hold until they received the results of Santo's tests. Normally, harvest would last from two to four weeks, depending on the weather and the ripening of the grapes.

Every year was different. This year, weather was not the threat.

Harvest might start as early as late July, or as late as the end of September. Out of habit, she plucked and tasted a tiny grape. Intense sweetness burst in her mouth. This could be a year of excellent wine, perhaps even the stuff of greatness.

Suddenly, she expelled the grape and spat after it. Had it been poisoned? Rage burned in her chest. She drew her sleeve across her mouth, wiping her lips.

When she reached the old vine section of the vineyard, she knelt in the dirt to inspect the rootstock. Had the vines been tampered with? She couldn't tell. She stood and brushed dirt from the knees of her denim jeans.

The vines rustled behind her, and she swung around, her heart pounding. Was someone in the vineyard? Ever since Luca's threatening letter arrived, everyone had been on high alert.

Seeing nothing, she shrugged it off as a breeze or a bird and turned back to inspect the old vineyard. She prayed they could use the cabernet grapes. Only her mother's vines from Bordeaux were more cherished. These gnarled plants, which had been planted at the turn of the century by previous owners, were the finest in their fields, perhaps even in the entire valley. Indeed, these grapes had yielded their special reserve that had taken the grand prize in Paris.

Poisoned?

In the center of the field stood a trio of vines that had been roped off, their lives dependent on Santo's test results. Or had they already received their death sentence? Reverently, she trailed her fingers along the perfectly groomed vines, stroking the lacy leaves and tight grape clusters.

Caterina couldn't imagine the hatred her father must have for them to have done such a thing. A bountiful vine was nature's beauty. True winemakers revered the vine.

She walked on, thinking about this year's crop. Raphael had

borrowed equipment from a neighboring vineyard for a short time to begin harvesting and processing certain blocks of grapes. The fermentation process had already started on the crops that had been harvested. They didn't add yeast to their fermentation; instead, they allowed the natural forces of nature to occur. During this process, the sugar in the grapes converted to alcohol. If there was too much sun, the alcohol content increased. A fine wine hung in the balance.

Caterina removed a destroyer beetle from her white cotton shirt with care and released it on a leafy vine. A cousin of the ladybug, destroyer beetles were beneficial in controlling mealybugs, which could damage their crop. She stooped to inspect another vine.

To make wine was to enter into a partnership with Mother Nature, one that sometimes turned adversarial. If springtime dealt a poor hand of rain, wind, or extreme temperatures, young grape clusters might fail to develop during their infancy, resulting in grape shatter, or *coulure* in French. A poor fruit set meant flowers failed to pollinate and develop into berries, or the weak berries fell from the vines. This was nature's way of aborting the frail.

The worst weather was a long, cool summer with intermittent rain. Grapes liked strong summer heat during the day and cool nights, which helped create complex flavors. The more extreme stress on a vine, the better the fruit.

Caterina was nervous with anticipation. Unlike last year, this was one of the best seasons anyone could remember. Would it be a spectacular year? Or would their vines die by poison at the hands of a lunatic?

She pushed her hair from her forehead and craned her head to the sky. She spied some clouds on the horizon, far out to sea. It looked like a marine layer that would hug the coast. She hoped the clouds would dissipate before reaching the valley.

Wind or rain could be disastrous at this time of year, with the potential to rob the valley and its farmers of the entire annual crop. She shielded her eyes, hoping their dry weather would remain.

The vines behind her rustled, and Caterina jumped back, ready to defend herself.

"Oh, it's you, Vino. You scared me." She knelt to scratch the dog behind its ears and looked up to see her mother approaching. "Stay close, will you?" she whispered. Her hands were shaking, and Vino pressed to her as if he understood her words and her need.

"Thought I might find you here," Ava said. "Vino is so happy you're back."

"Any word from Santo yet?" The mere utterance of his name brought a pain to her chest.

Ava shook her head. "No, but soon, I hope."

"I guess we can sit by the phone together. Marisa should be waking from her nap."

"I checked on her, and Nina will look in on her, too. She likes having a little one around again."

"Want to walk back with me?"

"Of course. I've missed you, Caterina. Speaking of Nina, I heard Juliana is dating a widowed vintner with two children up valley. Do you know anything about that?"

"Jules mentioned it. Why?"

"Nina is worried about her. But I've heard he's actually quite nice."

Caterina smiled. "She's still getting over Al's death. Maybe this is a good thing. They have something in common."

They fell into step with one another, while Vino trotted beside them. Though her mother chatted along the way about the pending harvest, Caterina couldn't shake her thoughts of Santo.

She doubted she ever would.

Ava paused to secure a heavy cluster of grapes. "*Chérie,* there's something I should tell you."

"What is it?" *More secrets?*

"As you know, Raphael has worked here for many years, and we wouldn't be where we are today without him, but over time, things change."

"He's not leaving, is he?" Caterina asked, alarmed.

"No, nothing like that," Ava said.

"What a relief—he's like family." Caterina put her hand over her mother's, tracing the tiny veins that ran along the back of her strong, capable hand. "What is it, Maman?"

"He's such a good man, *chérie*."

"He's the best." In a flash, she understood what her mother was trying to tell her. "Raphael is the man you should have married, isn't he, Maman?"

Ava's eyes glistened. "He's had a special place in my heart for many years. Now that Luca has returned, I understand just how lucky I am to have him. Though we haven't been together in *that* way," she added, blushing.

"Why not? You're still young, Maman." Caterina looked at her mother with fresh eyes. Ava was still a lovely woman. She was only forty-six. Why shouldn't she have a second chance? A memory clicked into place like a jukebox record. Raphael with Ava, touching her hand, gazing after her. Raphael's face was lined not with years of work but with years of desire. Caterina kissed her mother's cheeks. At least one of them should find happiness.

"While you were in Italy, I consulted with Brother Timothy, and he said a man as cruel and immoral as your father could not have entered a marriage with proper intentions. He has a severe psychological disorder; therefore, he was unable to enter into a valid marriage."

Caterina inclined her head. "What does that mean?"

"I'm filing for an annulment of my marriage to Luca."

In the space of a few weeks, Caterina had gone from idolizing a dead father to confronting the depths of his cruelty. Her mother deserved the right to pursue happiness in her life.

Even if she and Santo never could. Caterina swallowed hard, concealing her heartbreak.

Ava dipped her head and went on. "All these years, Raphael has worked alongside me, helping me realize the vision of the winery." Her face glowed with pure delight. "Raphael asked me to marry him."

"And you *will*, of course." Caterina hugged her mother. "I'm happy for you, Maman. I can't think of anyone I'd rather see you spend your life with." She drew back. "As long as this is what you want."

Ava dabbed the corner of her eyes. "Oh, it is, *chérie*."

They walked on, with Vino running circles around them as if to protect them. Caterina was truly happy for her mother.

Abruptly, Ava changed the subject. "Caterina, as long as I'm sharing my secrets, I feel I must speak my mind. With Luca back in our lives, I've been thinking about Marisa." Ava paused and held a tented hand to her forehead, shielding her eyes against the sunlight. "Though Luca was an evil man, I realize I should have told you about him."

Caterina slid a sideways gaze toward her mother. "What does this have to do with Marisa?"

"I'm drawing a comparison. I haven't pressed you about Marisa's father. But I'm concerned about the boy."

This was the question she'd dreaded, and yet, had she subconsciously invited the question again? "You needn't be. He's a good man, Maman. From a good family." That's what her mother wanted to hear. Caterina pressed a smile of assurance on her face to temper her distress.

The corners of Ava's mouth curved up. "You said you were in love. Would you ever reconsider this young man?"

Although the truth within her ached for release, Caterina laughed softly, camouflaging her roiling emotions. "Are you angling for a double wedding now?"

"Not at all." Ava spoke in earnest. "But whatever happened between you, know that pride hurts us in the long run. Perhaps it's not too late to rekindle your relationship."

"That's impossible." If only she could confide in her mother.

"Are you sure, *ma chérie?*" Ava put her arm around Caterina and drew her close. "It might not be too late to make amends. Does he know about Marisa?"

Her burden had become too heavy. Caterina rested her head on her mother's shoulder and made a decision. "Maman, Marisa's father is Santo."

Ava gasped, her face contorted with shock. "Oh, *mon Dieu!*" She flung her arms around Caterina as if to shield her, but even she could not right this travesty.

Caterina sank into her mother's embrace and cried. Two years of deceit, deception, and dissimulation had taken their toll on her emotional health. Now it was over.

Ava sobbed, clutching her daughter as she convulsed with grief. "My poor, poor *chérie*. I blame myself. Oh, how could life have been so cruel to my child?" Over and over she questioned God's wisdom in delivering such a cruel twist of fate.

After a while, Caterina regained her strength. Yet Ava looked pale, and her entire body was trembling. Had Caterina's revelation been too much for her?

"Maman, let's go inside. I think you need to rest."

Nina put Ava to bed and prepared a pot of tea for her. "I'll look after her," Nina said. "Find Raphael, see if there's any news from Santo yet."

Caterina sought out Raphael, who was working outside of the cave. They were all anxious to know the results of Santo's tests.

Raphael was overseeing the operation of the new machinery for de-stemming and crushing the grapes prior to fermentation. The equipment had just arrived, after approval of the new line of credit Caterina had rushed to arrange with Elsa Williams's bank in San Francisco.

With Vino trotting beside her, she signaled to Raphael. "Any word yet?"

Raphael pushed his straw hat from his head and drew a sleeve across his forehead. "Santo called with the test results." His expression darkened, and he put his hands on his hips.

Her heart nearly stopped. "Tell me."

"We'll have to destroy those three vines, sure enough, but the others are clean." He spat angrily on the ground.

"He's taunting us." No one was safe at Mille Étoiles until Luca was caught. *Though he's already destroyed my life,* she thought miserably.

Raphael motioned to several men sitting nearby who were wolfing down tortillas with beans and rice. "Nothing will get by us tonight. I'll make sure of that."

She nodded toward a new wooden structure next to the cave where they had moved the large vats. "I'm going to check the fermentation progress."

Vino plopped down to wait for her at the entrance while she went ahead. The doors were open wide to let air circulate. Everyone had worked hard to clean up after the earthquake and move equipment into new sections. The new funding had made it possible.

After she was satisfied with the progress, she stepped outside again, and Vino rose by her side. She stood still, watching the hawks soar lazily above the hillside, feeling a breath of warm air on her face as the sun sank toward the horizon. Everything in the winery and vineyard seemed under control. She exhaled a measure of tension. Though Santo was lost to her, she had finally told her mother the truth.

Yet she sensed an ominous undercurrent she couldn't articulate. "Come on, Vino. Let's go."

Caterina walked back to the house. Vino trotted beside her, sniffing, circling, and then sniffing again. The fur on his back prickled, and his ears flattened.

Even Vino knew that something was amiss.

After dinner with her mother and daughter, Caterina opened a French door to the patio. Raphael hadn't dined with them tonight as he'd started doing, because he'd told them he was working late. The encroaching twilight ushered in a refreshing breeze that was scintillatingly cool on Caterina's face after the heat of the day. The air carried the scent of ripening fruit, of darkened purple grapes, reddened peaches, and succulent pears.

Caterina inhaled deeply, comforted by the familiar scents. She turned back to Ava. "I need to talk to Raphael about the next phase of harvest."

Ava looked up from the table where she was finishing a glass of wine. "He should be in the cave. Do you want me to come with you?"

Caterina knew Ava was still upset over her revelation about Santo. "No, you take your bath and relax. It's not dark yet, and the air feels nice. I'll take Marisa with me. I'll only be a few minutes."

"Tell him we'll keep dinner warm for him."

Caterina picked Marisa up from her high chair, hoisted her onto her hip, and stepped outside. Before long she reached the open doorway of the cave. Inside she found Raphael, but she was shocked to see Santo with him. Feeling flustered, she clutched Marisa tighter. She hadn't thought to look for his car first.

"Caterina," Santo said, glancing up. He stepped toward Marisa and kissed her on the cheek. Clad in an embroidered pink dress, Marisa cooed and smiled up at him with adoration in her eyes. When he moved to kiss Caterina's cheek, she angled her head from him, but not before she detected pain in his expression.

Raphael cleared his throat. "Santo and I were just going over a plan to protect the vineyard." He leaned across a worn map of Mille Étoiles spread out on a table.

Santo stood with his hands on his lean, muscular hips, admiring her.

"I've posted people on each of the vineyard sections tonight." Raphael pointed out the specific locations on the map. "The sheriff and his men are looking for Luca, and the roads are blocked. We won't give him a chance to do any more damage."

Her eyes stinging, Caterina blinked and glanced away from Santo. Seeing him around Mille Étoiles and Marisa was proving more difficult than she'd imagined. "Has anyone spotted him?"

"No, but he knows all the back routes." Raphael traced a thin line on the map.

"My mother is worried you're going to take on Luca." She bounced Marisa on her hip.

Raphael looked up. "Your father—not that he ever earned that title—threatened everyone at Mille Étoiles. None of us will be safe until he's in jail—or dead."

"Caterina, let us handle this." Santo's voice was gentle but laced with concern.

"No, this is *our* land." Caterina jerked a thumb toward her chest, crying out with pent-up frustration and torment. Marisa frowned at her mother's sharp words.

Raphael leveled his gaze at her. "We've all worked this land together; it's our livelihood, too. More than that, it's our home, and we'll fight for it together."

Caterina bit her lip against the raging emotions within her.

"Anger is good, *signorina;* it gives you strength to fight," Raphael said. "But direct it toward the right person. Santo told me he tried to do the right thing by you. Regrettably, your mother and I committed a grave error in judgment. Now it's up to you and Santo to decide how to deal with this. We must go forward." He glanced at Marisa. "For her sake."

"There's nothing we can do about it." Caterina's eyes clouded, blinded by a mixture of hurt and hatred and rage for her father and the utter, gross unfairness of it all. She couldn't understand why their hearts sought out each other if their love was so wrong.

Seeing Santo was more than she could bear. Pressing Marisa to her chest and fueled by adrenaline, Caterina fled the cave, racing through the darkened vineyard toward the house. Leaves slapped at her arms, and she stumbled in her woven espadrilles. She careened down the hill, her hair streaming behind her, her face wet with angry tears. Marisa cried at the jostling chaos.

Caterina's shoes slipped in the dirt, and she pitched forward. She lurched to the ground, falling onto her knees but still clutching Marisa, who was growing even more agitated. As she went down, the air cracked above her. The old vine above her head exploded, showering her and Marisa with shreds of bark and leaves and fruit.

What the hell? In an instant, her muddled mind cleared. Caterina recalled with horror the sound of distant pings in the hills during hunting season. She pressed herself and Marisa down into the volcanic dirt, hardly daring to breathe, her heart thumping in her chest.

Another shot exploded the ground beside them. Dirt sprayed onto Marisa's face, and she screamed.

"Shh," Caterina whispered, clamping her hand over Marisa's mouth.

She heard a rustle behind her. Clasping her arms around Marisa, she crawled under the vines into the next row. She craned her neck and saw a man creeping through the rows.

Luca.

Her skin bristled. What she felt for him was far beyond hatred; it was an emotion descending into an intense, dark realm of abhorrence and loathing she didn't know she possessed. She leaped to her feet and raced through the vineyard with Marisa, trying to stay low.

Another shot cracked through the night air. Caterina ducked as a bullet whizzed past them, shattering a cluster of grapes and splattering dark burgundy-red splotches against her white shirt and Marisa's pink dress.

"Caterina, where are you?" Santo's voice rang out on the hillside above her.

"Get down!" she screamed. As soon as the words left her lips, another shot rocketed past her. She dropped and rolled through the dirt into another row, brushing leaves and dirt from Marisa's face. A laugh erupted behind her.

"Why run? You're trapped," Luca said.

Caterina blinked. Ahead of her was a shed, to the right a ravine. He stood angled behind her, blocking her escape, a gun leveled at them.

"You're an evil man! You never deserved my mother!" she screamed, edging away.

Another laugh. "She's next. She'll get everything she deserves." Her father—a rangy, menacing man with a haughty profile—advanced toward them. She pressed against a vine and turned her back toward him to shield her baby.

"Leave them out of this." Santo was striding toward them with determination, a shotgun wedged against his shoulder, squinting one eye down the barrel.

"You're not going to kill anything larger than a bird with that." Luca laughed again. "Ava stole everything from me. Now I'm taking it back."

Caterina felt her way along the wooden supports that held the vines and grapes. She'd reached the end of the row. A few steps behind her, the ravine fell away. A mule had once lost its footing and plunged to its death in the steep abyss.

That's exactly what he's planning, she thought. Caterina's hand quivered against the end of the wooden support.

"We'll give you what you want!" Caterina yelled, stalling for time. "Take Mille Étoiles!" Santo was closing in on them. Through the shadows, she spied another figure approaching him from behind.

"Santo, watch out!" Caterina screamed just before a man knocked Santo from his feet. Her pulse roared through her head. She was wild with fear for Santo. And for Marisa.

"What a shame; he almost saved you." Luca's eyes gleamed as he came closer to her, his boots crunching against the shattered vine. "Did you really think I'd be here alone?"

"You're disgusting." Santo and the other man were scuffling, but there was nothing she could do. *Or was there?*

His lips curled into a sneer. "Maybe, but I'll be rich once I get rid of this stinking place—and you and your mother."

"If you kill us, you'll be caught. You won't get the money."

"Sure I will. The sheriff will decide you all died in the fire." He reached the edge of the vineyard and took aim.

As Luca raised his gun, Santo sprang loose and dove for his legs. The gun exploded as they collided, and Luca slumped onto Santo, cursing. Precariously close to the edge, Santo clawed his way out from under him.

Luca clutched his side. Blood oozed from his wound. With effort, he raised his gun and took aim again. Caterina squeezed Marisa against her chest and shrank back, prayers on her lips.

But before Luca could bring Caterina and Marisa into his sight, Santo thrust out a long, powerful leg, smashing his foot against Luca's wounded area.

An animal scream erupted from Luca's mouth. Off balance, he

fired, flailing as he tried to maintain his stability. "Help!" he cried, waving his arms.

Caterina watched in morbid fascination as Luca slid backward in slow motion, the soft limestone soil crumbling beneath him, unable to stop his fall. Instinctively she reached for his hand, but he slid and flipped over, tumbling down the ravine. She could hear him grasping in vain at limbs and rocks. His screams reverberated through the mountains.

Caterina caught her breath, and even Marisa grew quiet. After a thud, the vineyard fell silent.

Santo wrapped his arms around her and Marisa. "*Cara,* are you two okay?"

"I think so." Shaking, she pressed against Santo, grateful he was there. She was still clutching Marisa, who began wailing hysterically. "Where's the other guy?"

"I got him," Raphael answered. He stood over the man, a gun pointed at his head.

"Do you think Luca is dead?" Caterina was still shivering.

Santo stared at the spot where Luca had gone over the edge. "No way could he survive that fall. The coyotes and mountain lions will take care of the rest." Santo's breathing was labored. "I never would've forgiven myself if he'd hurt you or Marisa."

Caterina's head grew light. She clung to Santo, her heart pumping. He took Marisa from her, stroking her tiny back with a broad hand to calm her cries.

Santo inspected Marisa's grape-spattered dress, alarmed. "*Dio mio,* is this blood on my child?"

Caterina looked down and clutched Marisa's pink dress, which was covered with dirt and stained a deep crimson. She ran her hands over Marisa's limbs. "No blood, just grapes," she said, expelling a deep breath. She and Marisa were bruised and filthy, but they were unharmed. "Luca was a lousy shot. Only the vines suffered his wrath."

Santo glanced down the black ravine. "He's surely dead." He rocked Marisa in his arms, stroking her hair with love. "When I saw him threatening you and my baby girl, I could have killed him myself."

Caterina's eyes misted as she watched Santo and Marisa together. In her father's arms, Marisa had ceased crying. Santo was humming to her. Caterina leaned into him and felt his heart pounding, matching her rapid pulse. "How did you know he was here?"

"I didn't," Santo said. "I came after you and Marisa, and then I heard shots. There's nothing I wouldn't do to protect this precious little one and her mother. So I grabbed the gun from the truck." He smoothed tangled hair from her face. "I never knew my parents. I wish I'd been there for Marisa from the beginning, but it's not too late to start now."

Under the tragic circumstances, that would be all he *could* do, Caterina thought, giving in to soul-crushing anguish. And for that, Luca was surely on his way to hell.

36

The next morning, Caterina lingered in the early predawn darkness at the rear kitchen door, cupping hot coffee in her hands. The house and vineyard were quiet, although the air still seemed charged with electricity.

Last night Santo had walked her and Marisa back to the house and made sure they were safe. She wanted to talk to him, but the house had erupted in chaos. The sheriff and the priest arrived after news of Luca's demise had reached the town. The sheriff had interviewed each of them and taken statements. The priest had counseled them, prayed with them, and reassured them of God's forgiveness for any sins they thought they might have committed.

He had no idea how many they'd racked up.

Caterina had barely closed her eyes to sleep before it was time to rise again, but this morning, she felt better knowing Luca was gone. She would mourn her father—not for the man he was but for the ideal her mother had created for her, for the father she had always wished she'd known.

Santo was a good man; he would be a fine father to Marisa. For this, she was thankful.

Yawning, she rubbed her puffy eyes. Life would go on, she thought sadly, though not as she'd hoped. After her mother's confession and confirmation of her worst fear, little hope remained for a life with the man she loved. All things considered, it was the best outcome she could have expected. Luca had done his despicable part, but she'd also mangled her life and lied to everyone who loved her.

As for the constant ache in her soul, she'd have to live with that for the rest of her life. She blinked back tears of despair. How she would manage that, she didn't know. One day at a time; that's all she could do. Caterina heard footsteps behind her and whirled around, her coffee sloshing over the rim.

"I didn't mean to frighten you," Ava said.

"My nerves are shot," Caterina replied, swallowing against a lump in her throat. Though Luca was dead, she couldn't seem to eradicate his disturbing presence.

"Mine, too."

Ava was attired in jeans and boots for the workday ahead. Even dressed casually, her mother looked chic with a printed cotton scarf at her neck, pearl stud earrings, and fresh citrus perfume. Then Caterina realized she was dressed the same way. Like mother, like daughter. Maybe the old adage was right, after all.

"You couldn't sleep either?" Ava put her arm around Caterina.

Caterina shook her head. "I still have a creepy feeling. Figured I might as well get started. I was just heading up to check the fermentation process."

"I'll come with you." They started off, hiking up the hill in silence. They each held a flashlight to light the uneven path. The grape pickers were already working a field farther down the hill. Caterina recognized Raphael in the illuminated section and relaxed a little, knowing he was close. Then she saw Santo and looked away.

Ava sidestepped a rock. "I'm so relieved that you and Marisa weren't harmed yesterday. Luca was always such a troubled soul."

"At least you won't have to get an annulment. Now you're really a widow."

"That's true," Ava replied thoughtfully. "Luca was never a father to you. He was just a cruel, egotistical, self-centered man. He professed to love Natalie, but that was obsession, not love."

"I'm glad you have Raphael now. And we still have Mille Étoiles. Luca had planned to burn it, with all of us inside."

Ava shook her head sadly. "But I'm devastated for you and Santo." Unlike in the past, Ava's voice now held a note of genuine sadness.

"We'll work it out, Maman. He'll be a good father to Marisa." At least Santo wasn't giving up on them, though their situation was tragic.

"Mille Étoiles would have been lost without you, *chérie*. You did so much—going to Paris, arranging the new credit lines, writing purchase orders, speaking with reporters. And making a phenomenal wine, of course." Ava's voice cracked with gratitude. "*You* saved Mille Étoiles, *chérie*. Your grandparents—my parents, and Violetta—would have been so proud of you."

"I couldn't have created the wine we did without Santo." Caterina kicked a rock in the path. Santo had been as much a part of the winemaking process as she had been. Their combined artistry and passion won the competition. And then she thought of Victor Devereaux and his comment about their wine label.

"When I was in Paris, the head of the competition saw the house on our label. He recognized it, but he called it something else. He mentioned a marquis, too. Was this my poppy?" Caterina used the childhood name that Ava had always used when she spoke of her family, although she'd never told her much, she realized.

"Yes, Alexandre-Xavier de Laurette was my father. Your grandfather, your poppy. It hurt so to speak of my parents after they died. They were fine winemakers and descended of an old, noble family. After I left France, it didn't matter anymore. We were pursuing our American dream." She waved a hand across the land. "This is our life now. I was determined to do whatever it took to succeed here. And for you to become a true American. I will always be French, but I wanted you to be accepted in our new country."

They arrived at the processing building adjacent to the cave. The doors were propped open to release carbon dioxide that built up during the fermentation process. They had a ventilation system, but everyone still took precautions.

Standing outside, Caterina shivered and looked around, still feeling uneasy. The sheriff had taken Luca's partner away, so they had nothing to fear, but she still couldn't shake the terror she'd gone through yesterday. Caterina followed Ava inside, glancing around the cave.

Caterina brushed against a stack of papers on a table, knocking them to the floor. "Go on, I'll catch up." As she picked up the papers, Ava went on ahead of her.

A moment later, a crash broke the morning silence. "Maman, are you all right?" When Ava didn't answer, Caterina rushed to find her. "Where are you?"

Caterina froze when she entered the room where large concrete vats of red wine were fermenting. On the catwalk that ran above the open vats, Ava stood clinging to a railing, her face white, her eyes filled with terror. Workers used the catwalks to monitor fermenting wine and punch down caps of skin that formed during the process.

Panic struck Caterina, but she tried to stay calm. "Maman, what are you doing up there?" She caught a glimpse of a man's hawkish profile and rangy frame shadowing her mother.

Ava angled her head, indicating someone behind her. "It's Luca."

A laugh rose in the air. "Thought you'd gotten rid of me, didn't you?" Luca stepped onto the platform behind her mother, a butcher knife gleaming in his hand. "But I know the secrets of Mille Étoiles. Fell right onto the ledge outside of the smuggler's cave used during Prohibition. People used to hide cases of wine there with rope ladders. Figured the authorities wouldn't search someplace they couldn't reach. I found the old mountain climbing equipment in there, too," he added, boasting. "After all these years, funny how so little changes."

"You won't get away with this," Ava said. "Raphael and the sheriff will be here any moment."

Luca laughed again. "I doubt it. Why would they be looking for a dead man? I was kicked into the ravine without a second thought. Now it's time to return the favor."

Caterina had to reach her mother. She slid along the shadows of the wall, fumbling for anything she could use as a weapon. When he looked away, she snatched a bottle of wine and tucked the neck into the rear waistband of her jeans under her shirt. The glass was cold against her skin.

Moving gingerly, she climbed the ladder that led to the catwalk.

"Come on up. Join the party," Luca said. "We'll make it a family affair. I'll kill two birds with one stone—or knife, as the case may be." He tossed the knife from one hand to the other, his expression one of gleeful hatred.

Caterina focused. She stepped onto the first rung of the ladder and hauled herself up, thinking as she climbed. Carbon dioxide was heavier than air and settled to the surface of the vat where it was the strongest. If a person fell in, he or she could quickly black out and drown.

Better Luca than us.

Another step, and she pulled herself up to eye level with the landing.

"Welcome, daughter." Luca held out a rough, dirty hand to her.

Caterina ignored it. She stood a few feet from him, drawing herself up to his height. She resembled him a little; she had his height and high cheekbones, but that was all. Unflinching, she stared straight into his cold, dead eyes. "You ruined my life, you're an evil man, and you're *not* my father. Now let my mother go."

Luca's mouth twisted with maliciousness. "You know I can't do that."

Ava gripped the railing. "Caterina, go back. This is between me and Luca."

Caterina shook her head. "I'm not leaving you."

Luca put a hand over his heart and feigned emotion. "How touching. Ava, did you hear your daughter? How brave she is, the little fool." As the last word left his mouth, he lunged for Ava with the knife.

Caterina screamed and Ava scrambled away from him.

But Luca was quick. He whipped the knife against the back of Ava's shoulder. Her shirt fell open, and blood oozed from a long gash. Arching in pain, Ava slipped and fell on the platform. She tried to crawl away from him as he stood over her, laughing.

"You stupid bitch, look at where you've ended up. Dying in your own wine, now that's justice." He spun around and waved his bloodied knife at Caterina. "You, too, pretty one. Down on your knees, now." His eyes lit with a wicked expression.

Repulsed, Caterina knelt on one knee but remained ready to spring. She looked past Luca and saw raw determination in her mother's eyes. Ava would not go down without a fight.

Caterina calculated the distance between them, formulating a plan. She glanced down. They had to stay on the platform.

"Other knee down, come on," he said gruffly, waving the knife. "Ava and I have a date, and you get to watch." His eyes glinted; he was clearly enjoying torturing them.

Caterina put her other knee down.

"There's a good girl. Maybe I'll save you for later. Or maybe I won't."

As soon as Luca turned toward Ava, Caterina reached around and whipped the wine bottle from her waistband. Lunging after Luca, she swung with all her strength and made solid contact with his head.

Luca wailed, cursing in Italian and flailing about. His knife clattered onto the catwalk, and he dove unsteadily after it, overshooting and crashing through the railing with his weight.

Caterina jumped back, watching him teetering on the edge. Ava rushed toward him, hatred blazing in her eyes. "Maman, no!"

Ava reached out to push Luca from the edge, but he caught her wrist as he fell back. Together they crashed from the catwalk and plunged into the vat, red wine splashing as they fought and gasped for breath. The knife wobbled on the planks and then fell in after them.

Thinking fast, Caterina began to kick a long piece of the wooden railing. "I'll get you, Maman."

In an instant, Ava disappeared under the surface.

"No, you won't," Luca said, sloshing around. "We're both dead now." He leaned his head back and bellowed with morbid laughter. "What a way to go."

No! Had the carbon dioxide already claimed her mother? Panicking, Caterina was poised to dive from the platform when Ava resurfaced.

Quick as a flash, Ava whirled around, flinging her arm across Luca's neck.

Luca's eyes bulged, and he gripped his neck, an expression of horrified surprise on his face. He tried to speak, but he couldn't. Ava threw the knife against the wall of the vat and began sinking again.

"Hold on!" Caterina kicked the rest of the wood railing loose. She stretched flat onto the platform and angled it toward her mother. "Grab it, and try not to breathe."

"Can't," Ava gasped.

Luca struggled a moment more and then slipped under the surface.

Caterina grimaced. "He's gone." She knew her mother didn't have long. "Come on, you can do it," she commanded. She'd go in after her, but they wouldn't stand a chance.

Ava caught the end of the railing and held her breath. Slowly, she dragged herself up.

Caterina stretched her hand toward her. *Come on, come on.* Her mother was struggling to maintain consciousness. "You're almost there; take my hand."

Ava blinked and shook her head. She was beginning to fade.

They only had a matter of seconds. Caterina hooked her knees against a post on the catwalk and flung herself down backward, stretching her arms out to grip her mother's hands. "I've got you," she said. "Climb up on me to the platform."

"Let me go," Ava said. "Save yourself."

"No!" Caterina cried. "We're both going to make it. Think of Raphael and Marisa."

A moment later, her mother reached up and seized Caterina's torso. Caterina supported Ava while she hauled herself onto the catwalk, grimacing in pain.

Ava rolled over and gave Caterina a hand, yanking her onto the wooden planks beside her. They lay with their arms around one another, sputtering and crying and catching their breath.

Luca had nearly claimed their lives again. "He would've killed us," Caterina said.

"At last, we're free of him forever, *chérie.*"

"Caterina? Ava? Where are you?" Santo's voice rang out, and footsteps echoed through the building.

"Above the vat," Caterina called out.

Santo raced into the room with Raphael right behind him.

"Up here." Caterina closed her eyes with relief.

Santo bounded up the ladder. Caterina guided her mother toward the safety of his arms. Ava was dripping with red wine, and blood gushed from her shoulder. Santo helped her down, and Raphael embraced her, while Santo returned to aid Caterina.

"What happened?" Santo asked. "We heard your screams."

"Luca came back to life." Caterina's feet touched the floor, and Santo hugged her close to him, rocking her in his arms in relief.

Ava turned her face up to Raphael's. "And Caterina saved me."

"Where's Luca?" Raphael demanded.

"My mother took care of him." Caterina jerked her head toward the vat. "This time, he won't bother us again."

The next morning, Caterina rose at dawn to continue the harvest. As she inspected the grapes, she thought about Luca's demise and their narrow escape. Raphael had rushed Ava to the hospital for stitches to her slashed shoulder, while Santo called the sheriff. The two men drained the wine vat to help the coroner remove Luca's purple body.

Caterina couldn't watch. "That must have been a gruesome job," she'd said to Santo after the coroner left.

"It was." Santo passed weary hands over his face. "But that man was *not* my father," he insisted. "I would've known; I would've felt it. I will never believe that he was."

Luca was finally out of their lives forever, but he'd left a wake of destruction.

At midmorning, everyone took a break from harvest duties, and Caterina walked to the house. Vino trotted beside her. Raphael's radio was tuned to classical music, and the operatic strains of *La Traviata* rolled across the hillside, reminding her of Montalcino and Violetta.

She was in the kitchen preparing a fresh pot of coffee and chatting with Nina when a knock sounded on the front door. "I'll get it," Caterina said, and made her way to the foyer, tucking her hair under her red bandanna. Vino followed at her heel. Since Luca had been on the property, the white sheepdog had stayed close to her and Ava.

"I have a trunk for Miss Caterina Rosetta." The brawny delivery man pushed a tattered cap back from his ruddy face.

Caterina peered at the label on the steamer trunk. *Montalcino, Italy.* It was from Santo's aunt Rosa. Her heart picked up a beat, and she held the door open for the man. Reinforced with knotted twine, the trunk carried with it the scents of age and Italy. Vino sniffed around it with caution.

Pointing to a spot in the living room, she said, "Put it there by the sofa." She thanked him and closed the door behind him. Standing before the large trunk, her mind whirred with anticipation.

In Italy, Caterina had asked Rosa to search for any letters Natalie might have written. Perhaps she'd confided an affair with Luca or an attack to a friend or relative. But would such writings disprove— or prove—Santo's blood relationship to her?

Nevertheless, a wisp of hope wound through her. *Had Rosa discovered something that would help them?*

Sunlight streamed through the French doors and rested on the trunk, illuminating the nicks and scratches it had sustained over years of use. Caterina fished a pocketknife from her denim dungarees. She rolled up the sleeves on her blue checked shirt and sank to her knees beside the trunk.

She sliced through the strands of twine and brushed them aside. Vino lay beside her, watching. Running her hands over the lid, she imagined what lay within. *Santo should be here,* she thought, but she *had* to see what Rosa might have uncovered. She couldn't wait, not a moment more.

Praying she would find letters, Caterina rested her hands on the lid before she opened it, willing it to reveal its secrets.

She drew a deep breath, flipped open the latches, and lifted the lid.

Rusted hinges creaked in protest while the aroma of dried lavender wafted from the trunk. The top tray fit snugly inside. Rosa had carefully wrapped packages in brown paper, tied them with twine, and labeled them. *Natalie's hair combs. Santo's baby clothes sewn by Natalie.*

She picked up one marked *family photos* and unwrapped it to reveal several tintypes developed on thin sheets of iron and mounted in cardboard folders. *Santo's grandparents,* one read. Other sepia photos of Natalie and Franco on their wedding day stared up at her. She smiled. Santo would cherish these. *How thoughtful of Rosa.*

She riffled through the packages but found nothing to help her in her quest.

Caterina tugged on the tray and lifted it from the trunk. On the top lay a letter from Rosa pinned to a tissue-wrapped package. She opened it and began to read. Rosa wished her and Santo a long life together, much happiness, and many babies. Caterina brushed errant tears from her eyes.

She parted the thin tissue. Nestled among many layers was a puddle of ivory silk and lace. She cried out at the sight.

Rosa had sent Natalie's wedding dress to her.

A dress she would probably never wear. Her heart sank at the thought.

Caterina lifted the dress to her cheek, stroking the smooth silk against her skin. Wistfully, she held it to her shoulders.

Maybe Marisa will wear this one day.

"You'd look beautiful in that." Santo's baritone voice rang out from across the living room.

Caterina flushed and dropped the gown in her lap. Vino barked and raced toward him, wagging his tail.

Santo ruffled the fur around Vino's neck. "Want out, boy?"

He opened the door for the dog and then crossed the room and knelt beside Caterina. The scent of fresh grapes and warm sunshine clung to his skin. He rubbed her shoulders, and she swiveled her neck, enjoying the touch of his hands.

Santo peered over her shoulder. "What's all this?"

"Your aunt Rosa sent some keepsakes from your mother." She

brushed a tear from the corner of her eye, remembering how she'd tried on the dress in Italy.

"And this dress? It looks like a wedding gown."

Caterina nodded. "It was your mother's."

Santo slid his hand over Caterina's. "I'd love to see you in that," he murmured.

"Santo, please. We don't know——"

"I know that I love you," Santo interjected. "Isn't that all that really matters?"

"And you have my love, but . . ."

Santo kissed her cheek. "I know," he murmured. He picked up a package. "Wonder what's in here?" He tore off the wrapping paper. In his hands lay an intricately inlaid wooden box. "What a beautiful piece." He shifted it in his hands. "It's heavy."

Caterina opened the lid. Nestled inside a plush lining of burgundy velvet was a yellow-gold, oval-shaped locket.

Santo drew it out. Mounted in the center was a cabochon amethyst, its vibrant purple hue mesmerizing. "For you, *cara*. My mother would have wanted you to have this." He placed it in her hands.

Caterina turned it over and touched the engraved letter *N*. She slid a fingernail in a small groove on the side, and the locket opened.

Staring up at her were two perfectly preserved photos. *Natalie and Franco.* On one side, Natalie in her wedding gown; on the other, Franco in a smart suit. *Until death do us part,* Caterina thought sadly. They were united even in death, for they died on the same day—Natalie in childbirth and Franco by Luca's angry hand.

Caterina exhaled a ragged breath. How close she and Marisa and her mother had come to being Luca's victims, too. She closed the locket, brought it to her lips, and kissed it.

"I'd like you to wear it for me," Santo said. He raised the long chain over her head and looped the locket around her neck, letting it tumble along the open upper buttons of her shirt to nestle between her breasts.

"Thank you. And someday, our Marisa will wear it." She pressed it to her chest.

They sorted through the rest of the items—Santo's infant christening gown, a family tree, and more photographs—but there were no letters, no answers for them, no final reprieve in Natalie's hand. When they reached the bottom of the trunk, Caterina sank her head into her hands, silent tears flowing for what might have been.

Santo massaged her shoulders again. "What's wrong, Caterina?"

"I'd hoped Rosa might've found some old letters from your mother about Luca. About your true parentage. But there was nothing."

"I wish it didn't matter." Santo drew her to his chest. "I suppose one of us must have a conscience."

Caterina leaned against him. She rested her hand on the locket, now warmed from her pulse, and drew a measure of strength from the fact that it had once touched Natalie's skin. *Santo's mother.* She would save it for Marisa. *For Natalie's granddaughter.*

Santo stroked her hair with a tender touch. "I'm glad we had Marisa, even if society and the church reject us. How can a love as strong as ours possibly be wrong?"

Caterina could hardly breathe. He was close, too close. The heat from his body was like a magnet, draining her willpower. One of his arms was around her shoulder; the other spanned her waist. His virile, musky, masculine scent overwhelmed her sense of propriety. His heart pounded against her rib cage, matching the intensity of her own. *Just a moment more,* she told herself, wishing this could last forever.

After a while, Caterina tore herself from him. She wiped her eyes and rose on unsteady feet. "Shall we store the trunk here?"

"Why not store it in our own home?" His challenge hung in the air. "I bought the old house and vineyard for us."

"For Marisa, you mean. Santo, how can we be anything more than parents to our child?"

He rose next to her, clasped her hand to his chest, and then bowed his head to graze her skin with his lips. "*Ti amo, Caterina. Senza di te non posso più vivere,*" he murmured. *Without you, I am nothing.*

"*Je t'aime, mon chéri,*" she replied, knowing she would always love him. Caterina wrested her hand from him, trembling. "We can't continue this," she whispered, stepping away from him.

Santo looked painfully adrift without her. Arching his neck, he swept his hands across his face and pushed his fingers through his thick hair. "Then you'll have to be the strong one, Caterina, because I can't be. I'm too much in love with you. I always have been, and I always will be. I don't care what people say. I know what's in my heart. And yours."

Caterina tugged her arms around her. "We can't escape the truth."

"I know the truth." Santo stepped toward her and brought his hands up to cradle her face.

As she gazed into his eyes, words failed her. How could they justify their desires? To risk medical complications and the condemnation of their faith . . . was that tempting God and fate beyond reason?

"Caterina, life is full of uncertainty. But there's also a damned good chance that we're *not* related. Have you thought of that?" He gripped her hands in his, imploring her. "Take that risk with me."

His strength flowed through his hands. If she never knew the truth, could she live with the ambiguity? To never know if they were living a sin? Caterina pressed her lips together. What would they tell Marisa when she was older? She couldn't live with a new generation of lies.

Did they have to risk so much to gain happiness?

She raised her eyes to Santo's. "I love you, but I cannot know-

ingly burden more children we might have with our history. As it
is, Marisa will have a lot to grasp. We will have to tell her."

"Then we'll be careful." Hope bloomed on Santo's face with this
seed of possibility. "We could adopt children."

She glanced at the old baby clothes Rosa had sent. White linen
shirts were embroidered with green ivy and yellow sunflowers, robes
for tiny babies who needed love and a home. Faith and Patrick and the
maternity home sprang to mind.

Santo grazed her lips with a soft kiss. "I can think of nothing
better, *cara*. I know what it's like to be alone in this world without a
mother or father."

Sincerity was evident in his voice. "And I know how a mother
feels when faced with the fact that she will never see her baby again."
How close she'd come to giving up Marisa. It still hurt just to imagine it.

"Does it have to be that way?"

Caterina searched his earnest expression. "No, we could change
things. Why not involve the mother in her child's life if she wants
and it's not to the detriment of the child?"

A smile grew on Santo's face. "We'll have plenty of room once
we renovate the old house on the vineyard." Santo drew a thumb
along her chin. "Say yes, *cara*." Santo's gaze held hers, the endless
sapphire of his eyes—Marisa's eyes—boring into her soul.

Could she do this? In her heart, she longed for Santo and the
future he painted. But could she really live with the uncertainty of
their blood relationship? She would always harbor suspicions. "I need
to think about it, Santo."

"I know you must be certain, and I respect that. I can wait, *cara*."

In her soul she knew the truth. They loved each other and always
would. But would love be enough to overcome their immutable
past?

"You should keep this for Marisa." On impulse, Caterina slipped the locket from her neck and picked up the jewelry box. Her hands were shaking so that she fumbled with the wooden box, and it slipped from her grasp. She shrieked, and Santo dove for it, but he was too late.

The lovely antique box crashed to the floor and splintered on the hard wooden planks.

"Oh no." Caterina fell to the floor, seizing the remains. The lid had burst on its old hinges, and the deep-weighted base had separated slightly from the main box. Hot tears sprang to her eyes.

Santo knelt beside her. "It's okay, *cara*. It's just a wooden box." With a firm hand, he pressed her to his chest and stroked her back in comfort. "At least I can put *that* back together, if not us." When she looked surprised, he added, "One of the things I most admire about you is your sense of right and wrong. You're a fine woman, Caterina Rosetta. You remind me of Violetta." He picked up the jewelry box and pressed the base to secure it to the main portion of the box.

As he worked on the box, Caterina stared at it. "Wait!" she cried. "Is that a little drawer?"

Santo fumbled with the box. "If it is, it's stuck."

"My hands are smaller. Let me see it." Caterina ran her fingers over the fine polished wood. A fingernail caught on a small indentation. She dug in and pressed.

The drawer moved. She gasped and tugged it open. "A secret drawer. No wonder the jewelry compartment was so shallow. Look, there's something in there." She lifted out a slim leather-bound notebook stamped with gold, small enough to fit into a lady's pocket.

She opened the cover. Written in a youthful hand was Natalie's name. "It's your mother's." She folded her legs under her and leaned against the sofa.

Santo sat next to her. "What's in it?"

The old yellowed pages crinkled under her hand. "Her most private thoughts." Together they read through several pages. Natalie had written about her wedding day, and she'd composed a love poem for Franco. "This is so sweet. Your mother was a very special woman."

"I wish I'd known her." Santo turned the brittle page and scanned it. As a native speaker, he read Italian much faster than she did. Page after page, he translated the feathery ink, telling her what his mother was writing about, his deep mesmerizing voice entrancing her.

Finally, he paused and looked up. His azure eyes were glistening. "I think this is what you want to see," he said with a husky edge to his voice.

Caterina squinted to read the small writing, translating the words in her mind. "She loved your father so much. Here she writes about what other girls were saying. Oh, it was awful . . . She mentions Luca and Ava. And what happened . . ." As she read, she pressed her hand to her mouth. "Luca threatened to destroy her marriage by spreading false rumors. He was trying to force Franco to leave her."

Santo went on. "Luca told her she would have no choice but to go to him. He planned to leave Ava and steal Natalie away to southern Italy. There, he would raise Franco's child as his own as punishment to Franco for taking Natalie from him in the first place."

"Poor Natalie," Caterina said, appalled by his devious plan. "Luca professed to love her, but he was cruel to her, too." She paused and then sucked in a breath as Natalie's words sank in.

"You know what this means, don't you?" Santo clutched her hand, his eyes shimmering. "There's no doubt now, *cara.* Franco was my father."

Caterina's tears spilled over her cheeks with joyful relief. "Oh, Santo, we're free!" In that moment, the chains of the past disintegrated, releasing them to live their lives.

"I knew we were meant to be together." Santo wrapped his arms around her, and kissed her with the passion of a man who'd waited far too long for the woman he loved.

She threw her arms around his neck, ecstatic at their discovery. Pure elation flooded her body, and her heart pounded with exhilaration. "Is your offer still good?"

"Absolutely." Santo's eyes glittered with happiness, his face lit with the radiance of love. "Let's fill that old home with love and laughter and children."

Caterina smiled. "And the finest wine in the world."

DISCUSSION QUESTIONS

1. The theme of family secrets is prominent in *The Winemakers*. Have there been any secrets in your family that later came to light? If so, how did this new information affect family members and their relationships?

2. Are parents ever justified in keeping family history from adult children? Ava kept vital information from Caterina under the assumption that she was sparing her daughter the abuse and heartache to which she'd been subjected by Lucan. Do you think she was correct in doing so? How might she have told Caterina about her father and her family history? What would you have done?

3. If Caterina had known about her parents' difficulties, do you think she would have kept her child a secret from Ava?

4. Fear of social condemnation forced Ava into a disastrous marriage in the 1920s, and yet Caterina was determined not to succumb to such a marriage. Even in the 1950s—Caterina's frame of reference— this was still an evolving social topic. What societal forces do you think have changed the way unmarried pregnant women are viewed? Are these views still held in your community? Why or why not?

5. Ava's heart softens toward Marisa after she meets her grand-daughter. Considering her anger toward Caterina, why do you think Ava had such a change of heart?

6. Ava speaks of reinventing her life in America, far from the trans-gressions of her past, and later, Caterina also considered rein-venting herself and her history after moving to Italy. Given modern communication, do you think it's still possible to recast yourself in a new environment, and to what degree? Do you think this an important skill for personal resilience?

7. As a woman, what impediments did Ava face in owning and running a business? Did the World War II years have an impact on professional and entrepreneurial women in your country or community? Have you faced any similar obstacles in business, and if so, how did you handle these challenges?

8. Do you know of any stories of emigrant experiences among your family or friends? Do you think this experience unifies or divides the generations?

9. If you enjoy wine, did you discover anything new or interesting about wine and its history from this book? What are your favor-ite wines? Do you have memories related to specific wines? Have you ever visited a vineyard?

10. If Caterina and Santo had been related, how might this have changed the ending? What would you have done?